MAEVE CLARKE was born in Birmingham to Jamaican parents. A graduate of Manchester University's MA in novel writing, she is an EFL teacher currently living in Italy and working for the British Council as Library and Arts Co-ordinator. *What Goes Round* is her first novel; her 'potent and supple' short story 'Letters A Yard' appeared in the prize-winning anthology *Whispers in the Walls*.

What Goes Round

Maeve Clarke

TINDAL STREET PRESS

First published in 2003 by
Tindal Street Press Ltd
217 The Custard Factory, Gibb Street, Birmingham, B9 4AA
www.tindalstreet.co.uk

Typesetting: Tindal Street Press Ltd

A CIP catalogue reference for this book is available from
the British Library.

ISBN: 0 9541303 3 2

Printed and bound in Great Britain by
Biddles Ltd, *www.biddles.co.uk*

To:

Mum

Aunty – the original Aunt B

Deloris, Phil and Paul

and

Oliver Hebron

Acknowledgements

Thanks to Jackie Gay and Emma Hargrave for their incredible patience, support and encouragement; to Lucy and Stefano for giving me somewhere to sleep when I had nowhere else to go; and to Norman and James for those emails!

1

12th February

The room was in semi-darkness and unfamiliar to him. He edged his way forward cautiously, but then stumbled, hands clawing at empty air as he lost balance. He didn't fall, but it was enough to stop him in his tracks. Instinct for danger took over from rational thought, and he sensed rather than knew that he wasn't alone. His personal menace guide had kicked into action, the pulse at the side of his neck pounding in time to the frantic rhythm of his heart, his stomach a mass of contracted muscles. He tried to concentrate, eyes and ears straining to see and hear in the darkness. But all he could hear was his own breathing and the pounding of blood in his ear. Maybe it was all his imagination? With that thought came a slight release of tension, a relaxing of his muscles, which was when he heard it. So quick, so quiet, he nearly missed the slither of a shoe on hard ground; the sound of someone creeping forward, trying not to be heard. As he instinctively moved back and to one side, he noted a shift in the quality of darkness from black to dark grey. Somewhere behind him was a source of light. If he could only move closer to it then maybe he could see who or what was making him feel physically menaced. He inched backwards, but as he did so, he felt his invisible companion matching him step for step, creeping forward stealthily and maintaining the space between them, even as he retreated.

With no idea of how long it took, he eventually found himself standing in grey half-light. He realized that this new position left him vulnerable, exposed to his invisible assailant – but he didn't care. If he was going down, then he wanted to see who or what was taking him there.

Suddenly he was rocked by a rush of anger – hard, brilliant fury – he wouldn't give up without a fight. He stood where he was, peering into the darkness. Long seconds passed before his straining eyes caught a flash of something light and silvery, about chest height from the ground. Intuitively he stepped back. He couldn't see a face, but knew there had to be one. In fact, he couldn't see anything at all except the gleam of silver coming closer. His hands blindly sought a weapon, an exit – anything that might help him out of this – but there was nothing.

His attacker continued moving towards him, slowly, deliberately tormenting him. He stumbled backwards and slammed into the wall behind him. His hands flew up, crossed in subconscious reflex. A desperate prayer of self-defence which went unanswered as his attacker lunged forward and plunged a silver-bladed knife deep into his chest. He sank to his knees, trying to stem the blood that poured from his wound. Somewhere, far in the distance, bells were ringing. As he felt his life-force seeping out of him, he slipped sideways, banging his head on the floor.

Thoughts drifted like an unmoored boat floating on a slow, easy tide – fragmented moments of his life. His wife, sparkling brown eyes and freckled nose, her smile on their wedding day, her tears when their daughter was born. His daughter, her first laugh, first tooth, first step. It hadn't all been in vain; he hadn't wasted his life. He'd managed to get parts of it right. He smiled to himself, or at least thought he did. He couldn't feel any movement in his face, no stretching of lips or bunching of cheeks. He forced himself to concentrate, to control his breathing, his reactions. He turned his face to the side so it lay flat on the cold ground. Grains of fine gravel stuck to his cheek, a slightly larger piece pressed into the delicate skin at the corner of his eye. It should have hurt, but it didn't. Funny, he thought, how in some moments you could be absolutely aware of everything, down to the minutest detail. He could feel liquid, his blood he supposed, running through the veins in his arms, his legs, his head. Strange he'd never paid attention to it before. Now he could feel his blood seeping out of his chest, a slow steady leak. His veins, narrowing channels as they trickled red into the moist, coagulating pool beneath him.

His assailant stooped beside him; though his vision was beginning to cloud over, still he saw her eyes. Deep inside he'd always known it was her. She'd come back – as he'd feared and as she'd promised. His eyes flickered. Once. Twice. Then closed.

Bells getting louder, ringing incessantly, filling his head, drowning out the sound of his own laboured breathing, until one shrill and insistent shriek had him opening his eyes and up onto his feet. He half tripped as his foot caught in the blanket he had wrapped around him, then he steadied himself and picked up the telephone receiver from the low table in front of him.

The sound of breathing on the other end of the line made him think for a second that he was back in the nightmare he'd just left.

Then his teenage daughter spoke. 'Put it down, Dad,' Jewelle said. 'It's Ambra . . . for me.'

'Huh? Yeah. Right,' he mumbled, rubbing his eyes.

'C'mon, Dad. Hang up!' she said impatiently.

He yawned widely before replying. 'OK,' he said, then yawned again.

'Hang up then,' she insisted.

'Five minutes!' Though he felt groggy and confused, he

was awake enough to warn his daughter to keep the call short.

'All right,' Jewelle said sulkily. She could sense him on the other end of the line and waited until she heard the receiver click before she spoke again.

'Hey, Ambra!' Jewelle smiled into the cordless as she jumped onto her bed and reached for the remote control in one smooth movement. 'How's it going?' With her free hand she used the remote to turn down the stereo until the music was a mere background murmur.

'Fine this end. All packed then?'

'No!'

'Don't take it out on me,' Ambra replied cheerfully. 'It's not my fault you're off to a sunny Caribbean island full of sand, sea, beautiful men and who knows what else.'

'Yeah, go on. Laugh,' said Jewelle, flopping on her back. 'It's all right for you. *You're* going to the party *tomorrow*. *You'll* get lots of Valentine's cards *tomorrow*. You'll probably get to lips up Roy, *tomorrow*. *Tomorrow*, I'll be stuck between my dad and Aunt B, on my way to an island in the middle of nowhere. Can't wait!'

'Don't know what you're moaning about,' Ambra chirped. 'I'd swap places with you any day. *You're* going somewhere new, meeting different people, seeing different things. Dan's parties are *always* the same. Brassneck will be there. If we're lucky he'll come without his briefcase and if we're really lucky he'll splash on some of his dad's Old Spice, put a bit of gel in that wild red hair of his and think he's trendy.'

'It'll take more than a blob of gel.'

'Too right.' They sniggered together.

'Then there'll be Trisha sitting in a corner picking her spots and playing with the peanuts before offering them round.'

'Ugh!'

10

'I know, but she does, doesn't she? Maybe she's trying to dry them out.'

'What?'

'Her spots, stupid. Salt.'

'Oh.'

'Anyway, she'll be there. And Matt and Simon from Year 5, Suzy "call the Fashion Police" Thompson in some little number she stole from her granny; Inderjit, Harry, Jazz, Christina Dalton and Christina Weston . . .'

'*We're joined at the hip and have one brain cell between us,*' Jewelle threw in.

'Yeah.' Ambra laughed. 'Plus a few other rejects that Dan felt sorry for and couldn't say no to. 'Like . . .'

'Seven-Eleven!'

'Oh yeah. Slagbag Sally! Probably come wearing an outfit as big as a three-year-old's headband.'

'She'll be all over Dan.'

'No, she won't. Anyway, I've already said I'll keep an eye on things. I'll twang her bra strap or something if she steps out of line.'

'It's not funny,' Jewelle said seriously. 'She'll be there and I won't.'

'Listen!' Ambra said. 'If Dan prefers her orange face and those purple Cumberland sausage legs to you, then you're better off without him. He's obviously got no taste and no sense of class. Right?'

'Right,' Jewelle echoed without much conviction. 'I won't get any Valentine's cards either,' she moaned.

'They'll be here when you get back.'

'But it's not the same, is it?'

'JEWELLE!'

She covered the receiver with the palm of her hand and crossed to the bedroom door. 'Yes, Dad?'

'Hurry up and finish your call. I need the phone.'

'OK.' She flung herself back down on the bed. 'I'll have

to go in a minute, Dad wants the phone. Anyway, it's not the same, is it?' she insisted.

'No,' Ambra admitted, 'but it *is* only for ten days. I'll keep an eye on Seven-Eleven. You already know who's going to the party and what'll happen, so you're not really missing anything, are you? Anyway,' she added, 'it *is* your grandad's funeral.'

'But I didn't even know him.'

'So? He might have left you something.'

'You mean like a mango tree?' said Jewelle.

'I'm being serious. Money, lots of it. Or,' Ambra's tone deepened, 'a mysterious letter that leads you to . . . to . . .'

'A mango tree,' Jewelle finished, even more sarcastically.

'Well, there could be treasure under the mango tree, but first, you've got to get help decode the hidden instructions, and the guy who helps you – cos of course there's always a guy – turns out to be the love of your life. You'll fall in love *and* find the treasure and *never* come back to England. I'll be stuck in class with Tranter the Ranter going on and on about how we massacre the English language, Snothead hawking up behind me and Patrick Smith scratching his balls in front of me.'

They burst into raucous laughter at the image.

'JEWELLE!' A voice cut through the laughter. 'GET OFF THE PHONE. NOW!'

'Wow!' Ambra marvelled. 'I can hear your dad from here. I've never heard him shout before. I'd better go. He sounds really stressed out.'

'He's not stressed,' Jewelle replied airily, 'he's just old.'

'Listen. I've got your number in Jamaica. I'll try and sneak you a call when Mum and Dad are out, OK?'

'Great. I'll need someone to keep me sane. You can tell me what happened at the party.'

'NOW, JEWELLE!'

'I wish you were coming, Ambra.'

'So do I.'

'NOW!!'

'Gotta go,' Jewelle whispered. 'Love ya.'

'Love ya, too.'

'It's all yours!' she yelled to her father.

'About time too!' he shouted back.

'Ungrateful so and so,' she muttered, kicking her bedroom door shut. 'One tiny little call. Anybody'd think I'd been on the phone for hours.' The duvet sighed as she flopped back on the bed and gathered to her chest a worn, furry rabbit. She'd had it since she was a baby and it was the only toy she still kept on her bed. All the others were arranged neatly on shelves around the saffron walls. On the back of the door hung an enormous poster of Tupac. His black eyes glinted sexily as he looked down at her. She smiled back, imagining that his smile was for her and not for some anonymous camera lens. His folded arms accentuated his tattooed muscles.

I'd go to Jamaica for him, she thought. She turned her head and caught sight of her alarm clock; it was nearly eight and she still had her packing to do. She tossed the rabbit to one side, rolled onto her feet and dragged a half-filled suitcase from under the bed. Then she pulled a few of her favourite items from her wardrobe and drawers, things she'd only been able to wear a few times the previous summer before the weather turned cold and she'd had to sacrifice fashion for warmth. At least I'll get to wear them properly now, she thought, dropping the clothes on top of the carefully selected assortment already in the suitcase. She wrapped her diary in a large beach towel and added it to the suitcase, then flopped on the bed again.

Downstairs, Frank replaced the receiver on its rest. He'd rung his mother to confirm their time of arrival. Was it only two days ago that she'd told him the news?

'Yuh puppa dead, Frank,' she'd said. 'It was his time. Nutten more, nutten less.' Her voice had broken up on the last few words and it had been impossible to tell if this was due to the crackly line or the emotion overcoming her.

He hadn't been able to hide his grief and she'd tried to comfort him. 'Wha' go roun' mus' come roun'. It simple. De only ting certain in life is death. No matter whether we choose it or it choose us. It was yuh puppa turn. Hush, son. Nuh cry.'

But he had cried. Burst into tears like a little boy. Like the little boy he no longer was and could no longer be because his father was dead. Then he'd switched onto automatic: making long-distance funeral arrangements, booking flights and organizing duties for his substitute at Burgess & Sons Accountants. He had a big auditing job on and a diary full of appointments, but there was no choice; somebody else would have to take over his clients. And even though everything was now prepared and there was nothing left to do – at least, not in England – he still felt as if he were standing outside himself, watching another Frank Galimore in action.

When Aunt B, his dead wife's sister, had offered to travel to Jamaica with them to keep an eye on Jewelle so he could spend time with his mother, he'd accepted gratefully. He didn't always see eye to eye with Aunt B. In fact, they didn't have much in common at all. Never happy unless she had the first *and* last word, she was loud, pushy, quick-tempered and full of superstitious claptrap. She in turn, he suspected, was annoyed by the fact that he was more measured and took his time before making up his mind. But she'd been unusually helpful and patient on this occasion and he could only hope that it would last for the duration of the trip.

He sank into the reclining chair Jewelle had persuaded him to buy years before, simply because she liked the way its various parts moved. He pushed the hand control so the footrest whirred and raised his legs. It felt like months instead of days since he'd had a minute to himself to just sit and be. That nightmare must simply be an indication of the stress he was under. It was no surprise that he'd dreamed of his own death – he felt he'd lost a part of himself with his father's passing away. The moment he settled back and closed his eyes, the doorbell rang. He recognized the impatient triple ring. Aunt B.

Jewelle's scalp itched. Her freshly plaited hair felt tight along her hairline and she rubbed the area carefully with her fingertips. Below, she could hear voices as her father opened the front door. Aunt B's voice rose loud and clear above the more muted tones of her husband, Sam. Jewelle rushed to put on a CD. Aunt B might like the sound of her own voice, but not everyone else did. She sat at her dressing table and sprayed her roots with some Isoplus hair sheen. It instantly reduced some of the itchiness and she massaged it in before pulling her hair back and examining her face first one way and then another. The plaits gave fullness to her rather narrow face with its wide and straight-lashed brown eyes. Her full mouth was set in a petulant pout as she heard a knock at her door. She barely had time to turn, let alone respond, before Aunt B walked in.

Jewelle's mouth tightened in exasperation. 'I didn't even say come in,' she muttered.

'Me all right. How are you?' Aunt B replied cheerily.

'All right, I s'pose.'

'Yuh pack yet?'

'Started not finished.' Jewelle nodded to the suitcase on the floor, then turned back to the mirror. She watched her aunt poke at the contents of the case and held her tongue as Aunt B held up a skimpy red jersey dress in one hand and a minuscule yellow swimsuit in the other.

'Where yuh goin' wid dis? Beach party?'

Their gaze met in the mirror, but Jewelle didn't speak. How could her aunt possibly understand *anything* about fashion when she dressed the way she did? All that bright, shiny material she liked to drape herself in. Today she had on a dark purple skirt, which wasn't too bad in itself, but on top she was wearing a salmon-coloured polo neck, whose knitted horizontal panels only served to accentuate her big bosom and thickening waist. To make matters worse she had on her favourite red lipstick, which didn't go with anything. With the dress and the swimsuit held in either hand she looked like a badly decorated Christmas tree. Jewelle stifled a sudden giggle.

'Nutten fi laugh 'bout, miss. Dere's nutten black in here.'

'I haven't finished yet, that's why.'

'Better get on wid it den,' Aunt B snapped.

'Can't concentrate when other people are in the room.' Jewelle turned and peered into the mirror as she swapped the fine gold ring in her nose for a dainty silver stud with a clear stone. The metal contrasted well with her skin and highlighted the delicate arch of her nostrils.

Turn roun' an' look at me, Aunt B willed, staring at Jewelle's back. Wh'appen to de likkle gyal who use to steal sweets from me handbag, den curl up and fall asleep on me lap lissenin' to me stories? Cho, Jewelle! I just don' understan' yuh any more, she thought.

She was looking forward to spending time with her only niece, even if the reason for the trip to Jamaica was a sombre one. She loved Jewelle dearly, but the older the girl got the less she saw of her, and Jewelle's attitude when they did see each other, made her want to shake her hard. Cyaan open me mouth to her dese days before she jump down me throat. She angry wid everybody all de time but she only seem fi tek it out 'pon me.

Whatever I do is wrong, Aunt B thought sadly. If I try

show likkle interest in her life, she call me nosy an' interferin'. When I try fi respect her privacy she start scream I don' care 'bout her and dat she hate me. Frank seh fi ignore her, dat is just a stage she going through. It all right fi him, she don' treat him like stray dog out a street. But she nuh stupid, she have her daddy twist so tight roun' her likkle finger she can get away wid anyting she like. Kuh 'ow she dress! Clothes dat barely cover her likkle maaga backside; six or seven rings pierce up one ear and dat damn *ting* in her nose like she some kind of cow. Now she talkin' 'bout gettin' a tattoo! Bad enough she look like apprentice punk, but a tattoo as well! No way any niece of mine gwine mark up her body like some kinda slave. No way! And if Frank don' put him foot down on dat one, den I will.

Aunt B's bosom heaved as she took a deep breath. In truth, all she wanted was for them to be friends – going to the cinema, shopping for clothes, just spending time together like they used to. She wanted her little girl back.

'Yuh hair look nice,' she tried.

'No, it doesn't. It looks horrible. Makes me look like a kid.'

'Once we out dere yuh soon glad fe de plait. Wid de heat and de sand and de sea, yuh waan someting yuh nuh haffi fuss over.'

'No I won't,' Jewelle complained. 'This is boring.' She flicked at her hair. 'I can't do anything with it when it looks like this. I can't gel it or colour it. Can't put it up. They're just stupid, boring plaits hanging around my face and getting in the way.'

Aunt B rolled her eyes and dropped the dress and swimsuit back into the case. Better leave before Jewelle really got her started. 'Yuh Uncle Sam downstairs. Maybe when yuh finish yuh packin', yuh can come down and seh hello. Dat is, if it not too much trouble,' she added.

Jewelle spun around on the stool. 'All right,' she said, staring at a point somewhere above her aunt's head.

Aunt B could feel her palm itching. Galang, Miss Jewelle, she thought. Yuh tink yuh big, soon show yuh who big 'bout here. She rubbed her palms down the sides of her skirt and left the room before she gave into the temptation to give one of the plaits a sharp pull.

Jewelle waited until she was sure Aunt B was downstairs before she moved. When she did, it was to slap the top of the dressing table hard. 'Why does she always make me feel bad?' she muttered. Aunt B could provoke her just by breathing. It was then that sullen, spiteful words she couldn't stop would spill out of her mouth from nowhere. The guilt she felt once the words were out only made her want to be nastier.

She pulled a few stray hairs from her eyebrows harder than she meant, bringing water to her eyes, then dabbed TCP on an incipient spot on her chin until it stung. Now I'm going to have a black burn mark, she thought angrily as she examined the damage in the mirror. And it's all Aunt B's fault. This trip was going to be a nightmare. She sorted out her make-up bag, fiddled with things on the surface of the dressing table and then brushed a few motes of dust from a large, framed black and white photograph which stood to the left of the mirror.

The photo showed Jewelle when she was a few months old, lying in the crook of her mother's arm. Their images were stark; their lines clean against the white of the background. Jewelle's bright baby eyes stared unblinkingly towards the camera, her round face framed in a hectic mass of soft black curls and her mouth puckered up in a small smile. The woman looked down at the child in her arms; her hair, pressed straight and curled into a bob, followed the line of her chin. Jewelle stared at the photo as she had so many times before, searching for some sign of resemblance to this woman who had died when she was only five years old. It wasn't the only photo she had of her mother, but it was her favourite.

She liked the way her mother held her against her bare chest, as if she wanted the closest possible contact between them; how her other arm lay across her body as her hand rose to stroke the rounded baby chin. Jewelle often imagined she could hear her mother's heartbeat beneath her ear as she lay against her chest, could feel the softness of her mother's skin against her own. She remembered sniffing at the photo after her mother died, trying to recall what she'd smelled like. It hadn't worked of course, and she'd cried with disappointment for days after. But the photo somehow brought her comfort. It had always made her feel safe and loved as a child. And even now, at fifteen, it still did.

Uncle Sam settled back in his armchair and savoured the dark rum in his mouth. ''Member fi bring me some back,' he said to his wife.

'Yuh already remind me a hundred times. Appleton Gold. Yuh never drink anyting else, anyway. Maybe I should bring a bottle of Wray & Nephew, mek yuh try someting different.' She nudged Frank.

'No, no. Appleton. Appleton,' Uncle Sam said quickly, missing the nudge. 'All set, Frank?'

'Yes, man. Everything's organized.' He stared down at the glass in his hand. 'Thanks for taking us to the airport. Really appreciate it.'

'Least I can do. I'll come an' pick yuh up as well when yuh come back. One less ting fi yuh fi worry 'bout. Yuh speak to yuh madda yet?'

'Called her just before you arrived. She sounded all right . . . considering.'

'Yuh madda strong. Mek certain yuh strong fi her too.

Cyaan be easy –' Uncle Sam stopped mid-sentence, but Frank finished what he'd been about to say.

'– now she's all alone. I know.' He massaged his temples between thumb and index finger before looking up. 'I don't know what to do,' he confessed. 'She can't stay out there all by herself, but Jamaica's her home. I know she doesn't want to leave but I don't want to go back there and live. I've been away too long. Anyway, this is all Jewelle's ever known and she's got her GSCEs coming up next year.' He shook his head as he spoke.

Uncle Sam patted his arm. 'Me certain once yuh out there, tings will sort themself out. Too many thoughts in yuh head right now fi yuh fi see anyting clearly . . . but another glass of rum might help . . . me,' he held his glass forward, 'seein' as yuh nuh really drink.'

'Sometimes I wish I did.' Frank shook his head and sighed.

'I tink yuh should bring Miss Jess back wid yuh,' Aunt B said firmly. 'She old. Me certain she not gwine argue.'

'Yuh not much younger an' yuh still love argue,' Uncle Sam teased.

'Wha' yuh talkin' 'bout?' Aunt B bristled.

'Me just sayin' yuh too fas'! Love interfere inna people business. Mek Frank and him madda sort tings out between dem.'

'I just waan fi help,' she protested.

'Well, wait till dem ask yuh before yuh leap in,' Sam warned. 'Remember de letter?' he whispered.

Whatever Aunt B had been going to say was cut off by Jewelle's entrance.

'Wha'ppen, Diamond?'

She smiled weakly. It was an old joke. Uncle Sam rarely called Jewelle by her real name. He called her Jade, Sapphire, Pearl, Ruby – even Jet when she was in a bad mood. But the funniest thing of all was that her name wasn't Jewelle at all, but Lauren. Her mother had always called her 'my little jewel' and the name had stuck.

'I've just come to do my hot water bottle and say good-night.' She went into the kitchen and switched on the kettle.

'Finish pack yet?' Aunt B called over the hum.

'Yes,' Jewelle lied.

'Yuh pack someting black?'

'Yes,' she lied again. It wasn't a real lie. There were black things in there, just nothing Aunt B would approve of. She filled the bottle and walked back into the sitting room.

'Nice hot water bottle yuh have dere,' Uncle Sam said, reaching forward to touch the transparent container with its multicoloured hearts floating inside. 'Pretty.'

'Glad you like it.' Jewelle grinned. 'You and Aunt B gave it me for Christmas last year.'

'Ah.' Uncle Sam raised his bushy eyebrows to his grey hairline. 'Sometime me figet me owna good taste.' Aunt B snorted while Uncle Sam took another sip from his drink, then looked at her. 'I choose yuh. Yuh choose it. So I have good taste,' he said calmly, winking at Jewelle.

For a moment the tension in the room disappeared and they all laughed, even Aunt B. As the laughter dissipated, she felt her smile grow inside. Thirty-odd years on and he was still happy with his choice. She blessed the day she'd said 'yes'.

'I'm going to bed,' Jewelle announced. She hugged the bottle to her chest as she kissed her father on his forehead.

'Waan me fi wake yuh?' Aunt B asked, hoping she would be granted a kiss too. But she had to content herself with a 'yes please'.

2

13th February

'Jewelle! We ready.'

'I wish she'd stop bawling my name like it's going out of fashion,' Jewelle grumbled under her breath as she hoisted her rucksack over one shoulder and hurried out the door. She waited by the car as Frank locked the front door behind them and Aunt B gave Uncle Sam last-minute instructions on how to best pack the bags in the boot. Early morning freshness brought water to her eyes, making her shiver and draw her jacket closer. The pavements shone seal-grey under the street lamps as fine rain fell insistently; enough to dampen and depress but not to clean.

'Soon be somewhere warmer, Ruby,' Uncle Sam said trying to cheer her up. She grimaced and he continued, 'Just think of me all alone in this cold country of pissy-pissy rain, where de only colour is grey.'

'Yeah, I know. But it's Valentine's Day tomorrow and there's the party . . .'

He gave her a quick squeeze. 'I know yuh waan stay wid yuh friend dem, but believe me, when yuh reach Jamaica an' feel true sunshine an' see real colours yuh won't waan come back,' he said. 'Come on, get in de car.'

Uncle Sam was nice. He didn't take sides or try to boss people about. Pity he wasn't coming instead of Aunt B, Jewelle thought. She pulled the tartan car blanket around her shoulders and turned to the window on her side. She wiped her hand over the steamed-up glass, then stared through the arc she'd created. They drove through Walsall to West Bromwich where they picked up the M5, and then there was nothing to see except motorway stretching for miles ahead; its grey monotony broken only by cars speeding past in the opposite direction. And, as the growing light pushed away night-time darkness, Jewelle fell asleep.

'Yuh have de passport dem, Frank?'

Aunt B's voice interrupted his reverie. He rubbed his eyes, which were red and watery through lack of sleep.

'Me seh, yuh have de passport dem?'

'How many times yuh gwine ask him de same damn fool question?' Uncle Sam said, expressing Frank's unvoiced thoughts. 'Anyway, too bad if him figet, 'cause we reach now an' me not turnin' back.'

'Nuh badda snap off me head! Is only askin' me askin'. It would be a pity to come all dis way only fi den find yuh leave dem behind. Anyway, I have mine.' Aunt B patted the front of her bosom where her passport lay damp but snug against her chest. 'So me won't badda worry 'bout anybody else,' she sniffed. 'Jewelle, stop jumpin' up an' down like dat. Yuh too big fi such antics.'

Jewelle kicked at one of the suitcases lying on the pavement in front of her, but was wise enough not to reply. Uncle Sam gave her a sympathetic smile.

'An' nuh badda dirty up yuh shoes,' Aunt B continued. 'Yuh tink yuh daddy buy dem new just so yuh can mess dem up before we even leave de country. Wha' wrong wid yuh? Yuh waan reach Jamaica a look like tramp, mek everybody tink yuh nuh have family?'

'They're *flat* and they're *ugly*,' Jewelle replied sulkily.

'Nutten wrong wid dem shoes. Is me choose dem.' Jewelle rolled her eyes upwards in irritation. 'If it did leave up to yuh, we all know yuh woulda live in a pair of trainers I wouldn't even mek dog play wid, or in a pair of yuh high-steppin' clod-hoppers.'

'I don't even want to go to Jamaica,' she grumbled.

'Yuh nuh have no feelings fi yuh father in him time of grief? Is yuh gran'daddy we gwine bury, in case yuh nuh 'member. All yuh can tink 'bout is yuhself. Well, I have news fi yuh – just watch yuhself 'pon dis trip. Me nah let yuh run wild like yuh do in England.'

'Cho!'

'Yuh tink just 'cause yuh have yuh own passport yuh can backchat me like yuh likkle English friends do wid dem parent. Better watch yuh step if yuh know wha' good fi yuh. Awoah!'

Jewelle rolled her eyes and pushed out her bottom lip as she fumbled in her rucksack for her Walkman. Aunt B was just warming up, so there was no point saying anything else and upsetting her further. She slipped a cassette into the machine and hoped she had enough batteries to outlast Aunt B and the nine-hour flight.

'Come, Jewelle.' Uncle Sam pulled her towards the news-agents. 'Yuh know yuh aunty love huff and puff – nuh mind her, her bark worse dan her bite. Come fi a likkle walk mek we buy some extra battery an' couple magazine.'

'Can't you at least wait until we check-in before you start arguing with everyone?' Frank hissed at Aunt B.

'So wha' yuh waitin' on?' Aunt B turned her attention to Frank. 'Yuh tink dese bags gwine walk to check-in by themself? Or maybe yuh just waan see me bruk me back carryin' dem.'

'Wouldn't mind,' he said under his breath.

'Mind me legs,' Aunt B ordered, as Frank heaved a bulging suitcase onto the trolley. 'Yuh waan rip up me tights?'

Frank ignored her and concentrated instead on loading

the trolley. He leaned forward so that his shoulder rested just below the base of the top suitcase, holding it in place yet at the same time giving him the extra leverage he needed as he tried to steer the trolley in a straight line. It hadn't taken long for Aunt B to revert to form. Now they were close to departure, she was grumpy and on edge. Anyone would think it was *her* father who had died, not his. If anyone was going to act up then it should be him. He was the one dreading the unvoiced recriminations in his mother's eyes when he arrived in Jamaica, not her. He was beginning to wish he'd said no when Aunt B had offered to accompany them. A moment of weakness he hoped he wouldn't live to regret, he mused, as Jewelle ran ahead of him and Aunt B puffed behind. The goodbyes had been brief.

'Mind yuh own business,' Uncle Sam whispered to his wife.

'Me cyaan help a fret, Sam. Yuh know why.'

'Me know,' he reassured. 'But wait till yuh have someting real fi worry 'bout before yuh start interfere.'

'But I don' waan nutten fi happen.'

'Me know, but me sure everyting gwine work out all right. Call me. Mek me know yuh arrive safe. Reverse charge. Nuh badda run up Miss Jess phone bill.' He gave her a quick hug before turning to Jewelle. 'Gimme a hug, Pearl.' He pulled her close. 'Look after yuh aunty an' yuh daddy fi me.' He slapped Frank on the back. 'Tek care, man, an' give yuh mumma my regards.'

Uncle Sam stood and waved until they entered passport control. When the trio turned for a final wave, all they saw was the back of his checked jacket as he walked away.

Jewelle pushed her way through the queue of people on the steps of the plane with teenage single-mindedness, and ran to her seat. She was already settled and peering excitedly through the small square of window on her left by the time Aunt B bustled her way down the aisle. She drew up short when she saw Jewelle sitting by the window.

'Come, move out of me seat now, chile.'

Jewelle merely nodded in time to the music coming from her Walkman and Aunt B tugged impatiently at the girl's sleeve.

'What?' she asked, pulling out one of the earphones.

'Yuh in me place. Move over mek me sit down.'

'But I'm sitting here. Dad said I could have the window seat,' Jewelle said. 'I want to see Jamaica from the air.'

'Hurry up!' Frank hissed at them. 'You're blocking the aisle and plenty of people want to sit down.'

'Tell yuh pickney fi move, den. She's in my seat.'

'But Aunt B, she's a child. Let her sit by the window.'

Jewelle replaced her earphone and turned back to the window.

'Dat's right,' Aunt B said loudly. 'She a pickney. She have plenty years left fi sit at any window seat she choose. Me old now. For all me know, dis could be de last flight me ever tek. First time in God know how many years I go back an' yuh an' yuh kin grudge me a piece of glass.'

Frank tried to push Aunt B into the middle seat, but the woman stayed where she was, defiant, her pink satin suit like armour.

'Ah waan dat seat!'

One of the elegantly dressed Air Jamaica cabin crew made her way through the knot of people concentrated in the middle of the plane. She gave Aunt B a sharp, surprised look, quickly replaced by an expression of professional neutrality when she discovered what the problem was. Aunt B glared at her obstinately.

'Listen.' The stewardess tapped Jewelle on the shoulder to get her attention. 'The plane's not completely full.' Her voice was melodic, a musical lilt to her accented English. 'Once we've taken off I'm certain we can find you a

26

window seat. But for now, can you please move over, otherwise nobody will get seated and none of us will be going anywhere. Oh, and switch off your Walkman until we're in the air.'

Frank gave Jewelle a nod and she slipped reluctantly out of her seat and into the aisle, her bottom lip pushed out sulkily, much like Aunt B's. He sighed deeply and hoped fervently that this was all these two women in his life would ever have in common.

Once seated, he watched Aunt B out of the corner of his eye, marvelling that she could remain upright despite the force of gravity that pushed everybody else's head back against their seats as the plane took off. Twenty-one years ago he'd been only too glad to feel that pressure against his body; it had held him safe as the plane took him from one island to another. To England and a new start. A new life. Or had it been somewhere to hide? He hadn't answered that question then and didn't want to face it now. All he was sure about was that it had taken him from a woman who'd been obsessed with him to one he'd truly loved.

'Why don't you take off your hat, Aunt B?' Jewelle whispered, good humour restored. 'You've already lost one of the feathers. You'll be more comfortable.'

'I waan look smart when I arrive, not like some people on dis plane.' She sniffed disapprovingly as she looked around. 'Mek people see dat *me* come from somewhere.' The two remaining feathers at the side of the hat moved as she spoke, as if nodding in approval. 'De hat stay weh it deh.' And it did.

Jewelle was given a window seat a few rows back once the plane was airborne, but she curled up and fell asleep almost as soon as she'd eaten, even before the in-flight films started. Frank set the alarm on his watch for thirty minutes before landing, enough time to freshen up and change out of his trackpants and T-shirt into something smarter. Aunt

B flicked through the in-flight magazine, but it held little of interest for her. The rigid brim of her hat meant that every time she dozed off her head lay at an awkward angle, causing her to breathe noisily as she slept until she snorted herself awake again. Her dreams were fragmented and unsettling; of Beth and Rose, Rose and Beth – of the sister she'd lost and the best friend she'd let down.

A few minutes before they were due to land, Frank pulled back the light blanket that covered Jewelle and woke her up. 'You don't want to miss this bit, Jewelle. Your first real sight of Jamaica. Look at it.'

She rubbed her eyes and yawned. 'But it's all so green,' she said, leaning forward.

'So, what colour did you expect it to be?' Frank laughed as he stroked her hair.

'I dunno. I didn't really think colour. Just beach and water, I suppose. I've never really thought about it. But it looks like a green pearl in a beautiful blue oyster shell.'

Frank kissed the top of her head and smiled again. 'I'd better get back,' he said, as the announcements began for passengers to take their seats and fasten their seat belts.

Jewelle pressed her nose up against the glass as the plane circled ever lower above the island, entranced. The shell-pink rooftops of houses lay dotted like tiny coloured stars among the deep green mountain peaks. The beaches outlining the edge of the island were a vibrant golden-yellow, gradually fading to creamy white as they ran into the sea. And what a sea! Not one shade of blue, but blues dark and light, aquamarine and greens, with a hidden depth of purple. Her fingertips traced the surface of the glass as if she hoped that somehow, magically, she could dip them in the warmth of the Caribbean Sea, rub the grains of sand between her fingers.

As the plane descended, the voices of the passengers did too until there was nothing to be heard but their whispers and the sound of the engines. Aunt B muttered a hasty prayer as she adjusted her hat. The plane bumped its way onto the runway, jolting passengers and cabin crew forward, before reducing speed and gradually coming to a halt. For a moment, there was nothing but silence, then a sudden outbreak of enthusiastic applause and cries of 'praise God'. Aunt B crossed herself and looked upwards.

Frank closed his eyes. The first part was over.

'Me know me reach me yard when me hear dis kinda music.' Even Aunt B couldn't stop herself from smiling as they walked into the arrivals area to be greeted by a four-man steel band and five or six dancing girls.

The men were dressed in light green cotton trousers with short-sleeved blue and yellow Hawaiian-style shirts. The array of flowers the girls wore around their necks contrasted vibrantly with their wash-faded, knee-length red or orange dresses. The girls danced barefoot, oiled skin gleaming as they moved among the recently arrived tourists, bestowing flowers and smiling for photographs. Then, as suddenly as the music and dancing had started, it stopped. The group of musicians and dancers retired to the room they'd come from to await the arrival of the next flight and the next group of tourists.

'Somebody should be here soon.' Frank pulled Jewelle closer to his side as he scanned the faces of those waiting in the arrivals area.

'Maybe we should wait outside,' Jewelle suggested.

'No, too hot,' Aunt B protested, but when she saw Frank and Jewelle moving forward, she pulled a red and black fan from her bag and hurried after them, her mouth moving in a silent grumble.

'Oh!'

'What?' Frank looked at his daughter. She stood open-mouthed, one hand on her heart.

'The heat. The light. It's so bright!' She stared up into the clearest of blue skies. 'Everything is so . . . I dunno,' she shrugged, 'so vivid.' Her hand moved as she spoke, as if she wanted to capture the quality of light and colour that she was finding so difficult to describe. She turned around slowly, smiling. 'It's just like a film, only better.'

Frank laughed and put one arm around her shoulders. 'Looks like Jamaica's working its magic on you already,' he said as a car roared into the taxi zone directly in front of the terminal building. It screeched to a halt, clipping the side of a parked taxi. The taxi driver jumped from his car cursing and raced to confront the other driver who was stepping slowly from his own vehicle. Then the two men were blocked from sight as other taxi drivers gathered around them. Frank watched the scene idly, the car park was emptying rapidly now that most people had collected their luggage and left.

He turned to Jewelle, who was sitting on one of Aunt B's suitcases. 'Mumma said she was sending one of the guys who do odd jobs for her to pick us up.' He looked around again as he spoke, suddenly his neck stiffened, then stretched forward slightly in surprise, as if jerked by an invisible string. Jewelle looked up as Frank's arm slipped from her shoulders. She followed his movement with her eyes and saw a muscular, dark-skinned man step out from the group of taxi drivers who were now arguing loudly with two crisply uniformed policemen. She saw Frank's mouth spread wide in a slow smile as he moved first hesitantly, then more quickly towards the tall man. His glance briefly met hers before her father's broad shoulders blocked him from view. Then both men were slapping and hugging each other hard.

'Who's that, Aunt B?' she asked getting to her feet. 'Is that the odd-job man?'

Her aunt stood frozen in shock. Aunt B's short, sturdy

legs seemed unable to maintain the weight of her upper body. The satin suit, no longer fresh, clung to her like crumpled tissue. Her eyes were bigger and rounder than Jewelle had ever seen them. She looked scared and that made Jewelle scared too. But of what? She shivered: icy fingers on her sun-warmed skin.

'Aunt B? Are you all right?' She tugged at her aunt's sleeve. 'Aunt B!'

'Huh?' Aunt B replied absently, her eyes fixed on the two men who were now making their way towards them.

'What's the matter with you? You deaf? Cho!' The sound of Jewelle's lips smacking as she kissed her teeth snapped Aunt B out of her trance. Her hand flew out, connecting smartly with the back of Jewelle's head.

'Nuh badda start gettin' lippy wid me, gyal. Yuh must tink –'

'See yuh nuh lose yuh touch, Miss B.' His voice flowed like gingered molasses into the spaces of the cracked silence. 'Wha'ppen? Yuh mouth favour grip dat cyaan close! Yuh not goin' to seh hello to me after all dis time? Wha' kinda manners yuh teachin' de chile?'

'Hello,' Aunt B said, as if the word had been slapped out of her. The cool freshness of his dark clothes – the black suit, casual but well cut and the dark grey T-shirt – only made her more aware of the damp brightness of her own clothes. 'Hello,' she said again, a little more firmly, but he'd already switched his attention to the girl at her side.

'So, you're Frank's jewel!' Sol raised one delicately winged eyebrow. 'I'm Sol. Bet yuh daddy never mention me before, eh?' He scrutinized her as he spoke. She had a woman's mouth in a girl's face and her father's eyes, but there was a spark of fire in them that Frank's lacked. He had a feeling she was used to getting her own way. Definitely a girl who was going to cause quite a few men more than a few problems when she was fully grown, he concluded.

'Pleased to meet you,' she said, offering him her hand. His sparkling black eyes seemed to see right into her and she clutched her rucksack closer to her chest. He made her feel self-conscious, more aware of herself in a way she couldn't define and she found herself standing up straighter with none of her usual adolescent slouch.

Sol's sharp-toothed white smile grew warmer, deeper, and pulled a smile from her in return, though she was unable to meet his eyes and kept her gaze fixed on one of his slightly pockmarked cheeks.

He chuckled gently at her confusion. 'I know yuh father since him was a bwoy. Far as me concern, yuh just like a daughter, so nuh badda gimme yuh hand,' he said, hugging her. 'Welcome to Jamaica!' His breath stroked the side of her face as he whispered, 'Everyting dat happen have a reason. Open yuh eyes while yuh here. Plenty fi see an' learn.'

Jewelle barely heard his words as she breathed in his double-layer scent; fresh but with an underlay of something rich, heady, that made her feel liquid warm inside. Lemon and cinnamon spice, she decided. It made her want to burrow her nose deep into his neck and not stop breathing it in. Sol was completely unlike any of the friends her dad had at home. This man seemed young, just like her. It wasn't just his hair, which he wore cornrowed back and then pulled into a tiny ponytail. Or the neat little goatee. This man was . . . she didn't know what he was, except he wasn't like her dad at all.

Frank smiled at the scene. Above Jewelle's head, Sol met Aunt B's frosty glare with a smirk.

'Car's this way.' Sol spoke over his shoulder as he hoisted one suitcase on to his shoulder wheeled the other behind him. It tipped perilously as he weaved his way around two taxi drivers arguing over a fare. Their potential passengers, two blonde girls, watched in bewilderment as their bags were dragged from one taxi to another, as each driver tried to claim them as his own.

'Yuh madda was goin' to send Jake wid de pickup, but I tell her yuh couldn't expect a lady fresh from England fi ride in a pickup.' Aunt B sniffed loudly in approval. 'Never tink *yuh* would like de pickup much either, Miss B.' Sol grinned as he opened the rear door of the car. He grinned again as he observed Aunt B's sour expression through the cracked rearview mirror as she viciously fanned the air around her with her red and black fan.

'Who's Jake?' Jewelle asked.

'One of de bwoys who do odd jobs fi yuh granny,' Sol said.

'Might as well go to sleep, Jewelle,' Frank said. 'We've got a good couple of hours' drive before we reach Brown's Town.'

'I'm not tired any more,' she said brightly. 'Anyway, I want to hear you chat in patois to Sol!'

'I've only just arrived,' he laughed, 'give me a chance to get back into it.'

Sol chuckled as he set the car in motion. 'All right. If yuh not tired, mek we drive through Montego Bay.'

Frank smiled. In the space of a few hours his daughter had gone from hating the idea of spending even one day, let alone ten, on what she referred to as 'that little island', to not wanting to miss a thing. It was the magic of Jamaica. A magic that had worn thin for him in the past, but one which he could now appreciate after so many years away.

Aunt B, likewise, was determined not to sleep, though her reasons were different. Despite having prepared herself to see Sol at the funeral, his appearance at the airport had thrown her. Still trim and muscular, he didn't seem to have changed in the intervening years, while she had grown shorter and stouter with the passage of time. Watching him saunter up to her in the airport in that lean, languorous way, looking so fresh and cool, and with that 'I've got your measure' look of his, infuriated her more than she could express. That way he had of lifting those girlishly fine eyebrows. Even his pockmarks only served to elongate his dimples and make his smile more dangerously attractive. With Sol around, bad luck was bound to be just a footstep behind.

From the moment she'd heard about Poppa Ben's death, she'd been uneasy. An unease that ate into her like a dog gnawing at a bone. Then she'd dreamed of Beth, which for Aunt B had been a clear sign. Sam might scoff, but she believed that all dreams had meaning; it just took time to understand them. Rather than take any chances, she'd insisted on accompanying Frank and Jewelle to Jamaica under the pretext of looking after Jewelle. The tickets had been booked and paid for before Frank could change his mind. Aunt B nodded to herself in grim satisfaction – she'd already lost her sister, she wasn't going to allow anything to happen to her sister's only child.

And as she nodded, an unsmiling Sol studied Aunt B through the fractured rearview mirror.

Jewelle looked around her curiously as they entered Montego Bay. Old and new buildings lined both sides of the main street. As they drove into the centre, Sol pointed out a little building set to one side of the main square.

'Dat place name de Cage,' he said, pointing as they drove past. 'It build 1806, 1807, someting like dat. It was a prison for runaway slaves.'

'Really?' Jewelle spun around in the car to look as they left it behind.

'Yeah. Back den it was illegal fi black people fi walk roun' freely after t'ree o'clock on a Sunday afternoon. So any black people on de streets after dat time, dem sling in dere too.'

'Oh.' Jewelle didn't quite know what to say. She'd always associated slavery with America and Africa and had never really thought about the fact that it'd taken place in Jamaica too.

'Dem teach yuh 'bout any of dis at school?' Sol asked.

'No. At least not at my school.'

'Over dere,' Sol indicated the corner of Union and East Street, 'is de Slave Ring. I suppose yuh can imagine what it did use for.'

She stared at the decaying stone amphitheatre. 'Fights?' She ventured a guess.

'Well, people seh dat first it use as a slave market, den after dat dem use it fi cockfight.'

'Oh.'

'So what kinda history dem teach yuh in England?' Sol asked.

'I know all about the Industrial Revolution,' she replied, but suddenly it didn't seem nearly enough.

'Why yuh tellin' de gyal all dis foolishness?' Aunt B asked. 'First yuh drag us out of we way an' den yuh show her all dese tings. Yuh nuh have nutten pretty fi show her?'

'Jamaica fulla pretty tings. Everywhere yuh look, yuh see dem. But is tings like dis people should see. We need fi 'member our history. Is up to us fi mek de youth know weh we come from. Dese things just as important as all dose "pretty tings" dis island famous for. Anyway,' he added, 'we never drive much out of we way.' Sol swung the car around at the next corner and headed out of town.

The further they drove from Montego Bay, the more the buildings changed – from banks, offices and structures that were clear evidence of Jamaica's colonial past, with their high entrances and thick-columned supports – to other, less grand affairs. As the scenery became more rural, so these buildings were replaced by ramshackle homes; many of them made of plywood, concrete or corrugated tin.

Anything their owners could lay their hands on was put to good use. Instead of shops, there were roadside stands and stores, often little more than flimsy shacks, selling fruit and vegetables. Mangoes, guavas, tangerines and guineps, yams, chocho and cassavas lay on broad green banana leaves, next to the roadside. They slowed for a corner and two children ran towards the car. The elder of the two, a bare-chested boy of about ten, held high a stick from which hung plump red and yellow fruit with black 'eyes'.

'What was that?' Jewelle turned around and stared through the back window as the car continued on its way.

'Ackee,' Aunt B replied.

'Ackee? That yellow stuff you cook with saltfish on Sundays?'

Aunt B nodded.

'I've never seen it look like that before. So why's it red, then?'

'How come unnu don' tell de gyal 'bout her heritage?' Sol laughed. 'What yuh just see is fresh ackee – Jamaica's national dish.'

Jewelle nodded.

'When de ackee ripe and open,' he continued, 'yuh find three yellow lobes full of black seeds, which we call eyes. Yuh scrape out de seeds, pull off de thin red membrane and den boil de ackee – de yellow part. When it done boil, not too soft now, yuh drain it and cook it up wid onion, pepper, saltfish, a little Scotch bonnet and salt and pepper. Yuh can eat it wid a whole heap a ting – roast breadfruit, or boil banana or fry dumplin'. Yuh like ackee and saltfish?'

'Not really.' Jewelle screwed up her face.

'Dat's probably 'cause yuh never eat fresh ackee. Tin ackee nuh taste de same. Look like we haffi cook yuh some true Jamaican ackee before yuh leave.' He turned around to look at her. 'All right?'

'All right.'

The heat, together with the slow rolling movement of the car, lulled the passengers into a relaxed, sleepy state. Sol whistled lightly under his breath. Frank lounged in his seat with his arm along the edge of the wound-down window and wondered how he could have so completely forgotten the feeling of hot sun on his skin, the intense blue of the sky and the salty taste of sea in the air.

The conversation between the two men was desultory, broken by the occasional question from Jewelle until even those died away. When Frank turned around, he saw both her and Aunt B asleep. Aunt B had finally given in. Beaten by the heat and the long hours of journeying, she'd kicked off her shoes, undone the buttons on her jacket and taken off her hat. Her fan lay in her half-closed hand. Jewelle's head had slipped down until it finally rested on Aunt B's shoulder, and the rise and fall of her chest and shoulders as she breathed echoed the rhythms of the island itself.

'See the road's got better,' Frank said eventually.

'Yeah. Some tings change.'

'Know something, Sol? When I left, I never thought I'd come back.'

'Never? Dat's a long time! Yuh mussi did know yuh folks would die at some point or other. Wha' yuh did plan fi do den?' Sol kept his eyes on the road as they spoke.

'You never really think about your parents dying, unless they die when you're young,' Frank replied, ignoring Sol's question. 'You just expect their lives to stop when yours does. It's like their lives only begin when you're born.'

'So yuh mean yuh never tink once 'bout de island or . . . or any of de people yuh leave behind in all de time yuh gone?'

'Course I did. I'm sorry I never contacted you more than such but I wanted to start fresh and that meant not looking back.'

'Nuh worry 'bout dat, man. Me did know yuh woulda come back . . . some time. Some memories,' he paused, giving Frank a long look, 'live on strong, much as we try fi bury dem.'

Frank turned his head away in silence.

'Frank, Frank, Frank.' Sol patted Frank's knee, then flashed him a quick, amused look and smiled as Frank shifted away in annoyance. 'Yuh still nuh change. Tink maybe yuh woulda learn someting from all a *dat* business.'

'It's over, Sol. Finished and done with. It's in the past. Where it belongs.'

Sol's dimples deepened as he concentrated on overtaking the bus in front. He swerved sharply to the left as an on-coming car sped towards them. 'De past is always present, my friend.'

'See you still love your riddles.'

'Until yuh learn to deal wid yuh past, it will always be yuh present. And yuh future. Jewelle future too, if yuh nuh careful,' he added, half to himself.

'I've come to bury my father – nothing else.'

'Den bury yuh past.'

His past. Unbidden, a sudden image of honey-brown eyes with flecks of green laughing up into his; long, smooth brown legs wrapped around his waist. The image cracked, was broken by Sol speaking: 'Yuh madda tell yuh how yuh father dead?'

'Of course she did. Heart attack. What kind of stupid question is that?'

Sol shrugged. 'Nutten. Anyway, yuh madda old. Is not right dat she should bother her head wid tings like dat.'

'Like what?'

'Like skeletons dat nuh waan stay bury. See dat place deh?' Sol continued, pulling a cigarette from his breast pocket.

'Which one?'

38

Sol slowed down and used the cigarette to indicate the charred framework of a low-roofed building on Frank's right. 'Recognize it?'

'Should I?' Frank asked, staring at what was left of the building. Burnt out windows gave a hollow-eyed, haunted look to the blackened façade of what had once been a general store. A faded, paint-flaked rectangular sign, incongruously still intact, hung from its front.

'Maybe yuh remember it as de Moonlight Club. Three time dem try fi burn it to de ground but de damn place wouldn't dead.' He flicked his lighter, then leaned forward and touched the flame to the tip of the cigarette, observing Frank slyly as he did so.

Frank sucked his teeth, making Sol grin. 'Galang!' he said. 'Kiss yuh teeth. But yuh can only run fi so long an' so far before it catch up wid yuh.'

'Before what catches up with me?'

'Yuh past, Frank.' Sol turned and looked at Frank directly. He smiled, dimples inverted commas in his cheeks and teeth gleaming vampire white against black skin. 'Yuh past. An' Rose . . .'

Frank's ears rang from the sheer volume of the sound system as he made his way to the lower floor of the Moonlight Club. Bass line, heavy and hypnotic, boomed into the night, spreading through the building like the lava of an unseen volcano and pounding in the chests of those gathered in the club. The creak of the wooden steps under his feet was lost beneath the chants of the DJs challenging each other over the music. He ducked to avoid cracking his head on one of the low beams that seemed designed to catch the drunk or unwary and entered the dimly lit basement room. He felt as if he'd stepped into another world. A nocturnal one, where the air was charged with the sense of sex, the scent of sensi and Friday night dance hall feeling.

Two large overhead fans, hanging like spiders suspended from a thread, spun lazily from the low ceiling, caressing the damp air and sending swirls of pale blue, shape-changing smoke floating like strips of fine gauze above the heads of the dancers. A potent cocktail of sweet-smelling ganja, perfumed bodies and sharp, salty perspiration filled his nostrils. He paused, giving his eyes time to adjust to the light, before making his way around gyrating bodies, stepping to one side as people jostled him, greeting friends, or making their way, just as he was doing, to a single wooden horizontal beam that served as the bar counter.

He pushed a handful of cents across the counter in exchange for a foaming Red Stripe and tilted the bottle to his mouth. The first cool drops of liquid tickled the back of his throat, chasing away the smoke that filled his mouth. He leaned casually against the bar, feeling the wood solid against his spine and elbows and scanned the room slowly. No sign of Sol or Bevan, but plenty of women to keep his mind distracted until his friends arrived, or at least until he finished his beer.

Though Frank had come deliberately later than arranged, Sol still managed to arrive after him. Not that Sol ever expected people to wait for him, but somehow they invariably did. Even in the midst of such good-time feeling Frank felt excluded. What was it about him, he wondered, that made it so difficult to relax with others, to be part of a group. Always wanting to join in but never finding the right door, let alone having the key. Was he really that different from everyone else or was it shyness and insecurity that made him feel that way? Tolerated but never quite accepted. Some people had a knack of being at ease – wherever they were. Take Sol for instance, he could chat to a complete stranger as if he'd known them for years. Frank couldn't, and the more he tried the more awkward and false and uncomfortable he felt – so in the end he'd given up trying. Though he told himself that people could take him as he was, or not at all, it wasn't easy and it didn't help in those low moments when all he really wanted was to feel as if he belonged.

The music had changed and now there was a live band playing. He watched the dancers in front of him; the women as they moved their bodies and ground their hips close to those of their dance partners. The men, somehow seemed to sense the movement of their partners a split second before, so they were always in step, dancing together and yet, at the same time, dancing apart. He was careful not to look too closely at any one woman; no point upsetting anyone or issuing an unintentional challenge. But, there was one woman that his eyes couldn't help but return to time and time again. He ran his fingers along the side of the beer bottle, the last drops of condensation disappearing unnoticed into the skin of his fingertips as he watched her.

She was tall and slim, with full breasts that seemed just a little too heavy for her slender frame. Her pale lemon dress hugged her body like a second skin and her shoulder-length hair clung damply to her forehead and the sides of her face. She danced with her eyes half closed, at one with the musicians who sang from a corner of the room and oblivious to the many men who danced around her. Her movements were slow, so slow, as she explored the dance she was making her own. She twirled around and opened her eyes. For a single, suspended second of time Frank felt she was looking at him and him alone. Instinctively, he lowered his eyes and shrank back against the bar. When he looked back, a little smile was playing around her lips and her eyes were again half closed. It was as if there were only the two of them in the room and that the dance she was creating was for him, and only for him.

Each gyration of her body seemed to bring her closer

until he could almost feel the length of her body against his and the touch of her skin under his lips. She danced, her hips undulating effortlessly, rippled by a lazy unseen tide. Her hands slid languorously along her thighs, her splayed fingers rucking up the material of her dress. Her neck arched backwards and her lips parted. He felt his own lips part in response.

'Ow!' He grunted as a large woman stepped backwards onto his toe.

'Hush,' she shouted above the music. 'Hope me never hurt yuh.'

Frank rubbed his sore toe on the calf of his other leg. 'Don' worry,' he lied. She was no lightweight and her feet were trapped in stilettos with treacherous spikes.

'Me sure a big man like yuh can tek a likkle weight every now an' den.' She laughed, before slapping him on his arm.

He smiled quickly to let her know it didn't matter and looked back to the dance floor but the dancing woman had gone.

'Waitin' on smaddy?' the large woman asked, watching him shoot glances to the dance floor.

'Yes, but him still nuh reach,' he replied, scanning the dance hall for another sight of the woman in the yellow dress.

'Well, me waitin' too, so we can keep each other company, eh?' Frank didn't look at her but merely nodded.

The woman reached into her purse before asking the barman for a small glass of rum and water. Better make it last, she thought before taking a sip. As she did so, a pair of hands squeezed her around her waist. Her hand jerked upwards, spilling the contents of her glass down the front of Frank's shirt. She turned around to face the woman, who was standing behind her.

'Yuh tek yuh time an' when yuh *do* come yuh mek me spill me drink an' me only just get it.'

'Don' fret. Me feel sure we a go get plenty offer tonight,' her friend shouted, pushing her damp hair behind her ears. 'Maybe yuh spar gwine buy us one.' She looked directly at Frank and smiled.

Frank, still in the process of wiping down his shirtfront, stopped, mesmerized by the energy that surrounded this woman. Her smile pulled one from him in return.

'Yuh not gwine introduce me to yuh friend, Beatrice?' the dancing woman teased.

'Not my friend,' Beatrice told her, draining the two drops left in her glass. 'Never meet him before. Me nuh even know him name. All me know is him put him foot under me shoes heel and start chat to me. Anyway,' she added, 'me tink him hand too big or him pocket too tight, or someting. So nuh badda count on getting any drinks from him tonight.'

'Maybe is someting other dan him hand makin' him pocket so tight,' her friend said with a wink. 'So, wha' yuh name?' She inclined her head towards Frank.

'Frank.'

'Big Frank.' She grinned. 'I'm Rose and dis is Beatrice, or Aunt B as everybody call her. She not normally so miserable, is only 'cause her shoes squeezin' her.'

'Oh,' was all he could think to say.

'One of de silent types, eh?' She smoothed her simple dress over her hips. 'But yuh look like yuh know how fi lyrics inna bed,' she murmured to herself, watching his eyes follow the movement of her hands. 'Me drinkin' whatever yuh drinkin',' she said more loudly, grinning and pushing the tip of her tongue through the small gap between her two front teeth.

Gap-teeth, just like him: he was surprised by how much this detail pleased him. He was just wondering what it would feel like to slip the tip of his tongue in there when Rose made a sudden movement and pushed her hand into

43

his trouser pocket. 'Need a likkle help gettin' whatever yuh have in dere out?'

He reacted quickly, bending forward slightly, lower body arched away from her as his hand circled her wrist lightly in an attempt to stop her from reaching any further. He could smell the musky perfume she wore – Khus Khus, he guessed; could feel the heat from her hand against the skin of his thigh through the lining of his trouser pocket, and took a deep breath.

She had clear skin, lighter than his and her eyes were wide, a light sparkling brown with flecks of green, the colour pure, the intent not. He imagined wrapping her hair around his hand and pulling her close; feeling those full lips pressing on his. She tilted her head up towards him as if she'd read his thoughts and stared at him, now with no trace of a smile. This time Frank held her gaze with his own, had just started to smile when he felt a slap on his shoulder.

'Too much bedroom tension here, man,' Sol whispered in his ear. 'Seein' as yuh have yuh hand inna yuh pocket, buy me one too.'

Annoyance clouded Frank's face. He dropped Rose's wrist and pulled away. 'Help me out, Sol,' he said in a low voice. 'Me nuh have money fi buy rum fi everybody.'

'Introduce me first.'

'Rose. Aunt B. Sol.'

Sol and Rose nodded to each other. She matched his cool look with one of her own, much as two boxing opponents might measure each other up, but it was impossible to tell what either of the two were thinking.

Sol's gaze flicked to Aunt B. 'Yuh look too young fi call aunty,' he said. 'Miss B soun' better. Unnu wait mek we go get de drink dem.'

'Weh yuh brother tonight?' Frank asked.

'Bevan get hol' up,' Sol replied pushing his way to the

44

bar. 'Look like yuh bite off more dan yuh can chew.' He smirked, jerking his head to indicate the two women standing behind them.

'How yuh mean?' Frank bristled.

'One too big fi yuh and de other one too much fi yuh.'

'Oh, so yuh waan her and yuh tink I cyaan get her?'

'No man. Just sayin' me know de type. Dat gyal deh rough. But as dem seh, wha' sweet nanny goat a go run him belly. So if yuh waan indigestion . . .'

'Yuh jus' jealous 'cause is me she waan.'

'No, bwoy. Too much trouble in de world already widout me lookin' fi more. Dat kinda woman bad news. Yuh can see it in her eye. Just remember – tek care, 'cause me have a feelin' dat once she have yuh she not gwine let go so easy.'

'Cho, man! Is just jealous yuh jealous.'

'Who me? Jealous! Nuh mek I laugh . . .'

'We reach, Frank.' Sol nudged him.

'Already?'

Frank opened his eyes and looked around. He was home.

'Franklin!'

His mother, Miss Jess, felt thin in his arms. Such tiny bones, so easy to snap. His joy at seeing her vied with his fear of being held to ransom on an island that was too small for him. He felt guilt course through him, realizing how frail she'd become; she seemed half the size of Jewelle. Another child to care for, but an old one. And she was on her own. No husband and virtually no son. He had barely arrived, yet already he felt trapped by the emotional ties of a frail old woman who had no choice but to be dependent on him. What good to her a son who lived thousands of miles away? A son not honest enough to admit that he didn't want to come back. Hot tears sprung to his eyes as he hugged her, keeping his back to Jewelle and Aunt B so they couldn't see his emotion, but his shaking shoulders gave him away. Jewelle wondered if he had cried this much when her mother had died.

Miss Jess rubbed the centre of Frank's back with the heel of her palm, just as she used to when he was a child and couldn't sleep. Eventually his tears slowed and stopped. She patted him, smiled then pulled away before turning, her hand resting on the head of a carved walking stick.

'Jewelle? Likkle Jewelle? But what a way yuh grow! Come here, gyal!'

Jewelle stepped forward and put her arms obediently around the grandmother she didn't remember. Miss Jess took a step back and scrutinized her.

'She have a look of Beth 'bout her, don' yuh tink, Frank? In her mouth, de way it curve up soft an' gentle. But she have a stubborn jaw.' Miss Jess grabbed Jewelle by her chin and turned the girl's face from left to right as if examining a horse. 'Dis gyal's a fighter, even if she nuh know it yet.'

'She nuh need fi know it yet.' Sol spoke from the doorway.

'Solomon.' Miss Jess raised a hand in welcome. 'Good fi see yuh again.'

'Behave yuhself, Miss Jess,' he joked. 'Yuh talk like it wasn't jus yesterday me did see yuh.'

'Aunt B! Excuse me. How yuh doin'? Never mean fi ignore yuh. Is just wid de excitement and everyting. Me one son come back and me finally get fi see me only gran'-pickney after all dese long years. What a way she grow!' she said again, as if amazed that a child last seen at the age of three, was not the same at the age of fifteen.

'Beth woulda proud of her,' Aunt B said, squeezing Miss Jess's hand. 'For all Jewelle stubborn, she's a good chile.'

'Still carry de scar, I see,' said Miss Jess, running a finger

46

along Jewelle's hairline and tracing the inch long line that ran into her hair.

'I waan talk 'bout dat,' Aunt B said eagerly.

'Beatrice!' Frank's voice was stern.

Sol spoke at the same time. 'Where yuh waan me put dese?' he asked, though his voice was soft and lazy, his eyes were actively observing and recording everything.

Aunt B felt squashed into silence. Miss Jess hadn't given any indication of having heard her words, and she knew that she couldn't say them again, at least not for the moment. 'Come, Jewelle,' she said, with resignation. 'Mek we leave Frank and yuh granny fi talk while we go freshen up.'

'Together? Me and you? Together?'

'Wha' wrong wid dat?'

'If yuh still snore like yuh used to, den I would seh plenty wrong wid dat, Miss B,' Sol laughed.

From where he stood propped up against the doorjamb, he had a good view of the frozen horror on Jewelle's face at the realization that she was to spend ten days sharing a room with Aunt B. True, there were two single beds, but the room was small. There was a simple wardrobe that didn't look strong enough to carry the weight of Aunt B's two empty suitcases, let alone their actual contents. A dark brown wooden bookshelf along one wall supported a dusty Bible and a few, yellow paged paperbacks. A large chest of drawers stood in one corner. The white crocheted doily on top stood out against the dark wood like a circle of spilt milk. Above the chest of drawers hung a picture of the Sacred Heart.

Sol snorted inwardly, he could recount a thing or two about bleeding hearts, about things that made Christ's persecution seem like a child's game, his thirty-nine lashes a mere numbered caress. But who would believe him? And would it matter if they did? No, this was all part of his learning, of his experience, and as such, was welcome.

'Don' worry, Jewelle,' he said to the girl who had flopped onto the bed nearest the window and whose mouth dropped even further as the mattress sagged under her weight. 'It coulda been worse.'

'Worse?' Her voice was incredulous.

'Yuh coulda been sharin' a bed.'

Aunt B sat cautiously on the bed nearest to her, held her breath as the mattress dipped, wobbled, and sank a few inches before slowly settling. 'Tek yuh bad breath mouth somewhere else and just clear off.'

'Me goin', but de both a we still have *plenty* fi talk 'bout.' He raised his eyebrows as he spoke. Aunt B opened her mouth to blast him to hell as she'd been dying to do since his appearance at the airport, but the reflection of Jewelle curiously watching the scene in the dressing-table mirror, caused her to limit her reply to a dangerous flash of her eyes.

'All right, Miss B. Me get de message. Nuh worry, me patient.' He half turned to the teenager. 'Jewelle, I'll be yuh guide. Show yuh roun' tell yuh how I meet yuh daddy. Tell yuh 'bout yuh family. Plenty fi yuh fi see an' learn whilst yuh here. Plenty.' He gave Aunt B a quick look before raising one hand in a quick salute and walking from the room.

'Aunt B?' Jewelle asked quietly. 'How did you meet Sol?'

'Big people business. Never yuh mind.'

Jewelle smiled to herself. 'He's an interesting man though, isn't he?'

'Don' get me wrong, Frank, but me glad yuh father die before me. Him always seh him waan go first. Dat him wouldn't able to manage otherwise. And him was right. Me know me strong. Him woulda just give up. Let himself

48

go. I have dis house dat we build an' de likkle money him leave me. I have de money dat yuh sen' me, so nuh worry yuh head dat yuh must come back here an' look after me, me all right. Dis is where I belong. Only one person yuh need fret 'bout, an' dat is Jewelle. Yuh hear me? Hush,' she said, seeing Frank's eyes fill with tears. 'Nuh cry. Yuh home now.'

Later that afternoon, they all sat outside on the front veranda drinking fresh ginger beer, so sharp it stung as it hit the back of the throat.

'Where're you going, Dad?' Jewelle asked, as Frank slipped his shoes on.

'Brown's Town. Funeral parlour.'

'Oh.' She frowned and rubbed the base of her glass against the whitewashed wood of the veranda step. After a second she said, 'Can I come?'

'Stay here wid us, chile,' Aunt B ordered. 'Yuh daddy probably waan go alone.'

'Can I, Dad? I don't remember him. I'd like to see him before he's . . . he's buried. I'm curious about my family . . .' she tailed off.

Frank rubbed his red-rimmed eyes and put his arm around her. 'Are you sure? It might not be very . . .' he searched for the right word, 'pleasant.'

'I'm coming.'

'Does he look the way you remember?'

'Not really. He always had a smile. Can't recall ever seeing him with such a serious expression.' Frank stared down at the man stretched out in front of him. He'd been a quiet man – his mother had always been the talker of the two. Slow but steady in movement, he greeted the world with a wide smile, and he'd always found something to smile about.

It was hard to match the immobile figure in front of him with his memories. This person bore no resemblance to the man he remembered. He knew it was his father yet it looked like someone else. Someone wearing a waxy mask and one of his father's suits. Guilt twisted like a slippery fish in his stomach. All those times he could have visited, all those phone calls he could have made. He'd had the money and could have made the time – but hadn't. And why not? Too much work, Jewelle too young, too soon after Beth's death – there were plenty of excuses – but none that really counted. Now it was too late. He wanted to touch his father, yet recoiled from doing so, using Jewelle's presence as an excuse. But he knew that at some point soon he'd have to. Wanted to. And he knew that then he'd need to be alone with his father.

'He doesn't look serious to me. Just relaxed. At peace.'

'You think so?' He seized at her words gratefully.

'Yes, very peaceful. I think . . . he looks like he was a nice man.'

Frank took Jewelle's hand and squeezed it hard. 'I think he would have liked you too.'

Though late afternoon, the sun still beat strongly as they strolled back from Brown's Town. They walked along the side of the road, under the leaf-laden branches that over-hung the uneven pavement and offered a little respite from the heat.

'Rain!' Frank said abruptly.

Jewelle looked up at the sky. It was still clear as far as she could see. 'How do you know?'

'I can smell it in the air.'

She looked at him puzzled and he shrugged helplessly. 'I just can,' he said.

They'd walked past St Mark's Church before Jewelle spoke again. 'Was . . . did, I mean . . . did Mum look at peace when she died?' She looked up at Frank quickly then

50

stared at her feet again, kicking at the stones in her path and sending up small puffs of dust. 'I don't remember, you see.'

'Yes. She looked beautiful. Serene.' He paused, searching for the exact words to convey what he wanted to say. 'As if she were lost in a beautiful dream.'

The first drops of rain that fell were light but warm. 'I wish I could have known her properly. That we could have had more time together.' She stared up at him, drops of rain on lying on her cheeks like fresh tears.

The rain came on more heavily. Frank dragged Jewelle along as he zigzagged his way through people rushing in the opposite direction, to a bar on the other side of the road. As he pushed the door open the rain began to fall in earnest; weighty, pregnant drops, that hit hard as they fell.

'It's warm!' Jewelle shook her hair and wiped drops of rainwater from her face and arms. 'It feels nice.'

'Maybe so,' Frank replied, 'but I'm not going back in it.' He shuddered. 'I don't believe in that English nonsense about walking in the rain for the fun of it.'

They found themselves squashed into a corner as more and more people crammed themselves into the already crowded bar.

'Come on, people. Dis is a bar not a bus shed. Put yuh hand inna yuh pocket if yuh waan stay in here,' the bartender encouraged, trying to drum up business.

Jewelle stood pressed against the window and looked out at the post office opposite. Its roof was made of ridged aluminium that angled downwards sharply, so that the rain slid along its grooves to the ground. People clustered under its simple porch, waiting for the rain to cease so that they could be on their way. Many of them were schoolgirls from the same school, Jewelle deduced, given that they wore identical uniforms. Long, broad-pleated navy blue skirts that reached mid-calf; checked blue and white cotton shirts and dark blue ties. Most of them wore black or blue shoes with matching ankle socks.

The girls were around her age but Jewelle couldn't imagine ever wearing a uniform like that. The kids at her school would go on strike if the headmistress even dared to suggest it. Even though the uniform was old-fashioned, the girls themselves looked nice as they stood together in little groups. They pushed each other playfully from the raised platform of the post office, out into the rain; or clasped their books close to their chests to stop them getting wet. One girl grinned to herself as she stood on the edge of the porch, hand outstretched as she tested the intensity of the rain. She glanced up, her gaze met Jewelle's; her hand extended as if in welcome.

'Dad?' Jewelle turned away from the schoolgirls. 'Tell me again how you met Mum. It was in England, wasn't it?'

She hadn't asked for a long time, but seeing her grandfather had moved something deep inside her. She hadn't expected to feel anything for this man she'd met only once, and yet seeing him had triggered some hidden emotion.

Frank understood where the need to talk about her mother came from as he looked at Jewelle's downcast head. A mother whose daughter only knew her through other people's memories and stories. Jewelle had been so young when Beth had died of cancer. A cancer so fast and aggressive that by the time it was diagnosed nothing could be done. They'd had just over three weeks left together then she'd gone. He'd told the simple story of their meeting a million times before and knew it was one that he would never tire of telling and his daughter would never tire of hearing.

'Yeah. In Smethwick where I used to live. Aunt B set me up with her. A blind date.' He smiled now, remembering how he'd tried to get out of it, thinking that Beth would be exactly like her big sister. But Aunt B had been bulldog stubborn and refused to accept any of his excuses. 'Aunt B came over to England soon after me, and although we weren't great friends here, over there it was different.'

'Why?'

'Well, for a start, we were all in the same boat – looking for work and a better life. When you're in a foreign country, everything's so new and strange that you tend to gravitate to anyone from home, and by home I mean the whole of the Caribbean. Aunt B and all those other people I met became my new family. I suppose it made me feel like part of a community. One where we all understood the "rules", even the unspoken ones, and could just be ourselves. It made me feel like I belonged somewhere.'

'And Mum?'

'Your mum came over to join Aunt B about six months after I arrived, and, well . . . less than couple of years later we had you.'

'Was it love at first sight?'

Frank laughed. How many times had Jewelle asked this very same question? 'Beth said it was for her.'

'But it wasn't for you?'

'I don't know. I wasn't looking for a girlfriend. I'd not long been in England, and the only thing I was concerned with was finding my feet and establishing myself. I didn't have anything to offer anyone. Beth said she didn't care, that the best thing I had to offer was right under my nose.'

'What was that?'

'My heart.' Frank turned his head and quickly blinked back the tears that were prone to come at a moment's notice these days. 'I always hoped that was enough,' he said, holding Jewelle's gaze with his own, 'and that I didn't disappoint her. I hope not,' he finished.

The rain had stopped. People left the bar just as quickly as they'd entered, smoothing back their hair and straightening wrinkled clothes.

The sun was out again and Jewelle could feel her clothes drying on her body as she and Frank walked homewards. When she glanced at her father she imagined she could see steam rising faintly from his clothes. The dust that was present earlier had been dampened into submission and the air smelt fresh and clean. Cars glistened as they drove past and the leaves of trees reluctantly shed diamante drops of water from their boughs.

'Even if you don't remember her,' he said, 'I do. Maybe the time you had together was limited, cut short. But she loved you. Loved you dearly. And every time I look at you, I see her in your face, that little dimple in your chin, in your movements. Hear her in your laugh. And I know she didn't go before leaving me the best present she possibly could.'

Jewelle stopped abruptly and buried her face in her hands, before turning to Frank and pressing her face into his chest. Her shoulders heaved as the tears that she'd been too young to cry when her mother died, escaped. Frank felt salty tears of his own slip from his eyes and fall into his daughter's hair.

They held each other for a long time.

The house was awake when they returned. Miss Jess met them on the front veranda.

'People soon start arrive for de Singing. Dem waan pay dem respects to yuh daddy,' she informed Frank. 'Yuh all right, little miss?' She stroked Jewelle's face.

'Uh huh. What's the Singing?'

Miss Jess patted the seat next to her on the veranda swing. 'De Singing,' she started, 'is a long time tradition. It come from Nine Night.'

'Nine nights?'

'People use to believe – in fact, plenty people roun' here still believe – dat after death de duppy come outta de grave an' visit de places de person used to go. So, during dis time, relatives and friends go to de house of de dead person fi entertain de duppy; welcome him return and speed him back to him grave. De ninth night is called de Singing. On de last of de nine nights, de duppy return one last time to visit him family and friends, look over everyting dat used to belong to him and den leave fi good.'

'But Grandad isn't buried yet. How come you're doing the Singing now?'

'Well, chile, over de years dem, tradition change. Now, a lot of people like fi have a kinda singing before de burial. Dis is how me waan seh goodbye, rather dan singin' after everyting done and tryin' fi keep yuh gran'daddy out. No, I don' waan none a dat. Don' even tink dat once him bury I'll change tings roun' in de bedroom.'

'Change things around? Why?' Jewelle turned to Frank, who returned her quizzical look with a shrug of his shoulders.

Miss Jess laughed and stroked Jewelle's arm. 'Don' ask yuh father nutten, him nuh believe in "ole time business".' She waggled her head from side to side as she spoke. 'Him call it superstition. Seh it turn people fool and ruin dem life.'

'So why do people change everything around?'

'Fi confuse de duppy. I don' mind yuh grandaddy comin' to visit me, but me don' waan him fi stay. Dis not him place any more. Anyway, my time soon come and I'll see him again.'

'You don't mean –?'

Frank interrupted Jewelle's half-formed question. 'No, she's not going to die. It's just a way of speaking. All she means is that eventually she will die, like we all will. Right, Mumma?'

Miss Jess looked at Jewelle. 'Me nuh plan fi go nowhere yet,' she said, pulling a hairgrip out of her almost white hair and scratching the side of her head with it. 'Is not my time.'

Jewelle gave an almost audible sigh of relief, causing Frank and his mother to exchange small smiles.

'Go eat someting. Yuh must be hungry.' Miss Jess pulled the end of one of Jewelle's plaits in a teasing gesture. 'Yuh nuh eat nutten since yuh get here.'

She waited until Jewelle had disappeared into the house then looked at Frank. He sighed. After a pause he said, 'She cry fi her mother.'

'Good. Probably long time due.' Miss Jess eased herself into the hard-backed veranda chair and put her stick to one side. 'And yuh?'

'Yes, Mumma. I'm all right.'

'Come sit down and eat.' Aunt B ordered, pointing Jewelle to a place at the Formica-topped table. 'Wha' yuh waan? Fry fish an' hard dough bread?'

'Not hungry.'

Aunt B ignored her, pushed a platter of fried fish towards her niece and busied herself cutting thick slices of hard dough bread, which she spread liberally with butter. Jewelle stared at the fish, brown pimento pieces covered the golden skin like a sprinkling of freckles. On top, the lightest of fried onion rings and fragments of spicy red Scotch bonnet peppers.

'Wha' what-him-name do wid de milk, Nancy?' Aunt B called to someone out of sight.

A thin, dark girl of about seventeen appeared from the back veranda. 'Jake? Him put it in here, Aunt B.' She reached into the back of the fridge. 'It already boil and cool, ready fi drink.'

'I don't like milk,' Jewelle said, playing with the bread on the plate in front of her.

'Don' worry. It won't upset no weak English stomach.'

'Dis is Jamaican milk,' Aunt B said, slapping Jewelle's hand away from the bread. 'Is not like any milk yuh ever drink before. Yuh hungry, Nancy? Waan some fish?'

'Wouldn't mind piece.' The girl slipped into the chair opposite Jewelle.

Jewelle looked up, saw how fresh and clean the other girl looked despite her well-worn and faded clothes and was suddenly conscious of her tear-streaked face, skin stiff where the tears had dried and of her dust-coated shoes. She wet one fingertip surreptitiously and rubbed at the sides of her face.

'Wha' yuh haffi cry 'bout?'

'None of your business.'

Nancy stared at Jewelle. Here was a girl not much younger than herself, dressed in the latest of fashions. She probably had a ton of stuff like that in her bags. Nancy's gaze wandered, took in the neat fingernails, the unstripped skin on the thumbs and knew without being told that these were not hands used to washing clothes or washing up. This girl – who'd never had to do without, never had to assume the responsibilities of an adult before her time and who didn't see her life spanning before her unchanging – was crying. And for what? Nancy was sure it wasn't about Poppa Ben. The girl hadn't even known her grandfather. Envy, sour like milk that had turned, rose in her mouth. 'Spwoil bitch,' she mumbled under her breath.

'Unnu gwine spend plenty time together over de next couple a weeks, so yuh just better learn fi rub along,' Aunt B announced.

'What?' Both girls turned to her with identical expressions of shock.

'Yuh hear me well enough, so nuh badda skin up, neither one a yuh.' Aunt B sucked loudly on a fishhead.

'I'll eat my fish outside.' Nancy picked up her plate. 'Me nuh have no time fi no spwoil rich gyal from England.'

Jewelle fiddled with a piece of the grey splintered Formica at the edge of the table with her fingernails, then heard chair legs scrape on the tiled floor and footsteps recede to the back veranda.

'Who's she?'

'Nancy?' Aunt B reached for her second piece of fish. 'She help yuh granny wid de cookin' an' cleanin'. Do a bit a washin' an' ironin' as well.'

'She doesn't like me.'

'She don' know yuh. Yuh different, dat's all. Drink yuh milk an' eat some a de fish.' Aunt B waved a fish bone in the air.

Jewelle sipped at her milk cautiously. It was cool, creamy and refreshing. Rich like no milk she'd ever drunk before. She took a second, longer sip, and then broke off a piece of bread. Still warm, it was firm, yet soft and full of freshly baked flavour. As she reached for a piece of fish, Aunt B started on her third.

The sound of singing filtered into her sleep so slowly that it took Jewelle a moment to realize she was in fact awake and that it wasn't part of her dream. She got up, washed her face hurriedly and rushed to join the others, but then felt shy and stood dithering outside the door until she heard a lull in the singing and only the murmuring of voices.

The room was filled with faces she didn't know. Young and old, male and female, dark and light-skinned, they all turned to stare at her. She felt naked under such open curiosity and shrank embarrassed into the corner between the doorway and the sideboard, where she fidgeted uncomfortably. Her dress seemed inappropriate: too short, too tight, too fancy. She felt out of place, as if she'd set off for a club, but had inadvertently ended up at Mass. Aunt B, her father, even Nancy were all seated on the far side of the room. She'd have to cross through a sea of strangers to get to them. She stood where she was, then felt someone appear by her side. Sol. He took her hand, walked her across the room and settled her next to her grandmother. She sat down with relief. Nestled between her grand-mother and her father, she felt much better. Opposite her sat a girl, who at first glance seemed to be dressed as in-appropriately as she. A second sly glance revealed that the girl's outfit was fine, it was more the way she was wearing it. Jewelle tried not to stare as she struggled to clarify her thinking. The girl wasn't fat and the clothes weren't too tight, she just seemed to be oozing out of them.

'Dis is me gran'daughter Jewelle.' Miss Jess touched her arm gently. 'Stan' up so people can see yuh.'

It was so stupid she almost felt like laughing. The very instant she felt she could relax and hide herself away from all these new faces, she was being forced to stand up like an animal on display for them. She straightened her shoulders and stood up slowly, and looked around to see people smiling up at her from their seats. Despite the fact that no words had been exchanged she felt unexpectedly warmed and comforted by their presence, by the feeling of solidarity, and gave a half smile in return. She felt Nancy staring at her as she sat down again and tugged the hem of her dress lower, making the girl opposite grin, but the material resisted and stayed where it was, too far up her legs for comfort.

A solo voice rose, strong and clear. The other voices were low at first as they hummed the melody; a humming that split into individual voices. The voices harmonized effort-lessly, intermingled, rose as a single voice in celebration of the soaring of a spirit no longer shackled. Voices singing songs of freedom. Of liberation.

And so it continued, one song after another. Different words. Different melodies, but always sung with joy. They paused, for food, for greetings, for stories and reminiscences about her grandfather which made her feel close to him despite never really knowing him. During one of the breaks she made her way to the large trestle table that had been set up in the front garden. Though it was late, the table was still laden with food. Her father was talking to a woman she'd never seen before, Nancy seemed to be arguing with the oozing girl and Sol and Aunt B were nowhere in sight. She picked up a carton of fruit juice but it was empty.

'A full one here,' said a young woman appearing next to her. 'Apple not orange, if that's all right. Or there's some June plum juice me mother make, if you prefer.'

'Apple juice is fine, thanks,' she said holding her glass up. 'I'm Jewelle.'

'Yeah, Miss Jess gran'daughter,' the woman said, not taking her eyes off the glass she was filling. 'I already hear 'bout you.'

Was that good or bad? Jewelle wondered. 'And?'

'You're Miss Jess gran'daughter and you come from England, that's all. I'm Daisy, I live next door with my mother,' she nodded towards the woman talking to Frank, 'and Nancy's sister Lil.'

'Lil?'

'Wha' yuh waan wid me?'

Jewelle turned to see the oozing girl right behind her. Up close she could see how the material of the girl's demure blouse struggled to contain breasts that threatened to burst out at the slightest movement. 'Just been talkin' to yuh daddy. Good-lookin' man fi him age!' She winked at Jewelle's shocked expression.

'Shut up and go home, Lil. You have school tomorrow.'

Lil ignored her and spoke to Jewelle. 'Fixit seh yuh must come and visit tomorrow or de next day.'

'Mrs Samuels, to you,' Daisy interrupted abruptly. 'My mother,' she added to Jewelle. 'Button up your blouse and go home. Look how you dress on an occasion like this. Shameless.'

'I'll go when I'm ready,' Lil told her unrepentantly. 'Yuh just jealous 'cause yuh nuh have nutten fi put inna blouse and 'cause yuh maaga and dark and nobody ever look 'pon yuh. All right, me gone.' She laughed as Daisy turned to her impatiently.

Daisy looked after her then put her drink down. 'Damn little wretch,' she muttered. 'I can see why Nancy don' bother with her more than such. See you when you come,' she said before setting off in the direction Lil had taken.

So Lil was Nancy's sister! Who'd have imagined? Jewelle thought. She looked around. People were drifting back to the house in twos and threes, so she followed them in.

As the evening progressed, she grew sleepy. She slipped into a vacant rocking chair in the corner and let the voices in the darkening room wash over her.

When she woke there was a pink bedspread covering her, and a flicker of blue-yellow light – a glittering teardrop, coming steadily closer. With the light came a smell her drowsy mind struggled to name – paraffin. Frank's voice materialized from the darkness a moment before his shadowy outline solidified and took form. He bent over her, a glass-bottomed paraffin lamp in his hand.

'Electricity's gone. Happens sometimes. Here, I'll take you to your room.'

Jewelle threw back the cover, stretched her legs and stood up. She stroked the lamp her father held and marvelled. She'd seen such lamps in Aunt B's house, but there they were nothing more than unused ornaments.

'Sleep well.' Frank waited until she had closed the door before turning away silently.

His lamp cleared a line of light along the dark length of the corridor, sending ghostly figures dancing along the walls ahead of him. He lit the candles in his room then blew out the lamp. A thin wisp of smoke drifted up into the air and an accompanying scent of paraffin filled his throat for a moment. The flickering candlelight and the warm night-time air, brought back memories of the past. Memories that he didn't wish to evoke. He slipped off his shoes and lay on the bed fully dressed. He thought idly that he should take off his black clothes so that the yellow lint of the candlewick bedspread didn't stick to them, but he was tired, too tired to care. Sleep eluded him – too much to think about. The candle flame flickered as he abruptly turned onto his side and stared into its flame . . .

The room seemed to be filled with hundreds of yellow teardrops. Candles of varying lengths had been placed on every available surface. In his family, candles were lit in moments of emergency, when storms brought unexpected power cuts and lamps couldn't be found. But Rose had used them to create atmosphere and a sense of intimacy. He propped himself up on one elbow, taking care not to sink into the dip of the old sunken mattress that would roll him closer to her. His gaze wandered: the plain wooden cross that hung above the bed; the treadle sewing machine that stood below the window framed by thin curtains, the same lemon colour as the dress she'd worn that night at the Moonlight Club.

'How many candles yuh have here? About a hundred, nuh?' He didn't really care, but spoke to fill the silence between them and to break the growing sexual tension he could feel building up. There was no answer and he turned his head to look at the woman lying only inches away. Against his will his gaze dropped to the invitation her cleavage offered and he quickly glanced away again.

Rose laughed. ''Bout ten, fifteen, twenty – I don' know.' Her low voice touched him all over like invisible fingertips.

'Yuh know how much money you're wastin' burnin' them all at once like that! Wha', wha', wha'ppen when yuh burn them all out an' we get power cut?' Nerves made him blurt out the first thing that came into his head.

'Me not 'fraid a de dark. Yuh?'

'No.' His first natural smile since he'd arrived. He moved until his weight was more evenly distributed between his elbow and his hip and then rested his chin in the cup of one hand. With his free hand he traced the shapes that had been carefully embroidered onto the bedspread – outlines of slender women in movement.

'But yuh 'fraida me. Nuh true?' Her finger casually flicked free one of the buttons on her yellow blouse.

'No man.' He laughed, but uneasily. She was older than the women he was used to. More assured. He felt sure she knew how to get what she wanted. And when she did – relished it. She scared yet attracted him at the same time. Made his head spin and drew him in a way he didn't understand.

'No man,' he repeated quickly. Too quickly. 'Yuh nuh frighten me.'

'Oh no?' She smiled. 'I can tell by de way yuh slippin' from yuh smooth Jamaican English into patois.'

He tensed as Rose gave the smallest of smiles and held his eyes with her own as she slowly undid another button. Now her breasts were in clear view, as they lay nestled together in the crook of her arm. The line between them ran deep – a valley full of secrets. Frank shifted the lower half of his body away from her as discreetly as he could, aware of the erection that strained against his trousers.

'Look like dem too tight.' Rose flicked a mocking look downwards. 'Maybe dem need adjustin'.' She arched an eyebrow. 'Me good wid needle an' thread.'

'Umhmm.' His mouth refused to shape itself around the words he wanted to say.

'Yuh nuh waan touch me, Frank?'

'Yy-yy-yes.' He swallowed hard, tried again. 'Uh, yes . . . but . . .'

'But. What?' Each word was punctuated by the popping of the last two buttons on her blouse. Now her nutmeg-brown breasts were bare before him. Her nipples, bright and firm as a tamarind seed, rose in pointed invitation. She encircled the base of one of her breasts between her fore-finger and thumb and leaned forward. 'Taste me.'

She smiled as he let himself roll towards her and gently touched the breast she offered. She brushed his hand away and raised her breast even higher towards his mouth. When she felt his mouth close over its tip, his teeth against her skin, the roughness of his tongue as it teased her nipple, she pulled him closer and they sank together into the welcoming dip of the mattress.

She unbuckled his belt before whipping it out through his trouser loops, then ripped open his shirt and bit one of his nipples hard. He cried out, but whether in pain or ecstasy he didn't know, or care, as she moved against him. Her fingers traced his skin as carefully as an explorer traces a map before an expedition, lingering at a point just below his left pectoral. She smiled and kissed the spot reverently, then her hands were everywhere as she explored his body.

The wooden bedframe groaned its protest beneath their weight as they rolled first one way and then another. Now their roles were reversed. Pupil became teacher and it was him who led. Teased and provoked. Promised yet kept waiting. Caressed and commanded. Rose laughed with joy as Frank buried his face in her hair. She felt his full lips move hungrily over her skin, along the curve of her neck into her shoulder. She sighed as his mouth moved further downwards as he traced her body with the tip of his tongue. When he paused, she wrapped one calf around the back of his neck and urged him on.

'Only one way fi go wid me, Frank,' she murmured, 'in all senses.'

They were suspended in time – a moment of mutual recognition. She held her breath for an instant, clenching her muscles and holding him tight inside. He was the one.

She would never let him go.

Ever . . .

Frank rolled over so he lay on his stomach. The soft fibres of the bedspread tickled his nose and brought him back to the present. His swollen penis burned hot between his legs. He buried his face guiltily in his pillow, ashamed that so close to his father's funeral he could still be aroused by a memory that was more than twenty years old, and that his thoughts were of a woman who had loved – and hated – too hard.

Aunt B, parcelled in a pink quilted dressing gown and with a red scarf tied around her head, lay in bed. On the night-stand that stood between the two beds was another paraffin lamp, this one of green glass. The wick was turned low so that its flame flickered shapeless shadows against the plain whitewashed walls. Jewelle undressed quickly, with her back to Aunt B, and slipped on an oversized T-shirt.

'Yuh nuh have nutten dat I don' already see,' mumbled Aunt B from beneath her mosquito net.

Jewelle slipped between the sheets and arranged her net around herself. Everything was so different to home. No duvet to snuggle under or heavy curtains blocking out the light. The mosquito net made her feel like an adventurer. Aunt B's voice interrupted her wandering thoughts.

'I let it pass tonight. It's been a long day, but mek certain yuh wash before yuh come to bed tomorrow.' She sat up and blew out the lamp before settling herself back under her net.

Jewelle turned on her side towards the window and flicked at a mosquito that had somehow found its way in. She liked the way the weak moonlight filtered through the slatted wooden shutters, along with the night-time sounds of rural Jamaica: the incessant chatter of crickets; dogs barking from a house further along the street; the whine of mosquitoes on a nocturnal search. From somewhere far away a lone owl hooted.

That night Jewelle dreamed of music: of a musical score which, when she looked closely, shimmered and moved, separating into hundreds of mosquitoes; of jumping crickets forming the notes of a celebratory song. A song that in her dreams she too knew how to sing.

3

Valentine's Day

A woman with browny-green eyes stepped off the bus and stopped for a second as she balanced the two scandal bags in her hands more evenly before setting off on her way again. Her hips swayed as she moved, drawing admiring glances and comments from the men she passed, but she ignored them. If someone had stopped to ask what she was doing in a little country town she hadn't visited in years, she would have been hard pressed to give a response. Her grandmother would have called it destiny, but Rose had more or less given up on destiny over the years. Destiny seemed to bring more of the unwanted than the desired. Destiny was a cruel friend. It had made her waste years, led her into doing things that her more rational side knew were unacceptable, forced her into solitude and ruined her life. Whatever compelled her to visit Brown's Town that day was nothing more than an easily satisfied whim. Destiny could go to hell.

'Wake up.'

Jewelle rolled away from the hand shaking her roughly out of sleep she wasn't yet ready to leave. 'What time is it?' she slurred.

'Time fi get up,' said Aunt B.

'It can't be! I've hardly had any sleep.' She burrowed even further under the sheet only to have it pulled back.

'Dis is not a hotel. Everybody else up long time. Dis is Jamaica, yuh know. If yuh wait till sun hot nutten get done.'

'But I haven't got anything to do. Why do I have to get up too?'

'Everybody haffi pull dem weight. Food fi cook, house fi clean,' Aunt B said. 'Funeral day after tomorrow. So we nuh have time fi waste. Yuh have fifteen minutes – breakfast soon ready.' Jewelle turned on her side and put the pillow over her head. 'Nuh mek me come back and see yuh still in yuh bed, otherwise is two corpse we a bury,' Aunt B snapped as she walked from the room.

Some holiday, the girl thought, as she dragged herself from bed, eyes half shut against the morning light. She gathered her things together and dashed into the corridor, bypassing the bathroom, which contained only a bathtub, and went to the shower room next door. What she saw was uninspiring: the original walk-in shower. No shower base and no shower curtain. The showerhead stuck out of the partially tiled wall like an obtrusive thumb, and the brown tiled floor sloped towards the centre so that the water drained there rather than flowing out into the corridor. The ceiling and upper part of the walls were painted a matt white which had cracked and flaked in parts with the passage of time. There was no key in the lock, so she pushed a plastic bowl full of what she assumed were dirty towels against the back of the door.

The floor was clean but cold beneath her feet and she quickly stripped, hung her clothes on a hook on the back of the door and turned on the shower. A spurt of cold water splattered onto her skin making her yelp. She stood back, shoulders hunched and turned the hot tap even further to the left. The water that fell was little more than a tepid drizzle. She shivered, skin raised in goosebumps, and quickly washed off the shower gel that had generated an alarming amount of lather. She couldn't decide whether the water here was softer, or if the gel just worked better in a hot country.

Using one of the towels from the bowl as a bath mat, she dried herself off briskly, applied a cursory layer of body lotion and hopped into her clothes. The lukewarm water had done little besides awaken her to the fact that she had always taken carpeted floors, a centrally heated bathroom and a power shower for granted. The floor was covered in water, but she could see no mop or cloths for drying it. She hesitated for a second, worried about leaving the bathroom in such a mess, but Aunt B had told her to get a move on, and she'd been in no joking mood. She tiptoed out of the room, nightshirt held high and her flip-flops flicking drops of water behind her.

Nancy, looking cool and fresh in a crisply pressed white blouse and skirt, gave Jewelle a mocking glance as she entered the kitchen. 'Enjoy yuh shower?'

'It was cold.'

'Funny. Sun been shinin' two hours now.'

'What do you mean?'

'Is de sun warm de rain water in de barrel.' Nancy turned her attention to the eggs she was scrambling. 'Better get used to it.' She laughed.

Rain? How much rain did they have in Jamaica? Jewelle kept her thoughts to herself, already aware of Nancy's willingness to laugh at her.

'Mornin', Jewelle. Sleep well?' Miss Jess asked, patting the seat next to her. 'Whole heap a tings fi do today. Washin'. Ironin'. Food fi cook. Animals fi feed. Wha' yuh waan do?'

'I'll do the washing if you want.'

'Sure?' Miss Jess scratched the side of her head doubtfully. 'Maybe dere's too much fi yuh.'

'No, no, Granny. If you show me where everything is, I can do it straight after breakfast.'

'Dis is de washroom.' Nancy opened the door to a small room set to one side at the foot of the back veranda. Jewelle peered inside.

'Where's the washing machine?'

'See it dere.' Nancy pointed to an oval aluminium bathtub that stood on two housebricks. In front of it was another housebrick that served as a perch for whoever was washing. She walked into the room. 'Fill de bathpan wid water from de stan'pipe outside. Separate dese clothes over here into whites and colours.' She indicated two plastic linen baskets full of clothes. 'Same time put a big pan of water on to boil. Soap over here, blue bag here.' She pointed to each object quickly.

'Blue bag?' What the hell was that?

Nancy shook a little blue bag attached to a long piece of string in front of Jewelle's nose. 'Put this,' Nancy spoke slowly, 'in de final rinse water for de whites. It mek dem look whiter. Anyting else yuh need?'

'Yes.' Jewelle looked at the pile of clothing in the corner. 'What am I supposed to wash with?'

'Yuh two hand!'

Back in the kitchen, Nancy giggled as she recounted the story. 'She ask me weh de washing machine deh!'

'Well, I didn't know.' Jewelle blinked quickly several times as she felt a warning prickle behind her eyes.

'Look 'pon her,' Nancy jeered, 'she ready fi bawl.'

'I am not!'

'Hush, chile,' Miss Jess squeezed Jewelle's shoulder. 'Plenty of other tings yuh can do. Yuh know how fi iron?'

'Er.' Jewelle looked at the sharp, crisp lines of Nancy's clothes, the ironed smoothness of Miss Jess's skirt, and she knew that her ironing skills were no match for the scrutiny her work would receive once she'd finished. 'Er, no, not really.'

The building was remarkable, Frank thought. Too striking for a pastor's house, for one who was supposed to live humbly as befitted a man of the cloth, in a property provided by the church. They'd passed the house the night before as it was only about half a mile from Miss Jess's place. Even in the twilight, the building had stood out, but he'd thought it was somebody's holiday home. This place, with its extensive landscaped gardens, could have easily belonged to a record company mogul. Although quite simple in design, the white-stuccoed two-storey building was clearly expensive. Its large windows were protected by metal grilles that locked into the cement casements and the front veranda was hidden from view by yet more grilles protecting the windows. The upper floor had what looked like a continuous balcony running around its edge. Large ceramic urns containing a lush variety of plants were the only decoration. A gravel path cut a line through the carefully tended lawns and ended in a cemented parking area on which stood a large shiny car. Japanese by the looks of it, Frank thought. Either the parishioners were extremely generous or the pastor wasn't as honest as he should have been. Whatever it was, he was unimpressed. Everything was either too big or too ostentatious. He just hoped that his mother wasn't contributing indirectly to the maintenance of this house with her weekly collection money.

Frank pushed one side of the metal gate, only to find it locked. When he looked more closely he saw a neat, handwritten sign, which said: 'Press the bell *once* and wait.' Not only did the pastor live in a house that could have belonged to a drug baron, he also locked himself away from the very people he was there to help. He pressed the bell once, turned his back to the house and waited. Even though his mother spoke highly of the man he was about to meet, Frank already knew that he didn't like him.

'Ah, you must be Frank, Miss Jess's boy.'

Boy! Frank turned around at the sound of the low, modulated voice. The gates were now open and a man of about his age, weight and build was standing watching him while wiping his glasses on a white cotton handkerchief.

'I'm Frank Galimore,' he said, holding out his hand, 'Miss Jess's *son*.'

'Pastor Sinclair,' the other man said, shaking his hand briefly. 'Right on time. Must be one of the things you picked up in England.'

'Punctuality is one of the things my parents taught me.'

Pastor Sinclair gave a stiff smile before replacing his glasses. 'We can talk in my office. Follow me, please.'

Frank walked behind him fuming. Who did he think he was? What power trip was he on? And that way he had of speaking so low that you had to strain to hear him – just another form of control. Perhaps he was supposed to feel privileged – after all, the pastor had come to meet him personally instead of sending his housekeeper. He felt like sticking his foot out and tripping Pastor Sinclair up. It'd be good to see him eat dirt. The thought made him smile, just as Pastor Sinclair turned to usher him into the house. His expression implied that Frank had been judged and found wanting. They turned into the first doorway on the right. The book-lined room was cool and simply furnished. The two men sat on opposite sides of the large wooden desk.

'I'm glad to see you've finally made the long trip home. Though of course I'm sorry that it was in such circum-stances. Many people like you only find themselves back when they lose somebody. These moments always make me think of Exodus 20 Verse 12.'

Why don't you just say what you mean? Frank thought to himself. He read the pastor's unspoken words in the eyes that flicked up and down him: another one from abroad trying to exorcise his feelings of guilt at abandoning his family in search of a better life.

'Were you thinking of one commandment in particular, or just in general?' Frank was pleased to see the fleeting look of surprise on the face of the man opposite him.

'So you've had some Bible training, I see,' said Pastor Sinclair with a brief smile. 'Actually, I was thinking of the fif –'

'"Honour your father and your mother that your days may be long upon the land which the Lord Your God is giving you,"' Frank replied, settling back in his chair. 'Funnily enough, I was thinking about the Bible too. You know, the verse that says "Let he who is without sin cast the first stone"?'

Don't get me started, his eyes challenged, otherwise one of my first questions will be where did the money come from to construct and maintain this place with its American air-conditioning, landscaped gardens and posh cars. The thing was, he knew it wasn't a question he could ask, and even if he did, he felt sure he wouldn't get an honest answer, but there was no harm in letting the man feel his suspicions.

Their meeting was brief. Neither had a taste for the other's company. Once the hymns had been chosen and the order of the service established, Frank handed over his list of readers and stood up. After an even briefer handshake than the first, he was on his way out. The pastor's voice stopped him as he reached for the door handle.

'I presume you'll be moving back here to look after your mother, now that she's all alone,' he said pompously.

Guilt caused Frank to retort sharply. 'Once my mother and I have decided what is best for her, we'll be sure to let you know.' He stalked out without looking back. It wasn't until he was back on the country road and the double gates had clanged behind him, that he stopped. His brief feeling of shame at having reacted to Pastor Sinclair's words soon passed. In reality he was pleased that he'd spoken as he had. Maybe the next time they met, the man would think twice before he brought that subject up again.

Now all the arrangements were made, he had the rest of the morning to himself, but he couldn't free his head of the pastor's words. He *did* still have to decide what to do about his mother. The easiest thing would be to take her back with him to England, but Miss Jess would hear nothing of it. True, she was independent – she'd pointed it out more than once – but even so she was still old, and getting older. He could of course pay someone to help her. Maybe ask Nancy to live in so that there was always someone she trusted at the house, but it wasn't the same as being with family. Yet what was the alternative? A personal move back to the island? His reaction to that idea was as strong as his mother's refusal to move to *that* island, as she called England.

His parents had visited him twice in England. The first time when he'd got married; that time the trip had gone well. They'd been involved with the preparations for the wedding, happy to see him so contented, and the weather had been good – at least for England. Their second visit had been a disaster. Christmas, when Jewelle had been about three and during one of the worst winters on record. Grey skies and snow every day. Miss Jess and Poppa Ben had been huddled up by the fire all the time and bored with what TV had to offer – 'Full a white people talkin' funny,' had been Poppa Ben's only comment. Apart from church on Sundays, they'd only gone out when forced to – so wrapped up in double layers of everything they could barely walk. They'd been so happy when it was time to leave, they hadn't even pretended otherwise to spare his feelings.

'Cyaan breathe in dis country, Frank,' Miss Jess had said. 'Yuh tek one good breath of air and yuh lungs freeze up it so cold. Me and yuh daddy feel trap here. Every day so grey and dark; everybody hunch up and miserable all de time. Dis is not de place fi us.'

Frank's rumbling stomach reminded him that he hadn't had breakfast yet and it was now close to lunchtime. He hurried towards the Tasty Patty shop ahead – two good curry patties and an ice-cold Ting would do the job.

He wolfed the first patty down so quickly he barely tasted the spicy minced lamb filling. The second one he ate more slowly, relishing the perfect complement of the sharp, tangy grapefruit drink to the flavour of the peppered meat. He was just wiping golden flakes of pastry from his mouth when he became aware of the insistent stare of the man sitting at the table opposite. Frank stared back. The other man rose to his feet, a broad grin splitting his face.

'Frank! Yuh nuh 'member me?'

'Benny?!' The chair screeched on the tiled floor as Frank stood up and pushed it to one side.

'Rahtid!' Benny exclaimed. 'How many years since we last meet?' The two shook hands and hugged. 'Life treatin' yuh good, eh?' Benny said, patting Frank's belly. Frank grimaced. 'Nuh worry, me have one too.' Benny laughed, rubbing his own.

'So, wha' yuh been doin' all dese long years?'

'Me run a likkle business now,' Benny said shyly. 'Yuh waan stop by? Yuh have time?' he asked eagerly.

'Well . . .' Frank started, then realized that he did in fact have time. Nothing for him to do at home that couldn't wait an hour or so. 'Well, yes.'

Benny's grin outdid the sun in its brightness. 'All right, man. Mek we tek two step. We cyaan talk in here wid all dese people squeezing us up,' he said, as the lunch hour brought a sudden surge of customers.

Frank adjusted his sunglasses and followed Benny out into the street where they stood chatting. Neither of them noticed the woman who stood just outside the door of the patty shop, two black shopping bags hanging from her hands.

Rose stared open-mouthed at the two men. It couldn't be, yet she knew it was. It *was* Frank. She would have recognized him anywhere. He still had a good head of hair, cut short and albeit receding a little around the temples. He'd put on a little weight, too, but it suited him. But those brown eyes of his that looked at you and into you hadn't changed. Her first impulse was to run and hug him but she held back, embarrassed by the way she looked. She'd gone out to shop; was hot and sweaty; didn't look her best. She didn't want Frank to see her like this. Not after all these years.

She dropped her bags to the ground as she felt a sudden hot rush of anger at the realization that Frank was back on the island and hadn't even tried to contact her. Hadn't even noticed her. She shrank back against the wall, half hidden by a broad-shouldered man in a dark suit who was waiting patiently to enter the shop. Frank and Benny were still lingering just outside the doorway and she cocked her ears as she heard Benny say, 'Me sorry fi hear 'bout yuh father. Him was a good man.'

What did that mean? What had happened to Poppa Ben? Was that why Frank was back in town? She pressed herself close to the broad-shouldered man as she strained to hear more. He turned at her touch and gave her a smile when he saw her face, but she was too engrossed in Frank's conversation to notice.

'Yuh right 'bout dat,' she heard Frank say. 'Funeral day after tomorrow if yuh waan come.'

So Poppa Ben dead and yuh come back fi yuh daddy funeral. All right, she reasoned, but even so, yuh still manage find time fi yuh old friends, like dat useless pot-bellied piece of string, Benny. The thought made her seethe. Yuh have time fi look up Benny, who never show him face unless him need someting; but as fi me – de woman yuh claim was de only one dat ever mean anyting to yuh, de one yuh did swear to love for ever – yuh nuh even drop look in my direction. Just look how you push straight past me. Too many people here, the rational side of her mind said, he didn't see you. But he should have sensed me, the emotional part argued back. He should have sensed me just as I sensed him. What drew me to Brown's Town today of all days? He did. His presence.

'Wha' time?'

'Ten o'clock. Thatchfield Church.'

'I'll be there,' Benny replied. 'How long yuh stayin'?'

'Ten days.'

Rose stood with her bags at her feet and watched Frank and Benny stroll away until they were lost amongst the lunchtime crowd. 'Yuh likkle raas!' she muttered after Frank's disappearing back.

'Excuse me, did you say something?' a petite American woman about to enter the shop asked.

'It look like me talkin' to yuh?' Rose snapped. 'Just gwaan 'bout yuh business before me give yuh someting fi stan' up an' look 'pon!' Her blazing eyes sent the middle-aged tourist scuttling to the McDonald's across the road.

Rose gazed after the men until her eyes burned. Even when they were lost to sight her eyes still traced the direction they'd gone in. Hurt and anger fought for dominance inside her as she mentally argued for and against Frank. She didn't know whether to stay in town or go home. Whatever she decided, she knew she couldn't stand outside a curry patty shop indefinitely. She slipped her hands through the looped handles of the bags, so they were suspended from her wrists, and stomped her way towards the bus stop. But with each step her anger grew, and the bags spun around noisily, the handles twisting and cutting into her flesh. She clenched the bags more tightly to stop them spinning but her nails split the thin plastic just below the handles and her shopping spilled out onto the pavement. The broad-shouldered man she'd hidden behind ran over to her. His lunchtime snack was in a brown paper bag that he tucked under his arm as he stooped to help her collect the tins and vegetables that lay strewn across the pavement. A bag of rice had burst open, white grains sprinkling the ground like carelessly flung confetti. The man tied a knot in the plastic so the rest of the rice couldn't escape and handed it to her.

'Move yuh raas!' she hissed venomously. He jumped back startled at the green fury blazing from her eyes. His lunch and the half-full bag of rice fell to the ground as he held both hands up in a conciliatory gesture.

'Ungrateful likkle bitch!' he muttered under his breath, as he snatched at the paper bag and backed away. 'Last time me go out me way fi help a woman, no matter how she sweet . . . Yuh mout' look good when it close,' he called to her, 'but when it open, bwoy – yuh jus' another rough-mouth gyal from outta bush.'

Rose stood, a lonely figure among her fallen tins. 'Him shoulda sense me!' she shouted aloud. The tall man quickened his step. 'Him shoulda sense me.'

Benny stopped in front of a shop tucked between Mr Lee's Linen Store and Graham's Grocery. 'Yuh like it?'

Frank stared at the pictures of rampant dreads, raging lions and marijuana leaves painted in bold red, green and gold across the record shop front. It wasn't to his taste, but all he said was, 'Yeah, man. Is yours?'

Benny rattled a large keyring in front of Frank's nose. 'Yeah. Is my likkle business.' He unlocked the various locks, bolts and padlocks across the front door.

The shop seemed smaller inside than it actually was, mainly because there were about ten massive speakers set around the room. Benny lifted the polished counter-flap and walked to one of the turntables.

'Mek me play a likkle tune.' He carefully pulled a record from its sleeve and dusted off an imaginary speck of dust. 'Dis one hot!' he said, setting the needle carefully onto the disc. Heavy bass boomed through the speakers. Benny shook his head wildly in time to the infectious rhythm.

'Baas, man!' Frank shouted above the music. Despite his mood he couldn't stop his feet from moving to the tune. It felt good not to think. Not to worry. To let himself go and just feel.

Benny grabbed a mike and beckoned Frank over. 'Papa Benny and de one Frank 'pon de mike,' he chanted over the music. 'We come to give de people wha' dem like. We nuh waan no worry, no fussin' an' no fight. Mek de people of the word get together and unite.'

Frank joined Benny behind the counter and the two sang and danced to the music as if they were still twenty year olds. When the song ended Frank sank onto one of the high stools on the customer side of the counter.

'Bwoy, I did need dat,' he said, catching his breath and wiping his forehead.

Benny popped a Red Stripe in front of Frank and the two clinked bottles.

'How's Florence?' Frank asked.

'She doin' all right. Yuh know she emigrate to Canada? Come back every so often.'

'Yuh never waan go too?'

'Me did go wid her. But me miss de island. De colours, de sun, ital food – yuh cyaan find none a dat anywhere but yard. I couldn't do like yuh an' stay away, but Florence never waan come back more dan such, an' dat business wid Rose . . .'

The beer suddenly tasted sour in Frank's mouth. 'Yuh mean Florence leave Jamaica 'cause of Rose?'

'No, man. Florence did waan go foreign long time, seh she waan better life, an' after Rose come back an' threaten her again –'

'She threaten her twice?'

Yeah, man. Me tink Rose did enjoy frighten her. Anyway, dat second visit give Florence de push she did need. She seh she never waan see blood shed, nor shed blood, so . . .'

'Me sorry 'bout dat, Benny.'

Benny shrugged resignedly. 'Is not yuh fault. Anyway, everyting happen long time.' He put another record on the turntable and set two fresh bottles of beer on the counter.

'Me know. Me 'member . . .'

Frank heard a harsh knock at the door. It came again before he'd even had time to react to the first.

'Wha' di raas . . .?'

He pulled himself from Rose's arms, slipped on a pair of faded green trousers and grabbed the paraffin lamp from the table by the window. He could hear a man shouting as he padded on bare feet to the door which he flung open.

'Benny! Wha' di pussy claaht . . .?'

'Weh yuh mad woman deh?'

'What?'

'Weh Rose deh!' Benny shouted.

'Rose? Calm down nuh, man. Wha' Rose haffi do wid dis?' Frank put one hand out in a placating gesture. 'Just sekkle down. Mek we talk 'bout dis. Come in nuh. Me nuh waan all de neighbours know me business.'

'Well, me waan everybody hear wha' me haffi seh,' Benny shouted, but he still came in. 'Weh she deh?'

Frank closed the door behind them. 'Rose!'

She appeared from the bedroom at the back of the house, her body clearly visible beneath the white night-gown, which flowed transparent in the half-light.

'Yuh cyaan cover yuhself up?' Frank snapped, angry that his friend should see her in this way. She was his woman, and what she had was for him and him alone.

'She need two slap,' Benny informed Frank.

'Wha' wrong wid yuh, Benny?' she teased, playing with the ends of her hair.

'Keep yuh likkle raas away from me woman.' He wagged a warning finger at her.

'Den yuh better keep yuh interferin' woman in order. Just tell her fi leave me man.'

'What?' both men spluttered.

'If she never trouble me and mine first, I wouldn't badda trouble her.'

'Wha' dis business 'bout?' Frank asked, looking from one to the other.

Rose laughed recklessly and turned to the kitchen sink. 'Tell him, Benny.'

'She find her way to my yard an' come slap up me woman! *My* woman!' Benny raged. 'Bruise up her two eye dem and cuss her off! Seh she know dat Florence waan yuh an' she just givin' her a likkle warning. Den she pull up knife under Florence chin an' ask her if she like de taste a steel. Seh if she haffi come roun' again, she gwine give her plenty fe nyam.'

'But me nuh have nutten wid Florence.' Frank turned to Benny. 'Me an' yuh is friend long time now. Why would I trouble yuh woman when yuh is me friend an' me have me own woman anyway?'

'Me know, Frank. Me know dat,' Benny replied, slightly mollified. 'But yuh better tek yuh woman in hand. She cyaan jus' go roun' a beat up innocent people as an' when she have a mind. She need two bitch lick. Me have half a mind fi give her dem meself,' he added darkly.

'Come lick me if yuh tink yuh bad!' Rose jerked her chin upwards, flashing the gap between her teeth as she stalked towards Benny, fish knife in hand, blade so thin and sharp that it cut the air as she moved towards them.

'Frank! Talk to her!' Benny shouted, pushing Frank in front of him. 'Me never come here fi fight nobody. Me come fi tell yuh fi keep her under control. Me seh wha' me haffi seh,' he edged towards the door, 'now de rest up to yuh.'

'Wha' wrong wid yuh, Rose? Why yuh cyaan behave like decent smaddy?'

Rose ignored him as she took another step towards Benny. 'Just mek certain yuh tell Florence me knife sharpen an' ready fi her if she gimme any trouble. An' beg yuh mek sure tell her I will cut her open just like ah do wid fish before ah clean it if she badda me again.'

'Stop talk foolishness, Rose.' Frank raised his arm to prevent her getting any closer to Benny.

She jabbed at him. 'Ah will chop yuh up too, Frank, if yuh ever give me reason,' she hissed. He watched a large drop of blood push its way to the surface of his skin.

'Better tek care, Frank. Find another woman before dat one put yuh inna early grave,' Benny warned before running out and slamming the door behind him.

Rose flung the knife after him. It hung quivering from the centre of the wooden panel. Frank looked at the blade of metal suspended four feet from the floor and then down at his arm again.

'Yuh cut me,' he said in wonder.

'Dat nuh nutten. Is just a likkle scratch.'

Rose laughed, and put her mouth over the wound. Drew his blood into her mouth and savoured it like the richest of wines. She took the lamp from his hand and placed it on the table. 'Nuh worry, Frank. Me soon mek it feel better.'

She did. So well, that the deep unease he felt at her behaviour receded until it was about no more than a pin-prick in his arm . . .

Benny stood up as the record came to a scratchy stop and carefully placed the needle on its rest.

Frank gave Benny's hand a squeeze full of meaning. 'Too much time pass.'

Benny cupped it with his other hand. 'Yeah man,' he replied. 'Too long.'

Jewelle forced herself to take shallow breaths as she dragged the shovel over the rough ground of the enclosure she was cleaning, but it was hard to ignore the stench and the squeals of the two fat pigs as they ran around their pens in anticipation of being fed. Her toes were cramped and pinched in the borrowed wellingtons and her hands already hurt, despite the thick cotton gloves she was wearing.

A waist-high wooden fence separated the pigs and stopped them from attacking each other. What about me? she thought to herself, as one of the pigs banged its snout hard against the back of her legs in its haste to get to the rice, stale bullah cake, vegetable peel and other leftovers she'd put down for it. The other pig squeaked with im-patience from its side of the enclosure.

'All right. I'm coming!' she shouted angrily and banged the shovel on top of the fence. The pig responded by grunting and rising on its hind legs, stretching its body towards her. Jewelle was shocked by how tall it was, and a little frightened. She soaked a piece of stale bread in water and threw it into a corner of the pen. When the pig turned, snout wrinkling rapidly as it snuffled its way to the bread, Jewelle quickly clambered over the fence and started cleaning the pen frantically, one eye on the pig all the time. Fear pushed away distaste. All she wanted was to get out of the pen in one piece. She hadn't been able to do any of the other chores – at least not well enough – but she knew that if she gave up on this one, Nancy would laugh at her for the rest of her stay.

She scraped the shit and leftovers into a special container and quickly swilled out the improvised trough – a truck tyre cut in half lengthways – before filling it with 'fresh' food. She lowered the shit, food and water buckets over the side of the pen, thought briefly about throwing the shovel over the side, but then decided to hang on to it just in case. She pulled herself over the fence one-handed and scrambled clumsily out of the enclosure. When she turned to watch the pig she'd just fed, she felt nauseated by the guzzling snuffling sounds it made, as if it were taking up the food and water through its nostrils as well as its mouth. Its thin tail curled back and forth in a long twisted comma as it flicked flies away from its rump.

Ugly, dirty thing, she thought. It turned and pinned a gaze on her as if reading her mind. She marvelled at its resemblance to Mr Harris, her history teacher. Same mean, little red eyes, same nasty off-white bristly hair. Mr Harris didn't smell too fresh either, most times. A sudden rush of nostalgia brought tears of anger and frustration to her eyes. That's all I'm good for, feeding goats and scraping up pig shit, she thought. Right now I'd give anything to be sitting in some boring history class. She was supposed to collect the eggs too, but had been too embarrassed to admit that chickens, with their flapping wings and sharp beaks, frightened her. I'll just pretend I forgot, she decided. I'm supposed to be on holiday, I shouldn't even have to be doing this kind of thing anyway. She gave the shovel a swift, resentful kick before dragging it behind her over the hard ground back to the house.

''Bout she a talk 'bout washin' machine.'

'All right, Nancy. I tink yuh done ride dat one joke enough fi today.' Aunt B spoke sharply before turning to Miss Jess. 'I leave her feedin' de animals. She seh she feel stupid 'cause she cyaan wash nor nutten an' we haffi give her likkle pickney job.'

'Stupid!' Nancy snorted and Miss Jess gave her an impatient look.

'It nuh matter. Is times like dese where every likkle count.'

It was mid-morning by the time Sol stepped into the kitchen. Miss Jess glanced up from the pimento seeds she was sorting. Her thin fingers moved slowly among the grey-brown spice balls as she searched for seeds and dry twigs. The woody perfume of the pimento berries filled the air. Aunt B turned away from him and stared into the enormous pot of oxtail she was stirring. Her rigid back expressed everything she dared not say in front of Miss Jess.

'Morning, everybody. 'Weh Frank deh?'

'Mekkin' final arrangement wid Pastor,' Miss Jess told him.

'Dem workin' yuh, Jewelle?' Sol enquired.

She jabbed her knife into one of the potatoes she'd been relegated to peeling and nodded miserably.

'Is yuh first full day here, me feel sure dem can do widout yuh help couple hour. Eh, Miss Jess?'

'Help?' Nancy laughed. 'She cause more work dan she help. Everyting she try fi do smaddy haffi walk behind her and do it again.'

'Yuh mouth too fast!' Aunt B gave Nancy a vicious flick with the tea towel she had hooked into the waistband of her skirt.

Miss Jess smiled at Sol, apparently oblivious to the scenes around her. 'She work hard, it'll do her good fi get out and see a likkle of Jamaica.'

'Thought I might tek her to Dunns River. It so close it'd be a pity if she never get fi see it.' Sol rolled a cigarette between his thumb and forefinger, but didn't light it. The yard or the veranda were the only places to smoke on Miss Jess's property – at least, when she was around. 'Leave yuh big people fi get on wid yuh preparation dem.' He strolled over to Jewelle and lightly squeezed her arm. 'So?'

'Now?'

'When else? Me tek de afternoon off work specially fi spend it wid yuh, so nuh badda say no,' he teased. 'Go get what yuh need. Towel, swimmin' costume, some sandals, an' a camera if yuh have one.'

'Is it a beach?'

'Beach!' Nancy smirked.

Jewelle bit her lip, angry she couldn't express herself the way she wanted to in patois. She could think of plenty of things to say to Nancy that would wipe that stupid smile of her face, but in English not in patois. And if she tried doing it in patois, her English accent would only give Nancy more fuel for the dislike she seemed to have taken to her. She wished she'd listened more to the way Aunt B and Uncle Sam talked instead of laughing at them as she'd so often done.

'Waterfalls.' Sol ignored Nancy. 'Yuh can climb up dem. Nuh worry, yuh'll like it.'

'Oxtail soon done.' Aunt B wiped her hands on the tea towel then hung it from the handle of the oven door. She had no intention of letting Sol out of her sight with her niece in tow. 'Just need another half hour or so. Don' figet fi stir it every now and den, Nancy. Ah don' waan it fi catch. Me a come too,' she said, hurrying after Jewelle.

Nancy slashed at the raw chicken as if she wanted to kill

it all over again. 'Everybody runnin' after dat stupid likkle English gyal,' she muttered under her breath. 'She cyaan even cook or clean. Any nine-year-old pickney could do better. So why she de one gettin' all de treats?' She hacked viciously at the chicken again.

'Easy, Nancy.' She sensed Sol move behind her. 'Yuh time soon come. Me see how yuh work good an' ah will mek certain yuh get yuh reward.' His hand squeezed her waist lightly. 'Today is fi Jewelle, but ah soon mek it up to yuh.' His hand tightened on her waist and his breath stroked the line between shoulder and neck. Nancy's face didn't show the smile she felt growing inside, but the next piece of chicken she cut as carefully as a surgeon performing a delicate operation.

'Better sit on de towel,' Sol instructed Jewelle as she got into the pickup, 'otherwise de seat gwine burn yuh.' Aunt B huffed and puffed as she squeezed in beside them and tried to make herself comfortable on the narrow front seat the three of them were sharing.

'So, what do you do, Sol?' Jewelle asked.

'I'm a lawyer, but I buy and sell houses too.'

'Two jobs?' she asked curiously.

'Why not?' he replied lazily.

'No reason,' she shrugged. 'Do you sell a lot, then?'

'Enough.' he smiled at her. 'Pass me one a dem cigarette.' He nodded towards the packet of Craven A lying on the dashboard as he concentrated on negotiating his way around a cow that had wandered on to the road. A thick, frayed rope was hanging from its neck and trailing along behind it. 'Look like one of Maas Bredda cow get loose. Hol' up.'

He stopped the pickup and ran back to the cow, grabbing the end of the rope before the cow had time to run away. Half pulling, half leading, he walked the cow to a small house set back from the road. The gate to the yard stood wide open.

'Maas Bredda?' he shouted. At his second shout, a woman wearing a faded floral dress and a headwrap of the same material appeared from behind the house.

'Wh'appen, Sol?'

'Find one of yuh cow out 'pon road.' He handed her the end of the rope.

'Thankin' yuh kindly. Waan someting fi drink?'

'No, man. Another time. Have Miss Jess gran'daughter a wait fi me in de pickup. Cyaan stop now. Tell Maas Bredda me will drop by when ah have time.'

'All right, Sol. Me wi' tell him. Tek care now.'

'All right, Molly. See yuh soon.'

Sol sprinted back to the pickup and started the engine. 'Everybody sekkle?' He put the pickup into gear and pulled out without looking back. A loud prolonged hoot came from the car behind them. Sol stuck his hand out the window and waved cheerfully.

'If yuh gwine drive like mad man, just turn de car roun' right now an' tek me an' me one an' only niece back home.'

'Aunt B!' Jewelle rushed to Sol's defence. 'It wasn't his fault, the other car was too close to us anyway.'

Aunt B grunted from where she sat squashed up against the passenger door. She searched in her bag for her fan, then clucked in annoyance at the realization that she'd forgotten it.

'Still want a cigarette, Sol?' Jewelle asked.

He nodded and took the cigarette she offered. 'Dunns River is where me meet yuh daddy properly,' he said as they drove. 'Still remember dat day, clear like it was yesterday.'

Sol shook his head and smiled to himself as he reached for the silver lighter that lay on the dashboard. A spin of its

wheel, and at the heart of the burning blue-yellow flame –
a teardrop of red . . .

Sol lay with his eyes closed. Sunlight flickered like tendrils
of silver on the red membrane of his eyelids. One blink sent
the red shimmering and the tendrils spinning into a hectic
movement of lines. He felt grains of sand on his face and
screwed his eyes tight shut until there was only blackness –
but the trickle of sand remained. He rolled on his side and
opened one eye. Saw a triangle of blue and white. Sky and
sand. Then an oval of brown as the light was blocked out,
he opened both eyes to see his friend Kurt leaning over
him.

'Cho, Kurt! Leave me nuh.'

'Come, Sol. Stop lying roun' like fla-fla dumpling and
mek we go find de others, play football or someting.'

'Too hot.'

'Sof'!'

Sol jumped to his feet and aimed a karate-style kick at
Kurt's head. Kurt blocked the blow and flicked his right leg
in and out in a lightning move, catching Sol in his side. It
left Sol winded and on his back. Kurt grinned down at
him, stuck out his hand and tried to pull Sol to his feet but
Sol resisted, yanked hard and pulled Kurt down on top of
him. Golden grains of sand sparkled like sequins in the
dark curls of their hair and stuck to their bodies where they
sweated as the two boys rolled around pummelling each
other.

It seemed to Frank, who was watching them from the
shelter of the line of palm trees set back from the beach,
that they were fighting seriously. He watched them for a
moment longer, then stood up and moved forward,
uncertain of what he was going to do. His silent footsteps
on the sand meant neither of the scrapping boys was aware
of his presence until they felt the heat of the sun blocked

from their bodies as he stood over them. They stopped, comically frozen, arms locked in place.

'Wha' yuh waan?' Kurt spoke abruptly. Frank wasn't to know it was his usual manner.

'N-nuh-nutten.' Nerves made him stammer.

'Well, n-nuh-nutten nuh here.' Sol rolled on his back and laughed up to the sky.

Frank stared at them for a moment, then walked back to where he'd been sitting without a word. He opened up his book and tried to ignore their shocked exclamations – 'Yuh see dat? Look 'pon him! 'Bout him a read book!' – and their hoots of laughter . . .

'Never imagine it would be de start of a friendship dat would last.' Sol glanced down, an expression of surprise crossing his face when he saw the lighter in his hand, as if he had no recollection of picking it up. He squinted against the flame that streaked out as he lit his cigarette and inhaled deeply.

Jewelle sat with one knee pulled up to her chin and waited. Her eyes followed every movement of Sol's lips as he spoke; her ears ready for unknown stories about her father.

'Never see Frank after dat for a good while. Never even 'member him more dan such. Next time I see him was at Ochy – we all lived near there, except Frank. I did think he was from town, never realize him come from bush, like me. Back then, in my mind, only town people act big, de way he did – readin' books when it wasn't even school time. Dat was one of de tings I learn from yuh father, just *how* much knowledge inna book. Now me grow, me realize – if a man wise, him nuh need fi show off him knowledge, him just need fi know how fi use it.'

Sol paused again. When he next spoke it was with a smile in his voice.

'Dunns River Falls – when I was a boy it did seem immense. Huge rocks, waterfalls cascading down so fast de water look like foam when it hit de bottom. Me and me spar dem did tink we was de greatest explorers, finding ways up de "mountain", conquering dose treacherous jets of water dat hit yuh as dem bounce off de smooth rocks. It easy fi slip if yuh nuh careful. I tell yuh, dat water strong enough fi knock yuh over. It much better if yuh feel yuh way, wid yuh hands and bare feet. Keep yuh eyes focused straight ahead, or upwards, but not downwards. Only one problem wid Dunns River – yuh needed money fi get in, and we never had any.

'Gettin' dere was never a problem. We was bwoy pickney and did have all de time in de world. Me 'member how we used to sit 'pon roadside, playin' jacks and waitin'. Eventually, smaddy passin' by would give us ride in de back a dem pickup. We never tek up much room and we never too fussy 'bout who or what we had to share wid. When yuh used to walkin' everywhere, yuh don' complain. Bwoy,' Sol rocked forward in his seat as if he were in that same pickup again, 'it was such a treat to be ridin' high in some ole Ford dat look like it shoulda dead long time. It felt like we were flyin'. If yuh lucky enough fi find space fi sit, de metal a de truck would burn yuh skin, but we hardly ever did. Sittin' was fi big people, not pickney. No, man! We just heng on. Just as much in de pickup as out. Jump down when we reach de spot and waited till everybody arrive.

'Dat day was another hot one, just like all de others. Nutten moving, except we bwoy – me, Kurt and de Gordon brothers Popeye and Shorty, in reality Billy and Bobby. Billy, we call Popeye 'cause of him frog eye. Bobby, we call Shorty 'cause him never grow. Him barely reach five foot and den only when him stand 'pon tiptoe. We were tired of de beach but we did waan de cool dat being near water brings. We got lifts in pairs and arrive in half an hour of each other. We stood outside de falls 'cause we never have enough money fi de entrance ticket.' Sol shrugged his shoulders. 'But even if we had, we wouldn't have paid. What!' He slapped his thigh. 'Tek good money, waste! Uh-uh,' He shook his head.

'So how did you get in?' Jewelle asked.

'Sometimes yuh could sneak in if yuh were quick and if yuh were lucky. We weren't, it was nearly de end of de tourist season and dere were four of us.

'Back then, de way we use to do it was to hit on a target an' offer fi guide dem up de falls. In return, dem would pay our tickets, an' usually give us a tip as well. When it was in US we were kings. Sometimes, instead of money dem buy us jerk chicken an' festival; or maybe give us a foreign T-shirt or a baseball cap instead.

'So anyway, de four of us stan' up at de entrance to de falls conspirin' to earn a few dollars from de tourists. Enough fi buy box juice, couple curry patty an' suck-suck shave ice. We had bread an' fish wid us, could pick fruit from anywhere we waan, but when yuh likkle, yard food not de same. Nutten bring more pleasure dan having money in yuh pocket an' buyin' yuh own food, even if yuh know yuh get better at home.

'Den me see her standin' alone . . . still 'member how she look. Her pale face round like football and her face already flush and shiny from de heat. She grease up wid sun oil, but she already start turn red. Her ugly blue nylon swimsuit so tight dat all dat grease-up red an' white flesh just shove out from de sides of it. Pure nastiness!' He shuddered at the memory. 'She look like piece a raw chicken ready fi fryin'. Me sure me wouldn't waan eat none of dat! Anyway, we guys did recognize de type: one a dem women who come to Jamaica alone – her fist full of dollars in de hope she can buy all de company she need.

'Ah hope yuh not tinking of tell my niece one a yuh dutty story,' Aunt B protested.

'She was a big woman. A likkle like yuh, Miss B.' Sol turned and grinned at her as she sat fanning herself.

'Just keep yuh eye 'pon de road. I don' waan dead out here.' Aunt B feigned disinterest but she was listening just as attentively as her niece.

Sol winked at Jewelle and continued. 'Ah point out de fat woman an' tell Kurt fi gwaan wid her. But Kurt never waan chat to her. She too big fi him. Ask me wha' gwine happen if she slip an' drop 'pon him. Popeye slap him leg an' laugh like him never hear joke before an' tell Kurt leastways him nah gwine dead seh him never see all of America!'

'What did Shorty say?' Jewelle asked.

'Shorty? Shorty short 'pon everyting. Him never seh more dan him usual "yeah, man".'

'So wh'appen next?' Aunt B asked curiously.

Sol grinned at her. 'Me tell him nuh fi worry. Tell him all him haffi do is talk nice to her. Dat she gwine love have pretty bwoy as her personal guide.'

'What did Kurt look like?' Jewelle asked.

'Kurt a pretty bwoy,' Sol replied. 'Have long gyal eyelash an' dimple dem. Him did proud of him soft Jamaican-Indian hair, always foolin' wid it, carry him pomade wid him all de time. We watch him slip up to de woman an' wait till him catch her attention.

'Him start him sweet talk. "G' morning, ma'am. Beautiful, isn't it?" Kurt wave one hand toward de rocks risin' up to de sky. High above, tourists in dem bright swimsuit an' T-shirt swarm up and down de rocks like . . . like rainbow insects crawlin' over a trail of spilt sugar.

'De woman couldn't help but smile back at Kurt as him

gaze up at her serenely, him dark eyes half close as him shield dem from de light.

'"Been up yet?" him ask ask, all innocent. We all know full well de woman nuh touch water since dawn break – her swimsuit still bone dry. She shake her head.

'Kurt decide fi pop some English 'pon her. "Well, I'm going up myself," he said. Him start act cute like him innocent. "If you want . . ." him begin, den him stop like him shy, den him start up again. "I mean . . . I can show you the way up if you like. Where to put your feet, where to hold on, that sort of thing . . . if you like."

'She look 'pon him widout sayin' a word but we could tell wha' she a tink. It shine clear in her face like moon shine in night sky. *Pity he isn't a little older*. Kurt could see it too. Fi a few seconds him act like him nuh care one way or another if she tek him or not. Den him flash her a grin. It was de grin dat sekkle it – it always did.

'"Well . . ." She gwine like she undecided and look all round behind her at de older official guides.

'"Won't cost you a cent, ma'am. As I said, I'm goin' up anyway." Kurt slip in nice an' easy. Him hold out him hand to her an' tell her fi come on before sun get too hot.

'We watch her shade her face wid her hand an' look at de falls again, den she seh, "All right then, but not too fast, you hear."

'Kurt spin and wink at us den him turn roun' an' follow her. "Carry your bag, ma'am?" was de last ting we hear. As soon as dem gone, we buss outta laugh.

'"De woman look like puss dat just get cream," Popeye seh. "Poor Kurt!"

'"Poor Kurt, nutten," me tell him. "Him know good business when him see it. Me sure dat in a couple of years him gwine offer more that just a tour of de falls."'

'Me nuh waan hear no more 'bout Kurt an' wha' him haffi offer,' Aunt B protested.

'What happened to him?' Jewelle asked, ignoring her.

'Last I heard, him livin' in Stockholm. Marry some Swedish woman who was here on holiday. Tink dem might even have a couple of kids too.'

Aunt B puffed and shifted as much as she could in her seat. Although they were passing through a green, tree-lined valley – and the cool air had that special fresh smell of vegetation – she was uncomfortable. The seat was too narrow for the three of them and she wished the journey was over.

'We soon reach,' Sol said before continuing his story. 'Popeye an' Shorty were next. We wait another ten minute before de next likely candidates pass by, an' dat turn out to be a group of Canadians wid two teenage kids. It never tek Popeye long fi get talkin' to dem. Him could chat to anybody about anyting alla de time. De Canadians soon invite him fi join dem an' where he go, Shorty follow. Dat just left me. People were comin' an' goin' in waves. By time me sort out de others, it look like me miss de tide.

'Den me see Frank wid a big black woman. I never see de woman before and didn't really know Frank, but at dis stage me never have nutten fi lose. From her clothes and de way she stand, I did tink she was American, but when I get close and hear how she talk, it clear she was a Jamaican who gone a foreign an' doin' all right fi herself.

'Me slap Frank on him back. When him see it was me, him cut him eye an' ignore me.

'"Franklin. Yuh not gwine speak to yuh friend?" de woman ask.

'Franklin! Me haffi cover me mouth fi stop meself from laughin'. Wid an old man name like that, no wonder Frank stutter, I tink to meself.

'"M-m-my name's Frank," Frank mutter.

'"Wha' yuh name?" de woman ask me.

'I tell her, an' den she invite me fi go up wid dem. Seh it

95

good fi Franklin fi have a friend wid him. Dat it not good fi a bwoy pickney spend so much time by himself.

'"Well, if Franklin," me seh, den change to Frank when him gimme dutty look, "if Frank nuh mind, den yes."

'As it turn out, it never matter whether Frank mind or not,' Sol went on. 'Cousin Milly, as I find out she call, done decide already. I soon discover dat Cousin Milly never lissen to anybody anyway. By de time we get to the top, me could see why Frank have so likkle fi seh fi himself. De woman never stop chat! She mek us stand together at de top wid our arms roun' each other to take photo after photo, dat mout' of hers workin' away just as fast as her automatic camera . . .'

'I know she family an' all –' Sol started to say.

'Distant,' Frank said quickly.

'Yuh ever feel like push smaddy down from here, just fi shut dem up?' Sol whispered.

Frank looked at him in surprise and then smiled – a slow smile that broadened into a big wide grin that showed the tiny gap between his front teeth. They laughed together and then heard a click . . .

'Me still have de photo, even now.' Sol gave Jewelle a brief smile. 'Dat was how it started.'

'Just like that?'

'Exactly like dat. It funny, me nuh see yuh daddy fi more dan twenty years, but it don' matter. Some relationships, we can never leave behind. Whether we accept dem or not, dem don' die.'

'Too right,' Aunt B snorted.

'We reach!' Sol announced suddenly. Jewelle leaned forward, peering through the windscreen. 'How it seem to yuh?' he asked, grinning at the expression on Jewelle's face.

Jewelle's first sight of the falls left her lost for words. The rocks stretched high to the cobalt blue sky; powerful jets of water dropped some six hundred feet in a series of white-foamed cascades; the echo of the water as it bounced from the rocks mingled with the excited voices of the tourists. It made her think of a watery ladder to paradise.

'It's incredible. So lovely.' She looked around her. 'To have all this beauty,' she opened her arms wide as if she wanted to hug it close, 'to have this *all* the time and to choose to go to England. I don't understand.' She shook her head. 'Dad's never told me about any of this. I didn't realize that Jamaica could be so beautiful.'

'Lot of reasons fi a lot of tings.' Sol shrugged his shoulders. 'When yuh live in a place all de time, it easy fi tek tings fi granted. An' anyway, some places, no matter how much yuh hear 'bout it yuh need fi see fi yuhself. Frank did right in lettin' yuh see it first.'

Aunt B refused to climb the falls, despite Jewelle's attempts to persuade her.

'I prefer keep my feet on dry ground,' she said, as she bundled Jewelle's clothes in her straw bag. 'Ah will meet yuh two in de market when unnu finish yuh climb.'

The algae-covered stones were slippery smooth beneath Jewelle's bare feet as she started up the falls. The first impact of the cool water, pummelling her skin like a jacuzzi, made her gasp in shock. Around her, the air was full of the echoing shouts and laughter of other tourists mingled with the deep roar of the water as it rushed downwards. She paused at one of the shallow spots and let the water swirl around her ankles. When she got her breath back she continued upwards, making her way against the force of the water to a miniature pool where she half swam, half crawled to a rock. From there, she watched Sol give a helping hand to a young woman and noted his look

97

of admiration as the girl moved on ahead, giving him a close-up view of her round, unblemished rear encased in the tiniest and tightest of leopard-print bikini bottoms.

It was with a sense of exhilaration that she slid and scrambled her way to the top without a guide. Now she could see how the trees along the side of the falls dipped their leaf-laden branches towards the water, sipping from the same source which nourished their roots. The sound of strangers joking with each other the way holidaymakers do, was loud around them. Sol took photos of her and then asked a passing guide to take one of the two of them together.

'De exact same spot me tek dat photo wid yuh daddy,' he whispered, as the guide clicked the button and the snap was taken.

They flicked water at each other then sat and chatted for a while as they sun dried their skin and hair. Around them, people took 'victory' photos: standing with their arms around each other, damp T-shirts and sandals held high above their heads. The leopardskin-bikini girl smiled at Sol in recognition as she passed him on her way back down.

'Time fi mek a move, Jewelle,' he said, suddenly spurred into action.

'Let's go down the same way we came up,' she suggested.

'Up *and* down?'

She nodded enthusiastically and he laughed as if it was the best joke he'd heard in a long while.

'Me too old fi dat kinda business. Check yuh later in de market. Nuh worry, it small, yuh cyaan get lost.' He walked quickly to one of the wooden platforms that served as exits for those who found the climb too arduous. 'Hol' on, daughter,' he shouted, hurrying after the leopardskin bikini bottoms.

Once at ground level, Jewelle turned away from the falls and strolled through the artisan market that lay to the left of the entrance gates. There seemed to be a stand or shop for just about anything a tourist could possibly want to buy. Stalls selling wood carvings of all types; shops where red, gold and green knitted tams and yellow straw caps with 'Jamaica' threaded through in crooked pink lettering jostled for space with 'Jamaica No Problem' T-shirts. Stands displaying posters of the island and its artists; stalls with cookery books; jewellery; leather sandals, cassettes and other souvenirs.

But only one stall really attracted her – unshowy, but with mobiles and wind chimes spinning lazily in the slight breeze, it drew her to a halt. Carved figures filled the two shelves that ran the length of its back wall: tall, elegant women carrying baskets on their heads, dreadlocked rastas beating drums, mother and child figures caught in a moment of mutual love. From the ceiling hung all manner of chimes – tubular bamboo, carved birds and fishes. Jewelle stretched up and touched the diminutive figures of one mobile gently. Female forms, entwined one around the other in such a way that it looked as if they were dancing, sleeping, making love all at once.

'Han' carve.'

Startled, she took a step back. Hadn't seen the boy who had been sitting on the ground in the far corner of the stall, well out of the reach of the sun.

'Sorry. I'm not buying. Just looking.' And I could look at you for a long time, she thought.

'It don' cost money fi look,' he said, staring back at her. His dark eyes looked like they could see through any amount of clothing and made her suddenly very aware of just how small and revealing her swimsuit was. She pulled it down at the back so that it covered her bottom more completely – only to feel it ride straight back up again a second later.

'Waan me fi tek it down fi yuh?'

He was standing closer now and she could see just how *dark* brown eyes could be. His winged eyebrows were delicate, as if painted on with a fine-tipped paintbrush. The tips of his short locks were bleached golden by the sun and the sea. His lips were well cut and his eyelashes curled up at the ends so they seemed to turn in on themselves. She wanted to touch the lines of his face and subconsciously put her hands behind her back to keep them out of trouble. She'd never met him before and yet she felt she recognized him.

'I haven't got any money.' She shrugged her shoulders with a little smile and turned the palms of her hands up as if to say 'see'.

He placed the mobile in her upturned hands very carefully. It was a little longer than the length of her palm. A golden wood, from which had been carved eight sensuous, slender ladies. Fully proportioned and utterly naked, their firm small breasts were topped with tiny nipples. Their curved buttocks, high and taut. Each figure was independent but when she held the mobile up by its piece of string, the figures twirled and seemed to reach out to each other. She looked at the figures again, ran her hand over the proud, provocative derrière of one.

'Jus' like *yuh* bumper.'

'What?' She raised an eyebrow at him. Didn't understand the words, but understood the look.

'Tek it as a compliment.' The voice came from behind her.

She half turned. 'Oh, Sol! Er . . . hi.'

She looked at the wind chime and then at the boy again. His gaze wrapped itself around her like a dark cloak and she felt the squirm of a tadpole tail flicking low in her stomach.

'So dat's where yuh reach! Cover yuhself up. Yuh not in de water.' Aunt B pulled Jewelle's T-shirt from the straw

100

bag hanging from one shoulder. 'An' put on yuh shorts too, yuh not in England now,' she added.

Sol took the mobile from Jewelle's hand as she dressed, and examined it. 'Nice piece a work dis. I once know smaddy who work wid figures like dese. Who mek it, Jake?' Sol's voice was unusually curious.

Jake. Jake. From under her T-shirt, Jewelle rolled the sound of his name around her mouth.

'Me nuh know. Yuh haffi ask me spar over dere. Is his stall. Me jus' mindin' it.' He nodded to the T-shirt stall opposite, where two young men sat chatting and drinking beer.

'Is where I see yuh before?' Aunt B asked, noticing the way the boy couldn't keep his eyes off Jewelle.

'Is me bring de milk to Miss Jess every morning.'

'So wha' yuh doin' here?'

He shrugged his shoulders. 'Never have nutten else fi do today, so I come wid a couple of friends. Then I see David an' him ask me fi mind him stall fi ten minutes.'

Sol looked at David with interest. 'Must 'member fi ask him where him get dese tings from.'

'Well, we goin' now, so we will see yuh, Jake.' Aunt B pushed past him and bustled Jewelle out onto the main path. 'Hurry up, Sol,' she shouted behind her, 'yuh seh a couple of hours. Couple of hours come an' gone long time.'

'Waan a ride, Jake?'

Jake's smile revealed perfect white teeth. 'Mek me just tell David me goin' and I'll be wid yuh.' He caught up with them as they got to the pickup.

'Weh *yuh* tink yuh goin'?' asked Aunt B.

'Sol seh I can get a ride wid yuh all.'

'Weh yuh live anyway?'

'Over Discovery Bay, wid me cousin dem.'

'Yuh daddy?'

'Never know him.'

Sol nodded almost imperceptibly as if a different, un-voiced question had been answered.

'Yuh madda?'

'She use to live Port Antonio way, but now she live St Ann most times.'

'How yuh mean most times?' Aunt B interrogated.

'She like fi come and go when it please her.'

'Cho, woman! Stop question de youth, nuh.' Sol's voice was unusually sharp. 'Jewelle, yuh waan ride in de back or up front?'

'It was a bit hot with the three of us in the front. Think I'll ride in the back this time.'

Jake climbed into the back of the pick up first, then showed Jewelle how to get up by using the wheel rim as a step whilst he held her hand. They sat in opposite corners occasionally smiling at each other but saying nothing.

'Trust him wid yuh niece out dere?' Sol teased, indicating the two in the back of the pickup.

'Him better nuh gimme reason nuh fi trust him, is all I seh,' Aunt B huffed, shifting herself until she was nestled in the hollow that was the passenger seat. She unwrapped her market acquisition – a leaf-shaped wicker fan with a bamboo handle and fine strips of bamboo around its border. 'Is yuh I don' trust,' she muttered under her breath.

They took the shorter, less scenic inland route on the way back, stopping once to buy sugar cane that was stacked, tepee-style, at a roadside stand. Sol stripped and cut the cane into long pieces before sharing it out between them.

The journey passed in a flash for Jewelle once they'd dropped Jake off. As soon as they reached home and the engine was switched off, she was out of the pickup and running to the house. The feeling still flicking in the base of her stomach. She wanted to be alone, to hug it to herself, to relive every moment of that afternoon since she'd met him, without having Aunt B prying and asking questions.

She wouldn't have wanted to share this moment, not even with Ambra. The realization made her slow her pace – she couldn't remember a time when she *hadn't* shared all her deepest thoughts with her best friend. It wasn't until she was at the front door that she remembered her manners and ran back to thank Sol. Her shining eyes and wide grin brought an indulgent smile to his face and he kissed her cheek. She could smell his citrusy scent but this time it meant nothing, smelled wrong, didn't excite her. She turned back to the house, leaving Aunt B and Sol alone, her mind full of Jake. With him she'd smelled nothing, yet his invisible perfume had filled her nostrils and left her wanting more.

Aunt B paused, hand on the half-open door. 'Nuh badda start playin' none of yuh games wid my niece.'

'Games?'

'Don' come play innocent puss wid me. Yuh know what I mean. Kissin' her an' flashin' yuh jackal teeth at her like dat. Mek she tink seh yuh is smaddy she can trust.'

'Wh'appen? Jealous? Waan some?'

'Yuh just keep yuh frowzy body away from me,' she retorted.

'Me talkin' 'bout dis.' His eyes teased her as he held up one of the strips of sugar cane in front of her. He sucked on it for a moment before grinding it between his teeth.

'Yuh know what I mean.' Embarrassment made her voice surly. She fumbled with the door handle, her suddenly damp hand slipping foolishly.

'Need a likkle help?' He leaned over, reaching for the passenger door handle.

Aunt B could feel the heat from his body – or maybe hers – as he inclined towards her, smell the faint scent of sugar cane on his breath. She pressed herself back into the seat as far as she could go, but still his chest covered her.

Her breasts seemed to melt into his body and she turned her face, trying to ignore the unexpected sensations she was experiencing. It took her a moment to react when he next spoke.

'Door open. Or someting else I can help yuh wid dat yuh nuh tell me 'bout?' His mouth curved upwards at her before he spat the shreds of sugar-cane fibre into a paper tissue.

Aunt B sucked her teeth at him and scrambled from the car. She stood up clumsily and felt her ankle turn. Her shoe slipped off as she keeled forward and fell onto her hands and knees. She heard footsteps coming from his side of the car and hurried to right herself, but before she could, Sol's hand was grabbing hers and pulling her to her feet. She resisted his pull but felt his other hand slide around her waist and pull her close. He dropped a kiss on her lips and she turned her head away.

'Jus' tek yuh crocus bag hands off me.'

'Not touchin' yuh, Miss B.' He held his hands high above his head, his smirk now a full-blown grin.

She picked up her shoe and flung it after his retreating back, but it glanced the side of his arm harmlessly and fell to the ground. He climbed into the pickup and waved before reversing in a wide arc, spinning tyres sending yard dust flying up into the air.

Aunt B's chest swelled with anger and something else she wasn't quite willing to name as she half limped, half stomped her way to the offending shoe. She dusted down her clothes, hoping that nobody at the house had witnessed the scene. A twitching curtain caught her attention and her eyes met Jewelle's for a moment before the curtain fell back into place and the girl's face disappeared from view.

Upstairs, Jewelle let the curtain drop. She hugged her knees tightly to her chest, just as she hugged her thoughts to herself: this is so secret, so special I don't want to write it

104

down. Jake! His name's Jake. This is the best Valentine's Day I've ever had.

Aunt B stormed into the house and flung her shoe into a corner. It bounced once before skittering to a halt under the window. She was perched on a chair, rubbing her ankle gingerly when Miss Jess walked in.

'Feet hurt?' she enquired gently.

Aunt B nodded. 'Twist me ankle gettin' out of de pickup jus' now.'

'A little bay rum would do it good. Come to me room, me have some dere.'

Miss Jess sat on the bed and placed a folded towel on her lap, then indicated that Aunt B pull up the elongated wicker chair that stood in a corner the room.

Aunt B settled back in the chair and sighed as Miss Jess began to slowly rub in the bay rum. The cool liquid drew the heat from her aching ankle; its pungent smell clearing a path through her murky thoughts.

'Not just yuh ankle troublin' yuh, is it?' Miss Jess asked after a while.

Aunt B nodded but didn't reply. Miss Jess continued to massage without speaking. Her old hands were firm as she smoothed and stroked Aunt B's skin. She could feel, almost see, Aunt B melt. Whatever was bothering her would come out; she just needed time and a little attention.

Aunt B closed her eyes and purred with contentment as the tension slowly began to leave her body. It felt so good to be looked after. How long had it been? When had Sam stopped doing these things?

Aunt B couldn't imagine her own mother doing for her what Miss Jess was doing now. So many Jamaican parents were strict with their children, rarely showing their affection for them openly. Her own mother had been like that, but she and Beth hadn't suffered from it, and they'd grown up knowing right from wrong and how to respect their elders.

And as far as Aunt B was concerned, English parents were often too busy hugging and kissing up their kids to discipline them properly. Just look at how kids behave today. Yuh could be a ninety-year-old great-gran'mother on a bus full of schoolchildren an' yuh tink one of dem would give up dem seat? Aunt B asked herself. Not a chance! Dem more likely fi sit an' eat crisps, crack joke an' laugh till dem drop if the old lady fall over.

Frank seemed to have got the balance right. But then with a mother like Miss Jess, how could he go wrong? Although Aunt B wasn't strictly part of the family it didn't seem to matter. Miss Jess treated her as if she were one of them – as if she were blood.

Miss Jess hands slowed as she gave Aunt B's ankle a final rub. It took a moment before Aunt B realized the easing movement had stopped, leaving her feeling suddenly bereft and almost cheated.

'Like dat?' Miss Jess grinned.

'Just what I did need,' Aunt B said in heartfelt tones.

Miss Jess wiped her hands off on the towel and watched Aunt B get to her feet. 'How it feel now?'

'Good as new.' She tested her ankle; there was no pain at all. 'Waan do something fi yuh now. Don' move.'

She walked carefully from the room and returned carrying a bowl of water, rock salt and a fresh towel. She threw liberal handfuls of salt into the lukewarm water then made Miss Jess sit with her feet in the bowl.

'But me feet already clean,' she protested in puzzlement.

'Don' doubt dat,' Aunt B told her, 'but dis only de first part.'

When she thought enough time had passed, she carefully dried off Miss Jess's feet, before resting them on her lap. She reached for a large bottle of cocoa butter and Miss Jess clapped her hands like a small child as she realized what was going to happen.

Now it was her turn to lean back and relax as Aunt B lovingly rubbed the cream into Miss Jess's skin, and the older woman's sigh brought a satisfied smile to Aunt B's face. She watched the dry skin beneath her hands soften as it absorbed the liquid, continued rubbing until the skin gave off a healthy glow.

'Enjoy yuh trip to de falls wid Sol?' Miss Jess asked, breaking the silence between them.

Aunt B's fingers tightened momentarily at the mention of Sol's name.

Hmm, Miss Jess thought, but all she said was, 'Mind me toes. I can never recall,' she continued innocently, 'yuh meet Sol or Frank first?'

'Meet dem both de same night.'

'Yuh an' Beth?'

'No. Me an' Rose.' Aunt B turned her attention to Miss Jess's other foot.

'Ah, Rose,' Miss Jess said flatly.

Aunt B chuckled.

'Wha' so funny?'

'Just tinkin' back to de first time me meet Rose.'

'Oh, yes?'

Aunt B missed Miss Jess's tone of deep disinterest. 'Lord! I cyaan believe how much time pass. Must be what, twenty, twenty-two years ago. I meet her in church of all places! Me friend Beverley cousin did a marry. Me new in town and Beverley invite me to de weddin' . . .'

The service had already started by the time Aunt B arrived. She stood in the doorway, scanning the heads of the people sitting in orderly rows. Beverley was way up at the front but it was too late to join her there. Aunt B looked to either side. There was one free seat to her left, at the far end of the row, nearest the door. She squeezed her way along, ignoring the tuts of annoyance as she stepped on toes and knocked hymnbooks off laps. When she sat down she realized why the seat was still free, it was in the hot spot, next to the window. She placed her handbag carefully under her chair and settled back to listen to the rest of the service.

'Family or friend?' the woman beside her whispered.

'Friend. Sort of. Me know de bride cousin,' Aunt B whispered back. 'Yuh?'

'Me don' know anybody,' the other woman said, laughing, 'but when me see de bridegroom enter me haffi follow. Him one hell of a fine man – couldn't help wonder which lucky woman get him. Never know, him might have a brother.'

'So?'

'When me see de bride, me realize – good-looking brother or not – me nuh waan hook up wid no pretty fool.'

'Is how yuh mean?' Aunt B asked from the corner of her mouth.

'De woman ugly is a shame. Only pure idiot woulda marry her.'

Aunt B grinned as she turned to look at the woman next to her. The woman grinned back, her browny-green eyes limpid clear.

'Yuh cyaan seh dat,' Aunt B protested. 'Is her weddin' day!'

'Weddin' day or not, she still favour hog!'

Aunt B raised one white-gloved hand to stifle the giggle that threatened to escape.

'Even wid her belly push up like watermelon under her frock,' the other woman continued, 'still she a wear white. Hypocrite!'

'Stop it! We in church,' Aunt B reprimanded. But her grin gave her away.

108

'If she a virgin, den me de Queen a Englan'!' The woman folded her arms across her chest. 'Talk 'bout she a wear white.'

'Unnu have some respec', nuh,' someone hissed.

The green-eyed woman sucked her teeth and stared straight ahead. Aunt B took the opportunity to look at her. Caramel-coloured skin, wide green-brown eyes and a mouth that looked too big for her face. No hat, but tall with straightened hair, long and easy to comb.

The service came to an end and the newlywed couple turned towards the door. The green eyed woman nudged Aunt B.

'Look 'pon dem good!' See how her eye dem a pop like bullfrog. Yuh ever see nose like dat? An' de mouth! Look like raw liver, but she still a come wid de lipstick.'

Aunt B hid her face in her hymnbook after the first look. Everything this woman said was true. 'All right. All right.' Aunt B chuckled hard. 'But even so, is her weddin' day.'

'So what! She still one ugly bitch,' the green-eyed woman pronounced.

Aunt B couldn't hold her laugh back any longer, she stuffed her handkerchief into her mouth but it wasn't enough to soften the guffaw that burst out. The bride and groom turned to look at the source of the noise.

The woman slapped her on the back. 'She have a bad cough,' she shouted to the congregation in general. To Aunt B she whispered, 'What a cow laugh yuh have. Rahtid! Why yuh never warn me?'

Aunt B shook her head, tried to speak but burst into laughter again.

'Come.' Her new-found friend grabbed her by the hand and pulled her outside, pushing past the bride and groom and flapping her hand impatiently at the cries of 'come out' and 'ignorant' that followed them.

Outside, she waited until Aunt B had stopped laughing

and had wiped the tears from her eyes. Aunt B took a deep steadying breath and straightened up. 'Beatrice,' she said, holding her hand out to the other woman.

The other woman took the proffered hand with a smile. 'Rose . . .'

'Never agree wid her alla de time,' Aunt B said to Miss Jess, 'but she not all bad. Just a likkle impulsive sometime. De type dat lick first and ask question after. If she nuh like yuh she show it clear, but if she tek yuh to her heart, she will give yuh anyting she have.'

'And what she love, she waan keep,' Miss Jess said with a surprising edge of bitterness.

Aunt B sighed deeply as she worked the cream in between Miss Jess's toes. 'True,' she admitted. 'Rose did have a likkle problem dere. Actually, one hell of a big problem if I tell de truth.' She laughed, caught Miss Jess's eye and stopped abruptly. 'Me agree Rose did have her faults but she help me more dan once in de past. Help me get dat first secretarial job at de Building Society. Help me keep it too, when de president waan replace me wid him likkle maaga galfrien'. Rose only problem was her gran'-mother. If she never lissen to her so much, she woulda live better.'

'Oh, yes?'

'Seh her gran'mother have de gift of sight and dat she inherit it too. Always chatting foolishness 'bout destiny. How dis meant to be and dat meant to happen. But when it never happen de way Rose waan, she never worry too much about givin' *destiny* a helpin' han' when it suit her.'

Miss Jess slipped her feet back into her slippers. 'Well, Rose in de past an' we in de present, so we can just figet 'bout her an' talk 'bout sometin' else.'

'Yuh right. Me know yuh never like Rose much an' me can imagine why. But she was a good friend to me one time. Don' know if I was such a good friend to her at de end.'

Don' want to know, Aunt B admitted to herself as she left the room.

Rose sat rigidly upright as the bus jolted over the pitted country track as it headed towards Bengal Bridge. Night had fallen and she'd lost hours wandering around aimlessly, her shopping weighing heavily from her arms and her head full of the conversation she'd overheard. The more she thought about Frank the more she fumed.

Likkle raas! All dese years an' not a single word from de bitch! Never a reply to any of me letters, not even dat last one I sen' care of Aunt B. Nutten! An' now suddenly him back inna Jamaica an' cyaan even badda himself fi let me know. All right. So him come back fi him father funeral, but him still find time fi run up an' down town wid him crusty friend. An' not even dat, tink himself so big dat him can push past me in de street like me a piece a dirt.

She remembered how her grandmother used to say that if there was a choice of roads, destiny would always take the longest one. Well, one damn long, rough route it tek, was all she could say.

Be honest wid yuhself, she thought. Yuh angry 'cause in spite of everyting him put yuh through, yuh still love him an' waan him back. But cho! Wha' wrong wid yuh? Yuh nuh have no pride? How yuh can love smaddy so much when dem treat yuh so bad. But pride nah keep my bed warm a night time, she admitted to herself, an' even though me have plenty others since him gone, is still him one me waan. Maybe I should just let go. After all, him mek a decision to leave me long time an' even end up marry smaddy else.

She remembered the day that she'd found out – from Constance 'Carry-Go-Bring-Come' who worked at the post office and knew everybody's business before they did.

'Oh, Miss Rose,' Constance had said. Rose was on her guard immediately. Constance never gave her the time of day normally, let alone the big wide-ass grin she was giving her now. 'Me sure yuh already know dat Franklin send two air ticket fi Poppa Ben and Miss Jess fi go a Englan'.' Constance's beady eyes watched Rose's face for the slightest reaction.

'Him not de first and me sure him not de last fi send air ticket to him people dem,' she managed to reply without losing her calm.

'True, true,' Constance replied, black eyes gleaming. 'But is him weddin' dem goin' to!'

Rose closed her eyes tightly, just as she had all those years ago, but she could still see Constance's malicious grin with the gold eye tooth she had gleaming against all the other irregular teeth in her mouth. It had taken all her willpower not to yank out that gold tooth with her bare hands and thump the woman down. Constance's husband was a policeman, which meant that she got away with a lot more than anyone else would have done. It was after her meeting with Constance that she'd written that desperate letter to Aunt B, even though in her heart she suspected it was probably too late. When, after months of silence, there was still no reply she'd given up.

But suddenly here was destiny stepping in. She givin' me another chance, Rose thought. Is not everybody get two tries, and bumping into Frank in Brown's Town was a sign. Me nah let go dis time.

'No, no, no,' she muttered, shaking her head emphatically, causing the woman beside her to shoot her a worried glance. Mr Franklin Galimore not gwine get away quite so easy dis time, she decided. If yuh nah come to me den me will jus' haffi go to yuh. Mek yuh suffer likkle den tek yuh back. Maybe there was something to be said for destiny after all.

Once she'd made up her mind, she relaxed. A smile played around her mouth as she shifted her bags and squeezed up on the seat so that the old lady who sat perched on the few centimetres of space Rose had conceded her at the start of the journey, could finally get both skinny buttocks onto the seat.

4

15th February

'One, two, three, four, five, six . . . Oh, no!'

Jewelle dropped the bucket where she stood. Her mind raced over possible excuses even as she re-counted. Three and three made six. Three cows, three goats. One goat missing. The one she liked best. The dark one with the lazy brown eyes and the old man's beard. She stumbled over the bucket as she ran back to the house.

'It's gone. Missing. I don't know how.' The words came out in a rush. 'I always check they're tied up. I don't know how it happened. I'm sorry,' she finished lamely as she pulled the heavy workmen's gloves off.

'Wha' yuh talkin' 'bout?' Miss Jess asked calmly. Her eyes didn't move from the green bananas she was deftly stripping with three quick movements of her knife.

'One of the goats.' This time Jewelle spoke slowly. 'It's run away. Gone.' She was too agitated to notice the look that passed between her grandmother and Nancy, who was busy seasoning a mound of chopped meat.

'Oh, de goat,' Miss Jess said casually. 'I know bout dat. Nancy done tek care of it. Yuh finish feedin' de other animal dem?'

'No, I came straight back when I realized that –'

Miss Jess cut her off. 'Well, go finish feed dem 'cause breakfast soon ready. And throw dis out fi me.' She pointed to the pile of banana skins which lay curled like thick green vines on a yellowed sheet of the *Daily Gleaner*.

'But –'

'Jewelle. I don' have time fi stan' up and talk right now. Too many tings fi do.' Her smile took the edge off her words. She wiped her hands down the front of her apron. 'Hurry, run go finish yuh chores. We have plenty time soon enough fi talk. Run now, chile.'

By the time Jewelle came back, the kitchen was empty bar Nancy, who was standing at the sink with her back to the door. Jewelle hurried past with her head down before Nancy noticed her. She peered into Miss Jess's room but the was nobody there. The large wooden four-poster bed was neatly made. The wicker chair held the white cotton cushion she'd often seen behind Miss Jess's head. A pair of house slippers sat neatly by the side of the bed, heels facing the door as if waiting for their owner to slip them on. The house felt big and heavy and empty. She realized that even Aunt B's loud presence was preferable to silence. Jewelle was surprised to feel a small twinge of loneliness when she walked into their bedroom only to discover that there was nobody there. If no one wanted her company then it was clear that she'd have to make do with her own. She put on her Walkman, grabbed one of the magazines Uncle Sam had bought her at the airport and made her way to the front veranda. There, she kicked off her sandals and slumped in one of the butterfly-winged carved wooden chairs.

Gloomily she flicked through the magazine, but she'd already read it and its pages held nothing new for her. She let it drop over the side of the chair and closed her eyes; one arm tapped the side of her chair lazily as she nodded in time to music only she could hear. A shower of pebbles bouncing beside her feet alerted her to the presence of another person. A smile flashed to her face when she looked up to see Jake peering from behind the front gate.

Over one shoulder he carried a stick adorned with the brightly coloured fruit she'd seen on her first day. He beckoned her with his free hand and she jumped to her feet, suddenly aware of just how glorious the day was, how vivid the green and brushed gold of the flowing coconut palms, the intensity of the purple buds of the flowering banana tree. She skipped barefoot down the veranda steps, pulling the earphones free as she went. They smiled at each other from either side of the gate. His red open-necked shirt accentuated the glowing tones in his skin.

'Hey!' Her eager tone betrayed her pleasure at seeing him.

He nodded towards the Walkman. 'Wha' yuh lissenin' to?'

'This.' She slipped through the gate and handed him the earphones.

'Like it?' she shouted.

He stood in silence and she turned the volume down a little.

'Like it?' she repeated.

He screwed his face up, 'It all right, I suppose, but me have some really good music. Yuh ever hear a Bob Marley?'

'Course I have!'

'Peter Tosh? Jimmy Cliff? Shabba? Buju?'

'I suppose so. Dad's always playing reggae, but it's not really my type of thing. Bit boring really, same rhythm all the time.'

'But yuh ever lissen to de word dem? Really lissen, de way yuh lissen to yuh likkle English pop star dem? If yuh know how much history and culture in what dem sing, yuh woulda never stop. Fi we music have ridim – from calypso to mento, ska to blue beat, den yuh have reggae an' dance-hall. Dere's a whole history in de music, man.'

'All right.' Jewelle held her hands up in mock-surrender.

116

'I never said there wasn't.' She laughed. She liked seeing him all fired up, the way his eyes shone and how he waved his free hand around as he talked.

'Yuh know what reggae mean? It mean sufferation. Poverty. Wisdom,' he told her before she had a chance to reply. 'Bad bwoy, rebel, dem man deh mek dis music. It come from kings an' plenty queens too, dese days.'

Jewelle giggled.

'Wha' yuh laughin' 'bout?' he asked, laughing too.

'You! You were so serious. You should've seen your face.'

'Yeah, yuh gwine laugh. I bet is people like yuh run give yuh daddy good money to all dem false prophet dat gwaan like dem black an' buy all dem white people version a reggae music. Yuh see, we Jamaican born wid talent. Even when we sufferin' we still produce good music dat have someting fi seh. Look 'pon Toots. Him learn from him experience. When him go a jail him mek a likkle record 'bout it: "54-46 Was My Number" him sing. Him prison number dat is.' Jake wagged a finger to emphasize his point. 'An' when him come out an' him situation get better, him sing 'bout dat too – "Pressure Drop". Ever hear it?'

Jewelle shook her head. 'Maybe,' she said doubtfully.

'Probably 'cause yuh fill yuh head wid UB40 and whatever dat white bwoy call an' him "Ice Ice Baby" foolishness.' He returned the headphones to her. 'Me will mek yuh a tape fi tek back wid yuh.'

'You seem to know tons about music,' she said. 'Do you want to get into the music business or something?'

'No, man. Music is fi pleasure.' He looked around before whispering, 'I like photography. But it cost too much.'

'Why're you whispering? Is it a secret?'

'Yeah. People love laugh too much roun' here. Love knock yuh back before yuh even step forward. I don' waan anyone know my business before me have someting fi

117

show dem. But it hard. Really hard. He stooped and picked up the churn. 'I better get dis milk inside before it spoil.'

'Can I carry something?'

'Dis not too heavy.' He handed her the stick of ackee. 'Careful. It delicate. Bruise up easy.' She shouldered it as she'd seen him do. 'Now yuh look like a real Jamaican,' he teased. 'Dem colours deh suit yuh,' he said, staring at the vivid red and yellow fruit which hung next to her ear like an exotic garland. 'Yuh look pretty.'

Before she had a chance to register his words he'd turned abruptly, picked up the container of milk and was striding around the side of the house. She struggled to keep up with him, just as she struggled to understand his sudden change of mood. The stones underfoot prickled the soles of her feet and slowed her down as she carefully picked her way over them. By the time she'd caught up with him he was in the kitchen and had already handed the milk over.

'Bring yuh some fresh ackee, Miss Jess.' He jerked a finger behind him at Jewelle.

'Thankin' yuh kindly, Jake. First time yuh bring me ackee in all de time I know yuh.' Her eyes teased him. 'Me 'preciate it, but look like me gran'daughter 'preciate it more.' She smiled openly at the boy's embarrassment. 'Cyaan let good ackee waste. Mek we cook it now.'

'But,' Nancy joined her in the doorway, 'I already cook cornmeal porridge.'

'Dat can keep,' Miss Jess answered serenely. 'Mek we start de day right. Full belly mek hard work taste sweeter. Weh yuh goin', sah?' she asked as Jake tried to slip past her.

'Me jus' a . . .'

'Is yuh bring de ackee, so yuh must eat from it too. Soon find yuh sometin' fi do. Yuh too, miss,' she added, as Jewelle gave an excited little jump.

'Aunt B? Jewelle popped her head around the bedroom

door. 'Breakfast is ready. It's ackee! Fresh! Jake brought it. For me!' she ended in a high-pitched, teenage squeal.

Rose drew the thin cloth that served as a curtain in front of the window so that the afternoon light was blocked out, then pulled the ottoman in front of the scarred dresser that sat solid in a corner of the room. She smoothed the quilted fabric that covered the wooden lid so that the excess material hung downwards and to the side. The padding that should have softened and protected the lid had long since escaped and she'd never got around to replacing it. A cracked mirror lay propped at an angle on top of the dresser and she shifted it so that it was directly in front of her. Around her were candles of all shapes and sizes, their teardrop flames dancing and shimmering each time Rose moved briskly by. She wiped the smoky surface of the mirror with her dress tail, without much effect.

That done, she pulled a tattered photograph of her grandmother – the only one that existed – from the bottom drawer of the dresser and spread it smooth with the palm of her hand. The photo was faded, its dark brown edges showing the passage of time. The face in the picture was no longer visible but that wasn't important – the face was clear where it mattered, in her memory. She set fire to the pile of crumbled roots and herbs she'd previously placed in a round enamel dish and set it on the floor near her feet, then perched on the lid of the ottoman. As the smoke began to rise, drawing up the scent of rosemary and mint and all the other ingredients she'd added, Rose stared into the mirror with the photo in her hand.

'Now, Mamma G,' she whispered, 'is now I need yuh fi help me. Tell me wha' fi do.' She stared intently into the mirror for a moment and then closed her eyes and concentrated. The candles burned down in the silence within the room, the smoke from the bowl petered into a wisp –

there was no movement or sound at all. Not from Rose, not within the room and not from outside. It was as if every living thing was in extended silent agreement, and then she was floating back and back and back . . .

'Rose! Just come right back here!' Becky screamed. 'Yuh likkle bitch yuh,' she added under her breath as Rose wriggled her way under the low wooden veranda. Becky interpreted the bump of the girl's arse as a gesture of defiance, and it spurred her into sudden action. She ran clumsily, one hand under the base of her stomach, which hung hard and low now that she was in her seventh month of pregnancy. Ignoring the flailing of the feet inside her as the baby kicked its protest against this sudden movement, she reached into the shadow cast by the veranda and grabbed hold of Rose's ankle. The girl grunted as she was pulled up short. For a moment neither moved as each waited to see what the other would do next. Becky twisted the ankle. How easy it would be to break this chicken-like leg of her daughter. She let the ankle slip from her grip and instead lowered herself heavily onto the middle step of the veranda, her belly rising like a hill between her legs as she leaned back.

Rose scrambled out on the other side of the veranda and brushed herself down. Her too-short dress rose up as she leaned forward to wipe grains of dry dirt from her knees. She used the sole of one foot to rub against the calf of her other leg, scratching an old mosquito bite. Mumma had chased her but her anger hadn't lasted long. Before the baby, Mumma would have pulled her out roughly and shouted, even though they both knew that she didn't mean it most times. Then they used to sit on the veranda steps and share a piece of fruit before doing their chores. Or, if everything was done, Mumma would sit and plait her hair, and that was the best time of all. But that was then . . . now

120

all she did was moan about how hot it was, how much trouble Rose gave, rub her stomach and talk to the baby. But Mamma G always had time for her. She'd read her palms and tell her who she'd become, even if the story was different every time. Rose loved these moments where she was the centre of attention. She sensed, rather than saw, that Mumma and Mamma G didn't like each other, and in her own way tried not to give one or the other cause for jealousy. But with Mumma so wrapped up in her belly, she was spending more time with the woman who had helped birth her.

Mamma G sat hunched in front of a blackened dutchy pot where she was frying fish. It was the usual spot used for outdoor cooking, set in the hollow that lay behind the bushes hiding the pigpen from view. The leaves from the trees overhead formed a dark green roof creating a cool area to work in. Smoke, rising in a twisted spiral from the dry sticks that crackled and snapped as they burst into flame, poked spitefully at her eyes, making them water until tears fell and mixed with the beads of sweat that ran down her face. Despite the beating sun, it was better than cooking indoors where the heat wrapped itself around you and the smoke and scent of fried fish would cling to your hair and clothes for hours after. She waved a piece of blackened cardboard in front of the flames, fanning them on, then jumped back as angry fat from the pot spat at her, pricking her skin viciously.

It was here that Rose found her grandmother, sitting on her heels and rubbing at her bare arm. She jumped lightly on her back, but the unexpected weight sent the old woman tumbling forward dangerously near the pot.

'Yuh a idiot?' she snapped at Rose, who lay on her side giggling. 'Dis nuh laughin' matter. Yuh nearly pitch me in de fire,' she added rubbing at her scraped elbows.

121

'Never mean fi frighten yuh, Granny,' Rose said, settling on her knees. Her heart sank as she looked at the stern lines of her grandmother's face. Now there would be no stories or play. 'Mek me help yuh,' she said picking up the long two-pronged metal fork and jabbing at the contents of the pot.

'Move from deh!' Mamma G ordered. 'Look how yuh a mash up de fish.' She grabbed the fork from Rose and prodded at the fish much in the same way Rose had, before turning them over. She glanced at the girl now sitting silently by her side, her greeny-brown eyes shiny with unshed tears.

'Do it like dis,' she conceded. 'Come.' Rose inched closer and placed her hand over that of her grandmother's. 'When yuh come fi tek dem out, tek dem out by de head or de tail. Then it nuh matter so much if dem bruk up.'

The two worked together in silence. The young one carefully hooking the fish from the oil and shaking them slightly before transferring them to the enamel plate the old woman held ready. When the plate was full, Mamma G busied herself chopping onions while Rose filled another, smaller plate with more fish. That done, Mamma G used two scraps of old towel to hold the handles of the pot as she moved it to a bare bit of ground, so scorched that nothing could grow there. When the oil was cooler, she poured most of it out, then threw in the chopped onions to what was left and stirred vigorously before adding a dash of vinegar and a little water. After a minute or so, she tipped the contents of the pot over the fish.

'Mek we tek it inside and leave it let de fish soak up de juice.'

They walked to the house in single file; the older one ahead with the larger plate, the smaller one trailing her steps and carrying her plate as if it were a royal, silver platter.

*

Late that afternoon, still hot but with a light breeze that took the edge off the heat, Rose was absorbed in digging holes in the dry earth with a piece of stick. As soon as she'd made one hole she used the sole of one foot to push loose dirt and dry leaves into it, before making another one and repeating the procedure all over again.

'When yuh last plait yuh hair?' Mamma G asked.

'Nuh 'member.'

'Look how it dry an' natty-natty! Run fetch de comb and de coconut oil.'

'Nuh worry, Granny,' Rose spoke hastily, as she patted down dry earth with the palm of her hand, 'Mumma seh she ah go plait it fi me later.'

It was a lie, but one Rose felt was justified as she thought about how different her mother's hands in her hair were compared to her grandmother's. Mumma would carefully part the hair, gently work at the knots with her fingertips until they fell apart, then rub and massage oil into the scalp and hair until both shone. She would sing to her all the time she worked and it was in these moments that Rose felt closest to her – just the two of them and no one else – until Poppa came along. But he would only sit down and watch them – a smile on his face as he smoked his pipe. Whenever she asked him what he was smiling about, he'd take the pipe out of his mouth and contemplate it. Then, almost as if he were talking to the pipe, he'd say, 'My big beautiful woman making my little woman even more beautiful,' before jabbing the pipe back into his mouth. If Granny happened to be around, she would huff and grunt until Poppa said something nice about her – but he never called her beautiful. It would have been too much of a sin for a religious man to tell such a lie.

Granny used the comb like an army tank forcing its way through thick jungle. She pulled so hard that Rose would feel her neck stretching way beyond its limits. If she murmured or if tears appeared in her eyes, it was an excuse for her grandmother to crack her on the forehead with the comb and mutter, 'Yuh waan me gi yuh sometin' fi cry 'bout,' before renewing her attack with more energy than before. It was only when she was actually plaiting and then, only if she were in a good enough mood, that the stories would start. Stories based on the shape of her head, the scar in her eyebrow, the lines in her hands.

'Yuh madda don' have time fi yuh dese days. Yuh nuh see how she big wid baby? But if yuh prefer run roun' wid yuh head lookin' like dat,' she folded her arms across her chest and looked away, 'is up to yuh.'

'But, Granny, Mumma said . . .'

'Me will tell yuh a story if yuh waan,' Mamma G offered sneakily.

Rose looked up, tempted but unsure; Mamma G cheated sometimes. 'Really?'

'Sure, man. Someting 'bout dem pretty eye yuh have . . .'

'Yuh already done tell me 'bout me eye,' replied Rose, who knew how to strike a hard bargain.

'But wait! Yuh never mek me finish,' Mamma G improvised hastily, ''bout yuh pretty brown and green eye and de man who boun' fi fall in love wid yuh sake a dem.'

'Soon come back!' Rose threw down the stick and jumped to her feet. 'Mek me run get de comb.'

They didn't hear Becky approaching and she was able to watch the two of them together. Mamma G sitting on an upturned pail, Rose on the ground between her legs as Mamma G parted her hair.

Cho, man, Becky thought bitterly, as she stood half hidden behind a banana tree, she even tief our together time, and after the morning's scene it would have been their make-up moment too. Why she haffi be de centre of everyting? She stood still, straining her ears so she could hear what they were saying.

'Yuh did promise, Granny.'

'All right. Me know. Just tinking weh fi begin.' Mamma G peered down at the head in her hands. She could have been talking about where to start in the thick hair. 'Mek me do some cornrows, dem last fi days.' Dat ways, she thought to herself, Becky won't have de slightest excuse fi hog de chile wid excuse 'bout her hair need doin' again. She just jealous 'cause Rose love me more dan she love she. She drew two straight lines down the left side of Rose's head, parted the line of hair into three and started twisting them expertly.

'When yuh gwine start?' Rose whined, beginning to feel that she'd been tricked into sitting still for at least an hour with her neck twisted uncomfortably.

Mamma G looked down into the golden-brown eyes with their strange flecks of green, staring up at her accusingly. Such pretty eyes – the way they changed colour depending on Rose's mood – so unlike anyone else's in the family.

'Come nuh,' Rose insisted. 'Yuh seh yuh would tell me 'bout de man me ah go get.

'Hope yuh nah tell de gyal more foolishness 'bout man. Plenty enough time in de future fi her start tink 'bout dem.' Despite herself, Becky's voice came out harsher than she meant as she stepped from behind the tree. Rose was already a dreamer, already showing beauty and Becky didn't want her daughter vain or thinking she could make her way through the world on the promise of a beautiful face and a sexy body.

Mamma G's face hardened at the sight of her daughter and she found herself speaking quickly – more for the sake of shutting Becky up than for anything else.

'De women in dis family have de gift of sight yuh know,' she started conversationally, 'not dat all of we have it.

Sometimes it jump one generation and pass straight to de next.' She glanced disdainfully at Becky.

'Me more dan happy me nuh have yuh kinda second sight!' Becky snapped back. 'All it mean is yuh chat rubbish 'bout wha' yuh cyaan see an' chat bad 'bout wha' yuh do.' She folded her arms across the bulge of her stomach as if the conversation was at end.

'Yuh, Rose,' Mamma G continued as if Becky hadn't spoken, 'yuh born wid a caul. Plus me boil it up, mek yuh sip de tea me get from it, so although yuh have de sight yuh also protected from anytin' evil roun' yuh.'

'Except yuh,' Becky muttered.

'Yuh seh someting, mam?' Mamma G demanded, holding the comb aloft as if ready to hit her with it.

Becky stared her in the eyes but all she said was, 'Tell us 'bout dis "special" man me ten-year-old daughter suppose to meet. Me interested fi know how yuh see him so clear when yuh cyaan see much further dan yuh left foot most days.'

Mamma G cut her eyes at Becky, but felt compelled to speak. 'Many men will love yuh but yuh will only truly love one, an' from de moment yuh see him yuh will know him is de one.'

'But how?'

'Good question,' Becky threw in. 'Me jus' 'bout fi ask de same.'

'Some people we suppose fi be wid we, and when we meet dem we just know. We nuh need no one fi tell us. We nuh need words nor signs. Dat type a bond come from other times, other lives and dem invisible to yuh and me . . . but dem dere and dem run deep. Just like de roots a dat banana tree over dere. Even though yuh cyaan see how deep de roots lie, yuh know de roots dere.'

Becky sniffed even as Rose askcd, 'But how I gwine recognize him?'

126

Mamma G pulled the girl's hair sharply. 'Yuh not lissenin' to me? Yuh never hear me just seh some tings yuh cyaan see?'

Becky laughed loudly. 'After all yuh done talk 'bout second sight dis and second sight dat; how yuh can see de past and de future, yuh mean yuh cyaan even see a likkle someting like what Rose man look like? Gyal,' she walked to Rose and looked down at her, 'yuh better off lookin' 'pon yuh schoolbook an' study yuh lesson dan waitin' 'pon yuh gran'madda fi talk sense.'

Provoked, Mamma G improvised wildly. 'It not always good fi know too much 'bout yuh future 'cause de minute yuh start wait fi it fi happen, it change. But sometime a likkle knowledge can help, 'cause it help yuh believe. Yuh will meet dis man through music, dancin' –'

'Considerin' dat everybody on dis island dance unless dem sick or dem foot bruk, yuh nuh need much sight fi see dat!' Becky interrupted. 'Rose, me met yuh daddy at a dance. Yuh granny meet yuh grandpa at a weddin' party. Mumma, yuh gwine haffi do better if yuh waan convince me or dat pickney sittin' dere between yuh legs.'

'Yuh wi meet him when yuh least expec', but only after yuh already meet de man yuh tink is de one.'

Both Becky and Rose stared at Mamma G in surprise. Her voice had deepened and sounded as if it were being pulled from within her. She sat lightly hunched forward, her eyes closed and the comb clenched in one hand.

'Yes, him a watch yuh dance and from dat moment on dere will be no one else fi him . . . or fi yuh. Him body mark in some way,' she screwed her eyes even more tightly shut, 'but me cyaan see how. All I know is dat likkle soon as yuh see de mark yuh will know him a de one. Is him one mek yuh complete, mek yuh whole. Him will be de moon to yuh sun, de night to yuh day an' when him tek yuh in him arms, yuh will never waan fi let him go.'

There was a moment of silence and then Mamma G opened her eyes. She looked surprised to see them, as if she had no recollection of where she was.

'But how I gwine know him?' Rose whispered, awed. 'How I gwine recognize him?'

'Uh? Him big an' like I seh him mark. I tink him have someting funny wid one of him hand or foot.'

'Like wha'?'

'But wait, chile! Nuh badda ask me no more question. I already tell yuh more dan yuh should know.' Mamma G picked up the comb and coughed. Forcing her voice to come out so harshly had made her throat hurt, but seeing the look on Becky's face when she'd opened her eyes had been worth it. She turned away from Becky's penetrating stare and continued plaiting Rose's hair.

Becky rested against the tree, rubbing her stomach. The baby was pitching about inside her, like a ship at sea, almost as if protesting at the story he'd just heard. The old bitch had always been a good actress, but that little show had been one of her best. The baby gave a kick that made her moan and drop to her knees in pain. Her last thought before she lost consciousness was that Rose was only a child and would have forgotten all that nonsense by the time the summer was over . . .

'*Him body mark in some way.*' The words and images came back to her – Mamma G sitting with her eyes tightly shut concentrating so hard it was almost painful to watch her. And she'd been right – she always was. '*Likkle soon as yuh see de mark yuh will know him de one.*'

Rose lay with her eyes closed, eyelids occasionally flickering. 'I find him mark, Mamma G. Him did mark like yuh seh. But . . . him don' waan me.' Tears slipped from her closed eyes as she admitted to grandmother's spirit what she'd never truly admitted even to herself.

'*Is him one mek yuh complete, mek yuh whole. Him will be de moon to yuh sun, de night to yuh day an' when him tek yuh in him arms, yuh will never waan fi let him go.*'

'I don' know wha' fi do,' Rose cried. 'Help me!'

'*Is 'cause yuh don' believe. I tell yuh once already – some people we meant fi be wid.*'

'But him don' waan me,' Rose repeated. 'Him mek a new life – no place in it fi me.'

'*Remember me words.*' The voice in Rose's head grew louder. '*'Member when yuh mumma waters break.*'

'Yes.'

'*Is not askin' I askin' yuh fi remember, is tellin' I tellin' yuh. Remember!*'

Rose frowned, eyes squeezed tightly shut as she tried to concentrate and recall what else had been said that day . . .

'Will Mumma be all right?'

'Yes, she restin' now and yuh daddy wid her.' Mamma G rubbed soap into her hands before scrubbing them hard.

'Me know. Me did waan fi sit wid her but Poppa tell me fi go weh 'cause she sleepin'. But she wasn't!' Rose's voice rose accusingly. 'She was jus' lookin'. Me did tink she was lookin' at me an' ah smile an' wave at her, but when she look at me, she look like she never even know who me was. Like she cyaan even see me. I don' waan her fi dead too.' The wobble in her voice turned into a shake and she started to cry.

'She nah go dead!' Mamma G spoke firmly. She dried her hands on the piece of old towel she had flung over her shoulder. 'She not going nowhere unless she give up. Yuh lissen to me, Rose. All dat happen tonight is destiny. Yuh madda never mean fi have dat baby, like him never mean fi live. Poor likkle ting spend nine months kickin' an' wearin' himself out so much him never have de strength fi kick when him need it. Yuh cyaan fight destiny, but yuh can tek every single chance it give yuh.' She shook the girl as if trying to shake the words into her head. 'Yuh haffi fight fi survive in dis world. Yuh haffi fight fi wha' yuh waan. An' if yuh cyaan fight, yuh go under, an' when dat happen,' she pulled the child to her breast and rocked her close, 'when dat happen . . . yuh might as well be dead! . . .'

Rose came around to find herself lying on the floor. She lay still with her eyes closed, lazily examining the images that drifted into mind, then she wiped the back of one hand across her forehead and smoothed back her damp hair. Eventually, a smile appeared on her face and she nodded, satisfied. She stretched slowly and got to her feet.

The session had been tiring but worth it. She stared into the mirror, poking her tongue out at the reflection that smiled back. The photo was damp in her palm; she smoothed it down before carefully drying its edges on the front of her dress and slipping it back into the drawer where she kept pieces of fabrics and remnants of material. As she put it away her hand came across the smoothness of silk and she pulled the material out. It was a pale lemon silk, bought many years ago and still uncut. Rose stooped on her haunches and smiled with pleasure. The signs were all there; this was another. She got to her feet and shook the fabric out. There was easily enough to make a dress and a wrap for her head or neck – whatever she wanted in fact.

She poured a little water into the bowl releasing a faint protesting hiss as the last of the herbs dried up. The remaining candles she left burning, but she flung open the curtain so that light flooded the room. She lay the material flat on the floor then turned to her sewing basket, selecting a sharp pair of scissors. The material spread across the floor like a yellow stream, and she cocked her head to one side as she considered it. She would make a dress that made its wearer both beautiful and bewitching. A dress that Frank wouldn't be able to resist. Like the light, figure-hugging ones she'd worn when she first met him. She picked up the scissors and started to cut. Clean, sure strokes. She didn't need a pattern, she never had. Besides, this dress was special. This dress would make itself.

Frank stood on the back veranda and looked down into the garden. It had done him good bumping into Benny yesterday. He'd enjoyed catching up on old times without someone pressurizing him to make decisions.

In one corner of the garden stood a single banana tree. Of course there were many others, but this one was in splendid isolation and he'd always thought of it as his own special tree. On impulse, he sought out his tree again and threw himself beneath the shade of its broad leaves, just as he'd done when he was a child and played alone. He looked up at the underside of the leaves splayed high above him, at a hand of unripe bananas which from his position looked like thick, curved green fingers.

His father had once told him that if he lay very still and put his ear to the ground, the earth would whisper its secrets to him. For a long time he'd believed the pounding he could hear was the earth speaking a language he couldn't understand, and not just the sound of his rushing blood. Even when he grew older and realized there was no magic there – he still liked the sound in his ear. Being close to the earth gave him a sense of peace and security. It seemed ancient, unchanging but in reality was constantly evolving. He loved smelling her scents, observing the life that went on at ground level. It never ceased to amaze him how much this miniature world paralleled the human one. He scooped up a handful of earth and sniffed at it. Dry earth had no scent, no personality, but when it was wet, it smelled so raw and fertile and strong. This earth was grey from lack of rain, and crumbled into lumpy grains when he rubbed it. He watched it trickle slowly between his fingers and form a tiny pyramid.

Lines of ants swarmed here and there, their bodies a dark brown that looked black, unless you looked closely. Ants were too much like him or maybe he was too much like them – always something to do and somewhere to go. Never letting up, never letting go. So controlled and busy being busy that they never had time to stop, be still and just enjoy the moment. Not like bees who buzzed around like crazy until they found the blossom they were looking for – but then would settle down and draw up the nectar like a baby sucking milk from its mother's breast.

Though he'd only ever seen them in England, he loved the perfection of ladybirds, with their glossy red shells that appeared as if they'd just been varnished, and their perfect black spots. He admired the symmetry of their parts; the way in which their shells slid smoothly back and their wings came out, just like a highly oiled precision machine. But best of all were butterflies. Beautiful multicoloured creations that lived to the full every moment of their short lives. Butterflies were so fragile, so delicate it made you want to hold them, protect them – but they weren't meant to be held, but to fly free. To come and go how they pleased. They knew how to be at one with what nature had provided. Their movements were leisurely, as if they had all the time in the world to float and explore the beauty they found around them.

A flicker of movement caught his eye: a lizard, tail flicking busily as it rummaged its way through blades of grass. Lizards weren't beautiful in his opinion, too rough and scaly looking, but they too knew how to be still, enjoy the sun on their backs until some sudden, abrupt movement sent them scuttling away to some other warm space.

Frank rolled onto his back and looked up at the sky through the patchwork effect of the overlapping banana leaves. He hadn't done this in so many years and it made him feel like a boy again. It just wasn't the same in England. How could you compare lying on a patch of damp grass, feeling the dew seep into your bones, to this? Even when the weather was good, the feeling was different. The parks were invariably full of half-naked people revealing pasty flesh that hadn't seen sunlight for years! He wished they'd do everyone a favour and keep it covered up. And when you did eventually find a bit of space, you had to check for dry dog shit, and a place where you weren't at risk of getting your head whipped off by a carelessly flung frisbee.

Even the so-called privacy of his back garden was no better. Once he'd overheard the couple next door whispering to each other on the other side of the garden fence, 'What's he doing? He's already got a tan.' The oldest joke in the book, and the most boring. It had put him off. He didn't like knowing that on the other side of the fence or somewhere above him, hidden behind a piece of dis-coloured net, one or more of his neighbours were watching and wondering why a black man would lie fully clothed on his lawn.

He rolled to his side and pressed his ear to the ground. A blade of grass tickled the tip of his nose and he pushed it away before sniffing at the dry, odourless earth. The leaves of the tiny flowers, hidden amongst the blades of grass were cool, a sharp green freshness to them. He closed his eyes and breathed in deeply, remembering that special time he'd had done this with Beth, in Lightwoods Park, Bearwood . . .

*

'Try it.'

'No. Don' waan mess up me hair,' Beth protested. 'Me only jus' set it.' She rolled her cardigan into a ball and placed it beneath her head. 'Cyaan hear nutten,' she said.

'How yuh expec' fi hear anyting when yuh ear about a foot from de ground?' He pulled the cardigan away and ruffled her fringe. 'Now yuh hair mess up yuh nuh have nutten fi lose.'

'Frank!' Beth slapped his hand away playfully and smoothed back her hair.

'Try it now,' he urged.

She laughed but put her ear to the ground anyway. He reached for her hand and studied her face as she lay there with her eyes closed. He loved the way her eyelashes cast spiky shadows onto her cheeks and how a funny pigmentation quirk had left her with a sprinkling of dark brown freckles on her nose.

'Yuh have some more freckles,' he teased.

'No, I haven't,' she said, as he'd known she would. She hated her freckles. 'Me never have more dan six or seven. Anyway,' she added as an afterthought, 'dem not real freckles.'

'Wha' yuh call dem then?' She stuck her tongue out at him. 'Hear anyting?' he asked in a low voice.

'Nutten,' she said. 'Funny,' she reflected after a moment. 'Silence . . . real silence, is loud.'

He stared at the brown beauty spot under her right eye. It lay so close to her lower lashes that it looked as if her hand had slipped when she was applying her eyeliner. Beth didn't like that either, he reflected. Yet all the things she didn't like about herself were in fact all the things he loved most. And he realized, suddenly and abruptly, how much he did love her. Loved the intimacy, the complicity he shared with her that he'd never managed to reach with

Rose. He grasped her hand more tightly bringing a smile to her face, but she kept her eyes closed.

'Mother Earth not sayin' anyting at all?' he asked, leaning closer.

'Uh-uh.' Beth grinned.

'Sure?' he asked, then whispered, 'Marry Frank, marry Frank.'

Beth laughed and opened one eye. 'Don' know,' she teased. 'Dere's a bit of static interference. Something 'bout someone name Frank.'

He shuffled closer to her and touched her nose with the tip of one finger. She opened both eyes. Now it was between them that the silence was loud.

'Marry me?' he said again, suddenly nervous.

She closed her eyes again and pressed her ear to the ground.

'Wha' yuh doing?' His heart was pounding so loudly it almost drowned out her words.

'Lissenin' fi de answer. Depend on wha' Mother Earth seh.'

'Wha' she seh?'

Beth opened both eyes. 'She seh yes . . .'

'Dad?'

Jewelle's voice was close, dragging him out of the memory he was reluctant to leave. He opened one eye and squinted upwards to see her staring down at him, hands placed firmly on her hips and a quizzical expression on her face.

'What're you doing down there?'

'Just thinking.' He smiled as he sat up and brushed dry grass stalks from his shoulder and arm.

'Will you come with me before dinner?'

'Where?'

'I've got to give the goats some water. And the pigs too, I suppose.'

'I could do with a laugh,' he said standing up. 'My daughter, who hates getting her hands dirty; who's always moaning about having to take the rubbish out or do the washing-up, cleaning out pig pens and not complaining. This should be fun.'

Jewelle grinned as she pulled on the cotton gloves and grabbed two zinc buckets. 'This place is like a park. Well, a wild park.' She stared at the untamed vegetation. 'How big is it?'

Frank looked up from the buckets he was helping her fill at the standpipe. 'I don't know,' he shrugged. 'About an acre and a half. Two?'

'But how big is an acre?'

'I don't know. You're the one who goes to school. My schooldays are long gone. You tell me.' He picked up the buckets. 'Lead the way.'

Once she'd refilled the animals' water container, Frank started pointing things out in the garden. 'See that over there – grapefruit.'

'Where?' She shielded her eyes as she looked up at the tree he pointed to.

'There!' He guided her forward and pointed again. 'See them now?'

'Man, they're massive!' she exclaimed when she saw the yellow fruit hanging like moons amid the dark green foliage. 'I thought they were something else. Lift me up so I can pick one?'

He placed his hands around her waist and held her up so she could reach the lowest branch. 'Hurry up,' he huffed, as her weight forced him to take a step back in order to brace himself, 'you're heavy.'

'It won't come off,' she puffed, yanking at the fruit.

'Twist *then* pull,' he instructed.

The sharp leaves from the branch prickled the skin on the inside of her wrist as she followed her dad's instructions. 'Got it,' she panted, kicking Frank in the stomach as the grapefruit suddenly came away in her hand. He let go of her with a grunt and she fell feet first to the ground, grapefruit held aloft triumphantly.

'Next time, use a ladder,' he said, rubbing his belly.

'It's heavy,' she said, weighing it up and down in her hand, 'and it's not shiny at all.' She held it up to the light. 'But,' she sniffed at it, 'you can really smell the fruit.'

'You're always asking me why I don't eat fruit at home. That's one of the reasons why. It's treated half the time, polished up to look nice and shiny. By the time they've finished with it, it's not real any more. When you've grown up eating freshly picked fruit, it's just not the same.'

She looked at him curiously. 'I always thought you were just being fussy, like me with cauliflower and broccoli.'

He smiled, then turned and pointed to a bunch of green fruit that hung in clusters like grapes. 'See that over there? That's guinep.' He pulled a handful of the fruit, each one about the size of a marble, from the branch and handed one to her. 'I used to love these when I was a kid. One of these would last me halfway through the school day.'

'How d'you eat them?' she asked rolling it between her finger and thumb.

'Like this.' He bit the leathery outer skin until it split to reveal a soft orange-coloured pulp. 'Suck, don't bite,' he warned. 'Otherwise you'll break your teeth. There's a hard stone inside.'

'Mmm!' She rolled it around her mouth. 'Not quite certain what it tastes like, but it's really nice.'

'Bit like lychees, I think.'

'No way.' She rolled it around her mouth again. 'More tangy. Much nicer.'

They continued walking around the garden. 'Look, yams over there.' Frank pointed to an unremarkable patch of green.

'Where? I can't see them.'

Frank laughed aloud. 'Under the ground, silly,' he said, slapping her lightly on the back of her head. 'Like potatoes.' He pulled her over to the patch and scrabbled at the ground with his hands. Here the soil was a moist, rich red colour; it looked as if it had been fed liquid iron. 'There's one.' He pointed to an irregular tuber.

'So, you just pull it out?'

'No. It's better to cut if off. Leave a bit around the edges so that next year it grows back again.'

'What's that over there?' She pointed at something that resembled an enormous avocado with smooth dark grey-green skin. He looked up.

'Calabash.'

'Can you eat it?'

'Don't think you'd enjoy it much! No, it's got a big stone inside. If you leave it long enough the insides dry out, then when only the stone's left you can use it like a type of maraca.'

'Wow! I wouldn't mind taking one of them home. Can you get one down for me, please?' Jewelle looked up, thrilled at the idea.

'Well, it's a bit high up,' he said doubtfully.

'Let's knock it down, then.' She looked around her excitedly. 'There are lots of old branches and sticks here, maybe we can use one of those.' She handed him a stick. Together they managed to knock a couple of the fruit to the ground. Jewelle ran and picked one up.

'It's really heavy,' she said. 'It weighs as much as a . . . a dictionary and it's . . .' she struggled for the right word, 'it's dense.' She held it in both hands as she shook it by her ear. 'I can't hear anything.'

138

'It's still young. You need to give it time to dry out.' He took it from her and juggled it in his hands. 'You can personalize this you know,' he added handing it back to her. 'Carve your name into it, or make a design or something.'

'I'm going to give it to Ambra,' she said. 'She'll love it!' She added after a moment, 'You know something? You're really different here.'

'Oh yeah? How?'

'You're more laid back. Plus you talk loads in patois. Sometimes it's weird listening to you 'cause you don't normally back home, not even to Aunt B and Uncle Sam.'

'Lost the habit I guess. When I arrived in England, if you wanted to fit in and if you wanted a good job, then you talked standard English.'

'But Aunt B's got a good job and she talks patois all the time!'

'Yeah, but even Aunt B tones it down at work.'

'But it doesn't really work though, does it?' Jewelle giggled. 'She still talks patois, she just puts on her posh English "Good Hafternoon" voice. She sounds really funny sometimes.'

'I know.' Frank smiled. 'But Aunt B is happy with that, she just goes her own sweet way. She doesn't care what anybody thinks about her.'

'But you do?'

'Used to – a lot. Now it doesn't matter so much any more. People know who I am and if I need to talk patois I can. End of story. Any more questions?' he teased.

'Yeah,' she considered him, 'this,' then gestured towards the garden. 'How come you know so much? You never do any gardening at home.'

He stood up, rubbed his hands down on the back of his jeans and looked around. 'I'm a country boy. I grew up here. It's not the same in England. Not the same at all.'

'D'you think you'll ever come back here to live?'

Frank groaned inwardly. Here was his daughter asking him the very question he'd been trying to avoid answering since he arrived. 'Doubt it,' he said honestly.

'Why not?'

Yes, why not? 'I don't know. I suppose it's because I've spent more than half my life in England now.'

'So? Lots of people live abroad for years and years, then as soon as they retire they go back to wherever they came from.'

'I know, but –' he frowned, 'maybe it's because when I went to England it gave me a chance to develop a part of my personality that wouldn't have come out if I'd stayed in Jamaica. I left the shy boy behind and became an adult in England. I used to stutter a bit when I was a boy.'

'You still do sometimes when you're really nervous, or mega-angry,' Jewelle said. 'Not much, though,' she added quickly, 'and not very often.'

'I don't know what it was, maybe I'd have grown out of it, but whenever I spoke English I hardly stuttered. Perhaps because it seemed like another language and I was concentrating so hard on getting it right that I forgot to stutter. Who knows?' He shrugged. 'Anyway, I was in England on my own, so it was a case of sink or swim. I didn't have much choice but to stand on my own two feet, take chances and accept responsibility for my actions. It made me grow up.'

'But you couldn't even be yourself half the time. It just all sounds so hard and . . . lonely.'

'It was,' he replied simply.

'So, I don't understand . . . I mean, why?'

'I couldn't come back.'

'Why not?' she insisted.

He shrugged again. How could he explain to this child, his daughter, the whys and why nots? He hadn't known

140

himself; he still wasn't sure. How could he explain what he'd been running from and would still be running from if circumstances hadn't forced him back? 'It felt right,' he said finally.

'What d'you mean?'

'I can't put it into words. It just did.'

'Try, Dad,' she insisted. 'I really want to understand.'

'Well.' He frowned and looked away as he thought how to phrase his words. 'I'd always been curious about our history, the connection between the "Mother Country" and here. So when I got the chance I went. It was hard, but I liked being there.'

'Weren't you homesick?'

'At first,' he confessed. 'Do you know what I used to do? It makes me laugh now I look back.'

'What does?' She smiled at him.

'Well, whenever somebody went back to Jamaica for a holiday, if they were from your district they used to bring things from your family. I remember the first time Mumma and Poppa sent me a bag . . . it was a type of canvas holdall with a brown nylon base and handles –'

'That tatty, dirty old bag that's full of holes but you won't throw away?' Jewelle interrupted.

'The very same.' He smiled. 'I won't throw it away because it's full of memories. I always used to wait a moment before unzipping it – just like a kid with a big present. You want to open it but at the same time you want to save it. When I opened it – the smells that came out were wonderful! Sweet Cup, pawpaw, mangoes, soursop, lime and sugar cane all mixed up with jerk pork and roast breadfruit. There was yam, chocho and sweet potatoes. They all smell of earth and I love that. Then there were pimento seeds and Scotch bonnet peppers. But best of all was the smell of white rum. I swear no other rum in the world smells like that.

'I loved unwrapping all the things inside. Whatever day of the year it was, it felt like Christmas. Fish and meat buried in layers of foil and thick brown paper so that if any grease escaped it didn't stain the bag. Fruit and vegetables wrapped in pages of the *Daily Gleaner*. I used to save the newspaper for later, reading scraps of old news about people I didn't know and didn't care about – but it didn't matter because it was from home.

'When the bag was empty, I'd zip it up tight and put it away – saved it for those secret homesick moments. That's when I'd open that bag and sniff deep inside it. If I closed my eyes I could see the colours, feel the earth the fruit and vegetables came from and for a few moments I was in Jamaica . . . until the spluttering of the gas fire or the cold seeping into my bones or the rain banging at the windows brought me back.'

'That sounds so sad, Dad,' Jewelle said when he'd finished.

He imagined he saw a touch of pity in her eyes and looked away, embarrassed. His little memory no longer sounded like the amusing anecdote he'd always thought it was when sharing it with other immigrants. Heard from the viewpoint of a different generation and someone who had never lived anywhere but in England, it seemed just as she'd said – sad. There was a moment's silence before Jewelle spoke again.

'And what about the way we were treated back in the sixties?'

'That was hard.' He stared at his feet for a moment. 'Really hard. I wasn't expecting it. I mean . . . we were invited over. There were announcements on the radio, ads in the newspapers. They asked us to help them; we didn't come begging. We were honorary English people and England was our Mother Country, or so we thought until we got there. It didn't take us long to realize that we were anything but. People wouldn't rent to us, they offered us the crappiest jobs, that's if they offered us a job at all. And most times they acted like we'd eat them the moment we got the chance. I sometimes used to wish that we could – give them what they were expecting.'

'So why did you stay?'

He held her gaze. 'Somehow it felt right,' he pressed his hand to his chest, 'here. And anyway,' he said playfully in an attempt to lighten the mood, 'if I hadn't moved to England I wouldn't have met your mum and then where would you have come from?'

'True.' She nodded and grinned. 'So, what about Granny? She shouldn't stay here all alone, but she doesn't seem very keen on coming to England, does she?'

Frank looked at Jewelle and marvelled: subconsciously she was pulling out all the stops, asking direct questions and expecting direct answers in the way that children did and adults had forgotten how to.

'I don't know yet. We'll have to sort something out over the next few days.'

'But –'

He interrupted quickly before she started asking more questions. 'Talking about your granny, have you collected the eggs she asked you for?' He watched her face fall, noticed the telltale sign of her bottom lip pushing out sulkily. 'What's the matter?'

'I don't like the way the chickens flap their wings at me,' she admitted. 'I'm scared they'll bite.'

'Is that all? We'll soon sort that out.' He set off to the fowl coop, Jewelle tagged behind him reluctantly.

'Come on.' He flapped a hand at her as she stood just outside the doorway, the bucket now containing the calabash on the floor beside her. 'Townie,' he teased. 'Come in and I'll show you a trick.'

She took a couple of steps inside but stood close to the

door, ready to run if necessary. Frank picked up the hen nearest to him, smoothed its wings back so they lay against its body, then raised the chicken in large clockwise circles. Slowly; one, two, three times. Then he set the hen down very gently and stood back. The hen sat where he had placed it, fast asleep.

'That's incredible,' Jewelle breathed, venturing closer.

'Come on. I'll show you how to do it.'

He picked up another hen and placed it in her hands. 'I don't want to.' She turned her face away from the bird and tried to hand it back, but Frank wouldn't take it. The bird felt so fragile with its brittle ribs and heart beating uncomfortably close to her palms. Something was tickling the back of one hand but she didn't dare look in case it was lice. She knew fowl had them, but right now it was one of the things she wished she didn't know.

'Now do what I did,' Frank instructed, stepping away from her.

She slowly raised the hen to head level and moved it in wide circles just as Frank had done. The hen remained immobile when Jewelle set it down and she chuckled softly.

'If you can do that, then you can collect eggs,' Frank told her. 'So, no excuses tomorrow. Right!'

She looked at her dad admiringly. Ambra wouldn't believe her when she told her she knew how to put hens to sleep.

5

16th February

Jewelle lay in the back garden and let the afternoon sunlight play on her face. She'd chosen a spot where she was half-hidden by a bush. Here, she was less likely to be seen and would therefore feel less guilty about lying around. She must have dozed off, for when she opened her eyes the sun felt much hotter and Nancy had appeared with an enormous basket of fresh washing. Jewelle rolled on her side and propped her chin in the palm of her hand as she watched Nancy clip clothes pegs all the way around the edge of her T-shirt so they hung like a row of wooden tassels. Her movements were fluid and the muscles in the back of her legs were clearly defined beneath her gleaming skin as she reached up to the line on tiptoes. Nancy had lovely skin, Jewelle thought; smooth and clear like that of a child.

Though hidden from sight she still felt uncomfortable about doing nothing. Nancy never seemed to stop. Jewelle got to her feet slowly and sauntered over. Up close, she could see how Nancy had stretched each item out fully before pegging it in such a way that it overlapped slightly with the previous one. Shirts and blouses were hung by the tips of their collars, dresses by their shoulder seams and trousers from their waistbands. Taut, with no spaces in between. Underwear was placed on a smaller line where it was hidden from view by other lines of washing.

'Want a hand?' Jewelle offered casually.

'If yuh waan,' Nancy replied without looking round. 'Yuh can start on dat line.' She nodded to the line in front.

'OK,' Jewelle said, even as she thought, bet you said that so you could watch how I hang things out. Well, I've been watching you. She dragged the wash basket to a point between the two lines where it could be easily reached by both of them and pegged the items just as she had seen Nancy do. The two girls worked in silence. Jewelle turned round to see Nancy sitting on the upturned wash basket observing her.

'Is it OK?' Her off-hand tone belied her desire for approval.

'Yeah,' Nancy replied, 'not bad – fi a English gyal.'

'At least I've managed to get something right,' she joked. 'Is there any more inside?'

'Sheets, but dere's no more room. We haffi wait till dese dry. Here.' Nancy got to her feet and handed Jewelle one of the two forked sticks that Jewelle only now noticed stood propped up against one of the trees.

'What's this?'

'Clothes stick.'

Nancy slotted the fork of the stick against the clothesline and hoisted it. When the line was far enough above the ground, she wedged the foot of the stick firmly into the ground so Jewelle quickly did the same. The line of washing rose high, clothes flapping briskly wherever the breeze caught them.

'Never seen one of those before,' Jewelle commented.

'Yuh nuh dry clothes in England?'

'Course we do! The washing line is already upright on a stand that is sunk into a block of cement. It looks a bit like a metal spider's web and it spins round in the wind.'

'And yuh use washin' machine too, don' it?'

'Well, I wash my underwear by hand but almost everything else goes in the machine. It's got lots of different programmes so you can wash clothes for as long or as little as you like.'

'Mek life easier, I s'pose.' Nancy sighed, thinking of the hours she spent each week washing things by hand. Two washes and a rinse were the minimum. Then there was the extra time needed to collect the water, do a special rinse for the whites and prepare the starch mixture for the cotton items.

'Why d'you turn the clothes inside out before you hang them out?' Jewelle asked after a moment.

'If someting drop to de ground when me hangin' it out, it mean I don' haffi wash it so hard fi get de dirt out.'

'Makes life easier I suppose,' Jewelle said, repeating Nancy's words. She stooped to take one handle of the wash basket. Nancy grasped the other.

'Thanks,' Nancy said.

A single word but it was a start. They walked back to the house in silence.

It had been a lazy day. Jewelle hadn't done much except read, eat and sleep. Now it was late afternoon and she could no longer put off the problem of what to wear to the funeral. She tiptoed into the semi-darkened bedroom where Aunt B lay on her bed with her eyes closed.

'It all right, me not sleeping,' Aunt B said without turning her head, 'Crack de shutter dem and let likkle light in. Yuh sort yuh clothes out fi tomorrow?'

Jewelle looked at her aunt, worry clear in her eyes. 'I haven't got anything to wear,' she confessed. 'I should've listened to you.'

Aunt B converted the smirk that had sprung unbidden to her face into a sympathetic smile. 'Well, me bring yuh a just-in-case dress,' she said, carefully easing herself off the bed. She burrowed in one of her suitcases, eventually producing a simple black dress which she shook open with a flourish. 'Maybe it not short enough fi yuh taste, but yuh cyaan go a funeral in miniskirt. It tie at de back so yuh cyaan complain it nuh have no shape.'

Jewelle put the dress on, then Aunt B stood behind her and adjusted the tie back as the girl looked at her reflection in the mirror.

'It's not bad.' She smoothed the dress over her hips. 'In fact, it's quite flattering.' She smiled at herself. 'Actually, it's perfect, Aunt B. D'you think Jake'll like it?' she teased, poking out her tongue at Aunt B's reflection. Aunt B rolled her eyes, making Jewelle grin as she realized that she was having fun with her aunt for the first time in ages.

'Just fooling with you, Aunt B.' She gave her a quick hug, missing Aunt B's expression of delighted surprise as she spun round to face the mirror again. 'Seriously though, thank you.' She peered at herself again. 'I thought something like this would make me look old. But it doesn't.' She considered for a moment, 'Just different. More suitable if you get what I mean.'

'Yuh can wear dis wid it.' Aunt B held up a wide black velvet hairband and watched through the mirror as Jewelle slipped it on. 'Yuh remind me so much of yuh madda right now,' she said smoothing Jewelle's plaits back.

'Do I?' Jewelle looked round at Aunt B, then turned to face the mirror. 'How?'

Aunt B stared at Jewelle's reflection. The girl's skin glowed from the sun of the past few days, reminding her of the sheen Beth had always had until she went to England. 'Is not so much how yuh look,' she started, lightly squeezing Jewelle's shoulders as an expression of disappointment crossed the girl's face, 'yuh do resemble her – yuh even have de same dimple in yuh chin.'

'So do you, but yours is a bit smaller than ours. It's funny, I never really noticed before but you've even got the same kind of nose as mum . . . but without the little freckles she had.'

Aunt B smiled, pleased that Jewelle had acknowledged not just the blood link between them but the physical one too. 'Yuh have yuh own face,' she continued, 'yuh own personality. But sometimes, yuh move or smile like . . . or t'row yuh hair back, exactly de way yuh madda use to do.'

They stared into the mirror. Aunt B remembered doing exactly the same thing when she was thirteen or so and Beth about ten. However, there had been no full-length mirror, only a small one with barely room enough for both their faces. She could see Beth's face in Jewelle's, the same shape, but Beth's face had been longer, narrower. Her hand reached forward to caress Jewelle's face, but as she made contact she stopped and turned around, her eyes seeking the shadow she could've sworn she'd seen in the mirror.

'Yuh see dat?'

'What?'

'I don' know. It feel like . . . nutten.' She shivered, took a final look behind her and then turned to the mirror again. But the moment of intimacy was broken.

Rose smoothed the dress over her hips. It clung like a second skin, snug at the bodice before lightly flowing downwards. She turned this way and that and laughed as the material gently swished and swayed around her knees. She'd worked well into the early hours of the morning and the dress had come out better than she could have imagined. With the remaining material she'd made a long scarf, which she slipped over her shoulders, holding the ends in the crooks of her arms.

Beautiful, she thought, peering into the fogged mirror. She pulled the scarf from around her shoulders and flipped it around her neck; so one end of its length ran down her front. It looked – elegant. Dat's how me ah go wear it, de way a Englishwoman would. I know in me heart dat Frank gwine like it.

Her hair she would wear loose. Right now, it was dry and coarse through lack of care, but there had been no reason to bother. It would soon be her crowning glory again. On bad days, she just twisted it up and wrapped it. But this was a good day. Better than that – it was the start of a lot of good days. This time round, nothing would part them.

One thing was missing – she rummaged in one of the drawers of her dresser and pulled out a balled-up scrap of material. Carefully, she untied its ragged edges and shook free a thin gold bracelet – tiny interlinked hearts. It was one of her most precious possessions and she hadn't worn it in a long time. She fastened the clasp around her wrist, stretched her arm out and waggled her wrist from one side to another, admiring the gleam of gold against her skin. Then she preened herself in front of the mirror again, laughing aloud and spinning in circles, the scarf held outstretched in her two hands. A shaft of sunlight entered the room and illuminated the scene, a beautiful yellow butterfly about to take flight.

'Psst!'

Jewelle looked up to see the oozing girl standing in the gateway, a green blazer in the crook of her arm.

'Wha' yuh doing?'

'Nothing much – just writing my diary. Finished now,' Jewelle replied, snapping it shut.

'Come next door wid me,' Lil said.

'What for?'

'Why not? Yuh nuh have nutten better fi do, otherwise it wouldn't be yuh one an' yuh writing book.' She nodded to the diary in Jewelle's lap.

'Yeah, all right. Why not?' Jewelle grabbed her diary and

ran to Lil who had already started walking next door. Though Lil was wearing a green school uniform, she didn't look like a schoolgirl, at least not the ones Jewelle had seen on her first day. She'd rolled her waistband over itself so that the skirt hung much shorter than it should have done and, despite the standard school blouse, the bra she was wearing underneath made her breasts look like she had two mini-rockets strapped to her chest.

'Yuh late,' Jewelle heard a woman say as they entered the house, but she stopped listening as her feet sank into something soft and she looked down to see thick wall-to-wall carpet.

Slowly she scanned the room, which was packed with furniture and ornaments and knick-knacks of all sorts. Wherever she looked, there was something taking up space: an overstuffed, swirly red and black settee; matching armchairs with their thick, brightly coloured crocheted wool squares that Aunt B called settee backs; a sideboard and two coffee tables with stiffly starched white crocheted decorative mats. Jewelle couldn't understand the obsession with these pieces of crochetwork. They were round and plain, with a flat circular centre, but the sides had been attached and sewn together in layers like the petals of a budding flower, and on what would have been the petals was a carefully balanced selection of china dogs and cats, shepherdesses and smiling ladies with parasols, all jostling for space. There was an old-fashioned electric gramophone with its lid down – Aunt B had one too, though she never used it. This one had framed pictures covering its surface, and a couple of lamps with red, blue and yellow blobs drifting around in what looked like oily water.

'I was chatting wid Jewelle fi bout an hour before we reach here.' Lil widened her eyes at Jewelle who held back the 'but . . .' she'd been about to say.

'So you're Jewelle!'

'Mrs Fixit.' Lil completed the introductions.

'Hortense,' the woman corrected, giving Lil a sharp look. 'Nice to meet Miss Jess gran'daughter finally. Never met you the other night. By the time things quietened down, you were sleeping. Sit down. Let me fix you something to eat.'

Lil giggled at her words. 'Ah haffi put on me yard clothes. Soon come back.' She grabbed Jewelle by the hand and dragged her into her bedroom and slammed the door behind them.

'Who is she?'

'I lodge wid her. De school here better dan de one near me in Kingston. Not so many people in de class.'

'Why did you call her Mrs Fixit?' Jewelle asked looking round the room.

'When she first come back to Jamaica wid her airs an' graces an' her speaky-spoky "I lived in Englan'" way a talkin', she still have de Jamaican accent but she don' speak patois. An' she an' her husban' set up a likkle business,' Lil said, undoing her blouse. 'She go all 'bout de place tellin' everybody dat her husban' can fix anyting, from bruk-up clock to bruk-up car.' She mimicked Hortense: '*Mikey soon fix dis, Mikey soon fix dat* – de name stick.'

She whipped off her bra and flung it across the room where it landed on the back of the chair. Jewelle looked away but not before she saw how high and firm Lil's breasts were, much bigger than her own. Lil started rubbing cream into them. 'Dem nice, don' it? Waan keep dem soft an' juicy, mek dem look like dem good fi suck.'

Jewelle coughed, embarrassed. 'Who's that?' she asked, pointing to a photo of a young man on the wall.

'Gunner.'

'Is that your boyfriend?'

'Yuh mad!' Lil stopped mid-stroke. 'Dat ugly brute!'

'He's not that bad,' Jewelle protested, half turning to Lil.

152

True, the guy wasn't wonderful, but he wasn't exactly hideous either.

'Him ugly like him madda!' Lil retorted. 'Mrs Fixit,' she added, noting Jewelle's puzzled expression.

'Gunner's a funny name.'

'Him name Gerald, but everybody call him Gunner 'cause him a gun runner. Fixit shame a him. She not too shame fi tek de money him mek from it, though. Tell people dat him a big-shot engineer in America, but everybody know him live a Kingston an' run gun all 'bout de island.'

'Does everybody have a nickname here?' Jewelle turned around to see if Lil was dressed. She was in her underwear, rubbing cream into her legs.

'Most people have a pet name from dem small, dependin' on how dem look or how dem behave. Me madda name Soon, bit like Fixit. Almost every sentence she seh start wid "soon".'

'You haven't got one, though?'

'Well, yuh cyaan do much wid Lilian except shorten it to Lil. Some bwoy dem call me "Cruise".'

'Cruise?'

'Seh me bubbies firm like cruise missile!'

Jewelle rolled her eyes upwards. This girl was obsessed with her tits. 'You ready yet?' she asked, peering at other photos of the family.

'Yeah.' Lil came and stood behind her. 'Dat's Fixit's husband before him dead. Dat black bitch dere,' she pointed to another face, 'is Daisy. Yuh meet her de other night.'

'Why don't you like her?' Jewelle asked, relieved to see that Lil had put some clothes on.

'She too uppity – just like her madda. Tink she nice just 'cause she speak posh and work in a bank.'

'I thought she had a nice voice,' said Jewelle.

'She only work inna back room, she too dark fi work out front.'

'What d'you mean?' Jewelle asked, frowning.

'Next time yuh go a de bank, tek a good look inside. Den tell me how much really black people yuh see dealing wid de public.'

'But that's – racist!' Jewelle spluttered.

'Surprise yuh nuh? Yuh tink is only white people racist?' she asked. 'Yuh wrong. We racist wid our own kind.' She peered into the wardrobe mirror, adjusted her short top, flicked a speck of lint off the side of her miniscule shorts and then turned to face Jewelle. 'Dat's why me intend fi use anyting me can fi get ahead.' Her face was deadly serious. 'Anyting.'

It was the first time Jewelle had seen Lil without a grin and she suddenly seemed far more knowing than any teenager Jewelle knew.

'C'mon, me hungry,' Lil said, the grin back in place. Now they were both fifteen again – but only on the surface.

Aunt B slipped Jewelle's dress neatly into the wardrobe next to her own funeral clothes. Jewelle had gone off to look for Frank. Poor likkle ting look so disappointed when I seh she nuh look like Beth dat me waan surprise her wid someting, Aunt B thought. All dis death business must be affecting her too. Is only natural dat Jewelle tinking of her own madda so much dese days. Me waan give her someting – maybe some jewellery to go wid de dress, but it already late an' I don' feel like de walk into Brown's Town. Anyway, me certain me won't find nutten even if I did know what I was lookin' for. Maybe me have someting of me own dat will do.

Once again she looked through her suitcase until she found the cloth purse she was using as a jewellery bag. She tipped it upside down and carefully separated the items

154

that fell out onto the bedspread. Several pairs of earrings – all too big and chunky for Jewelle's taste; a cameo brooch – too old-fashioned; a thin silver chain with a tiny silver cross – the present Beth had given her when she'd received her first English pay packet. Aunt B rarely wore silver now, preferring gold, but she'd always kept it. Dis is de gift fi Jewelle, she thought. It come from de madda, now is time fi pass it on to de daughter.

Aunt B put it to one side and scraped the other items together. An earring was trapped in the link of a gold chain and she patiently unravelled the knot, sitting back in surprise when she saw what it was – a lucky charm anklet. Six little figures – three in the 'see no evil, speak no evil, hear no evil' pose, dangled from it. In between each of these was a figure standing, jumping or sitting.

Rose had given it to her in the early days of their friendship. Aunt B had worn it once – and then only out of politeness. Too trampish for her taste. Only certain women wore chains around their ankles, but she'd accepted it with gratitude, appreciating the affection behind the gift. She gently tossed the chain from one hand to the other as she stared at it, puzzled. Hadn't she got rid of it all those years ago when Rose had sent her that final letter with the request she'd ignored? By doing so, she'd closed the door on her friendship with Rose and on the guilt she felt about what might have happened had she passed the message on.

Sam right, she reflected, after all dis time I should just let de whole damn ting go. But it hard. Rose and dat blasted letter keep come inna me mind. Cho! Just like Jehovah's Witnesses hangin' 'pon me doorbell. Ignore de bell, dem just keep ringin', open de door an' dem keep yuh fi hours. Some tings yuh just cyaan win. Same wid de business wid Rose.

Aunt B's thoughts knocked against each other like beads on a chain – if she'd passed Rose's message on, then Frank might not have married the barely pregnant Beth and Jewelle might never have known her father. So many ifs. The chain sparkled against her skin and the little gold figures seemed to slide down her fingers. Who'd have thought that so many years later she'd be holding the very same chain up in the air just as she'd done the day she'd received it . . .

'Wha' dis?'

'Jus' a likkle someting.' Rose grinned cheekily as she lounged against the wall that separated the Jamaica National Building Society where Aunt B worked from the main road.

'Wha' kinda someting?' Aunt B eyed the scrunched up ball of cloth in her hand suspiciously.

'Lord, wha' do yuh? How yuh love question everyting so? Just tek de ting and done.'

Silenced, Aunt B examined the cloth in her hand – a ragged remnant of something Rose had been making. The four corners of the cloth had been tied together into a tight knot and she picked at it with her fingernails, while Rose jumped around in front of her. Each time Rose tried to help Aunt B with the knot, Aunt B would pull away. They looked like two adolescent girls rather than the grown women they were. Once Aunt B had teased the centre of the knot loose, the frayed ends of the material quickly fell apart to reveal a narrow chain with tiny gold figures attached to it at intervals. She held it up to the sky and tried not to look at Rose's expectant face in the background.

'Uhmm.' Aunt B's first sound was non-committal as she carefully scrutinized the figures in movement. What was Rose trying to tell her? This bracelet would practically slide off her hand. Surely Rose didn't think she was that fat!

156

'Yuh nuh like it?' Rose's tone was flat, like a disappointed child trying hard to hide it.

'Course me like it,' Aunt B forced herself to smile.

'Liar!' Rose spat. 'I know how yuh gwaan when yuh like someting, so nuh badda pretend.'

'I do,' Aunt B insisted, 'is just,' her voice dropped, 'yuh really tink me wrist dat big?'

'Wha' dat?' For a second, Rose looked completely lost. After a moment she asked, 'Wha' yuh wrist haffi do wid anyting?'

'Dis a bangle, nuh?' Aunt B dangled the chain under Rose's nose, 'and bangle wear 'pon wrist!'

'But,' Rose started to laugh as understanding dawned on her, 'I never buy it fi yuh wrist, I buy it fi yuh foot.' She bent down and slapped one of Aunt B's calves. 'Fi yuh ankle.' She laughed up at Aunt B with shiny eyes and slapped her calf again as Aunt B's face cracked into a smile . . .

Aunt B rocked back on the bed, lost in thought. Rose must hate her, after all the secrets, dreams and disappointments they'd shared, and she could be vindictive if crossed. She always used to say she could hurt people from a distance, that she wouldn't settle until she got her revenge. Suppose Rose had somehow got rid of Beth, separated Beth from both Aunt B and Frank. A double hit – two birds with one stone. Even now she couldn't help thinking that if she'd simply given Frank his letter, then her sister might still be alive today.

No point thinking about it – she would never ever know for sure – and anyway, there was no going back. She caught sight of herself in the mirror, a frowning figure sitting hunched on the side of the bed. Suddenly she spun round, her eyes seeking the shadow, the hint of yellow she could have sworn she'd seen reflected in the mirror – but there was nobody there. *Is just yuh imagination*, she told herself. *Back in Jamaica after all dese long years an' wid yuh head full of tings long gone. Is only natural yuh mind jumping all 'bout de place.* She shuddered involuntarily, then threw the charm in the bin.

What was done was done. And what was past was past.

'I'll have to go in a bit, Lil,' Jewelle said. It was getting late, but it wasn't just that. The house was too full of furniture and was incredibly hot. She felt stifled and was glad it was nearly dinnertime. Even though she wasn't hungry, Hortense had stuffed her with snacks and drinks – at least she had an excuse to go.

'Surely you can stay little while longer,' Hortense encouraged.

'No, I'd better go,' she said putting her glass on the floor – there was no room on the coffee table in front of her. 'I only popped round for five minutes.'

'Another five minutes won't hurt. Tell me, *Coronation Street* still showing, and the Rovers Return? Deirdre and Rita still in it?'

Jewelle took a deep breath. Hortense had asked her about every soap going but she'd never even heard of half of them, like *Crossroads*, and the ones she had heard of, like *Coronation Street* and *Emmerdale Farm*, she'd never be caught watching. 'I can tell you about *EastEnders* if you like,' she started politely. 'There's a pub in that,' she added as Hortense's face fell.

Before Hortense could ask another question, the front door opened and Daisy walked in.

'How was yuh day inna de back room? Have any interestin' conversations wid de photocopier?' Lil greeted her.

Daisy gave her a big smile. 'Just pass yuh madda on de

158

road, she on her way here . . . and she look vex is a shame! I wonder what – or who upset her?'

Lil shrugged nonchalantly. 'Me nuh do nutten.'

Daisy shrugged back. 'Not my business anyway. I'm goin' to get changed.' She disappeared through one of the doors behind Jewelle's back.

'What you do now, Lil?'

'Nutten!'

'But –' began Hortense when the front door burst open making all three of them jump. A tall woman whom Jewelle had never seen before barged in. She had a darker version of Lil's pretty face, but not her grin.

'How yuh love shame me so?' she demanded of Lil.

'What I do now, Mammy?' Lil said innocently, playing with her toes.

'Yuh know wha' people a call yuh? Duracell! Ever Ready! Talk 'bout how yuh battery charge all de time!' She glared at Lil. 'Ah tired a tellin' yuh. Soon mek Uncle Tom talk to yuh!'

Lil was on her feet like lightning. Even Hortense was up and moving crabwise towards the bathroom. Jewelle frowned, but sat where she was, watching Soon, who was fumbling in her bag and talking to it like Uncle Tom was sitting inside.

'Lord, why yuh test me so?' Soon looked upwards as she wrung her hands together on the last words, then suddenly pulled a thin brown leather strap from her bag. She wrapped Uncle Tom round one hand. 'After all de sacrifice me mek fi yuh!' The belt whistled through the air, connecting with Lil's bare thigh, leaving a red stripe and sending Jewelle flying out of her seat on the sofa. 'An' look how yuh pay me back!' *Whish!* This time the belt caught the tip of Lil's little finger as she tried to fend off the blow, making her groan. 'Stan' 'pon street corner a chat to big man like yuh an' dem a size.'

159

'But, Mammy, I never do nutten wrong.'

'Liar! A smell yuh start smell yuhself? Tink yuh a woman an' can come contradict.'

'It was one of me schoolteacher me was talkin' to,' Lil protested, hiding behind Jewelle and using her as a shield.

'Yuh facety likkle brazen bitch! I send yuh to a gyal school, so don' talk shit! Yuh expect me fi believe dem rough-looking bwoy in a yard clothes a schoolteacher? Soon beat de facetiness outta yuh!' She tightened her grip on the belt and lashed round the side of Jewelle.

Jewelle closed her eyes as she saw the strap head her way; felt its breeze as it whistled past her and connected with Lil's backside. She kept one eye on Soon's red-eyed glare as she tried to prise herself out of Lil's grasp, but Lil hung on to her tightly, so the two were performing a comic two-step in the middle of Hortense's blue shagpile.

'Yuh ears too hard.' She flicked the strap out again but missed. 'If yuh nuh stop hide behind Miss Jess gran'-daughter, I gwine give yuh two bitch lick fi every second yuh stand dere a hug her up.' Lil was obviously as hard of hearing as her mother accused her of, for she clung on to Jewelle, shadowing her every movement and step. Soon lashed at the furniture in frustrated fury. *Whack!* The coffee table took a blow that made the ornaments wobble in their crocheted nest.

'Look 'pon Jewelle,' Soon ranted. 'See how she dress decent? Yuh see her inna batty rider wid her arse outa door fi every Tom, Dick an' Harry fi see? No, because she respec' herself.' *Slash!* Uncle Tom wrapped itself round a chair leg lifting it from the floor and sending it flying. The unexpected weight made Soon stop for a second and rub her shoulder.

In the pause, Jewelle wrestled with Lil. 'Get off me,' she panted, 'I don't want to get beaten too.'

'Just hold on a likkle longer,' Lil giggled. 'She soon tired.'

Jewelle looked at her in shock. 'I can't believe this,' she whispered, 'your mother's mashing you and the place up and you're laughing?'

'She cyaan hurt me less she use de buckle end,' Lil whispered back. 'All I haffi do is let her drop two lick 'pon me now and den till she tire herself out; when she start cry I know it done,' she said, grinning.

In the meantime, Soon had crept up to the side of them. 'Oh, a laughin' business dis? Soon give yuh someting fi laugh 'bout!' *Smack!* She brought Uncle Tom down on Lil's bare foot. 'Laugh nuh?' Lil yelped in real pain and loosened her grip on Jewelle as she jumped about on one foot. Her mother smiled maliciously. 'Mek me see yuh pretty dance step dem. Dance nuh!' She slung Uncle Tom from side to side chasing Lil round the room; forcing her to dance to Uncle Tom's erratic rhythm.

'Please, Mammy, don't,' Lil begged, crying noisily.

Jewelle had backed herself into the wrong corner – no doors that led to safety anywhere near her. She didn't want to taste Uncle Tom so she stayed where she was, too scared to move. Soon was wild with the belt and she'd worked herself into a rhythmic frenzy. Now in a position of relative safety, she began to feel sorry for Lil. What had she done that was so very wrong, except talk to somebody after school in broad daylight? She certainly wasn't dressed any worse than girls her age in England. At least Lil wore her shorts around the house; back home girls wore that kind of stuff out to clubs and nobody said a word. Jewelle felt doubly embarrassed for what she was witnessing and for how she imagined Lil must be feeling. Fancy being beaten like that, Jewelle mused, just for wearing a pair of shorts! And even worse, in front of a stranger. If Soon were her mother, she would never ever forgive her. In England, she'd be arrested for child abuse before she could lift that belt twice.

'Is who a dead?' came a voice from the veranda. Jewelle had never been so pleased to hear Aunt B's loud voice since the time in her first year at secondary school when she was being bullied by an older girl – Amanda Smith. Aunt B had cussed off Amanda, shamed her up so badly in fact that Amanda had run to her older sister who was at the same school. When her sister – a big pale lump of a girl – appeared, Aunt B merely rolled up her sleeves and said very slowly and clearly, 'Step forward if yuh tink yuh bad!' Amanda's sister had looked like a rat in a trap. She'd swallowed hard and grabbed Amanda roughly by the arm. 'Wharrov I told yew about pickin' on people?' she yelled as she dragged the girl off. 'Go fer the weak wuns, the wuns wiv no back-up!'

'Wha' all dis bawlin' about? Down to Brown's Town can hear yuh people.' Aunt B barged into the living room and then jumped back hurriedly as the tongue of the strap hit the door handle in front of her 'Yuh mad, Soon? Look how yuh nearly jook out me eye! Mind yuh don' lick me niece,' she ordered, suddenly spying Jewelle trapped in the corner. 'Jewelle, come. Wha' yuh doin' here?' She held out her hand towards the girl, who stumbled quickly across the room. 'Yuh all right? She ketch yuh?'

'Yes,' Jewelle started, 'I mean yes,' she corrected herself quickly as Aunt B glowered, 'I'm all right. She didn't catch me. I'm OK.' On the other side of the room Lil was still busy avoiding her mother whose energy was now beginning to flag. Jewelle decided right there and then that she would be extra nice to Lil; let her know that not everybody was as stupid and old-fashioned as her mother.

'Me sorry, nuh beat me no more,' Lil begged.

Aunt B pushed Jewelle in the small of her back towards the door. 'My diary!' Jewelle exclaimed, turning back.

Lil winked at her as she picked it up, then she screamed, 'It nuh gwine happen again. Me promise.'

'De only way dat gyal goin' is down. Look how her batty high like post office tower,' Aunt B said, staring disdainfully at the girl's tiny shorts. 'See how she laugh in her madda face even wid de crocodile tears stan' up strong in her eye,' Aunt B said. 'Dem shoulda give her two hot lick from de time her bubbies pop and she start hitch up skirt 'pon street corner. Too late now. Go home, Jewelle. Me stay wid Soon fi a while.' She nodded at Soon, now collapsed on the sofa. Lil sat on the floor; her head buried in her arms, her shoulders shaking.

'He who laugh first laugh last,' Aunt B shouted at the girl's heaving shoulders. 'Leave dem fi sort out dem fuss.' Aunt B pushed Jewelle out of the room and closed the door in her face. From outside, Jewelle could hear her taking control.

'Hortense, stop hide! Storm done.' Jewelle peered through the window and saw Hortense leaving the bathroom shamefacedly. 'Me shame a yuh,' Jewelle heard Aunt B say. 'Look how yuh let Soon work herself up; shout herself hoarse and she suppose fi sing a de funeral tomorrow. As fi yuh,' Aunt B nudged Lil roughly with the toe of her shoe, 'go change an' come tidy up dis room here.' Dry-eyed, Lil got to her feet and limped from the room without looking at anybody.

'Why yuh never stop her, Hortense?'

'Soon came in here so mad and angry I was sure she'd turn Uncle Tom on me too. After all, it's me her daughter's lodging with.'

'Dat wild beast need more dan a few belt lick! Come sit down, mek we sort dis out.' She settled Hortense next to Soon and then moved one of the armchairs so it faced the pair on the sofa. 'Wha' yuh doin' in dere, Lil?' Aunt B shouted from her seat. 'How long it tek fi drag off dem dolly clothes yuh sportin' an' put on someting decent? Don' mek I come in dere after yuh!'

'Soon come, Miss B.'

'Awoah! An' as fi yuh, Miss Jewelle,' Aunt B spoke with her back to the window making the girl duck below the windowsill. 'Unless yuh waan taste some Jamaican discipline yuhself, yuh better go home right now instead a lissen to big people business!'

Aunt B couldn't possibly have seen me from inside, Jewelle reasoned, she had to be guessing. I'll just stay quiet and listen, she decided. Whatever they say is bound to be juicy and I'm dying to see how Lil deals with Aunt B. Never know, I might even learn a few things. She stayed where she was for another minute or so, then carefully raised her head above the windowsill.

'Nuh mek me tell yuh twice, gyal.'

Jewelle ducked down again like a naughty child. She'd always thought Aunt B had eyes in the back of her head and now here was the proof. 'Yes, Aunt B,' she shouted obediently before straightening up and running down the veranda steps.

Aunt B smiled into the mirror that reflected the window behind her. Let Jewelle think she was all-seeing and all-hearing; it wouldn't do her any harm.

'Drop me here,' Rose said banging on the partition that separated the driver's cabin from the open trailer. She'd managed to hitch a lift without having to wait too long and now she'd got where she was headed, she was eager to be on her way. She had to bang twice before the driver noticed and pulled up at the side of the road. She climbed slowly over the side of the pickup, careful to keep her dress away from the dusty sides of the machine. Once her feet were steady on the ground, she smiled her thanks to the driver and his companions and then turned to face the direction they'd just come from.

A quarter of a mile later and she was approaching Miss

Jess's property. She'd only been there once officially and that over twenty years ago; but on a couple of occasions she'd gone there alone and fantasized a little about the day she'd be mistress of the house. But that was then. Now her only thoughts were how to make up for lost time. As she got closer to the house, she kept to the shadows until she found a good position where she could observe without being observed.

From where she stood she had a clear view of Miss Jess's front veranda. Frank was sitting on the veranda swing, his arms around a young girl – presumably his daughter. She hadn't been watching them for very long when the girl stood up, kissed Frank on his cheek and went inside. Nice de way dem sit together like dat, Rose thought. Mek me tink back to when I small an' me an' Mumma use to hug up close de same way. But after de baby stillborn, Mumma change. Keep herself to herself. No space fi me. Nuh matter anyway, Rose thought. At least Mamma G was dere. 'Yuh still here,' Rose said softly and smiled. Children better off wid dem gran'parents, look 'pon Mamma G, she did have de time and patience me mumma didn't.

If anybody had seen her they'd have thought she was completely mad. A woman dressed for town, half hidden in bushes on a quiet country road, talking to herself.

The night was dark and shiny; glittering stars that seemed sprayed onto the sky. It made Frank want to reach up and touch them. It'd be so hard, he thought, to see a night sky of this clarity and beauty in England. Fireflies flickered past, glistening briefly for a single moment before their light was spent. He got to his feet and walked down the veranda steps. He had no particular destination in mind and no particular reason for a late night walk, apart from the need to stretch his legs before going to bed.

Rose squeezed her eyes shut briefly, not quite believing

her luck. When she opened them Frank was so close she could almost have touched him. He hadn't seen her, hidden as she was by the gate of the house opposite. This couldn't have worked out better if she'd spent months planning it. Her heart pounded in her chest and a smile rose to her lips: it was meant to be. She'd always known it.

She watched him as he strolled to the corner of the road, and when she thought there was sufficient distance between them she set off silently behind him. She walked carefully, mindful of the fine gravel and loose stones of the path underneath the heeled sandals she wore as she followed him. Her eyes lingered on the broad set of his shoulders, the way he held his head erect as he walked and the easy, relaxed swing of his arms.

I wonder what him tinking, she thought. Please mek him 'member all de times we walk together, hand in hand on still nights just like dis one. Me sure him cyaan figet dem. Dem moment dem too strong fi de two of we. Him coulda stay in him yard wid him family or sit 'pon de veranda enjoyin' de night air. But no, him up and out. Him must sense me. Otherwise why leave de property, put space between himself an' him family if nuh fi mek space fi me?

'Go slow, Rose,' she muttered softly. 'Tink of all de times yuh act 'pon impulse an' regret it. Don' spoil it now. Tek yuh time an' speak nice to him,' she warned herself, 'nuh matter how long it tek tonight. Wha' it seh somewhere in de Bible? "Where you walk I will follow."' He was easy to follow. His white clothes seemed luminous in the moonlight and she was careful not to let him get too far ahead. He turned at the corner of the road and disappeared from sight.

She quickened her steps until she reached the corner, then stopped abruptly. No sign of him. A bitter taste rose in her mouth – so close and then to lose him. Then she spied him sitting on a log on the grass, a little way back from the road. He was leaning forward slightly with his elbows propped on his knees and his chin resting in the palm of his hands. Though his face was tilted up to the sky, his eyes were closed. She crept forward silently. For a moment she thought he'd heard her – his eyes flickered open for a second, but he remained still, so she slipped off her sandals and tiptoed until she was crouching behind him. Then she whispered his name.

Frank let the night-time sounds caress his ears: crickets busy chattering their business; owls on nocturnal excursions; dogs and cats at play and a host of other sounds he could no longer identify. He'd forgotten how noisy the countryside could be. He thought for a moment he heard his name called and half opened his eyes before chuckling at himself and leaning back silently. It was Jamaica working on him. All this talk of roaming ghosts and spirits after death, traditions and superstitions – all the things he normally laughed at – had rattled him.

The sudden touch on his shoulder and the sound of his name in his ear, as if whispered by some phantom, provoked an involuntary groan from deep within him. The invisible hand on his shoulder tightened and his name rang louder in his ears. He felt the touch of lips at the crease of his neck, the faint scent of Khus Khus in his nostrils and he froze rigid for a moment before jumping up and turning around, his arms held up in defence. It took him a moment to focus his eyes. He half expected to see some ethereal object floating before him, not a corporeal being in yellow. To feel some insubstantial creature, not flesh and bones pressing against his.

She wrapped herself around him, her body twisting and tightening like a stubborn vine. 'Frank,' she said looking up into his eyes, 'is me, Rose.'

Shock rooted him to the spot. His fingers still lay curled loosely around her shoulders. As far as he could tell the face beneath his hadn't changed. There were no signs of the past twenty years in her features. The softly curling hair had no telltale grey. This must be a joke. It just couldn't be Rose. He shook his head as if to banish the sight and memory of her from his mind.

She stood on tiptoes and stretched her body against his, and although he could feel her warm against him, his mind still couldn't quite make sense of what was happening.

'Frank,' she murmured, pulling his head down towards her and kissing him.

He obeyed automatically, as he'd done so often in the past, but his lips barely touched hers before he pulled himself away and asked, 'Rose, is it you?'

She purred against him. 'I been waitin' fi yuh all dese years. I knew yuh would come back to me. Knew if I did wait long enough yuh wouldn't disappoint me, couldn't keep away. Ah love yuh, Frank, just as much as in de past. Dis time we ah go stay together fi good.'

Her hands around his neck forced him to bend down towards her, but her words spurred him into breaking free, breaking the trance-like state he'd been in. He pushed her away, wiping his sweaty palms down the sides of his trousers.

'No, Rose. Me here for one ting. Fi bury me daddy.'

'Who yuh tink yuh foolin', Frank?' She laughed, wagging her forefinger in front of his face and taking a step towards him. 'Nuh matter anyway. I don' care wha' de reason was. All I know is likkle less dan a minute ago yuh was in me arms and yuh wasn't tinkin' 'bout yuh daddy, dat's fi sure.'

She was running her hands over him. Frank felt himself responding, against his will, to her touch. It was as if all the thinking about her he'd tried not to do since he'd arrived, his memories of her on the night of the Singing had summoned her.

'Don' tell me yuh nuh waan me, Frank, 'cause yuh eyes

168

an' yuh body tellin' me a different story. We can have wha' we had in de past,' she murmured against the base of his chin. 'All of it.'

His mind tripped over scenes of their time together – moments when they'd laughed and talked and made love and relished each other's company. When their world consisted of two – of him and her. But these scenes were quickly replaced by darker memories: of her anger, her violent reactions; the way she dominated his senses. Always worried about how she'd react, her jealousy, the way her mood changed from one moment to another.

She'd wanted too much of him all the time and it became too much for him; that feeling of continual oppression had eventually spurred him to make his life in another country. He'd always wanted to go to England, ever since he was a boy and had seen a picture of a snow storm – fat white snowflakes, drifting, covering a house and trees in a blanket of white. It had looked so soft and white and pretty that he'd wanted to see it for himself. His teacher had told him that snowflakes melted when you tried to catch them. What his teacher hadn't told him was how it was only pretty when it was falling, how snow could freeze your fingers and toes and make a grown man cry. Yes, he thought, he'd always wanted to go to England, but even now he couldn't be sure if he'd been running away from her, or if she'd just been a convenient scapegoat upon which to pin his decision to leave.

He pushed her away, more forcefully this time. 'I come back fi one ting,' he said firmly. 'To bury me father an' take care of me madda. What we have finish long time. No goin' back. Mek tings stay as dem are.'

'Dat's jus' talk, Frank,' she chuckled, 'even if yuh don' waan admit it. Yuh did always need persuadin'.' She ran the palm of one hand over his chest, her fingers lingering at the point where his shirt was unbuttoned.

He backed away from her. 'Wha' done, done.'

She tried to catch hold of his hand, but he pulled it away. 'Yuh jus' playin' wid me, usin' words to convince yuhself, but yuh nuh fool me.' She pulled the yellow scarf from around her neck and threw it around his, using the two ends to pull him towards her. 'Still playin' de same old game, nutten change. Runnin' 'cause yuh scared yuh waan what I can give yuh.'

He yanked the scarf from around his neck and let it drop to the ground. 'Keep away from me,' he warned.

'So yuh waan play rough?' she teased.

'I don't want to play anyting,' he said quietly. 'I haven't wanted to play with you these past twenty years and I don't want to start now. I have what I need in my life and it doesn't include you. My only concern is my mother. Keep away from me.'

'Don' mek I get rough wid yuh, Frank,' she said, her eyes echoing the sinister promise of her words. ''Cause yuh don' know jus' how bad I can be when me set me mind to it.'

'Keep away from me,' he repeated, slipping on the yellow scarf, grinding dust into the fine material, as he turned and ran back towards the house.

Rose picked it up and stared at it, his footprint loomed dark on the material. 'So, is only yuh madda yuh care 'bout?' she muttered, angry tears welling up in her eyes. 'I warn yuh!' she suddenly shouted at his disappearing back. 'Why yuh haffi push me? Mek me do tings I don' waan?' She pulled angrily at the material so that it stretched taut between her fingers. 'When dis business over, don' seh me never warn yuh.'

6

16th February

Rose pushed the thin cotton curtains to one side and opened the wooden louvre windows of her bedroom. It was cool – as if the gods had taken pity and allowed a little breeze to break the monotony of the merciless heat of the past few days. Outside, a goat nibbled lazily at the dry patchy grass of the yard before turning its attention to a well-tended, rectangular plot surrounded by a multitude of flowers.

'Move!' Rose screamed. She grabbed the first thing that came to hand – an empty Red Stripe bottle – and threw it at the goat. The bottle bounced off its skinny flank, making it yelp. 'Nuh mek me tell yuh again,' she shouted as the goat bared its teeth at her.

She kicked aside the yellow dress that she'd flung to the floor when she'd returned home the night before, feet and heart aching, and walked to the mirror. There she un-wrapped the towel from her head and shook her hair free. It fell soft and damp to her shoulders – the aloe vera pulp that she'd mashed and combed through her hair earlier was taking effect. Now all she had to do was rinse it, let it dry and then get dressed. She had a busy morning ahead.

The air was full of movement as the convoy of old but pristine vehicles filled with neighbours and friends set off behind the car carrying Miss Jess and her family to church.

Those who couldn't fit themselves in or on a vehicle walked.

The church was a small one. It had been built for worship by Poppa Ben's generation. Sweat and hope lay in the mortar between its bricks; faith and love, the varnish that sealed its wide beams.

Frank helped Miss Jess into the front row. Her blue-black dress hung from her shoulders and was cinched tightly around her waist by a narrow belt which emphasized her frailty. They sat within touching distance of the open coffin that lay on a wooden table directly in front of them. Frank stared straight ahead. He could see the pearl-coloured upholstery inside the coffin. He knew some people took photos of the dead at moments like these, a final attempt to hold the deceased to them, but he couldn't imagine anything more morbid. Who'd really want to have a final photograph like that? Someone lying stiff and rigid in a way they hadn't been in life. He'd prefer to look back at old photos, recall frozen moments of life rather than still frames of death.

Speaker after speaker stepped forward – each with a memory, an anecdote, a story of a man who had been friend to many. Frank half listened, his mind filled with his own stories, like the time he'd fallen out the mango tree he'd been told time and time again not to climb. Poppa Ben had blocked his fall and Frank had been lucky to suffer from nothing more serious than a broken finger. Miss Jess and Poppa Ben hadn't said a word, merely strapped his finger and then sent him to collect all the fruit that had fallen – ripe or not. They'd served it up to him morning, noon and night for nearly a week. It had given him the runs and put him off mangoes for life. Frank smiled to himself – a simple but effective punishment with more impact than a weekend of beatings.

A sudden movement among the bright wreaths caught

his eye and he stared hard. It came again, rapid quick, but this time near the base of the flowers. A green lizard, almost impossible to make out against the foliage, scuttled along one of the thick green stems of the flowers. Where had it come from? Had it been there all the time?

The lizard turned its head towards him, then relaxed against the stem as if lying in the sun. It seemed to be listening intently to the ceremony, moving slightly when-ever Poppa Ben's name was mentioned. For a moment, Frank felt that in some strange way his father had returned to say goodbye, but then immediately dismissed the thought as ridiculous, superstitious nonsense. Miss Jess squeezed his hand tightly and he looked at her. The smallest of smiles played about her mouth as she stared at the lizard, which had now raised itself on its Z-shaped legs, head cocked towards them. Once it had their attention, the lizard lay flat again, seeming to sink into the green of the stem as the service continued.

Awed by the ceremony, Jewelle decided it was best just to stand up and sit down when required. She didn't know the words to the songs and, not wanting to spoil the service, only joined in when the choruses were repeated. Aunt B sang a solo with an intensity and depth of feeling that moved many to tears. Frank sang low, his voice a bare murmur. Miss Jess moved her lips but no sound came out. It was only when the man she'd always called Poppa Ben was referred to by his full name of Benjamin Winston Gali-more that Miss Jess's tears escaped. Only once before had she heard his full name called out in such solemn tones – the day they were married – and she'd cried then too. The salty tears that had tasted nectar sweet in her mouth were now bitter and hard to swallow.

The lizard was suddenly alert again. Balanced on its short legs, it took a final look at the people seated in the front row. Miss Jess sniffed back her tears and gave a small

173

nod. The lizard moved its head and flicked its tail before it wriggled among the waxy petals of the wreaths and disappeared. Frank couldn't tell whether it was in response to his mother or not, but suddenly he didn't care. He didn't know if it was superstition, or spiritual or emotional hope – it didn't matter – he believed, if only for a moment.

Miss Jess and Poppa Ben had chosen their burial plot years before. It was at the far end of the graveyard, which was set in two acres of land behind the church and accessible on foot and by car. Sol handed Jake his car keys before joining Frank and four other men who had been present at the Singing. Together, they shouldered the coffin and slowly made their way over the field to Poppa Ben's final resting place.

Jewelle helped her grandmother into the back of the car and Miss Jess gave her a quick smile before her face returned to its previous immobility. Aunt B settled herself up front beside Jake, and then adjusted her hat so that its long black feathers fell to the side of her face rather than in front of it. No one spoke as Jake carefully manoeuvred his way around the people who had chosen to walk.

Jewelle was watching Jake's eyes, framed and luminous in the windscreen mirror. She felt the tiny tadpole flick once again in the base of her stomach, then quickly dragged her gaze from his.

By the time they arrived at the top end of the field the men were already in sight and making their way to the space that lay ready for its new occupant. Jewelle slid out of the car first. Her dress had stuck to the back of her thighs and she discreetly pulled it away from her skin. She and Aunt B helped Miss Jess out while Jake stood to one side, Miss Jess's walking stick in hand. The quartet made their way slowly alongside the low stone wall to the wooden-gated entrance.

When the mourners were standing together in a little semicircle, the pastor said his final words, his voice rising above the sighs and whispers of the gathering. Jewelle was only half paying attention as she looked round surreptitiously. This graveyard seemed like a garden in comparison to the one English graveyard she'd seen when Ambra's grandad had died. That graveyard had been full of old discoloured tombstones and wilted flowers flopping in jars. The names of the deceased were barely visible, though whether that was through wind, rain or general neglect she didn't know. Here, blossom-laden branches overhung neat headstones and trim grass borders. She looked for a hole in the ground. Where was the coffin, now lying on a pallet, going to go?

Miss Jess leaned heavily on her stick, her lips moving quietly as she said her final goodbyes to her partner of the last fifty years. The whispers and wailing of the mourners rose as the men moved to the sides and picked up the pallet that Jewelle now noticed lay on wheels. They stooped and fitted it into the entrance of what looked like a very low flat-roofed house made of cement and painted white. Mourning voices, singing voices rose to a crescendo as the men cautiously began to ease the coffin into its new home. Miss Jess looked away, tears rolling down her cheeks, as if she couldn't bear to witness this decisive moment. Jewelle, anxious that her grandmother might faint or fall and hurt herself, watched her closely.

All other eyes were fixed on the positioning of the coffin, but Jewelle saw the moment Miss Jess's eyes widened in acute surprise. Her neck stiffened and her tired eyes squinted at a point beyond the circle of mourners, out towards the road that lay behind them. Jewelle stared too, wondering what could have distracted her grandmother.

A woman, standing behind the wall, appeared to be waving at them. Miss Jess was transfixed. The thin skin covering her knuckles strained as she gripped her walking stick. Jewelle looked back – the woman seemed to be blowing them a kiss. Who on earth was she? And why was she standing behind the wall instead of here with them? The questions ran through her mind as the woman turned and stared at her with fierce intensity, as if she was trying to memorize her face. Her scrutiny made Jewelle drop her gaze. At the same time a thin wail rose from Miss Jess. It came again, rising higher and higher, a wail of anguish and loss and – fear? The walking stick slipped from Miss Jess's hands, and her knees buckled as she slid slowly towards the ground.

Aunt B moved quickly, catching Miss Jess mid-fall. Frank gave the pallet a final rough push before spinning around and taking his mother in his arms where she collapsed in a faint.

He stared down at her nonplussed, shocked by how light she was. Murmurs rose from the mourners as they gathered around.

'She all right?'

'Lord have mercy on us today!'

'She dead. She cyaan live widout him.'

'She waan go wid him.'

'Poor love! See how she look shrivel up inna Frank hand.'

Aunt B took control. Her voice was loud. Confident. 'Move, Frank!' she ordered. 'Get her into de car an' tek her home.'

'Go!' Sol said urgently. 'Me will finish up here.' He glanced over his shoulder quickly, scanning the length of the wall.

Before Frank could ask him who or what he was looking for, he felt a prod in the small of his back and looked round to see Aunt B brandishing Miss Jess's walking stick at him.

'Cho, man! Move yuhself. Wha' yuh waitin' on? Another funeral? Jewelle! Walk up. Where de bwoy Jake gone?' Her head spun from side to side as she barked orders and asked questions.

'He's gone ahead with the car keys I think,' Jewelle replied as Aunt B grabbed her hand and dragged her along in Frank's wake.

'Everyting all right,' Aunt B assured people as she strode away. 'We'll see yuh all back at de house.'

Miss Jess had been put straight to bed, even before the subdued wake, which was over much more quickly than planned. People had eaten and drunk a little of the victuals prepared, paid their respects to Frank, left messages for Miss Jess and departed. Now Frank, Sol, Aunt B and Jewelle sat together uneasily.

'Will she be all right?' Jewelle asked.

'Of course,' Frank said. He bit nervously at the cuticles of his thumb, belying the confidence with which he spoke. 'Sleeping. Let's hope she sleep de night through.'

'Nancy,' Aunt B instructed, 'pour likkle of dat soup fi Frank.'

'Me nuh have no appetite.'

'It's really good, Dad. You should try it.' Jewelle soaked up the last of the soup at the bottom of her bowl with a piece of hard dough bread before popping it in her mouth.

'So yuh like de soup, Jewelle?' Nancy enquired pleasantly as she gathered her things together.

'Yeah.' She walked to the cooker and filled her bowl again. 'What is it?'

'Mannish water,' Sol replied.

'What water?'

'Goat head!' Nancy said triumphantly before Sol could reply.

'Goat head?' Jewelle stared down at the brown liquid in

the bowl in her hand. 'I've been eating goat head soup?' She looked at Sol – a silent plea. Sol merely raised his eyebrows. 'The goat I fed the other day? The one I thought had run away?' She could feel the soup churning in her stomach.

Nancy tapped the pot on the cooker. 'Plenty leave fi tomorrow, Jewelle.'

'Yuh nuh goin' home tonight, Nancy?' Aunt B's tone was sharp.

'All right. All right,' Nancy said. 'Me gone.'

Jewelle put her still full bowl in the sink and sat down at the table. She stroked her stomach in ever-widening circles; her screwed up face a picture of misery.

'Wha' yuh tink Miss Jess did mean 'bout "Leave we. Past is past"?' Aunt B broke the silence that had fallen.

'When she seh dat?' Sol was suddenly alert.

'When she start fall an' I catch her.'

'Yuh sure?' His question came bullet quick.

Aunt B gave him a scornful look. 'Course me sure. She seh de same ting over an' over again.'

'Who was that woman?' Jewelle asked, still rubbing her stomach.

'What woman?' Frank said.

'Just before Granny fainted, I saw her staring at something behind the wall. When I looked, there was this woman doing something weird with her hands.'

'What! Talk sense, Jewelle!' Aunt B ordered sharply.

'I think de gyal talkin' plenty sense if only yuh would let her,' Sol said quietly. 'Wha' did de woman do, Jewelle?' he asked gently.

'I couldn't see properly, but it looked like . . . it seemed like she was wrapping one arm around the other, like this.' She demonstrated as she spoke. 'She put her palms together, then opened them out into a kind of cup and then she blew through them.'

178

Sol nodded. 'Was dat when Miss Jess fainted?'

'No. It was before. Then Granny started to make that funny crying sound.'

'Who was it? Did you recognize her?' Frank asked.

'Nope. Never seen her before.'

'Are you certain?' he asked sharply.

'Course I am. I already said so, didn't I?'

'Did she do anything else?' Frank asked.

'No, not much. After she'd blown through her hands, she flicked her fingers towards us and then walked away. So, d'you know who she is?'

She stared at them, hoping for a reaction, but they ignored her and talked among themselves in patois too fast for her to catch it all.

'See wha' I mean 'bout yuh past? Look how it buck up on yuh present,' Sol said to Frank.

'Just stop yuh nonsense,' Frank retorted.

Aunt B burst out, 'I never waan come! I did know from de start dis a bad lucky business. We should just take Miss Jess back to England wid we before someting really bad happen.'

'Who is she?'

'Wha' 'bout me, Miss B? Yuh gwine leave me all alone fi look after meself wid so much danger roun' me?' Sol grinned despite the tension that held them captive at the table.

'We nuh even move de furniture round in her room yet. Spirit soon come trouble her,' Aunt B said almost to herself.

'Pure stupid superstition,' Frank told her. 'De dead nuh harm. Duppy nuh exist. Is just live people we haffi worry 'bout.'

Sol glanced at Frank. 'Look like yuh learnin',' he said meaningfully.

'Who is she?' Jewelle asked again.

Sol flicked Frank a lazy look. His dimples appeared as he said with a smile, 'Ask yuh daddy.'

Frank glared at Sol before turning to his daughter. 'What did she look like?'

'I don't know!' Jewelle said impatiently. 'I told you, I couldn't see her that well.'

'Jewelle! Don't try my patience!'

The girl huffed and rolled her eyes before replying. 'Old.' She shrugged her shoulders. Frank slapped the table with the flat of his hand. 'Oh all right! About forty.'

Sol grinned to himself.

'Straight black hair. She looked a bit Indian like – that kind of brown skin? I think there was something funny about her eyes – but I couldn't really see them.'

'Why? She wearin' sunglasses or someting?' asked Aunt B.

'No.' Jewelle slowed down, trying to explain. 'I'm not quite sure what it was. I'm pretty sure her eyes were a funny colour, but I was too far away to see exactly what colour they were. Maybe they were clear. Oh yeah, there was one thing.'

'What?' the three adults chorused.

'She wasn't wearing a hat.'

'That's not funny, Jewelle,' Frank said.

'It wasn't meant to be. It was a funeral and she was the only woman, except for me, who wasn't wearing a hat, or at least a scarf or something. Who is she, Dad?'

Frank sat frozen in his chair, his thoughts chaotic. Rose? At the funeral? No, she wouldn't dare – would she? His head refused to accept the only answer his mind offered. Sol hummed as he rolled an unlit cigarette between his fingers. He looked as if he'd only heard what he'd expected to hear. Aunt B slumped forward and stared unseeing at the tabletop, where a line of ants ran in giddy circles around a crumb of bread.

'Aunt B?'

180

Her aunt only shook her head, mouth open but speechless.

'Sol? Sol! You tell me. Who is she?'

Sol looked at her. His eyes sparkled – not in shock or fear – but with anticipation. 'Rose. Her name's Rose.'

It was late by the time Aunt B and Jewelle went to bed and Frank and Sol were left alone.

'Yuh know dat was Rose at yuh father funeral?'

'Not tonight, Sol,' Frank cut him off. He didn't want Sol inspecting his mind and if he found out about what had happened the previous night . . . No, he needed to deal with his thoughts first; decide what he was going to do and, most importantly, do this alone.

'I can help yuh, Frank – but only if yuh let me.'

'I don' waan talk 'bout it, Sol. Me jus' bury me daddy.'

'All right. But 'member, tomorrow another day.' Sol got to his feet. 'Just gwine smoke a draw.'

Frank's thoughts were bitter as he stretched back in his chair. Damn Sol and damn Rose. Was he never to be free of her? He leaned forward, resting his head in the palms of his hands. Maybe he should have listened that first time Sol had offered to help . . .

'Dat Rose gwine be de death a yuh, yuh mark me words.'

'Stop yuh noise.' Frank drew damp circles on the scarred wooden tabletop with his beer bottle. 'I'm a free man. I can leave any time I waan. Yuh see any ring 'pon me finger?' He looked up at Sol challengingly.

'No. Just de one through yuh nose.' Sol tilted his beer bottle back and drained the last few drops. 'Waan another one?' He nodded at Frank's near-empty bottle.

'Nuh waan nutten,' he muttered sulkily.

'Junior!' Sol shouted to the barrel-chested man standing behind the bar. 'Another Dragon.' He played with the crumpled bottle tops as he waited, flicking them with the tip of his fingernail so that the pieces of metal jumped across the table.

'Stop dat nuh. Yuh cyaan see is tink, me a tink.'

'Seem like yuh only tink wid one ting far as dis woman concern. Wha' she have so special yuh cyaan get some-place else?'

'Dragon.'

Sol nodded his thanks as Junior placed a chilled bottle of Dragon stout on the table in front of him.

'Yuh don' understand, Sol.'

'I tink is yuh who don' understand. Is yuh don' waan open yuh eyes, see wha' real an' wha' not. Is yuh won't accept dis woman will suck out up to yuh eyeball dem if yuh nuh careful. Just like dat likkle bitch me brother did hook up wid.'

'Bevan?'

'How much brother me have?' Sol said impatiently. 'Anyway, seem like some woman over Port Antonio way did have him under pressure.'

'Wha' she name?'

'Don' know, but I have my suspicions. Bevan never name her, only call her "she". From him letters him soun' scared.'

'Bevan?'

Scared? Frank didn't know him well but from what he'd seen of Sol's older brother it was hard to imagine. Big, broad and with the same slightly pockmarked skin, Bevan had none of Sol's mercurial charm, but all the quiet assurance of a man who didn't lead but at the same time wouldn't be led. 'Must be some kind of bad woman,' he mused.

'Yeah, just like de likkle tegareg yuh tek up wid.'

Frank clenched the bottle in his hand. His friend spoke the truth, but how could he admit that Sol had been right all along and he was out of his depth? He wanted to explain – he always intended to end things with Rose when he was away from her, but somehow his resolve disappeared the minute he saw her. She could twist his words so that he found himself saying something different to what he meant, wrap her body around his till she left his head spinning and his senses reeling. He couldn't work out if his prevarication was because he didn't really want to leave her or because he was afraid of her reaction. It was as if she'd slipped him some magic potion that sapped his will and kept him tied to her. He loved her, at least he thought he did, but she scared him. So maybe what he felt wasn't love. Or was it?

'She not good fi yuh, Frank. I feel it deep down in me belly. Yuh haffi bruk free.' Sol's words interrupted his thoughts.

'Yuh just don' like her.'

'Nuh matter whether I like her or not,' Sol said, taking a swig from his bottle. 'I only haffi look 'pon yuh fi see yuh not happy. Look how yuh mash up already an' it not even a year since yuh tek up wid her. Imagine after two years, or t'ree – de longer yuh leave it de harder it get. Every time I tink of yuh an' she, me belly roll like ship 'pon rough sea. Do yuhself a favour, man, an' get rid of her – while yuh can.'

'Yuh don' understand,' Frank repeated, but this time calmly. He looked Sol in the eye, no anger or aggression but a silent request for help, which he was too proud to voice.

Sol shrugged. 'Well, I cyaan do more dan offer advice or help. Yuh a big man, up to yuh wha' yuh waan do. All I know is dat one a dese days, yuh gwine come runnin' to me fi help. Just hope de day yuh come it not too late . . .'

*

Out on the veranda Sol pulled a small bag of weed from his trouser pocket. He'd gone home and collected it, along with a couple of other things, after the funeral. Ganja helped him think. It wasn't called the weed of wisdom for nothing. He licked two Rizlas, stuck them together, then laid the marijuana along the papers in the palm of his hand. He rolled the spliff expertly, sitting on the top step of the veranda and staring up into the night sky. It was a little cloudy: a hint of wash-clean rain to come, but tomorrow would be clear.

Nothing like a little good weed and a still night. A woman in his arms right now and he'd be in paradise. The way he looked at it he had two choices. He could stand by and watch, let things take their course. In which case he'd smoke the spliff and then check out the bikini gyal. He held the draw under his nose and sniffed at it; it smelled good. Or – he held the spliff by one end and shook it gently – he could stay where he was and help things along a little, in which case the weed could wait. And if his reasons for helping were not strictly honourable and not just for Frank, who was to know?

From somewhere out of sight came the hoot of an owl. A wise bird, says little, sees all and knows how to wait. A sign. Sol slipped the joint regretfully into his breast pocket and peered into the kitchen. Frank sat slumped in his chair with his eyes closed. Sol glanced round quickly before pulling another bag from his trouser pocket. He opened it, releasing the scent of sulphur, spirit weed and rosemary, and began sprinkling the contents of the bag around the doorways, window ledges and walls of the house. When he'd worked his way back to the beginning he dusted his hands down on his shirttail and replaced the bag in his pocket.

The bikini gyal could wait, but why deprive himself of the rest? He took the spliff from his breast pocket, lit up and inhaled deeply. As the scent of burning weed rose, he chuckled in satisfaction.

When he'd smoked the spliff down to the end he flicked its tip over the veranda balcony onto the dry dirt yard below and turned inside.

7

17th February

'We haffi talk,' Sol started without preamble.

'Too early, man. Is barely eight o'clock.' Frank turned back to the Blue Mountain coffee he was grinding.

'Frank!' Frank kept his expression blank as he raised the chipped, red metal coffee pot towards Sol and flicked its hinged lid up and down several times.

Sol nodded, prepared to wait if necessary. 'I s'pose Miss Jess still sleepin', but where everybody else gone?'

'Jewelle feedin' de animal an' Aunt B 'bout someplace.'

The sound of spluttering coffee, bubbling in place of the unspoken words between the two men, filled the silence. There was a hiss as the coffee spilled over and hit the hot gas ring. Frank tutted in irritation, filled two large cups with steaming coffee, pushed one in front of Sol and then sat down and pulled the other towards him.

'Frank?'

'No, Sol. Why yuh haffi insist? Why yuh so concern?'

'All I was going to seh was how 'bout we spend some time together. We nuh talk good since yuh come, an' if we nuh look sharp we nuh go talk before yuh gone.'

The sound of running footsteps on the back veranda gave Frank an excuse not to reply.

'Morning, Dad. Hi, Sol. How are you?'

'All right, miss,' Sol replied. 'Yuh look please 'bout someting. Wh'appen?'

Jewelle smiled and, not for the first time, Sol thought how her big open smile made her resemble her father as a boy. But Jewelle was more carefree than Frank had been; her smile came more easily. When Frank did smile, though, it lit up his entire face and made you wish that he did it more often.

'Nothing.' Jewelle shrugged her shoulders quickly and pushed her plaits away from her face, revealing her hairline scar. 'I just woke up with butterflies here,' she said, touching her stomach lightly. 'I sort of feel as if . . . as if something really important is going to happen, but I don't know what. It feels a bit strange, but not bad strange – if you know what I mean.'

'Me hear wha' yuh a seh.' Sol nodded.

'How's Granny, Dad?'

'Sleeping last time I looked.'

'I'm just going to wash my hands and then take a peep.'

'Don't wake her,' he cautioned.

'Dad! What d'you take me for?'

'You sound like an elephant most times. You're not walking on carpet here, you know.'

'I know. Honestly!' She attempted to sound aggrieved but couldn't hold her tone. 'When I come back I want to ask you something. OK?' She was suddenly serious.

Frank nodded, only half listening. Aunt B came in with mangoes, sweet cup and lemon-grass wrapped in a tea towel, which she held by its ends so it hung like a bag.

'Thought I'd brew up some lemon-grass tea for Miss Jess. It light an' should settle her stomach,' she said to nobody in particular. 'De mangoes an' sweet cup ripe. We better eat dem before dem turn.'

'Morning, Aunt B,' Jewelle said when she returned. 'Granny's getting up. Says she wants some scrambled eggs.'

'No.' Frank jumped to his feet. 'If she's hungry, she can eat in bed,' he said, rushing from the room.

'Want me to check if there are any fresh eggs, Aunt B?'

Aunt B nodded as she pulled a heavy pot, black with age, from the cupboard under the sink, but Jewelle was already out of the door.

'Wha' yuh tink 'bout dis business, Miss B?'

'Mek me skin prickle.' She quickly washed some scallions before chopping them into small pieces.

'Yuh tink is Rose mek Miss Jess sick?'

'Rose enough fi mek anybody sick when she waan.' Aunt B poured a trickle of coconut oil into the pan and set it on a low flame.

'I don' know fi sure,' Sol continued in a tone of voice that implied that he did, 'but I don' believe it was Poppa Ben time. Know wha' me a seh?'

Aunt B looked at Sol properly for the first time that morning. Even though she'd been wanting to talk to somebody about her qualms since she'd arrived in Jamaica, now the moment seemed to have arrived, she wasn't quite so sure that she wanted the conversation to continue.

'All dese tings happen too quick. Poppa Ben, fi all him did old, was hale an' hearty, den from one day to de next – *bam!* Him drop down dead.'

'But is heart attack him did have.'

'Den before dog even have time fi bark,' Sol continued, 'Rose find her way to him funeral – and Frank.'

'Pure coincidence,' Aunt B replied, using the words Sam had so often said in the past. Whenever he'd said them it had annoyed her, but now they gave her unexpected comfort. Now that someone else was voicing her fears she suddenly hoped with all her heart that the events of the past couple of days were nothing more than coincidence.

'Too much "coincidence" 'bout here recently,' Sol said, watching her. He jerked his head towards the thin line of grey smoke rising from the pan on the cooker.

She spun round. 'Weh Jewelle wid de eggs dem?' she

muttered, snapping the flame off and moving the pan to one of the unlit back burners.

Sol waited until she'd seated herself opposite him before speaking. 'I need yuh help, Miss B,' he said stroking her arm. His voice was sweet like one of the mangoes she'd picked earlier. 'Jewelle too young fi understand; Miss Jess old an' Frank don' waan see. Yuh de only one usin' yuh God-given senses.'

'I did tell him!' she burst out. 'I tell him when we leave England dat is more dan a funeral we comin' for, but him never lissen.'

'Frank did always stubborn, but me more. If Rose so bold as to come to de funeral den we nuh have much time left if it nuh too late already. I waan talk to him today. Dat mean him cyaan come wid excuse 'bout him must sit wid Miss Jess all day or look after Jewelle. Yuh understand? So I waan yuh fi stay wid Miss Jess. Nuh badda her, but if she have anyting important fi seh mek sure yuh lissen.'

'Wha' yuh a do, Sol?' she asked warily, drawing herself out of the reach of his hand. 'I don' waan yuh stirrin' tings up fi yuh own ends an' drawin' everybody into yuh mess.'

'Miss B,' Sol said, opening his eyes wide as if injured by her lack of trust, 'Frank an' Miss Jess jus' like me own family. All me waan do is protect dem – jus' like yuh.'

Aunt B chewed her bottom lip thoughtfully as she stared at him. As far as she was concerned, Sol was a silver-tongued liar and she didn't trust him an inch, but . . . she didn't know what to think any more. Backside! Why wasn't Sam here? Even if she didn't always agree with him, he still had a way of helping her to see things more clearly.

'Wha' 'bout Jewelle?' she asked after a moment.

'Me already tek care a dat.'

'How yuh mean?'

'Jake.'

'Jake!' Aunt B screwed up her face like she'd been forced

to swallow a cup of serusi. 'Why yuh even badda fi ask me fi help when have all it plan out already?' she said angrily.

'Well, yuh cyaan expect her fi spend all day under yuh feet, specially if Miss Jess start talk.' He raised a winged eyebrow. 'Better she spend time wid someone her own age. Someone she like.'

'Dat is precisely what ah mean.'

'Come come, Miss B. Yuh too dark.'

'Jewelle like my own daughter,' she hissed. 'I don' waan her ruin her life before she even start live all 'cause of some stupid bwoy.'

'How yuh expect her fi grow if yuh rope her too tight? Me sure between yuh and Frank, yuh bring her up proper, teach her right from wrong. But time come when yuh haffi let go her han'. Give her space fi show yuh she learn well from yuh. Mek her mek her own choices an' her mistakes if necessary.'

'Him too old.'

'Sixteen or seventeen nuh too old. Me trust him.'

'As if me gwine mek dat convince me,' she snorted, missing Sol's muttered 'is him destiny'.

'Wha' yuh seh?' she asked.

'Nutten. Only dat is dese two years Miss Jess have him a work fi her.'

Aunt B compressed her lips, but Jewelle came into the kitchen before she could speak.

'There were only seven,' she indicated the eggs lying cradled in the bottom of her T-shirt which she'd stretched out so it formed a pouch, 'but they're big.'

Aunt B took them from her, cracked them into a bowl and added salt, pepper and milk. 'Mek yuhself useful,' she instructed, passing the bowl and a fork to Jewelle.

She put the pan back on to heat just as Frank entered the kitchen with Miss Jess in his arms. Sol quickly got to his feet and pulled out the chair nearest to them.

'Morning, everyone.' Miss Jess's voice was small. 'I don' waan no fuss.' She raised a hand stopping the 'how are yous?' mid-flow. 'Pass me stick, Sol.' She pointed to the corner behind his chair where her stick lay propped up against the wall. 'Thanks,' she said, tapping it on the floor a couple of times. 'Before yuh even badda me – me all right. Waan eat a couple egg wid yuh, den rest a likkle. Old people an' babies need dem sleep.' She smiled her thanks as Jewelle pushed a plate of fluffy golden eggs in front of her.

'Glad to see yuh on yuh feet, Miss Jess.' Aunt B touched the old woman's shoulder gently. 'Waan someting fi drink?'

'A cup of mint or lemon-grass tea would go down nice.'

'Jus' brewin' de lemon-grass, Miss Jess.'

Sol raised his eyebrows at Aunt B before turning to Frank. 'Come fi a ride wid me, Frank. We nuh talk good since yuh come.'

Frank glared at him. 'No, man. We done talk 'bout dis already. Me have plenty things fi sort out here.'

'Go wid him, Frank,' Miss Jess mumbled through a mouthful of scrambled eggs. 'Nutten fi yuh to do here anyway.'

'No, Mumma. I don' waan leave yuh alone today.'

Sol stared at Aunt B, opening his eyes wide so she could take her cue.

'Nuh worry 'bout nutten here, Frank,' she said, placing a cup of lemon-grass tea in front of Miss Jess. 'Go wid Sol. Feel sure yuh mus' have plenty tings talk 'bout, or some of yuh old friends fi look up.'

'No.' Frank turned and stared out of the window.

'Yuh waan me fi come kunk yuh inna yuh head?' Miss Jess asked, tapping the table with her knuckles.

Jewelle giggled at the thought. 'Don't give him another chance, Granny. Just kunk him.'

Miss Jess smiled as she chased the last of the scrambled eggs around on her plate with her fork. 'Dese old hands don' even have energy fi pick up scrambled eggs let alone do anyting else. Look 'pon dem.' She stretched one hand out on the table. 'Look how me knuckle dem wear out on dat tough head wha' him have.'

'I'll do it for you. My knuckles are strong.' Jewelle pushed her plate to one side and ran round to where her father was sitting. 'Where d'you want me to kunk him? Here?' She rapped Frank a few times on his forehead. 'Or maybe here?' Another series of knocks on the back of his head.

'Come out of my head, Jewelle.' He tried to push her hand away but she held on to it.

'Dad?' Her voice wheedling as she played with his fingers.

'What d'you want?' he asked, recognizing the signs.

'As everybody's going to be busy today can I go to the beach . . . with Jake? He asked me this morning.'

'Beach? Just you two? I don't think so.'

'But –!'

'How you going to get there?'

'Frank! Dem only going to de local beach,' Sol spoke up. 'De bwoy Jamaican born an' bred, in case yuh figet. Me sure him know weh de bus stop deh.'

'Just the two of them?'

'So wha' wrong wid dat? Yuh nuh trus' him 'cause him Jamaican?'

'Me nuh trus' him 'cause him a bwoy pickney an' me know how bwoys dat age tink, whether dem Jamaican or not. Sorry, Jewelle.' He turned to face her. 'I'll take you myself before we leave.'

'Oh c'mon, Dad. Please.' Jewelle's eyes filled up with tears as she spoke.

'Frank,' Aunt B interrupted, 'if Miss Jess trus' de bwoy Jake an' is dese past two years him a work fi her, I don' see why yuh cyaan trust him too.'

Frank stared at Aunt B in surprise. The one thing he'd

expected was her unconditional support over Jewelle, yet just look at how she was behaving!

'Is only yuh one see problem, Frank,' Miss Jess told him. 'Jus' hurry up an' come out, all of yuh. I tired an' I waan sleep.' Though she smiled, her voice trembled with fatigue. 'Frank, come help me up.' He picked her up in his arms. 'See unnu later,' she said as they left the room.

'Aunt B, thank you.' Jewelle wrapped her arms around her aunt for the second time in two days. Aunt B hugged her back warmly. For a moment Jewelle was her little girl again, not the obstinate teenager who delighted in annoying her whenever she could.

'Just tek care,' she warned her niece before hugging her again.

'Hope yuh please wid yuhself,' Frank grumbled sulkily.

'Wha' me haffi content 'bout?'

'Yuh get wha' yuh waan.'

'Cho, man. Hush yuh noise.'

Sol put the car into gear noisily and pulled out without looking back. A screech of brakes and a stream of curses split the air behind them.

'Nuh badda kill me, man!' Frank shouted, clutching at the handle above the passenger door.

'Is not me tink have reason fi kill yuh,' Sol replied.

Frank glared at him and gave him a dirty look before turning to face the road ahead. For a minute or so there was silence between them until Sol suddenly braked.

'Wha' de hell do yuh now?' Frank cursed as Sol stuck his head through the driver's window.

'Waan ride part way?' he heard Sol ask. Frank looked out the open window and saw his daughter and Jake at the side of the road.

'No thanks, Sol,' he heard Jewelle say. 'We thought we'd walk to the bus stop.'

193

'Yuh still have 'bout quarter mile walk, yuh know,' Sol warned.

Jewelle grinned. 'I know,' she shrugged, 'but who cares? We've got tons of time.'

'Yeah. Hours – nuh matter wh'appen,' Jake drawled.

'Just mek certain dat if anyting haffi happen it nuh happen to my daughter.' Frank's voice was gruff with concern and jealousy.

'Yes, sah.' Jake was suddenly rigid.

'Oh, Daddy!' Jewelle ran round to Frank's side of the car. She leaned through the window and pinched his cheek lightly before dropping a kiss on the spot her fingers had squeezed a moment before.

'Just be careful, that's all.' He trapped her nose between the knuckles of his first and second fingers and tweaked gently. 'Got enough money?'

'I have money,' Jake said.

Frank frowned. 'Weh yuh get money from?'

Jake narrowed his eyes, but Sol intervened before he could speak. 'He's a hard worker.'

'Sorry, Jake,' Frank's voice was gentler as he looked at the boy. 'I never mean nutten by it, but she my only pickney.' And I've been the only man in her life until now, he added, to himself.

Jake inclined his head, but didn't look at Frank. As the car pulled away, Frank watched his daughter and Jake dwindle in size until they were nothing more than two specks in the windscreen mirror.

'See de way him look at me when me ask him weh him get money?'

'De youth have pride. Never know him beg or steal nutten from nobody. Yuh daughter safe wid him,' Sol said curtly as he moved into a higher gear and urged the car forward.

*

194

The house was silent now everybody had gone. Aunt B observed Miss Jess from the doorway of the old woman's bedroom. She seemed little bigger than a doll as she lay in the double bed she'd once shared with Poppa Ben. Her skin looked sun-starved, a dry ashen-yellow against the whiteness of the sheets. Grey-white hair strayed from the plaits that had come loose as she'd tossed and turned in troubled sleep the night before.

Aunt B settled herself in the wicker chair next to the bed and opened the Barbara Cartland book she'd hastily bought at the airport. She loved these old-time love stories about women who knew how to wait and men who respected that, but despite her efforts to concentrate the words kept running together until they formed a single black line. Eventually she gave up and put the book on the bedside table. She'd read the same paragraph over and over again and still couldn't recall a single sentence. She pulled her chair even closer to the bed and willed herself to read the troubled and changing expressions on Miss Jess's face.

The bus that came was like an older, more decrepit version of Jewelle's school minibus back home. One side was dented and much of the dark blue paint scratched or scraped off in previous accidents. Inside, people sat squashed up: two, three, occasionally four to a seat. Jewelle and Jake followed a thin, light-skinned girl on to the bus and took a seat just vacated by a couple with a child. A fat woman with an ornately plaited hairstyle followed them closely behind, pushing Jake impatiently in the small of the back as she tried to squeeze past. She stopped next to the thin girl. 'Yuh maaga, nuh take up much space,' she said, sitting down next to her and spreading herself out so that the girl was pinned to the window for the rest of her journey.

Reggae pumped from the radio, bass line booming in time to the turning wheels of the bus. Snippets of conversation could be heard over the music:

'Bible seh "Thou shalt not covet thy neighbour's possession." So yuh tell me what pastor bicycle doing outside Mistress Sawyer's house at dat hour of de night!'

'Let those without sin cast the first stone.'

'Look like pastor need to read him Bible again dat is . . . if him don't already cast it away!'

Jewelle turned around in time to see two women sitting several seats behind her burst into raucous laughter. Despite the open windows, it was stifling hot. She shifted uncomfortably and pulled the skirt of her denim sundress down as far as she could in an attempt to stop herself sticking to the black vinyl seat. The bus conductor worked his way down the bus towards them as he collected fares. Jewelle took her purse from her rucksack, but Jake stopped her with a gentle touch of his hand.

'Mek me tek care of it.' He patted the pocket that held the money Sol had given him that morning.

'Puerto Seco beach.'

'Puerto Seco? That's Spanish, isn't it?' Jewelle watched as the conductor separated the bills he received and folded them in half lengthways, before putting notes of different denominations in between his fingers so the notes stuck up like spines.

'Yeah. It in Discovery Bay. Dem seh is where Columbus first land in 1494.'

Impressed, Jewelle raised her eyebrows; this boy knew his history.

The conductor stood with his legs braced against the side of the seat opposite them as the bus jolted its way over the rough road.

'Weh yuh goin', sah?' he asked the bald man in the seat behind them.

'Rio Bueno.' He handed the conductor sixty dollars.

'Sixty-five.' The conductor held his hand open.

'Sixty-five dollars? How yuh mean sixty-five when I pay yuh sixty for de same ride only two days ago?'

'Yuh nuh lissen radio? One US dollar worth 17.90 Jamaican dollars today.'

'No, man! Me not paying extra five dollars fi de same ride.' He folded his arms across his chest. 'Look how we ram up like hog inna pen. Koo de bus! Window crack! Seat mash up! Not even de Flintstones woulda ride inna dis.'

'Pay or come off,' the conductor warned.

The man remained where he was, arms stubbornly folded.

'Hol' de bus, driver,' the conductor shouted. The bus screeched to a halt. 'Pay or come off.' The conductor jerked his thumb towards the bus door.

'Hurry up nuh, man,' somebody shouted from the back of the bus. 'Yuh tink is yuh one haffi pay extra?'

A tall woman, with narrow, dangerous eyes and a sleeping baby in her arms, stood up. 'Yuh better hurry up an' pay, otherwise is me gwine throw yuh off,' she shouted.

Startled by the voices, the baby stirred. The bald man responded by sucking his teeth. More people were shouting now and the baby's whimpers turned into a loud cry.

'Look how yuh wake up me baby.' The tall woman started to rock the child in her arms roughly. 'Cho! Jus' come off.'

The man looked round for support, but there was none. He gave a final suck of his teeth before pulling out a crumpled ten-dollar bill.

The conductor slipped the bill between his fingers. 'Don' have no change right now. Soon come back.'

'Better mek sure yuh do.'

'No badda give de bitch no change,' the tall woman shouted after the conductor. 'Look how him mek me baby bawl.' She turned round and gave the sulky man an evil look. 'Cho!'

Jewelle rested her forehead against the sun-warmed glass and watched the world pass by through half-closed eyes. In some ways, except for the weather and the colours, it was like being at home. Exactly the same sort of everyday scenes she saw on her bus ride to and from school. Clusters of people standing outside stores, chatting or waiting for buses, long-limbed children playing tag and running among the shoppers. But instead of dense, bush-covered hills to her right and glimpses of beach-fringed sea stretching out into the distance, she'd be passing Boots or the post office or the back of Sainsbury's car park. The further the bus took them away from the town the greener the landscape became as the road curved its way between giant ferns and scenic hills en route to the beach-fringed coast. The heat, the rolling motion of the bus and the sense of time suspended lulled her to sleep.

'Waan a drink?'

'Too early.'

Sol's dimples flashed. 'Me 'member a time when it never too early.'

'Dem times pass.' Frank's voice was grumpy. 'Anyway, me nuh have de belly fi it any more.'

Sol threw his head back and laughed. 'When yuh never have de belly yuh drink like yuh might never get another chance an' now yuh have plenty belly,' he said, bending forward to rub Frank's stomach, 'yuh stop drink. I never meet a man so mix up.'

'Leave me.'

'Come, Frank. Is me yuh talkin' to. Sol.' He turned to the counter. 'Junior! Beg yuh bring two glass an' a bottle a Appleton Dark when yuh done.'

Junior raised a palm in acknowledgement as he carried a

tray full of gaudy drinks to a group of tourists sitting near the door.

'Yuh still don' waan believe dat was Rose at yuh father funeral,' Sol continued conversationally, ignoring Frank's frown. ''Bout time yuh face de situation. I did tell yuh long time dat Rose not de type of woman fi leggo. Maybe now yuh start believe me.'

'Couldn't be Rose,' Frank argued stubbornly, his mind working overtime. What on earth did Rose – if it had been her – hope to achieve by turning up at his father's funeral and upsetting everybody? If she really wanted him back then it was the worst way of going about it that he could think of. He hadn't told anybody about her appearance at the house the night before the funeral. Rose might be headstrong and impulsive but she wasn't that crazy – was she? Although deep inside he knew it was Rose, he refused to really believe it without proof. It was pointless stirring things up unnecessarily. 'She wouldn't be so stupid,' he said aloud. 'Anyway, how she know 'bout me daddy funeral or dat I even in Jamaica?'

'Look like Englan' soften yuh belly an' yuh brain. Yuh figet how Jamaica stay? Yuh cyaan even fart widout someone on de other side of de island tell yuh whether yuh eat cabbage or callaloo an' which field yuh pick it from. People talk, an' if yuh waan answers all yuh haffi do is ask question. Thanks, Junior.' Sol looked up as Junior placed the drinks on the wooden tabletop. 'Chalk dem up fi me,' he told him. Junior nodded, leaving as silently as he'd appeared.

Sol raised a tumbler of rum to Frank and waited as Frank raised the other one reluctantly. They clinked glasses and Frank took a sip of the liquid.

'Yuh family in danger!' Sol said calmly before sipping from his own glass.

Frank spluttered, sending amber droplets flying. He

wiped his mouth with the back of his hand. 'Wha' de raas do yuh?' he asked angrily.

'Only way fi get yuh attention. Don' know what else me haffi do apart from speak in Queen's English. You were never too fond of patois anyway, were you?' Sol continued. 'I could never quite work out why – if you spoke English to be different or if you did it because you were different.'

'It worked with the girls.'

'Rose too, I suppose.'

'It turned her on for some reason. Anyway, it doesn't matter any more,' Frank said.

'No, I don't suppose it does,' Sol replied. 'Funny though – you're speaking plenty of patois now you're back. Did you need to spend all that time away in order to get in touch with your roots?' Before Frank could reply, Sol suddenly changed the subject. 'Do you know what I've been doing since you left?' he asked.

'What? Besides your law and your medicine and all those other things you used to talk about.'

'What I talk about I do. I've studied law and medicine, astrology and graphology. I've studied ancient rites and religious customs –'

'So how come you're an estate agent?'

'I own the agency and I'm a lawyer. The best of both worlds and that's what I like. Buying and selling houses you get to meet people, you talk to them and they talk to you. You never know when something they say might come in useful. Being a lawyer gives me power. Do you know how many people owe me favours because I help the law work in their favour? Or how many people are frightened of me because they know I can tie them up with laws faster than a fisherman can tie up his boat? I'm happy with who I am and what I do.'

'All right, Sol. I wasn't trying to put you down.'

Sol was amazing, Frank thought, a little enviously.

Confident about who he was and what he did. He didn't seem to have any of the self-doubts that affected other people or, if he did, he never seemed to let them show. He wasn't scared, either, to plunge into something new simply because it had caught his interest.

Not like me, Frank mused. Studied one thing and had the same job most of my working life; and although I'd never give up Jewelle or the time I had with Beth, outside of them it all seems a bit colourless at times.

'I've travelled, too,' Sol said, his voice breaking into Frank's thoughts. 'To America, Canada, Latin America and to many African countries, including Egypt.'

'You seem to have missed out England on your travels,' said Frank dryly.

'It's not my time to visit England, but when that time comes I'll be ready. Maybe I don't have all the pieces of paper that are so important for so many people, but I've got the knowledge,' he pressed his forefinger to his temple, 'in here. And,' he continued, 'I've got the contacts. I try to learn from the people I meet, from the situations I'm forced into, and from the mistakes I make. I watch and I listen. Maybe you should think about doing the same.'

'I'm past the age of studying.' Frank kept his eyes fixed on Sol as he sipped cautiously from his glass.

'You think life is like your accounting books,' Sol mocked. 'That if you sit down and fool with your calculator for long enough then all the numbers will balance up at the bottom of the page. Well, life's not like that, my friend. We don't always get the numbers we want and the sums don't always add up.' He opened the bottle and filled both glasses up again. 'People aren't numbers you can just rub out when you decide they're not part of the equation any more. Or start a new page because you made a mess of the last one. People keep coming back.'

'All right.' Frank knocked his drink back in one and

reached for the bottle. 'Since you want to talk about Rose so much. Talk. I'm listening.'

'Rose is like me in some ways,' Sol started, then smiled at Frank's surprised expression.

'You and Rose?' Frank said incredulously. 'What? I mean, how?'

'I said alike not the same. I guess like recognizes like. We both want to come out on top, we both go our own way, but I suppose what links us most is that we believe in things we can't see, only sense. Chance, coincidence, what some people would call fate, destiny – call it what you will. I think that some things are meant to be and that no matter what happens, or how you try to avoid it, it's going to happen anyway in some way or other. You remember the night we met her?' Frank nodded. 'How I told you one was too big for you and the other was too much? You thought I wanted them both, but I was just trying to warn you. Rose had you marked as her man from the moment she saw you. What she saw I still don't know.'

'Thanks,' Frank said.

'You know I don't mean it like that,' Sol replied impatiently, 'but did she ever say anything?'

Frank shook his head, his forehead creased in horizontal lines as he thought. 'She just said that I was the one. Whenever I asked her how she was so sure, she just said that her grandmother had described me to her.'

'Nothing else?'

'Only that when I opened my eyes and saw what there was to be seen then I'd know the truth of what she was saying.'

'*Open your eyes*.' Sol laughed ruefully. 'Looks like she talks sense from time to time. It's what I've been telling you for years.'

'Everybody says open your eyes but nobody says what I'm supposed to be looking for or looking at.'

'When you really want to see, you won't need anyone to tell you what to look for. Like those movements Jewelle said Rose made. What do you think they meant?'

'I don't know.' Frank pushed out his bottom lip. 'Sounded like she was blowing kisses.'

'Rose? Blowing kisses!' Sol stared at him as if he were an idiot. 'You better drink some more rum.'

'I didn't say I thought she was, I said it sounded like she was.'

'You want to know what she was doing?' Sol held the bottle up. Frank put his hand over the top of his glass. 'When you hear what I have to say you'll want more than a glass.' He moved Frank's fingers and filled up his glass. 'Junior!' he shouted. 'Bring another bottle an' two plates of whatever yuh cookin' today.'

'Red snapper and steam vegetable!' Junior shouted back.

'All right,' he told him, 'just mek sure my fish have plenty pepper.'

'So?'

'Death Wish Breeze.'

'Death wish what?'

'Death Wish Breeze.'

Heat, dry as the inside of a hot oven, engulfed them as soon as they stepped from the bus. Jewelle stopped and turned her baseball cap around so that its peak faced the back and kept the sun off the nape of her neck. As they strolled the short distance from the road to the beach she felt a trickle of sweat roll down the hollow between her breasts. She plucked the front of her dress away from her chest and blew down it in an attempt to cool off. When they got to the beach she slipped off her sandals. The sand wasn't pale like she'd expected but like fine brown sugar; and she was surprised at the amount of twigs and litter at her feet.

'It's covered in rubbish,' she said.

'Dat's 'cause dis is a public beach. Beach just de same but cleaner round de other part, but yuh haffi pay before dem let yuh in. If yuh waan see some real nice beaches yuh should check Negril or Buff Bay, or one a dem place.'

Jewelle shaded her eyes as she looked along the length of the beach. To her right, the sea stretched as far as she could see. The staggered coastline, covered with dense vegetation, looked like a green staircase. To her left were a line of beach stands; the bases made from vegetable crates clumsily tacked together. Spindly frames rose up, supporting equally spindly and uneven roofs, giving the impression that the whole structure would fall down with one good puff of breath. About halfway up each stand, a wooden plank used to display wares ran across. A few of the stands were freshly painted, but on most of them only a few sun-dried flakes of paint hinted at their original colour. On display were necklaces and bracelets made from shells and coral; simple ceramic pots of beige and dark brown; and multi-coloured T-shirts, souvenirs of a Jamaican holiday.

Some traders chose to display their wares directly on the beach. Carvings of Bob Marley, turtles, pipes and fishes, and wooden pipes and amulets. Lines of intricately carved walking sticks made of cherry-brown and golden wood stood upright in the sand like a rigid line of gateposts. A naked toddler took a wooden pipe from a selection of the objects on display and started to dig a hole with it in the sand. He played quietly; his face showing the concentration of the very young when absorbed in something adults might not approve of. When his father realized why his son was so quiet he tucked the boy under one arm, surreptitiously shook the sand out of the pipe and quickly put it back among the other things before the vendor noticed. The child set up a loud wail when he realized his toy had been confiscated. His father hoisted him onto his shoulders and the child's wails turned into gurgles of laughter as his father galloped with him to the edge of the sea.

Jewelle and Jake strolled along the length of the beach, occasionally brushing arms. They passed women patiently plaiting the hair of tourists who wanted to adopt the local look, and more stands selling jewellery.

'Isn't this pretty?' Jewelle held up a necklace of pink knot-like shells carefully strung together.

'Is all right.' Jake shrugged his shoulders, feigning disinterest.

A youth with a mane of lion hair twisted into locks, and the start of a scrubby beard around his jawline, appeared from behind a basket stall. Lean and wiry, his muscles were clearly defined. A square gold pendant hung from a black shoelace around his neck. He pulled a spliff from the pocket of his knee-length blue shorts and lit up. As he caught sight of Jewelle he started to sing, 'Let de weed legalize.' She turned around and he danced towards her singing, 'Herb free, herb free, herb free.' His teeth flashed white as he sang and danced in front of her, making up the words to the song as he went along.

Jake turned away from the rings and necklaces he'd been inspecting and appeared at Jewelle's side. A look passed between the two young men, and the singing youth turned his attention to a tourist with a video camera and went into overdrive, weaving his way among the tourists and strutting the stretch of beach like a pop star.

People joined in with his 'herb free' chorus, moving in time to his simple tune. Another youth with cropped hair joined in, adding a rap dimension to the song with a chant of 'burn de weed'. He waved his spliff in time to the rhythm as he sang. The other vendors smiled but otherwise ignored them – they were used to shows of this kind and didn't have time to waste. There was money to be made, especially now the tourists were in a good mood – less inclined to haggle and more disposed to buy.

The last thing Jewelle heard as she and Jake walked towards the sea was the dreadlocked youth announcing 'dis a live someting' and the crowd clapping their appreciation as he broke into another improvised song.

'Race you in.' Jewelle was already pulling off her dress.

'Right in?' Jake sounded doubtful as he stood at the water's edge. 'It all right here.'

She stuffed her things into her backpack before running into the water. When she looked round Jake had taken his T-shirt off but otherwise hadn't moved. She beckoned him on. He took a couple of steps forward until the water lapped around his ankles.

'C'mon!' She waved him forward. He took another step then stopped abruptly. She waded back towards him. 'The water's really warm, what're you waiting for?'

Jake looked around helplessly. Behind him, a group of Jamaicans watched the scene with interest. He shuddered.

Jewelle held her hand out towards him. 'C'mon.'

He reached out for her hand and tried to ignore the voice that shouted from the beach bar behind them, 'Mind dat likkle gyal nuh drown yuh.'

Jewelle walked backwards, her eyes encouraging him on. He took three more steps before blurting out, 'Me cyaan swim.'

She pulled up short. 'But you live by the sea!'

'So!' He dropped her hand. They stared at each other. 'Yuh tink is me one cyaan swim? Why yuh tink everybody back up where it shallow?'

For the first time Jewelle noticed the distribution of the people in the sea. How the Jamaicans stood mainly in ankle-deep water or sat by the shore, close enough to the sea to get their legs wet when baby waves came in, but nothing else. Not one of them was more than waist deep in

206

water. Way beyond her only the tourists frolicked and played in water deep enough to cover their heads.

'I'll teach you. If you like. Over there.' She jerked her head. 'Away from these people.'

'Me nuh waan drown.'

'Ah don' waan yuh fi drown neither.' She smiled. 'See? I'm learning too.'

'Sam. Is me. Beatrice. Call me back quick.' She put down the receiver and waited tensely for Sam to ring back. Miss Jess was still sleeping and she didn't want the phone to disturb her.

'How's everything? Funeral go all right?'

'Rose come!' Aunt B announced.

'Well, bet dat did add a likkle spice to de proceedings,' he chuckled. 'So wh'appen?'

'Nutten. Is Jewelle see her. Seh Rose wave den leave.'

'She talk to yuh or Frank?'

'No. She never chat to nobody. Just watch de burial from behind de wall.'

'Funny she go to all dat effort just fi wave at yuh,' Sam said thoughtfully. 'Leastways she never come fi cause trouble,' he added reassuringly.

'Wish I could believe dat. But me worried,' Aunt B admitted. 'Feel in me bones trouble soon come. Bet she waan revenge.'

'Revenge?'

'Yuh know how Rose vengeful. If I did give Frank dat letter she send, den she wouldn't a come to de funeral lookin' fi me.'

'Whoa! Slow down!'

Aunt B could imagine Sam on the other end of the line, holding up one hand and with his mouth stretched out, the way it always did when he thought she was running ahead of herself.

207

'First of all, who seh she come lookin' fi yuh? Second, yuh don' know if Frank woulda even reply to her letter.'

'But she write an' tell him 'bout de baby!'

'Third,' Sam continued, 'how yuh know if she even have baby? After all, nobody ever seh she have pickney after Frank gone, an' yuh know how we love chat other people business. She write tell *yuh* she pregnant wid Frank baby. Maybe it was jus' excuse fi get yuh fi help her. Yuh don' know fi sure wha' she write to Frank. Coulda been someting completely different.'

'I wish . . .' Aunt B started.

'What? Yuh wish yuh did lissen to me when I beg yuh not to interfere? When I seh give de letter to Frank like Rose ask yuh to an' let tings take dem course?'

'But what could I do? Beth was my sister. Already pregnant fi Frank an' de wedding less dan two weeks away. Yuh tink I was goin' to mek Rose mash up everyting? Deprive Jewelle of her daddy?'

'Only yuh tink it would have,' Uncle Sam interrupted. 'Frank did love Beth. Nobody did have any doubt 'bout dat. Me sure him woulda married Beth no matter what Rose write.' He paused for a moment before repeating the words he'd said so many times before. 'Let it go. Look to de future an' stop live inna de past.'

'Is de future dat frighten me.'

'Stop it!' he said firmly. 'Is not 'fraid yuh 'fraid, is guilty yuh feel guilty 'cause yuh never do right by Rose. Yuh did what yuh tink was best at de time. Nutten more, nutten less. Even if yuh could turn back de clock, me sure yuh woulda do de same ting again.'

'Yes.' Her response was unhesitating.

'So wha' de point talk 'bout dis? Dis conversation cyaan change nutten. If yuh really waan do someting, go talk to Rose. Tell her wha' yuh did an' why. After all dis time she probably understand, even if she don' forgive yuh.'

'Yuh waan *me* fi talk to Rose! Tell her I help keep Frank from her? Yuh mussi mad!'

'Why? Wha' wrong wid dat?' Sam said impatiently. 'Better dan tellin' me de same ting every two month.'

'Yuh don' know women,' she muttered.

'Wha' dat?'

'Yuh don' know Rose,' Aunt B replied simply.

'Watch me!' Jake's arms moved erratically as if he had no control over them, splashing water everywhere. 'Me a swim.' But the moment he spoke he sank. 'I was,' he spluttered as he came up for air. He shook his head ruefully, little locks spinning around his face, sending hundreds of drops of water spraying up into the air around him.

'I don't know about swimming,' Jewelle said, laughing indulgently, 'but you were floating. You can't swim without getting your face wet, you know.'

She watched him try again, arms flailing and head arched back well away from the water. When he stood up she scooped water up in the palms of her hands and threw it into his face. He moved towards her, splashing her as he walked so that she cringed and half turned as she covered her face. When he was near she turned around quickly and splashed him as hard as she could, giggling as he wiped his eyes. Then he was after her, catching her by the waist and spinning her round. They laughed together, faces streaming with seawater. He twirled her round again so that her feet were out of the water, she shrieked loudly and her hands slipped around his neck.

Later, try as she might, she couldn't recall the exact moment that the game became serious. One moment they were laughing and joking together; the next, his face was serious. Purposeful. They were standing so close that she could feel the line of his body against her own. She saw the drops of water balanced delicately on the tips of his curling black eyelashes. Her eyelids felt heavy, too heavy to keep open and she let them close slowly. Her plaits fell through his splayed fingers as his hand gently cradled the back of her head. The short hairs on his chin and the side of his cheeks tickled the smooth skin of her face. His mouth when it touched hers was soft, yet firm. Warm, it clung to hers. His tongue pried its way into her mouth; she welcomed it. His lips moved on hers, drawing and holding her before reluctantly setting her free. Even when he stood back from her, she could still feel the imprint of his lips on hers. When she opened her eyes, his expression was difficult to read. She traced the line of his lips with her fingertips before touching her own lips gently.

'Me shouldn't do dat.' He gently stroked her hairline scar, then played with the ends of her plaits. 'Not wid all dese people a fas' inna we business.'

'They don't matter.'

'Dat's wha' yuh tink. Yuh don' know how tings go here. People love carry-go-bring-come.'

Jewelle frowned, not certain what he meant.

'Look,' he said trying to explain, 'we have a saying: "Likkle bit a someting, me tek tell aunty. Aunty run tell cousin, cousin run tell uncle, uncle run tell bredda, till it become one big someting." Me nuh waan cause yuh no problem, yuh understand?'

'That was my first real kiss.'

He smiled at her and cupped her face in his hands.

'Death Wish Breeze is a sign of impending death.' Sol sliced into his fish serenely as if they were talking about the latest West Indian Test victory.

Frank stared at him, willing him on, but Sol chewed away, dabbing occasionally at his mouth with a paper napkin.

'The fish is good.' He pointed at Frank's plate with his knife. 'Better eat it before it goes cold.'

'Sol!' Frank pushed his plate away impatiently and leaned forward with his elbows on the table.

'All you need to know is that the movements of the arm are designed to link the "victim" to the "sender". All that entwining,' Sol moved his arms quickly in demonstration and a piece of fish flew off his knife, 'bind the two together. The tighter the arms the closer the bond. Death Wish Breeze is when the hands are cupped and the person blows through them. When the "victim" feels this breeze physically it's an indication that they're in danger. When the breeze is strong, it means death is close.' Sol speared a piece of potato. 'Unless the "sender" is stopped of course.' He popped the potato in his mouth and looked directly at Frank, his eyes wide open, the expression ingenuous.

'Are you trying to tell me that Rose, if that's who it was, is going to blow my mother to death? No, no, man. Can't believe that, Sol.' Frank's laugh was high with relief. 'That one's too far-fetched even for you.'

Sol shrugged his shoulders and looked at Frank's plate. 'Aren't you going to eat any of it?'

Frank shook his head and pushed the plate towards Sol.

'Hate to see good food going to waste,' he said as he scraped the fish and a few of the vegetables onto his plate.

'Is that it, then?'

'I've told you what you need to know. All I have left to say is: bury your past.'

'What're you saying, Sol?' Frank's voice was serious. 'That I should go and kill Rose? Bury her that way?'

'Dry ground's too good for her in my opinion. I know what I'd do.' The expression in Sol's eyes was ambiguous.

'So, what would you do?' Frank asked curiously.

'I'm me and you're you.' Sol shrugged. 'How you choose to deal with it is up to you.'

'I don't even know where to start looking.' Frank spoke half to himself.

'Stop making excuses, Frank.' Sol wiped his mouth on the crumpled paper napkin. 'You know how bad Rose can be.'

'I know,' Frank said with feeling. 'That woman marked me for life!'

Jewelle walked backwards for a while as they left the beach. The play of light made the whole scene look like an elaborately designed theatre set. The hulk of a rusting ship, once used for transporting bauxite, now took on the appearance of a deep-rose yacht. The line of palm trees in the distance looked like a superimposed shadowy silhouette in the fading light, and the branches of the Fancy Ants tree, which Jake had pointed out earlier, seemed draped with short wrinkly brown snakes. The setting sun cast dark gold shadows over the incoming tide so that the gentle waves looked like rippling molten bronze. Her camera was in her rucksack but she preferred to let her eyes memorize the scene to add to the store of memories of a day she knew she'd never forget.

Rose sat perched on the veranda rail, her knees drawn up under her chin. She had no idea of the time and didn't care. She drank steadily although the beer was warm. Her mind ran like a video recorder, pausing and rewinding moments of loving with Frank; fast forwarding scenes of disagreement and discontent. The more she thought about him the stronger her desire to see him became. He hadn't noticed her at the funeral, but his mother had.

The other night hadn't been enough – over much too soon, and she'd lost her temper. But she'd had two days to calm down now. She didn't want Frank thinking she was still quick-tempered. There had to be some way of letting him see that she was calmer, had changed. She swigged from the bottle, pensively.

If me was Frank me wouldn't tell Miss Jess nutten 'bout me visit, but I wonder if Miss Jess gwine tell him I turn up at de funeral. Me nuh tink so. Frank is Miss Jess only son. Bet she waan keep him to herself, keep him from de woman him love. Probably only tell him me around when him at de airport. Me cyaan mek dat happen. Won't mek it happen. Ah know him still waan me. See how him respond to me de other night? Is stop him stop himself 'cause him feel guilty 'bout him madda, but me sure we can fix dat. Nuh have much time though, she mused. Wha' Frank tell Benny? Dat him here fi ten days? Who know how long him already here? Him could all due fi leave tomorrow.

Rose reached for another Red Stripe, but they were all gone. That seemed to make up her mind, and she got to her feet. There was no time to lose, she had to see Frank. She'd go and look for him now.

'Come in, Jewelle. Come sit down.'

She lay on the bed next to her grandmother. 'You look well, Granny.'

'I am. Yuh not looking too bad yuhself. Any special reason?'

Jewelle smiled, but didn't reply. How could she explain these strange new sensations? She couldn't talk to Aunt B about boys, and even though up until recently she'd been able to talk to her father about almost anything, she suspected he wouldn't be such a willing listener if Jake were the topic. Anyway, he'd been looking increasingly worried over the past few days and she didn't want to add to his problems. Her grandmother was a completely different generation and Jamaican; she doubted very much that she could talk to her either.

'It have someting fi do wid Jake?'

'What? How did you –?' Jewelle's face cracked into a surprised smile.

'Me old. Me don' have nutten fi do but watch people.'

'He's wonderful,' she said, her voice full of fifteen-year-old feeling.

'Wha' so wonderful 'bout him?'

'Don't you know? Can't you see?' she replied, surprised that everybody else didn't share her infatuation. 'He's gorgeous! And he's funny.'

'An' dat mek him wonderful? Yuh barely know him.'

'I know that,' she said a little impatiently, 'but don't you think you can meet somebody and know straight away that they're special?'

'I'm not saying dat, Jewelle. Me like Jake.' Miss Jess patted the girl's hand reassuringly. 'But den, I know him fi over two years. Not everybody yuh meet is wha' dem seem. Some people pretend to be wha' yuh waan till dem get wha' dem waan. Yuh understan' me?'

'Yes, but Jake's not like that.'

'Me never say him was. Me just sayin' yuh haffi give yuhself time fi get fi know people. I tink yuh honest an' show yuh feelin's. Dat's good, but it also mek yuh prey to people who not like dat, so yuh haffi be careful. Mek people show dem worthy of yuh feelin's an' yuh trust. Mek dem earn yuh respect.'

'And how am I supposed to do that?'

'I don' have de answers. Everybody haffi do it dem own way.'

'Yeah, but where do I start?'

'Don' put yuhself above other people an' act like yuh superior. Don' say "yes" when yuh mean no an' nuh say "it all right" when it not. Learn fi ask fi wha' yuh waan calmly but firmly. Give an' expect respec'.' Miss Jess wagged her finger to emphasize her point. 'Yuh nuh haffi jump up an' down an' mek a scene. De minute yuh start shout "respec' me, respec' me" yuh lose de battle. Who yuh tink will respec' yuh when dem can see yuh nuh

214

respec' yuhself? Expec' not demand respec'. Yuh see wha' me ah try seh?'

'I think so.'

'An' don' try live yuh life how Jake or some other bwoy –'

'Another boy!'

'Anybody! – man or woman – say yuh should. Live how yuh feel yuh should. But always wid dignity an' pride.'

'I . . . I . . . let him kiss me.' She kept her eyes downcast.

'Dat nuh nutten. Is how yuh behave before, during an' after de kiss dat important. Was it wid dignity?'

Jewelle frowned. What was dignity for Granny? She nodded. 'Yes, I think so.' After all, they'd only kissed and held hands. She nodded again, this time more firmly, and looked up. 'I think he behaved with dignity too. He wouldn't kiss me again even though I sort of . . . wanted him to . . . said he didn't want to cause me any problems.'

'Dat good. Look like him already respec' yuh, so nuh badda lose it now yuh have it. Wha' yuh feelin' is normal, but tek yuh time. Nuh badda run ahead. Let tings develop naturally an' what meant to happen will happen as an' when it should.'

'Sometimes I wish Mum was here to talk to.'

'I know, chile. I know. But 'member yuh madda did love yuh enough to honour her contrac' wid yuh.'

'Contract? What contract?'

'Yuh spiritual contrac'. Beth love yuh enough to give yuh up early so yuh could learn de lessons yuh have to. Lessons yuh can only learn widout her in order to grow into de woman yuh meant to be. If she never die, yuh wouldn't learn de tings dat yuh need fi dis life.'

'Spiritual contract?' Jewelle repeated, frowning. 'What's that?'

'I believe dat children an' parents choose one another. A spiritual contrac' is an agreement a chile mek wid him parents before him born. It mean yuh choose yuh family, when an' where yuh born, if yuh have brothers an' sisters, if yuh parents divorce or not – all kinda tings which together help create de circumstances yuh need fi help yuh grow in dis life.'

'I don't understand,' Jewelle said.

'All right,' Miss Jess said, 'mek me try it dis way. Maybe yuh were too dependent or easily led in a past life, so dis time round yuh might be an orphan an' haffi fend fi yuhself.'

'So does that mean an orphan chooses to be an orphan?'

'Yes an' no.' Miss Jess smiled. 'I know dat soun' like contradiction but as soon as yuh born yuh figet de agreement.'

'Well, that sounds stupid!' Miss Jess raised her eyebrows and stared at her in silence. 'Sorry, Granny,' Jewelle said after a moment, 'I didn't mean to be rude. Go on.'

'Who pay attention in class if dem tink dem already know de answers?'

'Huh?'

'If a student tink him know it all him don' bother lissenin'. Look,' Miss Jess spoke more quickly as if she had a lot to get through. 'Maybe yuh were intolerant in a past life so yuh have a chile who is a drug addict for example; or yuh were a racist, so dis time round yuh born black. Life's a bit like a test where deep down yuh know de answers but yuh can never 'member dem when yuh have to, so yuh end up just a work it through.'

'So, I'm black because I was a racist before?'

'Not necessarily. All it mean is dat is yuh choose to be a first-generation black girl growin' up widout a mother or brother an' sister in Britain for some reason specific to yuh development. I don' know de reasons for dat choice any more dan yuh. De point is dat Beth honour fi her part.'

This all felt new and strange, and didn't really make sense for Jewelle, but she didn't want to hurt her grand-

216

mother's feelings by saying so. She decided to think about it some more later; for now she'd just listen and try to accept it.

'But I feel so lonely sometimes,' Jewelle said eventually, 'even when I'm with other people. It's as if –' she bit her bottom lip '– I don't really belong anywhere. Like I don't really fit in. And sometimes it makes me so angry – that I don't have anyone to talk to.' Her eyes sparkled with unshed tears.

Miss Jess stroked her granddaughter's face. 'Yuh madda is dere for yuh when yuh need her. All yuh haffi do is call her.'

'It's funny, I don't even remember her really, but sometimes I feel she's close.'

'She is. Yuh just have to believe it. Yuh born wid caul –'

'Caul? What's that?'

'Some babies born wid a thin membrane covering dem head and face.'

'Ugh! I must have looked like a monster when I came out!'

Jewelle looked so disgusted that Miss Jess burst out laughing. 'Yuh only favour monster when yuh screw up yuh face like dat!'

'But it sounds like something out of a horror film.'

'It natural. Some baby born wid hair, some born wid teeth – yuh born wid a caul, dat's all. Anyway,' she continued, 'we believe it mek de chile more sensitive dan most.'

'Does it?' Jewelle interrupted excitedly. 'Does that mean I'm special?'

'It mean,' Miss Jess said firmly, 'dat it mek yuh life more difficult sometimes, specially when yuh young – mek yuh sense tings yuh cyaan explain.' Jewelle nodded in relieved recognition. 'But,' Miss Jess continued, 'it also give yuh an advantage, so nuh waste it. When yuh head sayin' one ting an' yuh gut sayin' someting else, lissen to dat gut feelin', den decide if yuh head wrong. Dat feelin' dere fi a reason. Use it.'

'Whenever I feel like that,' Jewelle said, playing with her grandmother's fingers, 'I want to tell someone. But I don't, because I think they'll think that I'm stupid or mad.'

Miss Jess chuckled. 'Well, if yuh stupid or mad, I don't know what people woulda call me.'

They laughed together. Eventually Jewelle spoke, breaking the silence that had fallen. 'I wish you lived with us.'

'Me here fi yuh whenever yuh need me.'

'But it's not the same. I can't talk to Aunt B like this or even Dad.'

'Dat's 'cause I'm yuh gran'madda. When tings get difficult me can pass yuh back to yuh daddy an' mek him deal wid it. Is me have de easy part. I know if I did have a daughter yuh age, I couldn't talk wid her like dis. Is de fact yuh is me gran'daughter mek it easy fi me to talk to yuh like we talkin' now.'

'Jewelle?' The voice came from the back of the house.

'Yuh aunty lookin' fi yuh.'

'But I want to stay here with you.'

''Member wha' I say 'bout respec'?'

Jewelle grinned ruefully. 'Yeah.' She slid off the bed and smoothed down her skirt. 'Can I come and talk to you again tomorrow if you're not too tired?'

'Yuh can come an' talk to me whenever yuh like, darlin'. Yuh can even talk to me when me not here.'

Rose paced the outside perimeter of Miss Jess's garden, uncertain what to do next. All she knew was that she couldn't let Frank slip out of her life for a second time. Maybe she could talk to Miss Jess. All right, so de woman don' like me, but Frank is a man now an' not just her likkle bwoy. It would also be to Miss Jess's advantage, Rose reasoned, to give her blessing to her relationship with Frank. At least that way Frank would stay on the island – they could even pretend that he'd decided to stay for his mother's sake only.

Who dat likkle dry old lady have now, anyway? Nobody! Her husband dead an' bury an' she herself cyaan have much longer till she join him. Me sure she waan live out her last few years knowin' dat her only chile come home fi her? Me nuh mind, me an' Frank will know de truth an' to hell wid other people. De way I see it, she thought as she walked, every dog have him day.

She stopped in her tracks. She must have circled the property at least three times, but didn't seem able to walk up the path. It was as if there was an invisible barrier holding her back, one she didn't have the strength to get past. Obviously a sign, she decided. The wrong moment for the chat she had in mind. Miss Jess was probably still in shock from seeing her at yesterday's funeral and she didn't want to kill her with her sudden appearance; although, she mused, it would have saved a lot of time all round if the old lady had died years ago. Her hands clenched at the thought and she made herself stand still and breathe deeply until the tension left her body. She'd waited years for this moment. A few hours more when she was so close couldn't hurt.

8

19th February

Aunt B stared at the ground, puzzlement clear on her face.
She turned slowly, then stooped to examine the light layer
of dust that covered the speckled red-tiled floor of the
veranda. There was dust everywhere, even on the windowsills. She rubbed a little of it between her fingertips; it was
grainy, with a yellowy tinge and didn't look like normal
dust at all. She grabbed the yard broom, the one Jewelle
called a witch's broomstick, and swept the floor vigorously
before turning her attention to the windowsills and their
hidden corners. Yellow dust clouds went flying up into the
air. She sneezed loudly and turned her head to one side as
she quickly collected the last of the dust and threw it into
the bin. As she washed her hands she made a mental note
to talk to Nancy the next time she saw her – the girl wasn't
doing her job properly.

Now that mess was cleaned up there was nothing left to
do, at least nothing that couldn't wait. Aunt B pulled up
one of the veranda chairs, positioned it so the sun wouldn't
hit her directly and sat down. For the first time since she'd
arrived she had a moment to herself. Miss Jess was
sleeping, Jewelle had taken herself off to phone Ambra,
and Frank had gone to the travel agents to see if he could
get Miss Jess a seat on their flight back. Aunt B hadn't even
bothered to question this sudden change of plan. Frank
had seemed charged with a strange energy ever since the

funeral and perhaps this, together with Miss Jess's very obvious vulnerability, had done more to make up his mind than all her nagging had. She closed her eyes and relaxed, smiling to herself as the sun caressed her face. It was beginning to look as if all her worrying had been for nothing.

'Ambra? It's me. Jewelle.'

'Jewelle!'

'Ambra!'

'Where are you?' Ambra squealed.

'In Jamaica, of course.'

'I know that, fool. But where?'

'Phone box. Outside Charlie's. Look, I don't know how long this phone card's going to last so I'll have to talk quickly.'

'Charlie's? You've met somebody? Already? Wicked!' Ambra's voice was high with surprise. 'Who is he?'

'Wait! You've got it wrong.' Jewelle tried to interrupt, but Ambra was like a runaway train. There was nothing else to do but let her run out of steam.

'What's he like? Where is he? Put him on, I want to speak to him. Just wait till I tell Dan.'

Jewelle tapped her fingers on the receiver impatiently and rested her forehead on the sun-warmed glass of the phone box as she waited.

'Go on, then. Tell me something,' Ambra eventually said. 'It's me doing all the talking here, you know.'

'I know.'

'So, what's Charlie like?' Ambra persisted.

'First of all, Charlie's is the local department store.'

'Oh!' Ambra groaned with disappointment. 'You're having me on, aren't you? Haven't you met anybody, then?'

'Well . . .'

'You have, haven't you?'

'Don't really want to talk about it right now.'

'God. Must be someone special if you don't even want to tell me anything about him. All right,' she said after a second, 'I can wait. But just give me a little clue. Please. Anything. Just so I've got something to go on.'

'Ambra! I'm not calling about that. It's just that so many things have happened since I arrived I've just got to tell you.' She spoke quickly, describing Miss Jess, Sol and all the things she'd seen and heard until she'd filled her friend in on the events leading up to the appearance of the mysterious woman at the funeral.

'Wow!' Ambra exclaimed. 'It's so exciting. You've only been away five days and look at all the things that have happened. God, I wish I were you. Your life is so interesting.'

'Who do you think the mystery woman is?'

'I dunno. I'm not there, am I?' There was silence for a moment as Ambra considered what she'd just heard. 'Well, what you need to do –' she started.

'What?' interrupted Jewelle.

'Give me a chance, will you? You need to be a detective.'

'A detective?'

'Stop repeating everything I say! Listen. You're always going on about wanting to be a journalist. Well, now's your chance. Journalists have to go out and investigate. Go out and investigate.'

'Investigate what? All I know is that her name's Rose, but nobody will tell me anything else.' She didn't tell Ambra of her vague suspicions about who this woman could be. The less her family told her the more she found herself watching and listening, just as Sol had told her to when she'd first met him.

'Mysterious, very mysterious.' Ambra broke in on her thoughts. 'There's a secret there somewhere, you just need to find out what it is. You've got five days left. See what you can discover.'

'How?'

'Jewelle!' Ambra said in exasperation. 'D'you want me to do everything for you? Talk to people. Ask Aunt B for a start, she always knows what's going on.'

'Aunt B will just say "dis a big people business", you know what she's like.'

'True,' Ambra admitted. 'What about your gran?'

'She's not feeling well. I can't really bother her about something like that.'

'Try Sexy Sol then?'

'Sexy Sol? I didn't say he was sexy.'

'Yeah, I know. But from the way you described him he sounds seriously cool, even if he is old. Try him.'

'I suppose I could.' Jewelle giggled despite herself. 'You're mad, and I'm just as mad for listening to you.' She scratched at the arm that was getting all the sun and changed position again. 'Look, we're going to get cut off any moment now,' she warned as a voice informed her she had thirty seconds of credit left.

'Go on. Give me a clue, quick,' Ambra begged.

''Bout what?'

'About him. Pork or Beef?'

'I'm in Jamaica!'

'So? It's full of tourists, isn't it?'

'Beef. National. Prime.'

'Lucky thing. Wish I was –'

The line went dead in Jewelle's hand, cutting off whatever Ambra had been about to say.

Aunt B nodded, satisfied. Miss Jess had managed to drink several spoons of Cock soup. Packet made – there hadn't been time to prepare anything else – but warming and nutritious nevertheless. Now Miss Jess lay propped up

223

against two pillows, her eyes staring way into the distance. She sat obediently as Aunt B carefully and gently washed her. The warm water seemed to revive her, for she smiled her thanks at the woman in front of her.

'Did have yuh all worried. Nuh true?' she whispered.

'Just a likkle,' Aunt B conceded. 'Maybe later when Frank come back, we can move yuh into de sittin' room an' turn de bed round.'

'Don't worry 'bout dat. Poppa Ben never hurt me in life, sure seh him nah go start now him dead. Is live people we haffi watch out for. Specially those we tink gone long time.'

'How yuh mean?'

'She come to me last night.'

Aunt B froze. The facecloth she held fell into the bowl on the floor, but she was oblivious to the water splashing onto her sandals as a memory of Beth flashed to her mind, clear as if it had happened only yesterday . . .

'She come to me last night,' Beth said. 'Yuh friend in de photograph yuh did show me.'

'Who yuh talkin' 'bout, Beth?'

'Cyaan 'member her name, but is de clear-eye gyal from town – de seamstress.'

'Rose?'

'Yeah. Same one. She come to me last night . . .'

Beth had said those very same words before, twice in fact. And then what had happened? The first time, Jewelle had mysteriously fallen down steps she'd never fallen down before, knocked out two of her milk teeth and ended up with six stitches in her hairline. The second time, Beth had got knocked down by a car. Nothing too serious – a cracked rib and mild concussion. But while she was in

224

hospital Beth's test results had come through, results that showed she had cancer.

Pure coincidence, Sam had said, and whenever she tried to talk about it he pulled the face he pulled when his false teeth hurt and he wasn't in the mood for company. In the end she'd given up trying.

'Rose?' Her voice trembled. 'Rose? she said again, this time more firmly.

'She visit me,' Miss Jess repeated.

'In yuh dream?' Aunt B asked.

'Claim she have score fi sekkle,' Miss Jess continued as if she hadn't heard the question. 'I only meet her de one time. Franklin never bring her back an' I never ask 'bout her. Poppa Ben did try talk to him, but yuh know how stubborn Franklin can be and we never waan lose we only son. Yuh know how many baby me carry an' lose before me have Franklin? Couldn't tek dat chance.' She shook her head. 'When him say him goin' to Englan', I did cry. Cry 'cause I was goin' to lose him anyway, but at least I know him would be safe over dere. Why yuh tink we help him pay him passage? Away from Rose him have a chance . . . to have a life, a family. Be a man. Wid Rose . . .' she pressed her lips together and looked down at her hands.

'Yuh see dese two han'?' She held her hands up in the air. Aunt B clasped them in hers and gasped at how hot and dry they were. 'If me did have me time again,' Miss Jess said, 'I woulda wring dat damn gyal neck. First time roun' me too 'fraid. "Thou shalt not kill," it write in black an' white in de Bible. I couldn't break de Lord sacred commandment. Now me old and dese han' dem too weak.' Aunt B gently squeezed the hands she held.

'If me did have me time again,' Miss Jess repeated. 'I woulda bruk dat commandment an' face God when Him come. And if Him ask me why me do it, I woulda tell Him me birth my son once, but me give him life twice.'

Tears rolled down her thin cheeks as she spoke and Aunt B gathered her to her chest where the tears fell and were lost.

Rose turned slightly to attract the barman's attention, then quickly clutched at the bar counter for support as the top of the barstool wobbled unexpectedly. She tipped herself forward and fumbled under the base of the seat with her free hand. When her seeking fingers confirmed that two of the four screws that attached the seat to its stand were missing, she sat upright.

'Hey!' she shouted to the barman. 'Dis damn stool nearly kill me! Me must get a drink fi dat.' She held her glass up and looked around as she waited. Club 54, which was not a club at all, but a bar with pretensions, had been practically empty when she walked in. Now it was filling up with early evening customers. The regulars stared with some curiosity at the woman sitting alone at the counter.

'Wha' yuh doin' later?' the bartender asked, opening a bottle of white rum.

'Depend on wha' happenin' later.' Rose smiled at him from under her eyelashes. The look in her eyes encouraged him and he filled her glass to the brim.

'Well,' he said slowly, 'dat up to yuh.' He leaned towards her. 'Allow me to introduce myself. Me name Mikey. Me shift soon finish an' de night young.'

'Younger dan yuh, dat's fi sure,' she joked.

'Young man, dem come and go.' He flapped a hand dismissively. 'Yuh cyaan trust dem. An older man,' his voice took on a lower, more confidential tone, 'an older man more constant – him come fi stop.'

'Dat if him come at all,' Rose mumbled into her drink before knocking it back in one.

'Wha' yuh seh?' He raised the bottle again.

'Yuh invitin' me to all dese drinks?'

'Darlin', me invitin' yuh to anyting yuh waan.' He ogled her, his eyes fixed on her cleavage.

'All right. Leave de bottle mek me tink 'bout it.'

'Is dat a yes?' He held the bottle out of reach.

'Is not a no.' Her eyes challenged him.

She prime an' she ready fi it, he thought quickly as he held her gaze. A few drinks won' cost me anyting an' might mek her more agreeable – wha' me haffi lose?

A little further along the counter a customer hissed at him impatiently and he shot the man a sour look. 'Check yuh later,' he said, leering at Rose as he put the bottle down in front of her. 'A who yuh a hiss after?' he demanded, moving towards the customer. 'Me look like puss to yuh?'

'How me look now?'

'Yuh look lovely, Miss Jess.' Aunt B rubbed the end of the final plait between her finger and thumb. It sprang up into a comma-like curl as soon as she let it go.

'Mek me see.'

Aunt B placed the square wooden-framed mirror that normally sat on top of the dresser, in front of Miss Jess. She gripped it tightly as she peered at her reflection, then she smiled, pleased.

'Pass me one a dem grip dem.'

Aunt B handed her a brown hairgrip that had long since lost its original shape. Miss Jess used it to scratch the side of her head while she held on to the mirror with her other hand.

'Poppa Ben did always like my hair like dis.' She smiled at her reflection again. 'Him woulda please,' she added under her breath.

'Wha' dat?'

'Jus' say me please fi see yuh again an' I grateful fi every-ting yuh do fi me an' de family. No, lissen.' She rushed to continue before Aunt B could interrupt. 'I know yuh an'

Frank nuh always see eye to eye, but him 'preciate yuh in him own way.'

Aunt B snorted inwardly. If Miss Jess hadn't been so weak she would have happily recited the numerous occasions on which Frank hadn't appreciated her in the slightest.

'When dem come back, tell dem me waan see dem. But me tired now.' Miss Jess let the mirror fall gently onto her knees and Aunt B picked it up and returned it to its place on the dresser. 'Go rest, Aunt B,' Miss Jess instructed. 'See yuh later.'

Rose poured herself another generous measure, then stared into the transparent liquid in her glass. She thought back to the funeral. She'd been surprised to see Aunt B there, after all she'd never had much to do with Frank's folks. She was a lot fatter, but looked well and it would have been nice to chat to her. They'd had some good times together, but time and distance and one thing or another meant they'd lost touch. Maybe once she'd resolved things with Frank, she'd have her old friend back – but there was time enough for that. For the moment, Frank was the main issue.

Although she hadn't ventured beyond the perimeter of the veranda the night before, she'd stood behind the garden gates for a while. There were nightlights set above the front and back door, but they weren't on and the moonlight had protected her as she peered through the gates, trying to guess which window led to Frank's bedroom and how he'd react when he saw her. The funeral had been her first chance to observe him properly in daylight – that morning in Brown's Town didn't count; she'd seen more of Benny than she had of Frank. He'd looked so smart and handsome at the funeral. His shoulders were still as broad as she remembered, and the cut of his black jacket had only served to enhance them. The thought of his shoulders made her smile, for his shoulders made her think of his chest, his back, his legs, the way he'd felt in her arms. It made her think of all the times she'd kissed and caressed him, moved on him and under him. The memories of how they'd loved and made love made her catch her breath. She could feel herself growing warm, even where the rum didn't flow, as images of careless, abandoned love with Frank came one after another. Anywhere. Anyhow. Anytime – it had always been right. And although it had been so long since she'd last held him for real, she knew that the moment she did, it would feel as if no time had passed at all.

Jewelle popped her head around the bedroom door. 'Are you awake now? Can I come in?' she whispered.

Miss Jess beckoned her in. 'I'm not an invalid, yuh nuh haffi whisper. Was just feelin' a likkle tired yesterday, dat's all.'

Jewelle sat on the bed gingerly, careful not to throw herself down as she normally did. 'You look much better, Granny.' With her hair freshly plaited and her skin shining from the cocoa butter Aunt B had rubbed in, Miss Jess had a healthy glow.

She patted Jewelle's hand. 'Someting on yuh mind?'

'It's about Dad,' Jewelle replied after a pause.

'I'm lissenin',' Miss Jess said as the girl lapsed into silence again.

'Did he have a girlfriend before Mum?'

'Yuh daddy was young once. Still is. At least, compared to me.' She laughed. 'Course him did have girlfriends.'

'But one he really liked?'

'Yes.'

'But I thought he loved Mum.'

'Yuh nuh tink smaddy can love more dan one person?' Her old eyes smiled warmly. She could imagine what her granddaughter was asking, and why. However, the words needed to come from her. All Miss Jess could do was wait until they did.

'So Dad did love someone else?'

Miss Jess observed Jewelle's profile as she sat half facing the window. 'I don' know. Yuh better ask him. Bet yuh did like someone in England before yuh come here an' meet Jake,' she added slyly.

'Uhm,' Jewelle admitted grudgingly.

'So yuh like two people a de same time,' she pushed.

'Yes, no.' She played with the hem of her dress. 'I like Jake better. A lot better.'

'So yuh choose one over de other?'

Jewelle furrowed her brow as she thought. 'I suppose so, if you put it like that.'

'Just like Frank. He coulda choose she or any other, but him never. Him choose Beth. Him choose yuh madda an' so him choose yuh.'

Rose sat at the bar nursing her drink. She'd refilled her glass over and over again and her head was beginning to spin. She normally drank beer, not rum. It was time to go home, but she didn't want to go home. Home was lonely, empty – no point being there.

'Me waan see Frank,' she suddenly muttered aloud. She topped up her glass and raised it to her lips. Me sure if we have a chance fi chat proper, him soon see dat what we had once we can have again. She took a swig from the glass, as she considered the situation. Maybe I should chat to Miss Jess first, get her on my side. If after twenty years me an' Frank still feel de same 'bout each other, den even she must realize dis ting meant fi be. She knocked back the remaining rum in her glass and got to her feet a little unsteadily. No time fi lose. Me must go to de house now.

'Good timin'. Me jus' finish.'

230

Rose turned to see Mikey at her side, a wide smile on his face. 'Wha' yuh waan?'

'Is party time, daughter!' He slipped his arm round her waist.

She stiffened against his arm. 'But me look like yuh daughter to yuh? Look 'pon me good. Yuh see any ugly genes in me face?'

'But is jokin' yuh jokin' wid me?' he asked, his smile faltering slightly.

'Just move yuh ugly raas from me!' She shrugged him off and reached for her jacket.

'We did have a likkle agreement,' he said, angrily plucking at her arm. 'Me buy yuh drinks an' yuh spen' some time wid me. Is only now yuh done drink de place dry yuh waan come change yuh mind? Yuh must tink me name Boops.'

Rose brushed his hand away. A single step forward closed the gap between them. 'No mek me cry rape,' she warned very quietly, 'otherwise is de last ting yuh do.' Mikey opened his mouth to protest, but Rose continued. 'Unless yuh like de taste a Babylon stick, come put yuh han' 'pon me again.'

One of the other barmen pushed Mikey into an empty chair, with a warning: 'Sekkle down, man. She nuh wort' it.'

Mikey rapidly calculated his options: me cyaan mek up too much noise, otherwise me might well lose me job. An' if dat happen me babymother gwine mek me life a livin' hell. But cho! Cyaan mek her handle me so in front of me bredren. No, sah! Me haffi mek her see who she dealin' wid.

He jumped up from the chair roughly, sending it flying and shoved off a couple of friends who tried to hold him back. 'Me never waan yuh anyway,' he roared. 'Yuh frowzy bitch. Come in here a drink an' a flirt wid everybody den expect me fi tek yuh home. Yuh better tink again.' He curled his lips in disdain and looked around. 'Yuh too easy,' he concluded in an attempt to get male support.

Rose stared at him and then gave a crooked half-smile. 'Yuh see dis?' She raised her forefinger, licked its tip very slowly then quickly flicked it off the side of her bottom dismissively. Those watching burst into laughter.

'Cho, Mikey! Leave her,' one of the bystanders shouted. 'She look sweet like candy but she rough like hell. Mek her gone.'

Mikey slumped sulkily into the chair the man pulled out for him. Though he feigned disinterest, he couldn't stop himself from watching Rose's bottom as she half strutted, half wiggled her way out of the bar.

Outside, the fresh air only strengthened Rose's resolve to talk to Miss Jess and to see Frank.

'Evening, Mumma. Jus' waan see how yuh doin' before me seh goodnight.'

'Me all right, son. Just a likkle tired. An' yuh?'

'All right.' He wondered how to tell her about the ticket he'd bought. Maybe he should wait until she felt better. But when would that be? They were due to leave within a few days – he couldn't wait until they were actually at the airport. Miss Jess suddenly chuckled. 'Wha' so funny?' he asked, laughing nervously.

'Yuh. Yuh jus' like Jewelle. Come in here wid someting on yuh mind. Waan fi talk but don' know where fi start.'

'Wha' de matter wid Jewelle?'

'Nutten. She just growin' up, dat's all. She like talkin' to me an' me like talkin' to her. We nuh have much time left so we mekkin' de most of it.'

Frank seized at the opening. 'If yuh come to England, yuh could both spend plenty more time together,' he said.

Miss Jess looked away. 'We done talk 'bout dis already, Frank.'

232

'No,' he said. 'We talk 'bout yuh comin' to live in England. Dis time we talkin' 'bout yuh comin' fi a visit. Jamaica yuh home an' I respec' dat but I would like yuh fi visit me in my home.'

She stared at him, her eyes watery. He pulled the ticket from his back pocket, unfolded it and pressed it into her hand. 'Dis ticket open return. It date so yuh can travel wid us when we leave. Me leave it open so dat any time yuh ready, any time at all, even if it's de day after yuh reach, yuh can go home. Me nuh gwine pressurize yuh or beg yuh or force yuh. Me gwine let yuh decide, jus' how yuh always let me decide de big tings in my life.' He folded her fingers around the ticket.

She looked at him and smiled. Watery eyes transformed into bright, shiny eyes.

'I love yuh, Mumma.'

She reached up her arm and he clasped her in a warm embrace. The edge of the ticket she clutched in one hand tickled the back of his ear. 'I love yuh too, son,' she whispered.

'When yuh ready, let me know yuh decision.'

'All right, Frank.' She held him tight. 'Me will do dat.'

She hadn't said no. It was a good sign.

The jolting motion made Rose's stomach lurch and she clung on tight to the side of the pickup trailer. She was beginning to feel a bit sick from all that rum. It wasn't far from Brown's Town to Huntley, but the road was rough from periods of heavy rain when the road turned to mud and vehicles got stuck, their spinning wheels churning up great grooves. These long grooves, like deep scars in dry skin, caused the pickup to jerk and shake from side to side as the driver picked his way around them, negotiating the blind curve up ahead.

The rough rocking motion made Rose's head wobble and

nausea rise in her throat. Her head was pounding and all she wanted right then was to separate her head from her body until it stopped hurting. *Cyaan talk to Miss Jess in dis state*, she thought, *maybe me should come back tomorrow.*

'*Fi wha'?*'

Rose looked around abruptly, ignoring the increased pounding in her head from the sudden movement. That was Mamma G's voice. But it couldn't be – she hadn't called her.

'Yuh all right?' asked the woman sitting opposite her.

'Me belly a hot me,' she answered. 'Me nuh eat since dis mornin'.'

'Me nuh have nutten but dry bun. Waan some?'

Rose nodded, gratefully accepting the small piece the woman broke off for her. She nibbled on it slowly. She just wanted to go home and lie down.

'*If yuh give up now, yuh might as well dead!*'

Rose half stood up, dropping the piece of bun. The motion of the pickup threw her forward and she fell into the lap of the woman in front of her.

'I cyaan do it, Mamma G,' Rose shouted to the night air.

'Who yuh talkin' to?' the bun lady asked, cringing away from Rose. 'Is duppy yuh see?'

Rose heaved herself back into her corner. Her stop was coming up. It was now or never.

'*Is yuh destiny.*'

'No.' She shook her head. 'Is too late.'

'*Is yuh destiny.*' The words were a mere whisper.

'Drop me here,' Rose shouted to the driver.

Miss Jess turned and pulled the sheet up around her neck until its edges tickled her ear lobes. Though the night was still, there was a breeze circulating in the room. It had been so hot earlier that Frank had left the window ajar when he'd gone to bed. Now it was cooler, but she didn't have the energy to get up and close the window. Trapped between a half-dream and half-awake state, she felt the same kind of restlessness and uneasiness she'd felt so many years ago in the hours preceding Frank's birth. Nothing was wrong, yet nothing was right. She sighed as she turned on her side and waited for the embrace of sleep. When it came it was fitful. Moments of calm were interspersed with vivid dreams of snakes twisting and entwining themselves around her. Of faces changing before her, solid and real one moment, then blurring into something unrecognizable before transforming into yet another face, somehow familiar, yet at the same time totally strange. Of shape-changing, ethereal forms, floating above and around her, penning her in so that there was no escape.

It took her a while to realize that the shadowy figure standing by her bed was real and not another dream image. Miss Jess lay still, clutching the sheet in her hands, willing herself to stay calm until she was able to speak without a tremor in her voice. Outside, the night breeze blew a whispery accompaniment to their conversation.

'Rose. Why yuh cyaan let go after all dese years? Yuh nuh tired of fightin'? Of hatin'?'

'Nuh have no choice. Is me destiny.'

'Is we one choose we way forward. So nuh come tek destiny mek excuse.'

'From me likkle bit, me gran'madda tell me me woulda know me man by him mark. And dat when me find him me mus' keep him 'cause is him one can mek me whole.'

'Which mark dat?' Disbelief was clear in Miss Jess's voice.

'She say him would have two. First, him would have sometin' wrong wid one a him han'. An' if yuh look good, Frank likkle finger on him left han' crooked.'

'But Frank fall outta mango tree an' bruk him finger! Yuh know how many people fall outta tree an' crook up

235

demself? Look how yuh mek dat nonsense come turn yuh fool.'

'But she also tell me is him second mark would prove seh him de one.'

'Wha' mark dat, den?'

'De white half moon him have on de right side of him chest,' Rose announced triumphantly.

'But dat him birthmark! Me sorry, nuh mean no disrespec', but it seem like yuh gran'madda lead yuh astray.'

Rose continued as if Miss Jess hadn't spoken. 'Yuh see me have a mark just de same. It in exactly de same place but on de left han' side of me chest.' She opened her blouse and lifted her breast to display the silvery white birthmark at its base. 'Yuh see it? When we lie together, we mek one full moon an' I am complete. Is Frank complete my circle an' dat is why me cyaan figet him, why me cyaan let him go. 'Cause is only wid him dat I am whole.'

'Tell me someting den,' Miss Jess demanded. 'If is him mek yuh complete, why yuh waan hurt him an' him people?'

'Me give him plenty chance already, but him never waan tek dem. Me beg him nuh leave me. Me write him in Englan'. Me tell him 'bout de pickney –'

'Which pickney?' Miss Jess tried to sit up.

Rose pushed her back down gently. 'Nuh worry yuh head 'bout dat. Dat a Frank an' me business. So,' she continued conversationally, 'now me haffi mek him come to me. Him come to Jamaica an' never once try find me. Run up an' down de place wid him bruk-up friend, but nuh even spare a minute of him time fi me. Me waan yuh blessin'.'

'Blessin' fi wha'?' Miss Jess screwed up her face in puzzlement.

'Me an' Frank union.'

'Union?' Miss Jess repeated stupidly. 'Which union?'

'Me an' Frank waan stay together,' Rose said, her voice rising as she spoke. 'Yuh de only ting stoppin' it.'

'Yuh mussi mad, gyal! After all yuh do to him?' Miss Jess sat up. This time Rose didn't stop her, merely stared at her with a faraway look in her eyes.

It seemed that Rose was paying more attention to the whispering outside, as the wind rustled the leaves of the banana trees, than to Miss Jess.

'I bless de day Frank leave dis island an' leave yuh behind. Yuh tink after all dese years when him finally find him way, find likkle peace, I gwine put him in yuh hands?' Miss Jess laughed quietly. 'Yuh good fi joke, Rose.'

'Is yuh a de one problem,' Rose repeated stubbornly. 'Me nuh have no more patience. I must mek him come. Any way I can.'

'Go home, Rose,' Miss Jess told her softly.

Rose wasn't listening, at least not to her. 'Yuh right, Mamma G,' Miss Jess heard her say to the night air. 'Yuh always right. I shoulda lissen to yuh before.' She shook her head as she slipped one of the pillows from behind Miss Jess's back and pushed her down so she was lying flat. 'Me sorry, Miss Jess. Me already try all ways possible, but dis is me destiny an' dat mean it yours too.'

She placed the pillow on Miss Jess's face and pressed down. The scream was stifled before it fully sounded. Miss Jess struggled; the night-time noises of geckos calling to each other and crickets chattering seemed magnified as she blindly slapped and scratched at Rose's hands. The gold bracelet around Rose's wrist snapped and fell to the floor.

'Me sorry it come to dis,' Rose murmured, watching the old lady's feeble struggles. She shifted position as she put her full weight on the pillow, knocking Miss Jess's walking stick to the floor. The clattering sound shocked Rose back to the present. She froze for a second and an expression of surprise ran across her face as she looked down at the bed.

Quickly, she replaced the pillow beneath Miss Jess's head. Then she brushed her palm over the old woman's face and tucked her arms under the bedcover as if protecting her from the cold. Miss Jess looked at peace.

'Me nuh have no real grudge 'gainst yuh, but me haffi mek him come,' Rose whispered in her ear, then turned and slipped silently out through the window.

In the adjacent rooms, only Jewelle slept peacefully as she dreamed of black eyes that shone like polished onyx and lips that tasted of the sweetest of fruit.

Frank shivered in his sleep and wrapped the bedspread more tightly around him until his head was covered and he was cocooned mummy-style.

Tears slipped from Aunt B's eyes as she dreamed of Beth: *She come to me last night.* The words echoed in her head over and over again like a warning mantra until she was jolted out of sleep and onto her feet.

9

20th February

'Nobody will tell me anything, Jake. All they do is push me out the way.' Jewelle hugged her knees tighter to her chest. The early morning air was cool. 'How could it have happened? She was better yesterday and now suddenly she's in bed again – and this time it's a hospital bed. It just keeps getting worse! And from the way everybody's acting I know there's something really wrong,' she said, turning to look at the boy sitting beside her, 'but I don't know what.'

Jake contented himself with an abrupt hug before pulling away. Jewelle nodded, appreciating the brief contact. He rubbed the heel of one baseball boot backwards and forwards over the patch of green in front of him, releasing the scent of fresh grass as they sat in silence under the broad-leafed banana tree. It was barely five thirty a.m. He'd come with the milk as he always did and had been surprised but pleased to see Jewelle sitting on the veranda steps. The expression on her face had soon shown, though, that she wasn't sitting there waiting for him.

'All de tings dat happen,' he said eventually, 'maybe it too much fi her.'

'You don't really believe that, do you?' He stared away out to the coconut tree, heavy with fruit, at the end of the garden. 'Do you?' she insisted. His only response was to shrug his shoulders and scratch at the back of his neck.

'I finally meet my grandmother,' Jewelle continued after a

pause. 'I mean, meet her properly.' Her eyes glistened. 'She listened when I talked to her. She understood me,' she said, jabbing at the centre of her chest. 'I don't want her to die. Not her too.' She buried her face in her knees and burst into tears.

Jake gently stroked the exposed nape of her neck. Jewelle half turned to him and suddenly he was holding her in a clumsy one-armed embrace.

'But she not dead. She jus' need rest an' plenty lookin' after,' he said, trying to comfort her as her tears wet the cloth of his shirt. 'All right, so she inna hospital fi couple a days, but at de same time,' he stressed the words, 'she right here wid yuh. Wid all a we. Yuh just haffi believe it.'

'Easy enough for you to say,' Jewelle said, snuffling against his neck, 'it's not your grandmother.'

'Learn from yuh gran'madda.' Jake spoke into Jewelle's hairline and she felt his breath on her temples. 'Look how she behave 'bout Poppa Ben. She cry fi him physical loss, but she know she still have him essence. Yuh still have her physically. Nuh cry.'

Jewelle sniffed noisily, then wiped the back of her hand first across her eyes and then across her nose. She pulled slightly away from him and he felt a mixture of emotions: relief that her father hadn't returned from the hospital and caught them together like this, glad that she trusted him enough to show her feelings in front of him, but also regret that he couldn't totally relax with her, knowing her father would think the worst if he came back and caught him with his arms around Jewelle. He waited until he caught her eye, then gave her a smile.

She leaned into him and let her forehead rest against his. 'Yeah. I suppose you're right.'

'Me nuh business if doctor call it natural causes, me nuh believe him.' Aunt B paced up and down the living room.

240

'Yuh have a better reason?'

'Me feel sure dat blasted Rose have someting fi do wid it an' after dat likkle chat we have yesterday, me surprise yuh even haffi ask. Since she turn up at Poppa Ben funeral, Miss Jess nuh right.'

'Yuh know,' Sol looked down at his fingertips which were pressed together forming a triangle, 'if it wasn't fi de fact dat me did protect de house meself, me woulda agree wid yuh. An' even though me know right down to me toe bone dat someting not right 'bout dis, me know no way Rose could get in here last night.'

'How yuh so sure?'

'Just one a me ting dem.'

'Cho, man, talk straight fi once!'

'Call it magic dust.' Sol waved one hand dismissively as if what he was saying was of little importance.

'Magic dust? How yuh love talk riddle!' Aunt B snapped in exasperation.

'Me sprinkle magic dust all roun' de house, de doorways an' windows. Everywhere. No way on earth dat woman coulda get in.'

Aunt B stared at him, her eyes narrowing. 'Wha' colour was dis magic dust?' she asked in a low voice.

'Yellowish.' Sol stared at his hands.

'Oh Lord!' Aunt B raised one hand to her mouth, while with the other she sought blindly for support. 'Oh Lord,' she repeated again as she sank heavily into the nearest chair.

Frank had found himself driving to the churchyard after leaving his mother at the hospital. Unplanned, and yet here he was again – twice in two days. 'We born in order fi die.' The words came back to him as he trampled blossoms underfoot. Their crushed perfume rose up to fill his nostrils with a cloying scent. His head was filled with a strange silence. Everyday sounds like the distant rumble of traffic from the road behind him, the crick of whispering insects and the roar of a plane as it passed overhead, were all broken by blocks of silence, so that in his mind this strange lull lay like the white spaces in a black dotted line.

He squatted beside his father's grave. Maybe it was your turn, he thought, but is it hers? No reply. No response. Nothing. Yet what had he expected anyway? The answer was to be found within. He knew that he needed to lengthen the gaps between the dashes so that there was space, not to think, but to allow his unformed thoughts to fall into place. But, try as he might, he couldn't reach that hush, that soundlessness. The dashes lengthened into a solid black line as his thoughts tumbled over each other and the chaos in his head reigned free.

He reflected on what he had – Jewelle, and through her he would always have Beth. He had good friends, a life of his own back home and maybe his mother there soon, if she pulled through this. If he were honest, he didn't want for anything. Occasionally, a little bit of excitement, but he'd had his fill of that with Rose – more than enough to last this lifetime and beyond. Rose had been the first woman he'd felt deeply about, and at the time he'd thought it was love. Now he was older and more experienced he could see that he'd mistaken first-time infatuation and sexual gratitude for love. He'd moved on, but Rose hadn't – and that he realized was partly his fault. It was clear he couldn't achieve the inner silence he desired until he made his peace with his past.

He sighed, weary of feeling pulled in different directions. Just as he thought things were resolved, that there was a good chance his mother would come to England and give them both time to decide what to do next, this happened. He knew what he had to do, but he didn't want to deal with it. If I don't, he wondered, what'll happen next?

Mumma dies? Jewelle gets ill and I lose her too? Are things going to keep happening to the women I love until I've got no choice but to walk into my past, into my pain and face the outcome? Maybe it was as Sol said, fate and coincidence were one and the same – no way out.

Two or three leaves had drifted down on top of the cement casing of Poppa Ben's grave and Frank brushed them away with the flat of his hand. The top was warm and specks of grit stuck to his hand. He ran his fingertips over the space that the headstone, once carved, was to go. No – no answers to be found here. The only answers were inside.

He got to his feet and walked slowly back to the car. Right now, his mother was lying in a hospital bed, weak but out of danger. He switched the engine on and put the car into gear. He would face Rose. Eventually. He just had to decide when. Problem was he was running out of time.

'Frank?' Aunt B rushed forward to greet him as soon as he entered the kitchen. Her round face looked peaky with the stress of the last few days. 'Frank, I need to talk to yuh.' She shot a quick glance at Sol, but Frank stared beyond her.

'Daddy?'

'She's weak but she's all right.' His eyes sought his daughter. He reached out for her and pulled her close. 'She's all right,' he repeated. Over her head he looked at the boy in front of him. 'Jake? Do me a favour? Look after Jewelle fi today? I know she safe wid yuh.'

'Yes, sir.' Jake held Frank's gaze.

'Thank yuh,' he said.

'Frank?'

'Aunt B, not now. Dere's time later.'

'Dat's just it, Frank. Dere isn't time. Last night I had a dream. Well, I have plenty dream since yuh daddy dead. I never waan worry yuh more dan yuh already worried, so me never seh nutten. Now I wish I did speak up, but I 'fraid yuh might not let me come wid yuh on dis trip. I knew smaddy was in danger. Never tink it would turn out to be yuh mumma.'

'Aunt B!' Frank roared, making Jewelle jump and Aunt B's mouth close tight on whatever she'd been about to say.

'Frank.' Sol's voice was calm. 'We can all imagine wha' yuh goin' through right now an' wha' yuh tinking. But maybe yuh should lissen to what Miss B haffi seh. Wha' we both haffi seh.'

'Daddy! That hurts.' Jewelle peeled Frank's fingers away from her shoulder and massaged the spot where his hug had turned into a squeeze.

'Sorry, baby.' Contrite, he rubbed her shoulder gently.

'Me find dis in Miss Jess room.' Sol held his open palm above Jewelle's head towards Frank.

'Dad?' Jewelle craned her neck to see. 'Sol's trying to show you something.'

'I don' waan see nutten. I don' waan hear nutten. An' I don' waan talk 'bout nutten. Is your arm OK, Jewelle?' He stepped around her before she even had time to respond, then looked straight at the others. 'I waan fi be by meself fi a few minutes. Me 'preciate it if yuh would all respec' dat need.'

Do someting Aunt B's eyes flashed at Sol. He took a quick half-step and grabbed Frank by his sleeve.

'Frank!' Sol's eyes burned dark, the look compelling. 'I find dis in Miss Jess room.' He pushed the object into Frank's hand. 'Look 'pon it, Frank,' he commanded, as Frank turned his fist face downwards as if to drop the object to the floor. ''Member how yuh ask me fi go wid yuh de day yuh choose it? Look 'pon it an' tell me yuh nuh recognize it.'

Frank slowly opened his hand – and what he saw made

244

him gag for breath. Then slowly he seemed to fill up with air, increasing in size like an angry cat under attack.

'No.' He shook his head in an instinctive gesture of denial.

'Is she do dis, Frank.'

'Impossible!' The word was strangled, but in his heart he knew the truth.

'Wha' it tek fi mek yuh believe it?'

'Who's "she"?'

Aunt B poked Jewelle in her side with her elbow. 'How yuh love stick yuh nose inna big people business.'

'But he's my dad so –'

'Come out of here,' Aunt B ordered. Jake pulled at Jewelle's arm, but she shrugged him off.

'Go, Jewelle.' Frank spoke without looking at her. She pouted, but allowed Jake to lead her away.

'Why it so impossible, Frank?' Sol asked the minute Jewelle and Jake were out of the room. 'Yuh tink Rose wouldn't run to dis? Look like yuh memory short. Yuh figet dis?' He poked at Frank's chest with his forefinger.

Frank turned away. *Stop*, he screamed inwardly. All these people and these events pushing him. Never letting up. Forcing him into a corner. It was too much. Too much.

'Yuh carry her mark, man,' Sol said, his voice suddenly quiet. 'Look how she do yuh when she did love yuh. Imagine what she capable of when she hate.'

'Wha' she do? Wha' she do?' Aunt B stepped forward, curiosity clear on her face.

'Dis.' Frank spun round and opened his shirt with one hand. With the other, he traced the thin raised scar that ran diagonally across his chest from just below one nipple to the base of his collarbone. 'She do dis . . .'

Rose took Frank by surprise as she appeared from behind the door and jumped on his back. Her perfume filled the air around them. 'Frank! Yuh come back. Me know if me did give yuh long enough, if me did give yuh enough space, yuh would come back to me.'

'It's not what you think,' he muttered, pulling her arms from around his neck and shrugging her off his back.

If she noticed his tone of voice she chose to ignore it as she kicked the door closed and pushed him fully into the room.

'Come.' She pulled him by the hand to the large double bed which served as a seating space during the day. 'Why yuh act like yuh a stranger? Sit down.'

Frank resisted her pull and looked away from the bed. He had spent too much of his past there and had no desire to rekindle old memories or retread old paths. Instead, he slipped his hand from hers and moved as close to the window as the treadle sewing machine in front of it would allow. He felt his usual exasperation as he looked down at the clutter of objects on its extended worktable. Remnants of material and pins stuck haphazardly into an old piece of sponge fought for space with a pair of tailor's scissors, fragile paper patterns and gaily coloured spools of thread thrown carelessly into a fraying wicker basket. He'd never been able to understand how she could work and, more to the point, how she could produce such beautiful work amid such disorder.

He cleared his throat, uncertain how to start, glanced at her over his shoulder before quickly averting his eyes. He tried to move closer to the window, but found himself blocked. When he did speak it was hurriedly and with his back to her.

'I'm leaving. Going to England. This summer.'

She leapt at him, knocking him off balance and pressing him up against the side of the worktable. She kissed him and in her kiss he tasted the same invitation which had drawn him back time and time again. Felt himself slipping, eyes half closed in memory of those times, but her next words jerked him back to the present like a dash of cold water.

'England! Me so happy. When we goin'?'

He took a step sideways and walked around her to the centre of the room. 'I said I'm going, Rose. Not you.'

'But wha' yuh sayin', Franklin? Dat yuh goin' widout me? But yuh cyaan do dat. We belong together. We have a future together. Yuh cyaan jus' up an' leave me behind.'

'Listen to me.' He spoke decisively but avoided her gaze and the mute appeal in her eyes. 'Listen to me,' he said again. 'We've already talked about this. Why can't you accept that things have finished between us? That it's –'

She shook her head. 'No, Franklin. Yuh always say dat. Every single time yuh walk away from me yuh use de same old words. If tings did really finish yuh wouldn't be here today.'

'No, Rose. This thing between us is over. I only came to say goodbye.'

'Frank,' she interrupted him, 'yuh know me cyaan live widout yuh. Yuh know dat. Me woulda rather kill meself, or yuh,' she added darkly, 'before me let yuh go.'

'I shouldn't have come, Rose. I made a mistake.'

She brushed away his words as if they were a persistent mosquito. 'Me know wha' do yuh. Yuh still vex 'cause of dat other woman. Dat Angela. Me admit me was wrong.' She twinkled up at him. 'I know dere was nutten between yuh, but when I see yuh in de street wid her – me was so jealous dat . . . I'm sorry. All right? Sorry, sorry, sorry, sorry! How many times I haffi say it before yuh believe me? Me get mad an' me don' always tink properly when me mad. I promise it nah go happen again.'

Frank tried to speak but she silenced him with a wave of her hand as she walked towards him, held his eyes with a glittering gaze that shone black against the clearness of her skin, commanded his attention just as she had done the day they met.

She opened her blouse and raised her left breast high. When she spoke it was with a force that made him listen. 'Is dis bind us together. Dis.' She pointed to the silvery birthmark. He avoided looking at her breast and stared instead at her face, trying to make sense of her words. What did a birthmark have to do with any of this? She saw his bewilderment but pressed on. 'It go wid de mark on yuh chest – it unite us, mek us one. Just tell me wha' yuh waan me fi do an' me will do it. Tell me how yuh waan me fi be an' me will be dat. Yuh know me pride, nuh mek me beg yuh no more.'

He felt a mixture of emotions fight for space inside him – embarrassment, pity, distaste – as she sank to the floor in front of him. So where was her pride? How could she behave like this, knowing that he no longer wanted her, was no longer willing to make room in his life for her? If he'd been her he'd have just walked away, no matter what he was feeling inside. He hated scenes. But no, she couldn't do things that way – couldn't make things easy for both of them. She was too ardent, too volatile, always had been. It was one of the things that had attracted him at first, but now he hated it. She was too quick to react, too explosive. He couldn't understand why they'd stayed together for as long as they had, given this fundamental difference between them. Perhaps it was as Sol said. Maybe he was emotionally distant, detached, so afraid of his own feelings that he gravitated towards people who were ardent, impetuous, wild. Lived his life through their expression of emotion because he was too scared to live his own.

Rose remained crouched on the floor, arms wrapped around her knees as she rocked herself. He moved reluctantly towards her and forced himself to stoop down and touch her. 'Stop it, Rose. I don't want any more of this.

This isn't how love's supposed to be. You have so much to give – but to the right man. A man who can match your love, your intensity one hundred per cent. I can't, Rose.' He didn't want to admit to her that he didn't want to, or was scared to. His voice faltered. 'Lord knows I've tried, but I can't.'

He shook her slightly, intent on making her understand that this time there would be no going back, no more tempestuous separations and passionate reconciliations. She sat like an obedient child in his grasp. 'If you really love me as you say, then let me go. Please.'

She seemed to shrink beneath his touch, the glitter in her eyes disappearing as she leaned away from him, pushed herself to her feet and buttoned her blouse.

Frank straightened up, at a loss as to what to do next. He wanted to leave, he'd done what he'd set out to do. There was nothing to keep him there any longer. He'd braced himself for a string of curses, a flurry of flying objects. This silent acceptance threw him, made him feel guilty. At least you had the balls to tell her yourself, he thought. How many men in your position would have done that? Most men would have taken the easy option and disappeared without trace. A part of him wanted her to recognize his decency in facing her rather than allowing her to hear it from somebody else.

He moved towards her but she held one hand up, palm outwards, a silent plea for a moment to compose herself, to hold back the tears burning in her eyes. She turned and looked out of the window. He could see the thin veins raised along her arms as she leaned heavily against the sewing machine. Impatient to be on his way and unwilling to acknowledge the depths of her hurt and anger, he stepped towards her again. Guided by an ill-timed, mis-judged prick of conscience he moved forward and laid a hand gently on her shoulder.

His touch released a tension which lay curled up inside her like a taut spring. She whirled round so lightning fast that he only had time to register the blur of silver in front of his eyes, but no time to react.

The scissors slit his flesh as smoothly as a hot knife entering butter. He felt searing pain as Rose slashed him from collarbone to nipple. Blood surged from his chest splattering her face and her dress. And as he stood rigid in this first moment of shock, he marvelled at how thick and dark and warm his blood was.

Adrenalin kicked in. Half doubled up, his right hand holding the flaps of his skin together, he used his left hand to grab hers and force it down, banging it sharply on the side of the sewing machine table. The scissors fell to the wooden floor and skittered out of reach. An open-handed blow sent her spinning and he sidestepped her, then turned and stumbled towards the door. He'd taken no more than two steps when he felt her hands round his ankle pulling him back. He kicked her shoulder forcing her to loosen her grasp – a few vital seconds in which to back away. She lay where she'd fallen, watching as he fumbled behind him for the doorknob. He looked away for a single moment, desperately seeking his exit to freedom.

She made a final breathless appeal: 'Franklin. Me pregnant. A fi yuh baby.'

The words held him. He shook his head in disbelief – she was bluffing. It was a lie. Impossible. For Rose, that gesture was his ultimate rejection of her and she screamed her furious hatred of him.

A second was all she needed to launch herself at him again, scissors held high. Frank twisted, drawing his head back and feeling the breeze from her arm as the shiny blade whistled past his left cheek. This time he didn't hesitate to swing his fist in her face, knocking her to the floor. A moment's pause as he registered in amazement that she was trying to rise to her feet even after a blow like that. He reached for the doorknob once more and this time felt it reassuringly solid as his hand, slippy with blood, curled round it.

'Me nuh rest till yuh dead,' she screamed.

He turned and ran, closing his ears to the curses that damned him to hell and back.

Run. Run. Run.

The words pounded through his head and his legs automatically obeyed the message. The street was full of people but he ran through their midst as if in a dream. Felt their silent yet unanimous parting; the curious but knowing looks in their eyes as they drew themselves in to avoid contact with him.

Run. Run. Run.

But where?

Run . . . Run.

Only one place to go.

Run.

He felt the wooden door warm beneath his forehead. Knocked so softly that even he couldn't hear it.

The door opened. He fell into welcoming darkness . . .

'Hey!' Frank blinked hard as Sol snapped him back to the present with a sharp click of his fingers.

'Lissen to me, man. Maybe me wrong, maybe me right. Only one way fi find out.'

Frank shook his head. Opened his mouth. Closed it again as the words refused to come. Looked down at his open palm and shook his head again.

'If yuh really believe Rose nuh have nutten fi do wid Miss Jess den fly back a Englan' wid yuh conscience clean. But if yuh have even de slightest doubt dat maybe, just maybe

Rose involve, then yuh haffi deal wid it. I help yuh once. Yuh 'member?'

Frank stood immobile, staring down at his hand.

''Member, Frank?'

'I remember . . .'

The scent burned the inside of Frank's nose, creeping upwards ever stronger until it brought water to his eyes. His face wrinkled and he turned his head away, weakly raising one hand to push away whatever was being held under his nose.

'Wha' dat?' he whispered.

'Piss.'

He opened his eyes. Blinked. Saw Sol's face coming into focus – the long white teeth, the pockmarked cheeks, the quirky grin gradually filling his field of vision. 'Piss?' he repeated.

'Oh all right, if yuh insist. Smelling salts. Me never have enough piss. Yuh shoulda warn me yuh was plannin' fi drop in.'

Sol laughed heartily at his own joke, as he helped Frank sit upright. He took a long sip from a tumbler of white rum before putting the glass in Frank's hand. Then he pulled down from the top of a cupboard a leather surgeon's bag from which he selected a pair of scissors, needle and thread, tweezers and a clamp. He removed the towel he'd hurriedly put on Frank's chest to stem the flow of blood and stared at the mess below. Carefully, he cut away at the dried crusted edges of the shirt before meticulously tweaking out loose threads that were stuck to the wound.

'Why yuh so rough?' Frank protested. His voice was stronger now that he felt sure he wasn't going to die.

'Relax, man. Drink some rum,' came the reply.

'Yuh know me nuh like dis stuff more dan so,' Frank complained as he handed the glass back.

Sol took a sip, swilling the liquid around in his mouth as he stared at the glass in silent contemplation. 'Sure?' he asked raising the glass to Frank's face. Frank shook his head, staring down at the bloody mess that was his chest. Sol shrugged his shoulders. 'Shame fi see it waste,' he said and quickly threw the contents at Frank.

Frank screamed as the liquid seeped into the wound. He gripped the edge of the table so tightly that the bones of his knuckles threatened to burst through the skin. He couldn't stop himself from trembling, felt bitter bile rise to his mouth. The pain was as bad, no, worse than when Rose had slashed him. Then it had been a single sharp searing flare of pain matched by an equally sharp surge of adrenalin. But this; this was a burning that seemed to reach far below the skin and now the adrenalin was gone. As tears trickled from the corner of his eyes, he silently cursed Sol as a sadistic bastard.

'Sorry, but me never have nutten else fi clean de wound.' Sol sounded genuinely sorry as he threaded the needle. 'At least de worst part over.'

Frank looked at him in disbelief. The impact of the pain was now beginning to recede and he felt able to talk in an almost normal tone of voice. 'Maybe I should go to de hospital, mek dem look on it.'

'Dis look worse dan it actually is. A whole heap a blood but de wound not as deep as it did seem.' Frank wasn't too convinced by his friend's easy dismissal of his injury but Sol continued. 'Anyway, wha' dem gwine do fi yuh dat me not doin'? Stitch yuh up an' ask plenty question, dat's what. Get de authorities involve an' is yuh might end up wid police record.'

'Me? But me nuh do nutten.'

'So what! Who know how many Babylon dat woman have fi friend. Suppose she start chat lie 'bout how yuh beat her up an' den claim she cut yuh in self-defence.'

'But I never hit her in my life. Except fi today.'

'Maybe if yuh did give her two bitch lick from time, yuh wouldn't have dis problem now,' Sol grunted. 'Anyway, it nuh mek sense involve de police, dem have a tendency fi lock up de innocent an' let de guilty walk free.'

'But me is me de victim.'

'Since when life fair? Yuh get a likkle police record an' people start ask question. "Is dis de best of our youth? Is dis de kinda man we waan send to de motherland?" Englan' have plenty criminal of her own, yuh tink dem waan more? No way. Yuh know dat as well as I do, otherwise yuh wouldn't have come here.'

Frank had to admit that Sol had a point, but he wasn't completely reassured. Sol hadn't even washed his hands before starting work on him.

'Yuh turn up on me doorstep, half-conscious, wid yuh chest wide open an' blood drippin' everywhere. Yuh look ready fi dead, like yuh buck up on slaughteration butcher who not too choosy 'bout weh him get him meat. But did I say a word? I ask yuh any questions? No. I open my door to yuh an' tek yuh in. No questions asked. I already know de answers anyway.'

'I never believe she would run to dis,' Frank objected.

'I did warn yuh right from de start wha' kinda woman yuh tekkin' up wid, but would yuh lissen? No, not yuh. Yuh tink yuh bad? All right. Now yuh know she badda dan yuh. As my good madda used to say, "If yuh cyaan hear yuh must feel." Feelin' it now, Frank?' Sol grinned as he pushed the needle through Frank's flesh.

Frank winced, but willed himself to sit still. He was at Sol's mercy and, given his friend's warped sense of humour and his sometimes quick temper, it was probably better not to provoke him in any way. After all, he didn't want to spend the rest of his life looking like Frankenstein's monster. 'All right, man. Yuh mek yuh point. I just cyaan believe she ready fi kill me. She say she love me but she try fi kill me.'

Sol smiled to himself. Frank sounded like a puzzled little boy. 'Dat kinda love too strong,' Sol told him as he sewed. 'And yuh know why? 'Cause it too close to hate, dat's why. And dat is precisely de kinda love yuh cyaan trust, 'cause when it go wrong dere's no turnin' back.'

'Maybe I was stupid, I did only waan say goodbye, show her I wasn't one of dem bastard dat jus' up an' leave him woman as an' when him have a mind. But when I try fi explain, she turn crazy. I don' understand. Is a good likkle while now we nuh see each other. Last time we talk, it seem she finally . . . at least I thought she finally understan' dat dis time it fi real; dat everyting over an' we nuh have no future together.'

'Dat's always been yuh problem. Yuh tink yuh can talk everyting over. Reason wid people. Rationalize. No wonder Miss Jess baptize yuh Franklin Winston Churchill, she mussi see one great negotiator in yuh, heh? When yuh gwine learn dat wid some people yuh jus' cyaan reason?' Sol made a final, careful stitch before cutting the thread quickly with a pair of surgical scissors by his side. 'Me finish now. Better mek me give yuh a shot of dis. Hope yuh not allergic to it. Is de only ting me have.'

Now he was out of immediate danger, was no longer in shock from the woman who professed to love him trying to kill him, Frank could pay more attention to the moment. Sol's slim fingers moved quickly but surely as he sorted through the items in his bag. Frank looked at the man he'd known since he was just a kid and wondered, not for the first time, just what kind of friendship it was they had. It was unbalanced, something slightly out of sync. It seemed that Frank could turn to Sol in need, but Sol never asked anything of him. He didn't know if this was because Sol believed that Frank would always be too weak to help him, or because Sol seemed not to need anybody at all.

'Weh yuh get all dese things from? Yuh better equip dan de hospital. Anybody woulda tink yuh studyin' medicine not law.'

Sol raised an eyebrow. 'I mek it my business fi learn anyting dat might serve me in dis life an' de next. An' dis business,' he said, indicating the surgeon's bag and accompanying paraphernalia, 'is just one of dem.'

'Lucky for me den, isn't it.'

'Yuh better stay here fi de time being,' Sol told him as he put the implements he'd used on to boil. 'Yuh never tell her when yuh leavin'?' he added as an afterthought.

'Well – yes.' Frank hung his head as he realized his error.

'Frank! Why yuh badda tell her anyting? Yuh shoulda jus' left her an' gone. Yuh a idiot? Cho!' Sol sucked his teeth in disgust. 'Me can jus' see it. Yuh wid de likkle English accent yuh love use.' He mimicked Frank: *'I'm going to ruin your life in the next five minutes but I do hope you won't take it too personally and I'm sure we can still remain friends once this is over.* Bwoy, yuh lucky she only scratch yuh!' He gave Frank no time to respond, but continued briskly, 'Dat leave us about six week. Yuh chest shoulda heal all right by den. Yuh can stay here till yuh leave. I'll sort everyting out.'

'No, Sol. She mad. I don't waan put yuh in danger too.'

'Me?' Sol's eyes flashed. 'But, bwoy, yuh fool. Yuh nuh see Rose 'fraid a me. Yuh see we already know each other from way back,' he said as piled up the bloodied strips of cloth and thread he'd removed and the cotton he'd used.

'How yuh mean?' Frank twisted round to stare at his friend, wincing as he did so. 'First time me hear dis.'

'Not from dis lifetime, fool. Other ones.'

Frank shook his head. 'Yuh already know wha' I tink 'bout dat past life business.'

256

'And dat is precisely yuh problem, my friend,' Sol snapped, leaning forward and pressing his long fingers into Frank's good shoulder. 'Yuh tink if yuh nuh see it den yuh cyaan believe it. If yuh nuh feel it, it nuh exist,' he hissed. Sol stood so close that Frank could feel spittle on his face as he spoke. 'If yuh only more willin' fi learn from yuh past, from other people, then maybe yuh coulda avoided dis,' he said, touching Frank's wound and forcing a groan from him. 'I meet yuh before, I meet her before an' so have yuh. She know as well, dat's why she nuh mess wid me 'cause she know dat between me an' her is only one winner. I'm tellin' yuh, bwoy, better start lookin' to yuh past startin' from now. 'Cause if yuh don', yuh pig-headedness,' and he rapped Frank hard on his forehead, 'yuh refusal fi learn from yuh past wid her, yuh past wid me, from all yuh past, gwine kill yuh. Galang!'

Through with speaking, Sol set light to the dirty things he'd gathered together. There was silence between the two men as they watched a spiral of smoke rise from the burning cloth, then Frank spoke. 'It shouldn't have ended like dis.'

'Well it did an' yuh damn lucky it not yuh throat. Good ting yuh never breed her.' Frank opened his eyes wide. Sol stared at him. 'Wha' do yuh now?'

'I cyaan believe I figet. What wid de way she just launch herself 'pon me, de way she attack me, de blood an' –'

'Get to de point.' Sol's tone was brusque.

'What wid everyting . . .' Frank saw Sol's expression darken and continued hurriedly. 'Her words went out of my mind just like dat.' He snapped his thumb and index finger together.

'So?'

'Sol. She claim she pregnant.'

'Cho! A woman like dat will say anyting fi keep her man.' Sol grunted as he threw the leather bag back onto the top of the cupboard. He shot Frank a swift look. 'Yuh believe her?'

'She always tell me she can't have pickney an' we were together for close on two years an' she never pregnant, so why now?'

'Maybe yuh been firin' blanks, Frankie baby.' Frank cut his eyes at him. Sol flashed him a grin that showed his dimples, then busied himself finding a pillow and a spare sheet. 'I know fi a fact dat woman can breed,' Sol added casually, throwing both pillow and sheet onto the hammock before walking over to the sink to wash his hands.

Frank moved awkwardly towards him and pulled Sol around to face him, wincing as his wound protested. 'Wha' yuh mean?' He narrowed his eyes, bringing Sol into sharp focus.

Sol rubbed his hands dry on his shirttail. Pulled a cigarette from a crumpled packet in his breast pocket. Took his time before answering.

Frank stared at him. He wanted to hear what Sol had to say and he knew Sol wanted to tell him, but he wasn't going to ask, wouldn't satisfy him by showing any curiosity. He hated it when Sol did this, kept him waiting in anticipation of whatever it was he was about to do or announce. It went beyond playfulness, it was a power trip – what else could it be? He'd told Sol more than once how much it annoyed him, but Sol just laughed, said there was nothing wrong with a man getting things straight in his mind before spitting them out. Lying bastard! Sol only spat out what he wanted when he wanted and to hell with anyone else's feelings.

'She already have a chile,' Sol said, looking down at the cigarette in his hand. 'Leastways, according to rumour,' he added in a different tone of voice. He took a drag from the cigarette, blew out smoke from between his teeth. 'Must be walkin' an' talkin' by now.'

Frank opened his mouth to speak. Deny. Question. But nothing came out.

'Franklin!' Sol raised his eyebrows in mock surprise. 'Nuh tell me yuh never know? Maybe it was meant to be a secret.' He pulled on his cigarette again. 'Yuh mean she never tell yuh – I always imagine dat in between de sex yuh chat to each other. Maybe it jus' slip her mind. I mean, what's a pickney here or dere?'

'Who say she have chile? When?' Frank demanded.

'Doesn't matter.' Sol shrugged. 'Maybe it nuh even true.' He waited, relaxed, his cigarette loosely held between two fingers, and a smile flitted across his face as he watched the muscles in Frank's jaw tighten. Maybe one day Frank would let himself go. Actually show what he was feeling when he felt it, instead of always holding back and torturing himself in private. But from the way Frank was tightening up his face – like he had a bad case of the runs without a toilet in sight – it wasn't going to be today. 'One ting I notice 'bout yuh, Frank,' he said with resignation, 'yuh have a funny habit of gettin' angry wid de wrong people at de wrong time.'

Despite the advantage of his greater height and build, Frank couldn't hold Sol's black-eyed stare. Sol had a way of looking – no, more than that – he had a way of being that made it difficult to outstare him, to outdo him. He commanded attention, respect, but he also commanded fear. Frank looked away; despite what his friend had done for him he felt something close to – hate? For a moment he almost hated Sol for being right about Rose. For always being right.

Sol turned off the saucepan he'd put on to boil and tossed his half-smoked cigarette into the sink behind him where it hissed lazily before going out. Frank didn't move as Sol brushed past him.

'Have my bed tonight,' Sol told him over his shoulder.

259

'Tomorrow we can talk 'bout bringin' forward yuh departure. Dat woman will fight fi yuh till de last.'

Frank turned round and watched the door close behind Sol. He heard the sound of a match being struck against the side of its box, and through the window he saw the brief arc of light before the match was tossed casually to one side. He closed his eyes, felt his wound itch and throb just like the thoughts that raced through his head. Felt his hands clench into fists of frustration as he bit down on his lip until the taste of blood filled his mouth . . .

'Is only yuh can stop dis business, Frank. But yuh haffi decide.' Sol stepped forward.

Frank turned mechanically. His look was inscrutable, but when he spoke his voice was decided. 'Yuh right. I gave dis to Rose.' He held the bracelet up in the air. 'Help me, Sol.'

10

21st February

Aunt B tugged at Frank's sleeve, as if she was a little girl pleading for sweets. 'Wha' yuh plannin' on tellin' Jewelle?' she whispered urgently as she saw her niece approaching.

'Only wha' she need fi know.'

'Beg yuh don' go, Frank.' Her eyes implored him. 'I don' waan no more trouble. Yuh mumma safe in dere.' She gestured towards the hospital building they'd just left. 'Mek we jus' go home. Please.'

In the early morning light the worry lines that danced across her forehead stood out clearly. Frank was shocked by how vulnerable she looked: for a moment he saw Aunt B not as a stubborn middle-aged woman who argued with everybody, but as a woman who loved her family dearly and would do whatever she could to protect them. And this realization, this perceived softness, broke the impenetrable barrier he'd erected around himself ever since Miss Jess had taken ill.

'I don' waan no more trouble either, dat's why me haffi do dis.' He'd worn a suit so he would look smart for his mother; now he was outside he hooked a finger behind the knot of his tie, pulling it down so he could undo the buttons behind. 'Take Jewelle home wid yuh. I waan de two of yuh stay together till I get back.'

'Dis nuh feel right, Frank.' She tapped him on the arm, but he stared at her impassively. 'Yuh cyaan just up an' leave like dis.' She spoke earnestly, examining his face as she did, but it was impossible to imagine what he was thinking or feeling. 'All right. Seem like yuh mind set,' she said, disappointment threaded her voice.

Frank nodded, relieved that she wasn't making it any harder for him.

'Beg yuh one ting though.' Her fingers pinched through the material of his suit jacket trying to impress on him the importance of her words. 'Don' react!' The way she spoke made her words sound like they were written in capitals.

'How yuh mean?'

'If yuh react den she gwine react – and if she react de wrong way she might back a machete an' drop yuh two good chop!'

'No, Aunt B, me nah go let it happen again.'

'Yuh tink Rose gwine give up now?' Aunt B hissed. 'NOW? When she finally get yuh fi come to her? Cho!' She sucked her teeth long and hard. When Frank didn't respond she shook her head in a gesture of surrender. 'All right, Frank. Galang! Is fi yuh goose a go cook inna enamel pot!'

'Dad?' They both turned at the sound of Jewelle's voice. 'Sol says you two are going somewhere. Can I come with you?'

'No, Jewelle. This is something I need to do alone. It's long overdue.'

'It's to do with her, isn't it? That woman.'

'Yes.'

'Will you tell me what's been going on when you get back?'

He was surprised by how adult she was. She sounded . . . mature – none of her sulky monosyllabic teenage remarks. Even her face seemed to have changed, the difference so subtle he couldn't quite pin it down – except that she was a young woman. His little girl had grown up during the few

262

days of their holidays. When had that happened? Was he always going to see things after the event? Her words broke through his thoughts.

'I'm so sick and tired of people not answering my questions, or telling me,' she screwed up her face and mimicked Aunt B, '*dis a big people business.*'

Frank inclined his head slowly. 'I'll try to answer your questions as honestly as I can. All right?'

'But you won't tell me everything, will you?'

He forced a tight smile. 'I'll tell you as much as I think you need to know.' He raised an eyebrow as she started to protest. 'Which is more than you know right now. Right?'

'Frank!'

He glanced round. Sol was jabbing at his watch face with the tip of one finger. 'Coming,' he mouthed, then turned his attention back to Jewelle. 'I have to go.' He gave her a quick peck on her forehead, then beckoned to Jake. 'Tek Jewelle an' Aunt B straight home an' stop wid dem till we come back.'

He watched as they made their way to the pickup, then turned to face Sol.

'How yuh find her?' Frank asked once they were in the car.

'It never too hard. After all, yuh both waan de same ting.'

'Foolishness!'

'Is it? Yuh waan find her an' she waan find. Look like de same ting from where I'm standin'.'

'Why yuh puttin' yuhself out so much for me?'

Sol kept his eyes on the road. 'It nuh matter,' he replied simply.

'But it does, Sol. It tek me a long time fi start askin' instead of just acceptin' tings. Years back yuh say yuh know Rose from before. When? How? Why?'

Sol smiled to himself, but the smile didn't quite reach his eyes. 'It tek me a lifetime to understan'. Now yuh waan me fi try explain it all in five minutes. When we done wid dis business we can talk. But right now, yuh need fi concentrate on de matter in hand.' He settled his sunglasses on the bridge of his nose.

The conversation was over.

'D'you think Dad will be OK, Aunt B?'

'Hope so.' Aunt B was so worried that it didn't occur to her that Jewelle might be equally concerned.

'Me sure everyting all right,' Jake reassured, closing the pickup door and following them into the house.

Jewelle raised the blinds, which had been pulled down low to keep the heat out – but somehow it crept its way in, slipping through the seams of the house and hanging heavy in the air. Even Jake, used to the heat of the island, felt breathless in the suffocatingly damp humidity.

Aunt B flopped heavily onto the sofa. 'Beg yuh bring me some sorrel, Jewelle. It already mix. An' please mek sure it have plenty ice.' She unpinned her hat and threw it onto the table where it slid to a stop. Jewelle came back with three glasses of sorrel on a tray.

'Thought you would be thirsty too,' she said, handing a glass to Jake, then standing by his side.

'Sit down nuh,' Aunt B instructed. 'Yuh mek me nervous hoverin' above me like dat.'

The three of them sat in silence. Jewelle twirled the glass in her hand so that the ice clinked against the sides. 'Aunt B?' she started timidly. 'Who is – I mean, can you tell me anything about this woman?'

Aunt B closed her eyes as if deeply exhausted, the lines around her mouth seemed scored into her face. What could she say? Where could she start? There were so many facets to Rose, to this whole story. How could she put into words the affection she'd once had for this woman? A woman who loved and hated equally hard; a woman who lived each day intensely as if it might be her last; a woman who had helped her with things that even Sam didn't know about and whom she'd betrayed. Betrayed was too strong a word, Sam claimed. It was just a job inna building society she help yuh keep – and now yuh feel yuh owe her someting when yuh don't, he'd said on more than one occasion. But it wasn't just the job. If only. Sam didn't know about the baby she'd once carried and lost. That had happened before she'd met him. She sighed, opened her mouth to speak, but Jewelle interrupted her. 'I know. Big people business! Forget it.'

Aunt B sighed again. 'Yuh right, is big people business, but yuh not such a chile any more. Yuh growin' up an' dis affect yuh too. She smaddy yuh daddy know when him growin' up. She was my friend too, once upon a time. She cyaan accept dat tings not de way dem use to be, dat's why she causin' all dis fuss. Yuh daddy will tell yuh wha' yuh need fi know when him get back. Is not my place to interfere. I already interfere too much . . . though at de time I did tink I was helpin'.' She lapsed into silence again.

'Dad will be all right, won't he? He's with Sol, so –'

'Hmm. Sol have him uses, I suppose,' Aunt B conceded, 'but me cyaan help wonder why him so determine fi help now. Him mus' have someting fi gain from it – but me don' know what.' She fished a piece of ice out of the tangy dark red liquid and crunched on it loudly.

'We haffi walk from here.' Sol switched off the engine. 'She live likkle beyond dat electricity pole dere.' He pointed to the crown of a small hill.

'Lead de way,' Frank said, slipping off his jacket and throwing it onto the front passenger seat. 'Me ready.'

'Hold on a moment.'

Sol opened the car boot and pulled out a machete with a thin, murderous-looking blade. Frank's eyes bulged. 'Might be useful,' Sol said cheerfully, waving the machete in the air.

'Me nuh waan see no blood shed,' Frank protested.

Sol's response was to whistle as he hacked back the branches that snatched at his arms and shoulders as they followed a narrow path – worn by countless feet into the grass and shrubs over the years. The dirt track was rough and uneven. Half-hidden tree roots pushed up through the dry, baked earth. More than once Frank slipped on round stones, smooth as marble under his leather-soled shoes. He grew tired of brushing down his shirtsleeves and picking burrs from the material. The air was heavily moist, making it difficult to breathe and he took off his tie and shoved it into his trouser pocket. Rain was due; he could taste it in the air.

'Slow down, man,' Frank panted.

Sol merely swung the machete in wide arcs in front of him as the undergrowth around them thickened.

'How yuh know Sol?' Aunt B asked Jake abruptly as he nursed the drink in his hand.

'Me see him around a few times. Enough fi seh howdy but nutten else. One day him start chat to me. Seh me remind of smaddy him did know well.'

'Who?'

'Him never tell me. Just seh it was smaddy dat get led astray an' pay fi it. Him ask me 'bout me people an' when I say I never know me daddy, him seh it not good fi a bwoy grow widout a man around. Seh if me ever need a han', if me ever have any problem, den come check him an' he woulda help. When I tell him I lookin' a likkle work fi earn me keep, him say him know smaddy dat might need some help now an' den. Dat's how I meet yuh granny,' he finished, directing his gaze to Jewelle.

'Yuh mean fi tell me,' Aunt B said, sittings up straight,

266

'Sol come to yuh out of nowhere an' say him waan help yuh when him never even know yuh more dan so?' Aunt B snapped her black and red fan open with a deft flick of her wrist. 'Strange. Very strange.'

'But Sol's really sweet. He's kind and generous and he's always got time for everyone,' Jewelle blurted out.

'Leopard cyaan change him spot much as him might try,' Aunt B sniffed. 'Tek it from me, Jewelle. Sol is him own number one priority. Him not de type fi go out of him way fi help smaddy outta de goodness of him heart unless him stand fi gain.'

'But he's been so good to us. All of us. He's funny and he knows how to listen.'

'I hope time don' prove me right, but me know Sol, so me sure it will.' She saw Jewelle's crestfallen expression and softened her voice. 'Just remember dat some people will be anyting dem tink yuh waan, till dem get wha' dem waan.'

'That's exactly what Granny said to me the other day,' said Jewelle.

'Yuh granny nuh stupid. Why yuh tink she live as long as she live?' Aunt B pronounced. 'Is only yuh daddy stupid. Lose him head over dat damn woman an' come follow her till she turn him fool.'

'Which woman?' Jake asked.

Aunt B stared at him. 'Family business,' she said. 'Yuh nuh have nowhere fi go?'

'Jewelle daddy say I must stop here till him reach.'

'Well, me certain dere is plenty yuh can do instead of answer back yuh elders. Come. Soon find work fi yuh.'

'Dem seh she live here,' Sol announced presently.

'Who seh?'

'Bwoy! How yuh love ask question at de wrong time? She live here. Dat's all dat count.'

Frank stared at the pink-painted house front. The net

curtains were drawn and the louvre windows closed flat. 'Nuh look like nobody home,' he ventured.

Sol sucked his teeth in exasperation. So close now and Frank was forming fool. 'Only one way fi find out,' he said, pushing Frank forward and then following closely behind.

'You tink I should knock first?'

'Yuh tink Rose knock before she walk into yuh madda house? Jus' come on!' Sol gave Frank another little push so that his nose was almost touching the front of the white panelled door. It swung open to reveal a square entrance beyond which he could see the kitchen. They stepped into the waiting silence of the house and looked around. The whitewashed walls were bare; the kitchen equipped with the minimum of objects. A small dutchy pot stood on the stovetop. A dusty orange tube ran from behind the cooker to the blue gas-bottle that stood at its side. Three white plates lay face down on the enamel draining board. To one side of the plates was an assortment of cutlery in a yellow Tupperware container.

Past the kitchen was another square of corridor with a closed door on either side. Directly in front of them, the back door stood open, beyond it a yard overrun with jasmine and hibiscus, azalea and magnolia. Frank took the three red-stained steps down into the garden, paused for a moment and then spoke.

'Rose.'

She pivoted smoothly as if on a revolving pedestal. Her face held no trace of surprise at seeing him, her body, as slim and inviting as ever, showed no apparent change. She was wearing pale yellow, just like the first time they'd met. A girlish colour – but on her it didn't look silly. Though he knew it couldn't possibly be the same dress, he felt transported back. Felt the familiar hypnotic pull that separated his brain from the rest of him. She held out one hand to him and smiled, a big open smile that pulled him forward.

'Frank.' Her voice wrapped itself around him with the light, yet deceptive strength of a spider's web.

He took a step forward. Their fingertips touched and then there was no sense of time. No past. No future. Only present. She stood close, not quite touching, yet still he could smell the perfumed heat of her body.

'Kiss me.'

He felt her arms tighten around him, her fingers gently moving up and down the base of his neck, as her lips reached up to his. Then she stiffened in his arms, her nails biting into his skin. He opened his eyes to see her gaze fixed on a point over his shoulder. He turned and took in the photographic quality of the scene – Sol relaxed against the doorjamb, black clothes stark against the white wood, machete slung casually over his shoulder like a scarf.

'Come outta me house,' she hissed. Her eyes were no longer brown but a clear icy green. Frank had never seen them so uniform in colour, but they held the same murderous look as on that day years before. And it chilled him to the bone, as if the sun had withdrawn its warm embrace and left him unprotected. Slowly he withdrew his arms and pulled away from her.

'Wha' yuh doin' in me house?' Rose moved forward as Frank stepped backward.

'We just come from hospital an' decide fi pass by an' seh howdy,' Sol replied pleasantly.

'Yuh nuh answer me question.'

'Me come wid Frank. An' in memory of Bevan.'

She stopped in her tracks and shot Frank a swift look. When she next spoke her tone was slightly less aggressive. 'Dat time long gone.'

'But him memory live on. If,' Sol said, arching an eyebrow, 'yuh know wha' I mean.'

Rose narrowed her eyes. 'Dat time long gone,' she repeated stubbornly.

'Oh?' Sol said innocently. 'Yuh mean past past an' alla dat?'

'It finish an' done wid.'

'Oh?' Sol raised his chin slowly. 'Just like yuh an' Frank?'

'Dat different. Anyway,' she added quickly, 'it nuh concern yuh, so just come out.'

'Me not leavin' widout Frank. So hurry up chat yuh business an' done.'

Rose rushed at him, but he stood firm. Held her gaze while he lazily traced the blade of the machete with a fingertip. She drew up a few inches from his face.

'Me nah go tell yuh again. Come outta me house!'

Frank squeezed his way between them. 'Stand back, Rose,' he ordered. To Sol, he said, 'Dis is my fight. Is only me can end dis.' He turned sideways, palms splayed between them and arms wide apart. He felt as if he was absorbing electrical current that had nowhere else to go but through him. 'Wait fi me out front. I don' waan fight but me nah go run no more. Yuh understan'?'

'Just come off me property.' Rose clawed at Sol around the side of Frank's body.

'Which property?' Sol sneered. 'Yuh born wid nutten and yuh wi' dead wid nutten. Who yuh sleep wid den dash 'way fi get dis little piece a dust yuh call land?' He looked at Frank. 'Me out front. But just 'member – use yuh head.'

'Put on yuh shoes,' Aunt B ordered. 'We goin' into Brown's Town.'

'But Dad hasn't come back yet,' Jewelle said, sitting up carefully in the hammock she had stretched out in.

'It mek no difference whether we here or in Brown's Town. It won't bring him back quicker. Jake. Yuh know a car rental place?'

'Yes, mam. Dere's one opposite de church.'

'All right. Write a note tellin' Frank we gone fi rent a car.

I don' intend ride one more time in Sol bruk-up old Ford him one tink is a Ferrari.'

The bell above the entrance clanged nosily as they walked into the wooden interior of the car rental shop. A large black and chrome ventilator fan spun in one corner of the room, holding the heat at bay. Jewelle stood with her arms wide open in front of it and looked around. The walls were covered with framed pictures of the latest sports cars and of a man – she assumed he was the owner – with his arm around celebrities who had rented from him. One of the faces looked like Madonna's – but it couldn't be, Jewelle thought. Madonna would go to one of the posh resorts, not a little village like Brown's Town.

Aunt B walked to the counter. Through the glass panel of the office door in front of her she could see two men playing dominoes.

'Hey!' She waved her hand at them. 'Unnu not workin' today?'

One of them caught sight of her and waved back before slapping another domino onto the table. 'Tre!' they heard him shout.

Aunt B rolled her eyes and waved her bamboo fan vigorously as she waited. After about ten seconds she delved into her bag and pulled out a whistle, which hung from a length of purple ribbon. 'I gwine count to t'ree,' she informed Jewelle and Jake, 'if dem nuh come out by de time me finish countin', just watch me an' dem! *One. Two. T'ree.*' She blew the whistle as hard as she could, producing an ear-piercing blast which had Jewelle and Jake covering their ears and the two men running out of the office.

'Wh'appen? Weh de fire deh?' asked the oldest of the two. A stout bald man wearing a yellow T-shirt with '100% Jamaican' emblazoned across the front in big red letters.

'Wh'appen is dat me waan some service,' Aunt B replied calmly.

'Yuh mean fi say yuh raise me blood pressure nearly give me heart attack all 'cause yuh waan serve?'

'Yes.'

'But why yuh never ring de bell like normal people?' He pointed to the hotel reception-type bell that stood on the counter. 'Wha' wrong wid yuh?'

'Oh, yuh mean dis?' Aunt B banged it hard with the flat of her hand. It gave a tired little ping. 'I tink yuh'll agree dat my bell work better.' She waggled the whistle in front of his nose.

'How can we help yuh?' asked the younger man, shooting his partner a 'keep calm' look.

'Well, sir,' Aunt B said politely, 'I would like to rent a big car. Five seats. Fi de day after tomorrow. Wha' yuh have?'

The young man opened a ring binder of plastic wallets filled with pictures of different models of cars. Below each picture was a handwritten price list, cost of insurance and conditions of hire.

'I waan dat one.' She jabbed at one of the pictures. 'It free?' The man nodded. 'How much fi one day?'

'One thousand, five. US!' he quoted, making Aunt B squint. She pulled a boiled sweet from her bag, slowly unwrapped it and then crunched on it loudly.

Jewelle raised her eyebrows at Jake. 'Come on,' she giggled, pulling him to the counter. 'This'll be wicked!'

'What? Why?'

'When Aunt B starts crunching on those sweets she means business.'

'Dat a tourist price,' Aunt B informed the young man. 'Me come from yard. One hundred per cent. Just like yuh spar dere.' She nodded to Baldy. 'Give me an honest Jamaican price.'

'Where yuh come from? America? England? Yuh not

272

Jamaican. Yuh nuh live here,' Baldy told her. 'Yuh only come to Jamaica fi spend money.'

'Yuh just lissen to me.' She pointed her fan at the centre of his chest. 'Me mumma Jamaican. Me poppa Jamaican an' I born here. Dat mek me Jamaican.' She brought the fan down with a thwack on the counter.

Baldy blew on his little finger and glowered at her.

'Me catch yuh?' she enquired. 'Thought it was a mosquito. So, how much?' she continued conversationally.

'One thousand,' the young man said. His partner glared at him.

'Dat better,' Aunt B told them, 'but it still not good enough. After all, is round here me born an' grow. Probably know yuh people an' all. Come to tink of it,' she said, peering into Baldy's face, 'me know dat nose! Yuh family name Johnstone?' Baldy nodded. 'From round May Pen?' He nodded again, surprised. 'I know yuh. Yuh did love run up an' down wid yuh belly outta door an' yuh nose a run. Wha' yuh name now?' She pinched the bridge of her nose between forefinger and thumb as she concentrated. 'Pepper!' she announced triumphantly.

'Pepper?' The young man stared at his partner. Baldy looked away.

Aunt B pinched Jewelle's arm. 'Peppercorn!' she declared.

'All right,' Baldy said quickly. 'Seven, five,' he whispered, putting his forefinger against his mouth and making a shushing sign.

Aunt B gave him a vindictive victor's smile and continued. 'Yes, yuh head did always knot up. Mek yuh look like yuh have peppercorn fi hair. Wh'appen to it, anyway?' She leaned forward and stroked his head.

'Peppercorn!' Baldy's partner chortled.

Jake and Jewelle covered their mouths trying not to laugh. Baldy pushed Aunt B's hand away. 'Dat's my final price!' he said angrily.

'Yuh sure?' Aunt B challenged.

'Me sure,' he said rubbing his hand over his bald pate.

Aunt B tightened her scarf. 'Now me mind start run . . . didn't I hear someting 'bout yuh an' one a Maas Foster cow?'

Baldy's partner slapped the counter and doubled up with laughter. Jake had to lean on Jewelle for support, tears streaming from his eyes. Jewelle looked perplexed. 'I didn't get that,' she whispered to him. Aunt B merely looked smug.

'All right!' Baldy shouted. 'Name yuh price.'

Aunt B placed her hands on the counter and smiled with satisfaction. 'Now dat's how me like fi do business.'

Frank waited until Sol left, then turned to Rose. They stared at each other in silence. Now the first flush of emotion had passed he was able to look at her impartially. Her face *had* changed, he just hadn't noticed at first. Her mouth was thinner and less inviting, as if the juice had been slowly sucked from her lips. The lines that ran from the corner of her mouth, lines he'd always associated with her smile, were now deeply scored. Discontent? Bitterness? He could only guess. She was still a tall, beautiful woman, imposing, but there was a new brittleness to her slimness. He wondered how much of this hardness was due to him and his role in her life.

He walked towards her slowly. Although his heart was beating wildly and his head was telling him to leave, this time he refused to run. Step into it and through it, he chanted mentally. He would step into it too. If he really believed it, then he could just maybe come out bruised but otherwise unscathed. It was a journey that was long overdue. She turned her back to him, just as she'd done all those years ago when he'd told her he was leaving for England.

'Rose?' She didn't move, but this time he didn't fall into her honeyed trap of physical contact. Instead, he walked carefully round her until he was facing her. 'I've come to finish what I should have finished years ago.'

'Yuh cyaan finish wha' meant fi be.'

'Your destiny, not mine.'

'Ours.' Her voice was stubborn. 'Yuh cyaan fight it, Frank. It stronger dan any life we know. It have root. Deep root. Just like dat tree over dere.' She pointed to a tall yacca tree with dainty, dagger-shaped leaves. 'Yuh cyaan pull dem up.'

'I'm pulling them up now, Rose. Enough is enough.'

'Yuh don' mean dat. If tings did really finish yuh wouldn't be here today.'

He took a deep breath, careful not to let his nervousness show. Exactly the words she'd used the last time he'd seen her before he left for England. He'd never forgotten anything said or done that day. How could he? It was indelibly marked on his body.

'Two halves. One whole,' she said and gave her gap-toothed smile.

His mother's words came back to him. Her face when she'd first seen his wound. 'Well, Frank,' she'd said stoically, 'yuh nuh even leave wid quarter moon. Look like two mash-up mango.' And, remembering those words, he suddenly knew what to do.

Rose had been right. She'd known him better than he'd known himself. In a way, some deep, hidden part of him had been fooling around with her. Begging her to let him go, yet knowing that she wouldn't, couldn't in fact, until he set her free – allowed her to move on. Deep inside, buried as deep as the yacca tree roots she'd pointed out, was the knowledge that he'd always known what to say to her – and how. He knew the effect of his lightly accented English, knew it turned her on yet at the same time made

275

her feel like a lady. How could she possible take anything he'd had to say to her seriously if that was the effect? He'd chosen and used his words well, used them in such a way that it was guaranteed she wouldn't listen. Known that she'd think, it's just Frank, being Frank.

So what did that say about him? The answer was simple – but it was an unpleasant one, hard to accept. He was weak and selfish. Pure and simple. Even when it had all gone wrong between them, he'd still let the relationship continue. Preferred to suffer, unwilling to let go with both hands until he met somebody new.

Was that all Beth had been? Someone to cling on to?

No. That, if nothing else, was clear in his mind. Beth had been the right one. The only one for him. Never a day's doubt, or a moment of regret with her. He'd done Rose wrong. It had taken him a long, long time to accept his role in the stupid games they'd been playing, but enough was enough. For both of them. It was to time to use the language they both knew and understood.

'Still scared a wha' yuh feel fi me?' Rose asked softly, interrupting his thoughts.

'Not any more,' he whispered, slipping his hands around her slim neck. His thumbs caressed the soft skin at the base of her jaw as he ran a delicate line of kisses along the length of one shoulder. 'So smooth, so soft,' he murmured, 'just like the first time I touched you. You still wear the same perfume.' He inhaled deeply, nuzzling the skin beneath his nose and making Rose purr with pleasure. 'You see, I haven't forgotten.' His hands gently traced the clean lines of her neck. She closed her eyes and smiled, arching her neck so her throat lay exposed. 'So slim, so beautiful,' he murmured. She pressed herself against him and he knew it was now or never. 'So easy fi break,' he continued.

Her eyes flew open. 'Frank?' Her hands fluttered over his.

276

'Yuh love talk 'bout how we two mek one, but yuh cut my moon in two, in case yuh figet.'

Deep in her eyes he saw something flicker, sensed her uncertainty and pressed on. He pushed her hands away from him and unbuttoned his shirt. 'Look!' She looked away but he held her face firmly in both hands. She stiffened in resistance and tried to pull away. 'Touch it.'

'No.' It was barely a whisper.

He forced one of her hands onto his chest. She twisted and struggled in his grip. 'Touch it!' he insisted, dragging her hand along the hard line of flesh. 'Is yuh do dis to me. Is yuh split de moon. Is yuh kill it. I don't love yuh, Rose.' There. It was out. Not 'I can't love you as I should' or 'You deserve a better man.' None of the half-truths of the past. Nothing but the truth.

'I don't love yuh. It's finished, Rose. Over.'

She yanked her hand violently out of his grasp, stumbling backwards with the momentum. 'It nuh done, Frank. It nuh done.' But her voice betrayed her.

Just as her voice wavered, so his strengthened. 'Yuh cut me free all those years ago an' I too fool fi even know. Waste so many years feelin' guilty 'bout how I hurt yuh. Is stupid when is yuh hurt me – mash up me body an' if I never stand strong yuh woulda mash up me life. All dat time I too scared fi look behind me an' face de past, our past, all 'cause I 'fraid a what I might see. Yuh know what I see now, Rose?' Rose stood frozen to the spot as Frank leaned towards her. 'I ask yuh if yuh know what I see?'

She shook her head reluctantly.

'Nutten.'

She seemed to crumple in on herself before him – her skin softening and slackening. The lines of her face seemed to ripple, tremors moving below the surface. And suddenly she was old. Her eyes, now a tired brown, looked as if she'd lived too long and seen too much.

'Whatever yuh done,' Frank said, his nostrils flaring as he inhaled sharply, 'whatever yuh choose fi do, I don' waan know. Me not like yuh, Rose, an' me glad. I cyaan hurt or maim fi get wha' I waan. But I can walk away.'

He turned on his heel, galvanizing her into action. She ran to the door, then spun around, blocking his exit.

'Yuh ever tink 'bout yuh daughter?' Her hand fell on his chest.

'Wha' Jewelle haffi do wid dis?'

'No! Yuh first born. My daughter. Our baby!'

Frank shook his head as he contemplated her. Stared at her as if she'd just pulled her knickers down and peed on the ground in front of him. Her touch no longer soothed or stroked but left only a mild sensation of irritation where her skin had made contact with his. 'Yuh just won't give up, will yuh?' He flicked her hand away disdainfully; ignored the tears that sprang to her eyes.

She watched him leave in silence.

Aunt B signed the contract, then held her hand out for the keys. ''Bout yuh a rob one of yuh mumma old friend,' she chided. Baldy slapped the keys into her outstretched hand. 'How yuh mumma, anyway?' she asked.

'She dead,' he muttered.

Aunt B turned to look at him. 'Least she spare see how yuh turn out. De shame woulda kill her. Come on yuh two.' She hustled the two teenagers ahead of her.

'Maas Foster cow!' she heard the young man crow as she stepped into the street. 'Wait till me tell de bwoy dem tonight!'

'Nice doing business wid yuh,' she called over her shoulder.

'Come back anytime,' the young man shouted back, shooting a sly glance at Baldy. 'Anytime.'

Out on the pavement, Jake slapped his thigh. 'Bwoy,' he

chortled, 'yuh aunty rough, Jewelle. Yuh see how she do de man?'

Aunt B joined them. 'Wha' do yuh seh?'

Jake wiped his eyes and straightened his face. He could feel his stomach muscles tightening, and his chest constricting as he fought to hold back his laughter. 'Nutten, mam.'

'Yuh better choke back dat laugh before it choke yuh,' she warned before joining him in raucous laughter.

Sol watched Frank as he sauntered towards him. He looked taller, leaner, his step lighter. He noticed Frank's leisurely pace and the fact that he never once looked behind him. His open shirt flapped in front of him as he strode to the car. The shirt was still white, creased around the edges and marked with two irregular patches of sweat under the arms, but apart from that there were no other signs of wear and tear.

He slapped Frank on the shoulder. 'No blood shed den?'

Frank held him in a one-armed embrace. 'It never as bad as I expec'. I feel so free, man. Cyaan believe how light an' young I feel.'

'Waan tell me 'bout it?' Sol asked as they started down the hill.

'Nuh seem like nutten much fi tell, except it over. It over fi good.'

'Over?' Sol's expression was inscrutable as he watched Frank hunch his shoulders and rub the back of his neck.

'Yuh feel dat breeze, Sol?'

'No.' Sol looked behind them; saw the outline of a figure in the doorway of the house they were leaving behind. 'Walk up, man,' he instructed and hurried Frank along.

Frank slipped on his jacket once he got to the car. 'How yuh brother Bevan mix up wid Rose?' he asked as Sol turned on the engine.

279

Sol narrowed his eyes. 'Bevan hook up wid a woman some years before yuh meet Rose. Him never tell me her name.' He spoke briskly, glanced at Frank to see how he was taking the news. Frank lay slouched in his seat, head propped against the headrest, sunglasses perched on his nose, his face a picture of relief.

'Mek me guess. Long time back yuh tell me Rose did already have baby. I never waan lissen at de time but me lissen now. Is Bevan di babyfather, right?'

'I still don't know if dat woman is Rose. All I know fi sure is dat Bevan have a chile somewhere 'bout de place. Him tell me in him last letter dat de woman have pickney fi him an' den run off wid de baby. Him ask me fi find de chile an' dat's what I intend fi do. I lose too many years. Dat letter follow me all 'bout de world. Every time it reach one place, I already move on. By de time I get Bevan letter it too late. Bevan dead. Too late fi answers – dead man don' talk! But even if I never get de chance fi question him, from de type of woman Bevan describe an' dat old-time rumour dat Rose have pickney, I tink it could be her. Is she kill him!'

'But yuh tell me Bevan commit suicide. So it couldn't have been Rose, even if she was Bevan's woman.'

'Is she lead him to it.' Sol's expression was hard, his voice categorical.

'So dat's why yuh did waan help me so much. Yuh waan revenge fi Bevan.' Frank sat up and nodded in understanding. 'Wh'appen to de baby? Must be big man or woman now. Yuh have any idea weh to find him? Her?'

Sol fumbled in the dashboard and pulled out a bent cigarette which he clamped between his lips. 'Me workin' on it,' he muttered. 'Very damn hard,' he added under his breath.

Frank rubbed his neck again and closed the car window on his side. 'Win' up yuh window, Sol.'

'Wha' do yuh?' Sol asked, cranking up his window. 'Yuh cyaan feel how sun hot?'

Frank turned up his jacket collar and looked around the car in irritation. 'Dere's a breeze in here,' he grumbled.

Sol glanced at him. 'Ah,' he said.

'Nancy? Got a minute?'

The girl turned round in the middle of shrugging on a light cardigan. Outside, the darkening sky threatened angry rain. 'Why?'

'Listen, I know we didn't really hit it off or anything . . .'

Nancy looked Jewelle up and down. Her eyes took in the other girl's stance and the tense set of her shoulders. She lifted her chin. If Jewelle wanted to argue, she was more than ready for it. She was only surprised that it hadn't happened sooner.

Jewelle took a deep breath. 'The other day I saw you wearing a really pretty red dress and I thought . . . maybe these could go with it.' She opened her fist to reveal a crumpled ball of tissue paper.

Nancy stared at Jewelle's palm, but otherwise didn't move. Jewelle shoved the clumsily wrapped gift into Nancy's hand.

'Wha' dis?'

Jewelle nodded. 'I'm leaving tomorrow and – I dunno – I wanted to give you something. Don't ask me why,' she added quickly, seeing the beginnings of a smile on Nancy's face.

'For me?' Nancy said, peeling back the tissue paper to reveal two silver earrings. 'Look how dem pretty.' She held one up by its hook; a fish with delicate silver spines and a cornelian red stone eye in its solid silver head.

'They're earrings,' Jewelle said helpfully.

Nancy flashed her a look – 'Me not blind yuh know' – but her smile took the sting from her words.

'They're not new, but I thought they'd suit you and the fish shape is to remind you of the first time we met.'

Nancy grinned. 'How can I figet Aunt B sitting at de table suckin' on her fish head an' telling us dat we "just better learn fi rub along together"?'

'That's right,' Jewelle continued. 'Every time you look at them you'll remember dat spoil likkle English gyal.' Jewelle put her hands on her hips and waggled her head from side to side just as she'd seen Nancy do.

For the first time they laughed together – an unexpected truce.

'Thanks,' said Nancy softly.

'Don't start going all nice on me otherwise I'll have to take them back.' Jewelle grinned with satisfaction as Nancy's hand curled protectively around the earrings. 'Go on then! Try them on.'

Nancy carefully slipped them into her ears. She pulled a compact mirror from her bag and turned her head from side to side, watching how the earrings swung as she moved.

'Yuh not so bad,' she conceded.

'Oh come off it,' Jewelle scoffed. 'You hate my guts. Why don't you just admit it?'

'When yuh hear me seh I hate yuh?' Nancy argued. 'Just never tek to yuh much, dat's all,' she added, smiling at her reflection again.

'Why not?' Jewelle asked. She finally had the chance to ask the question that'd been bugging her since her arrival.

''Cause yuh have everyting.'

'But I haven't –'

'Open yuh eyes! We almost de same age but look at de difference between us,' Nancy interrupted. 'Look 'pon yuh clothes an' den look 'pon mine. Me nuh even seen half dis island, let alone another country, yet yuh go from one side of de world to another just like dat,' she said, snapping her fingers together to illustrate. 'Yuh tink me can ever have a holiday like de one yuh just have? Have a chance fi follow my dreams? Yuh ask an' yuh get. Tek a good look at my life den look 'pon yours an' tell me yuh nuh have every-ting.'

'I – I hadn't thought about it like that. I don't know what to say. I'm sorry.'

Nancy sucked her teeth. 'Nuh badda come wid yuh pity 'cause I don't need it.'

'Just who d'you think you're talking to?' Jewelle snapped. 'It's not my fault I was born in England and you were born here. It's not my fault I've had things that you haven't, so nuh badda come wid yuh damn facetiness 'cause me nuh need it either.'

They eyeballed each other until Nancy smiled. ''Bout time yuh answer back.'

'Maybe me not as renk as yuh, but me learnin'. Next time I see you, I'll give you a good run for your money.' Jewelle watched the other girl button up her coat. 'Nancy? Have you ever thought about going to England?' she asked suddenly. 'Wait!' she shouted, seeing stormclouds gather on the girl's face. 'Maybe my father can help out.'

'Everytime smaddy come from foreign dem promise fi do someting fi help yuh. Send money. Buy yuh schoolbook. Sponsor yuh. Whatever. But dem promise only last as long as dem holiday. An' my own family de first wid dem empty promises,' she added bitterly.

'Your family?' Jewelle repeated, surprised. 'What about them?'

'Me have a big sister in New York, yuh know.'

'Have you? I thought there was just you and Lil.'

'Lil!' Nancy snorted and thrust her hands hard into the pockets of her mac. 'No. Marlene in New York dese past ten years, if not more. She promise me when she leave she would send fi me so I could get me education in America;

go to university an' den get a good job – dat way I could help Lil an' de rest of de family in turn.'

'So what happened?' Jewelle asked in a low voice.

'Me still here, don' it?' Nancy retorted sharply. 'Workin' like a damn slave in dat hotel where everybody tink that just 'cause yuh mek bed an' clean up after people, yuh nuh fit fi anyting else. Dem nuh even see yuh – yuh invisible – only 'member yuh name when dem have someting fi complain 'bout.' She pulled out a chair and slumped at the table.

It was the first time Jewelle had seen Nancy anything but sure of herself. She wanted to say something to make her feel better. If she'd been Ambra she would have hugged her. But, looking at the stiff set of Nancy's shoulders and the rigidity of her neck, she knew that if she touched her the moment of contact and communication between them would be broken. Instead, she sat down in the chair beside Nancy and quietly asked, 'So why didn't Marlene send for you? Didn't she have the money?'

'She always send a cheque fi de family,' Nancy started defensively. 'Every month. Sometimes more sometimes less, whatever she have.'

'So?'

'First she seh it difficult wid all de papers de American authorities want. Den she have a pickney an' need de money fi her baby –'

'Well,' Jewelle started, 'I can kind of understand that –'

'But she coulda taken me anyway,' Nancy shouted. 'Me coulda look after de baby instead of she payin' out good money to a chile minder. I coulda get a likkle part-time job fi help pay me keep an' I coulda go to night school.'

'It sounds very – hard,' Jewelle ventured.

'Tink it any harder dan dis?' Nancy snapped. 'Yuh right,' she said after a moment, 'it woulda been hard but I'd have a reason – someting fi work towards. What I have here?

Nutten! Just one day after another after another. Knowin' dat I'll never go nowhere, never do nutten, never amount to anyting.' She banged the table suddenly with a clenched fist, then buried the heels of her palms in her eyes.

Jewelle tentatively put out a hand and touched her lightly in the middle of her back. Nancy shrugged her off word-lessly. 'Want something to drink?'

'Why not?'

'Will sorrel do?' Jewelle asked as she opened the fridge door and took out a jug of the drink. It was as she was getting ice cubes from the freezer compartment that she noticed the bottle of white rum on the shelf next to the fridge. 'Do you want some of this in it?' She grinned, holding the bottle up.

'So yuh a old drunkard now?' Nancy teased.

Jewelle laughed. 'Nope, but it'll pep it up a bit, won't it?' She poured sorrel into the glasses and then topped them up with rum.

'Yuh waan drunk me off?' Nancy said, putting her hand over the top of one of the glasses.

'It's only a bit!' Jewelle said, licking the side of her glass where some of the rum had spilled down the side. 'Uhm! It's nice. C'mon. Drink up!' She held her glass up to Nancy's. 'Cheers,' she said and took a sip. She pulled a face. The drink was strong and she wanted to add some more sorrel, but Nancy didn't seem to be having any problems with hers, and if Nancy could handle it then so could she. 'So, what happened with your sister?'

'Last year when I hear she pregnant again, I glad. I tink to myself, she mus' send fi me now. Wid two small pickney, she bound fi need help.'

'What happened?'

'Dem send fi her husband bandy-foot likkle sister instead a me. I never even bother ask Marlene why, I jus' give up. Couple weeks back I hear from one of me cousin dat dem send bandy-foot back to Jamaica a few months ago 'cause she lazy, facety an' was slappin' up de children.'

'So why don't you write to your sister or something?'

'I write too many times. Me not beggin' nobody fi nutten – whether dem family or not.'

'You don't have to beg, you just want to know once and for all so you can get on with your life. That's not much to ask is it?'

'I call her just before yuh come –' Nancy started.

'Your sister? What did she say?' Jewelle interrupted eagerly.

'Huh. Just like I expec'.' Nancy took a long swallow of her drink and then lapsed into silence.

Jewelle topped up Nancy's glass and waited.

'I call her 'cause I waan hear her seh why she nuh send fi me. So she couldn't not give me an answer like in her letters. She tell me she not sendin' fi me 'cause me too old now an' it too hard fi get papers fi someone my age. When me seh a no so it go, she tell me dat even if dem send fi me, dem sure dat likkle soon as me come, me find man or pregnant meself an' den all dem sacrifice stay fi nutten. She seh dem decide fi tek Lil; she only fifteen an' still young enough fi shape an' go to high school an' dat.'

'Lil!' Jewelle almost shouted. 'Lil's not easy to shape – at least I don't think so,' she added, suddenly remembering that Lil was Nancy's sister. 'It's just that Lil's not into school, she's –'

'She ah breed,' Nancy announced flatly.

'She's what!'

'Nuh badda shout,' Nancy said, shouting herself. 'She pregnant!'

'Who for?'

'Preacher? Teacher? Who know an' who care?'

'So what does that mean for you now?'

'It mean Lil belly full an' me still here. Not a damn ting

286

change.' She looked at the jug on the table. 'Dere's a bit left,' she said, nodding to it.

'Let's finish it,' Jewelle said. She added more rum to the liquid, swirled it around in the jug and then divided it between the two glasses. She held Nancy's eyes as she raised her glass. 'Down in one!' Nancy nodded. They downed their drinks, slammed their glasses down on the table and burst out laughing at the same time. Jewelle couldn't stop laughing and the more she laughed the more she made Nancy laugh, until the two girls were howling with tears streaming down their faces.

This feels good, Jewelle thought. I can't be drunk, because when you're drunk you feel sick and I don't feel sick at all. I feel great. In fact, I feel better than great, I feel wonderful.

'Me gone,' Nancy said eventually, wiping the tears from her eyes.

'I can't promise you anything,' Jewelle said as Nancy got up from her chair. 'This is a "maybe". I have to talk to Dad first. Do you want to visit us in England?'

'Maybe,' Nancy said, shrugging. 'Not sure if I do.' Then she smiled.

'Everything packed then?' Frank asked, looking round the room that Aunt B and Jewelle shared.

'Nearly finished,' Aunt B and Jewelle replied simultaneously. They looked at each other and started laughing.

'You and Aunt B agreeing on something! Never thought I'd see the day,' Frank joked.

'Neither did I,' Jewelle said, laughing some more.

'Sure yuh nuh mind stayin' wid me an' Sam till yuh daddy get back?' Aunt B asked, twisting her wedding ring round and round on her finger.

'Don't worry, Aunt B,' Jewelle said, slapping at Aunt B's fingers lightly. 'I'd rather Dad stayed with Granny until she gets better. I don't like the thought of her being all alone here.'

Aunt B let out a silent breath of relief. She'd been over-joyed when Frank had asked her to look after Jewelle, but apprehensive about how her niece might react. 'Yuh certain?' she asked nervously.

'Certain,' Jewelle replied.

Aunt B beamed. 'We can do a whole heap a tings together,' she started enthusiastically, 'like –'

'Going shopping!' Jewelle interrupted. 'I can't wait to show you how to dress – you need someone to help you out before you get arrested by the Fashion Police!'

Frank left them laughing. They'd be all right together. Jewelle would be fine.

11

22nd February

The rain of the previous night had brought out the scents of the ferns and pines and left the vegetation freshly washed. Heavy mist filtered the blue of the sky. Jewelle wrapped her arms around her body – a futile attempt to keep warm given the morning freshness – as she watched Jake and Sol load cases on top of the car. They lifted them easily – they were almost empty, most of their contents having been given away. Jewelle had packed a bag of clothes she thought Nancy would like, but she had a feeling that Nancy with her pride would refuse to accept them if she gave them her directly, so the bag now sat on the kitchen table with a short note. By the time Nancy got it, Jewelle would be on her way to England and there'd be nobody to argue with.

Aunt B joined her. 'At least we goin' back in someting yuh can call a car.' She smirked, stroking the shiny front of the two-year-old Toyota.

'You were great yesterday,' Jewelle told her.

'Yeah, me know,' Aunt B replied without the slightest trace of embarrassment.

They stopped briefly at the hospital but it was too early for visits, and the young nurse on duty, as stiff as the uniform she wore, refused to let them onto the ward even when they showed her their plane tickets.

'Don't fret,' Frank whispered to Jewelle as they turned

and headed to the airport. 'Your granny's agreed to come to England as soon as she can travel.'

Jewelle beamed and clapped her hands together. 'How long for?'

'Well, it's an open return ticket. Let's just keep our fingers crossed and hope she forgets to use the other half.'

It was an early morning flight and few people were about. The atmosphere inside the building was heavy and dull, with none of the vibrancy, noise and colour of their arrival. No singers or dancers to speed them on their way.

'I don't want to go!' Jewelle suddenly blurted out. She put her fingers to the corners of her eyes trying to hold back the tears that threatened to spill now she was so close to leaving a place she'd come to feel at home in and people she'd come to care for. Jamaica wasn't just a place Aunt B and Uncle Sam were always talking about; it wasn't just a mark on a map. It was real, and part of it was in her, just as she was part of it.

Sol put his arm around her. 'Dat's good. If yuh feel dat strongly 'bout it, yuh soon come back.'

'Jake.' Frank turned to the boy who was watching Jewelle silently. 'Dere's not much time, so why yuh an' Jewelle nuh say yuh goodbye while I go check in an' pay de departure tax?'

Jewelle stared through the glass door of the departure terminal – her last sight of Jamaica from the ground. The sky was beginning to clear, bringing the promise of another golden day, but all Jewelle could see were long days ahead in England; colourless days without Jake.

Two fat tears fell onto her cheeks. She rummaged in her rucksack for a tissue. 'Sorry,' she muttered.

'Fi wha'?' Jake asked.

'This.' She waved her hand vaguely.

'Better fi show wha' yuh feel dan pretend yuh nuh feel nutten at all.'

She sniffed and wiped her eyes, then searched in her rucksack again. 'This is for you.'

'Yuh Walkman,' he said in surprise.

'Is it? Oh yeah . . .' He poked her in her ribs and she gave a soggy smile. 'Take it.' She thrust it at him.

'No, it's yours.' He put his hands behind his back.

'Well, you haven't got one, so how are you going to listen to this?' She waved a cassette under his nose.

'Wha' dis?'

'A letter.'

His face lit up. 'Fi me?'

She nodded shyly. 'Promise you won't listen to it until after I've gone, though.'

He smiled as he slipped the Walkman and the cassette into his shirt pocket. 'Left or right?' he asked, grinning and patting the sides of his trousers.

'Left.' She grinned back.

He pulled a plastic box from his trouser pocket. 'Is de tape I did promise yuh. I got dem to record it fi me at de Music Shack. Hope yuh like it.'

'I'll love it,' she said, taking the cassette. 'Thanks.'

They stood and stared at each other. Time was running out, neither of them quite knew what to say.

'Left or right?' Jake asked again.

'Again?' He nodded. 'Er . . .' she said, pretending to think. 'Right,' she announced. He handed her a small gift-wrapped box. 'For me?'

'For me?' he mimicked. 'Fi who else, stupid? But I waan yuh fi open it before yuh leave.'

She ripped the paper off excitedly and opened the box. Lying on a nest of cotton wool was the pink shell necklace she'd admired the day they'd gone to the beach.

'You bought it! When? I didn't see you,' she said, half

crying, half laughing as she held it between two fingers.

'Not surprised. Yuh was too busy wid dat dread an' him "herb free" foolishness fi notice anyting I was doin'.'

'I was not!' she retorted, slipping the necklace on. 'Can you do it up for me?' He put his hands around her neck and fastened the catch. A brief moment of contact, then his hands were gone. 'How does it look?'

'Beautiful.' His voice was sombre. 'Like yuh.'

She threw her arms around him and they hugged hard. Clumsily. The Walkman in his breast pocket pressed into her chest.

'I'm going to miss you,' she whispered into his neck. 'Jake?'

'Uhm?'

'I think I lo –'

'Don' seh it,' he interrupted hurriedly. She froze, then sprang back, embarrassed and hurt. 'It just mek it harder,' he whispered, pulling her close and hugging her tight.

'Dem comin' back.' Sol pointed towards Frank who was approaching them, trailed by Jewelle and Jake. He looked at Aunt B. 'Yuh nah go gimme a hug?'

Aunt B stepped forward reluctantly and Sol put his arms around her waist. 'Uhm,' he said in a naughty voice, wiggling his hips a little closer, 'nutten like a big woman in a man's arms fi mek him feel like a likkle good lovin'. Hey, Miss B?' She slapped at his shoulders but he held her firm. 'Just jokin' wid yuh.' He grinned. 'Seriously though, we mek a good team, nuh true? At least once in a while.'

'Leastways me can rest easy in me bed now I know dis business over,' Aunt B replied.

'Who seh it over?' Sol whispered. 'Nutten ever finish when or how we expec'.'

Aunt B stiffened. 'Wha' yuh mean?' But Frank was upon them and her question went unanswered.

*

'Nuh cry.' Sol comforted Jewelle.

'I can't help it.'

'Me have a feelin' dat yuh nuh done wid Jamaica, so dese tears not necessary,' he said as she sniffled against his shoulder. 'It in yuh heart,' he said softly. 'Yuh'll be back.'

'Don't forget to make sure that Nancy gets the clothes – they're on the kitchen table,' Jewelle told Frank as he hugged her close. 'She'll take them from you.'

'I won't,' he promised, wiping her face with the palm of his hand. 'I love you. See you soon,' he whispered. 'And don't give Aunt B too much trouble.'

'Yeah, OK.' She blinked back her tears and tried to smile. 'Love you too, Dad.' Make sure you look after Granny.'

Even as she spoke they could hear the final calls for their flight. Nobody moved. Nobody wanted to prolong the goodbyes but, by the same token, nobody wanted to finish them. Aunt B, so anxious to leave, now found an unexpected lump had risen in her throat. She'd spent so much of her stay being apprehensive, protective and worried that she hadn't actually looked at the island she'd last seen so long ago. She hadn't lived its warmth or vitality; hadn't seen its beauty or drunk in its scents. And now, on the verge of leaving, she suddenly felt cheated.

'Come.' Sol kept one hand around Aunt B; with his other he beckoned the others to him. 'Come mek we all hold each other fi a moment.'

They formed a tight little circle. Heads touching, arms around each other's shoulders and waists. A brief moment of feeling and affection – then they parted.

Aunt B led the way. Jewelle followed closely behind; she walked quickly with her head down and didn't look back, even when Aunt B stopped for a final wave.

'Jewelle!'

She turned to see Jake jumping up and down, waving

both arms at her. 'Me too,' he shouted between cupped hands. 'Yuh understan'? Me too!'

Her radiant smile showed she'd received his message loud and clear.

Frank rubbed the back of his neck with one hand as he and Sol strolled from the airport. 'Hungry?' he asked Sol. ''Cause me starvin'. Never have time fi breakfast.'

'Dumpling shop?'

Frank smiled. 'Sounds good to me. Yuh know,' he said as he got in the car next to Sol. 'I'm considerin' gettin' a likkle place out here . . . close to Mumma. Yuh in de business, maybe yuh can sort someting out.'

'Yuh comin' back?' Sol asked, surprised.

'Not sure. We'll come over in de holidays – at least fi start wid. Jamaica is my home just as much as England. But I haffi admit though, I feel better fi comin' back. Don' feel I need to be one ting or another any more, just me – Frank Galimore, Jamaican and "adopted" Briton. And if anybody have problem wid dat den is dere business. If I can deal wid Rose, me sure as hell can deal wid anyting else life haffi throw at me.'

'Yuh sound pretty sure,' Sol commented.

'Is true?' Frank grinned.

'How yuh feel 'bout Rose now?' Sol asked.

'Yuh know,' Frank sighed, 'it hard fi say. Everyting still mix up deep inside. Part of me feel guilty 'bout her. I let her hang on to a dream dat couldn't ever come true. Part of me angry wid her – angry 'cause in some way I feel is she keep me 'way from Jamaica fi so long. But den, if me honest wid meself, I know I coulda come back any time I waan. I did have de money and I coulda mek de time, so it never really have so much fi do wid her at all. I tink I did 'fraid dat if I did come back I would slip into de old Frank – just shrivel up. No confidence. No balls. Nutten. Just driftin' along

294

waitin' fi sometin' fi happen; sometin' dat mek me feel like me born fi a purpose an' dat me life have a reason. I don' tink I sure till now, just how real de "new" me was. Understan' me?'

'Tink so,' Sol said, giving Frank the space he felt he needed to talk.

'Is like,' Frank continued, 'is like yuh go into a coffee shop but wha' yuh really waan is a beer. So of course, nuh matter wha' dem offer yuh, yuh nah go satisfy. If yuh waan beer, yuh better go to de bar next door.'

'Me wid yuh.' Sol nodded. 'If yuh waan discover de world under water, better yuh learn fi dive dan learn how fi fish!'

'Yeah, man,' Frank said, pleased that Sol understood what he was trying to say. 'So yuh see, Sol, I cyaan even blame Rose more dan such fi de way I live my life an' de choices I make. After all, if it never fi Rose, I might never have met Beth. An' even if I had, maybe I wouldn't have 'preciate her in de way I did after dat experience wid Rose. Den dere woulda been no Jewelle an' I cyaan imagine my life widout my likkle gyal. So, in a funny way, I feel grateful to Rose . . . if yuh know wha' me mean,' he finished sheepishly.

Sol nodded slowly. 'Me catch yuh meanin',' he said. 'Just don' let yuh gratitude mek yuh figet all de other tings Rose do to yuh an' yours. All right? Nuff respect to yuh, Frank.'

Frank touched fists with Sol before squeezing his hand. 'Respect.' He smiled, then jerked his neck a couple of times. 'Raas!'

'Wha' do yuh?'

'Neck still stiff,' Frank said, massaging it gently. 'Must get it check out when me back in England.'

Might not be in England dat yuh sort it out, Sol thought. 'Just mek sure yuh look after it,' was all he said aloud.

12

8th March

Sunlight chased shadow in an early morning game of tag. A final lunge had sunlight winning; illuminating the street with sudden blinding light and sending Sol in search of his sunglasses. He cruised along Brown's Town's main street, one arm hanging lazily out of the wound-down window. But his relaxed pose belied the thoughts running through his mind.

Much as Frank might think it was all over, that he'd dealt with everything – and he had, to the best of his ability – stories of life and death never start or end as expected. The past few weeks had merely seen the ending of one chapter and the beginning of the next. Just as shadow would patiently wait its turn to mask sunlight, so the game would begin again.

Jake stepped into the road from under one of the stone arches of the post office and Sol swerved to a noisy halt, making the boy jump. Sol raised his sunglasses to his forehead as the boy pulled the earphones from his ears.

'Dat's why yuh never hear me call yuh. Must be someting good yuh lissen to. Yuh smile broader dan de street wide.'

'Is de letter Jewelle record fi me,' Jake said proudly.

Two weeks on and Jake was still listening to his letter as if he'd only just received it. 'All right, bredda. Me won't keep yuh. Can see yuh have important tings fi do.' Sol's eyes twinkled. 'Where yuh gwaan anyway?'

'Goin' fi check me madda. Is a good while now me nuh see her.'

'When yuh see her tell her me say howdy.'

'Yuh know her?' Jake asked in surprise.

'I know everybody.' Sol grinned. 'Don' waan hold yuh up.' He touched fists with Jake. 'Check yuh soon. Me have a likkle story fi tell yuh.'

''Bout what?'

Sol slid his sunglasses down over his eyes. ''Bout a man call Bevan.'

'Who?'

But Sol had already gone.

The sun was casting golden flecks of light over the pink-fronted house by the time Jake arrived. The kitchen was empty but the smell of cooking still lingered in the air. He peeked into the dutchy pot on top of the stove and took out a piece of fried chicken.

'Momma?' he shouted.

'Out here,' a voice came back, 'an' nuh badda nyam off all de chicken. Yuh see yuh sister?'

'She seh she will reach before night fall.' He helped himself to another piece of chicken before walking to the kitchen doorway. His mother was in the yard with her back towards him. He could hear her muttering to herself and his heart sank. She was so unpredictable that it was hard to relax with her, and that kept his visits infrequent. Even when he was a child and had lived with his grand-parents he'd never known what to expect. No Momma for months at a time and then a sudden flurry of unexpected visits, often with his great-grandmother in tow.

On her good days, his mother had been happy and girlish and would play and sing with him for hours. At other times she seemed to hate the sight of him and he'd run and hide behind his grandfather, as she stalked up and down,

297

ranting about people and things he didn't understand. His great-grandmother seemed to be the only person who could calm her down. But then, he reflected, his great-grandmother frightened him into silence too, talking as she did to people he couldn't see and who never replied. His grandfather would hold him in his arms and comfort him. 'Dem only bad when dem together,' he would whisper as the two woman sat huddled together. The relief that he and his grandparents felt at the end of one of these flying visits was almost as palpable as the calm which descended on the house.

His mother didn't sound in a particularly good mood right now, but then she never was when she stood in front of the small rectangular-shaped plot hidden by a mass of honeysuckle and ginger lilies. He'd once asked her what was buried there. 'My memories,' she'd said. One day, bored and curious, he'd taken advantage of her absence to dig up these memories.

He remembered how he'd watched her walk away, waited until she was out of sight before taking from the kitchen the enormous metal spoon they used for cooking curry goat. His heart had beaten frantically as he dug into the earth. He hadn't found anything and continued to dig, thinking she must have buried her memories very deeply. He'd been so absorbed in what he was doing that he lost all sense of time and fear. After a while, he'd thrown the spoon to one side and used his hands. His roving fingers had come across a ragged ball of cloth with what looked like a curl of hair inside. Before he'd had a chance to do more than poke at it timidly, he'd heard a scream and turned to see her bearing down on him, murder in her eyes.

Jake licked his lips, his mouth suddenly dry, as dry as it had been when his mother had grabbed him by the scruff of his neck and he'd felt his feet leaving the ground. She'd given him a beating that he still remembered and it had taken both his grandparents to hold her off. Afterwards, he'd never had the courage to ask her where her memories had gone and why the plot had been empty except for that screwed up piece of material.

Sometimes he wished he were capable of walking out of her life as she'd walked out of his. Almost every family he knew had a similar story; a mother or father leaving at least one child with grandparents as they sought work – something better for the family. Those left behind would brag about how they'd soon be in England, Canada or America; the parental promise a golden hope shaping days and months until the passage of years left nothing more than a dusty broken dream. Jake had never bragged. He'd had no promises, no dreams to boast about. But he couldn't leave her behind. When all was said and done, she was his mother. He sighed as he took the three red-stained steps down into the garden and moved reluctantly towards her.

'Yuh tink dis ting finish, Frank?' she muttered, pulling petals from a Jamaica Rose whose blossoms, bathed in the last of the day's sunshine, seemed lit from inside. Their glow faded as they fluttered to the ground. 'Well, yuh wrong! When yuh feel soft breeze blow round yuh neck, it mean me comin' fi yuh. Me nah rest till dis ting come full circle an' I see yuh eat dirt.'

'Seh wha', Momma?' Jake asked.

'Nutten, son,' Rose replied. 'Only wha' go roun' must come roun'.'

'How yuh mean?'

She sank to her feet in front of the flowers and gestured to Jake to do the same. 'Sit down, son. Me have someting fi tell yuh.'

HARD SHOULDER edited by Jackie Gay & Julia Bell
ISBN: 0 9535895 0 1 * £6.99

THE PIG BIN by Michael Richardson
ISBN: 0 9535895 2 8 * £6.99

SCAPEGRACE by Jackie Gay
ISBN: 0 9535895 1 X * £6.99

A LONE WALK by Gul Y. Davis
ISBN: 0 9535895 3 6 * £6.99

SURVIVING STING by Paul McDonald
ISBN: 0 9535895 4 4 * £7.99

HER MAJESTY
edited by Jackie Gay & Emma Hargrave
ISBN: 0 9535895 7 9 * £8.99

JAKARTA SHADOWS by Alan Brayne
ISBN: 0 9535895 8 7 * £7.99

THE CITY TRAP by John Dalton
ISBN: 0 9535895 6 0 * £7.99

BIRMINGHAM NOIR
edited by Joel Lane & Steve Bishop
ISBN: 0 9535895 9 5 * £7.99

THE EXECUTIONER'S ART by David Fine
ISBN:0 9541303 1 6 * £7.99

BIRMINGHAM NOUVEAU edited by Alan Mahar
ISBN: 0 9541303 0 8 * £7.99

All Tindal Street Press titles are available from good
bookshops, online booksellers and direct from:

www.tindalstreet.co.uk